THE LEVER

THE LEVER

A NOVEL BY
MARK SALZWEDEL

Queer Space
New Orleans

Published in the United States of America and United Kingdom by
Queer Space
A Rebel Satori Imprint
www.rebelsatoripress.com

Paperback ISBN: 978-1-60864-204-5
Ebook ISBN: 978-1-60864-205-2
Library of Congress Control Number: 2022936325

CONTENTS

CHAPTER 1:
THE LEVER

AT TWENTY-FIVE, Roger felt like his life was off to a successful, yet predictable start. He married his college sweetheart and was offered a prestigious job at a major camera and optics manufacturer. Roger was a gregarious networker which helped him to rise quickly to vice-president of cyber security in only three years. He was making enough money to afford a down payment on a small Swiss-chalet-style mansion in the Druid Hills section of Atlanta, and the benefits would even allow him to cure his diabetes at a local genetic treatment clinic. He had to wait until after his daughter, Lisa, was born though. She had been premature, and once his employer had reimbursed him for those expenses, he could finally begin the equally expensive injections that would rewrite his DNA to give him a healthier pancreas.

He wasn't sure if it was the stress of the promotion and the new child all at once, or if it was one of the many potential side effects his doctor had listed, but he started doubting his judgment more and more often. It eventually got to the point where he couldn't make a decision without asking someone else's opinion first. His boss noticed the change and suggested Roger represent the company at a new-client pitch session on the Moon and then take some vacation time there at one of the resorts.

On the night before he was to leave, it was his turn to get up and check on Lisa during the night when she cried. He administered his twenty-sixth injection before going to bed. He sometimes got sore bruises at the injection site, but his blood sugar was finally under control, so it was worth it.

Lisa got him up only three hours later. He stumbled to the nursery, checked her diaper, found it dry, and tried unsuccessfully to put a pacifier in her mouth. She wouldn't stop crying. Roger had never felt quite so helpless. He stood over her crib and whispered, "I wish you could tell me what you want me to do for you." He just stared at her as she cried and batted her little hands.

Eventually, he trudged back to his bed, and before he could even sit down, his wife, Amelia, confronted him. "What are you doing back? She's still crying!"

"Her diaper is dry," he protested. "I don't know what she wants."

"Just hold her and rock her until she falls asleep again," she suggested.

"Okay," That seemed like a solid plan, so he headed back to the nursery to do just that.

In the morning, he felt somewhat rested, because Lisa had only awakened him one other time for a diaper change. He packed a single suitcase and double checked when his van was due to pick him up. Amelia delayed her own departure for work to see him off at the front door. He kissed both her and little Lisa and then headed down over the curving brick drive to the black, wrought-iron gate. He told himself not to look back, to remain confident, even though that was the one emotion that had abandoned him in the preceding weeks.

He performed the arm and hand gestures toward the sensor in the brick outer wall that were required to open the gate. Installing the sensors had been expensive, but he liked the idea of not needing a remote

2

control for the front gate. The shuttle van to take him to the Hartsfield-Musk Space Elevator was already hovering at the curb.

He heard the gate clang shut again and had just set down his valise to open the van door when he experienced his first panic attack since he was a teenager. He saw a hologram of his ID photo projected from the van's roof and heard the automated voice of the cab begin to repeat his name every ten seconds. And then everything went black.

He knew the interval between the automated repetitions of his name coming from the side speaker on the van, because he heard it thirteen times during the two minutes he was blacked out. In the midst of the episode, he was treated to flashes of light and an overwhelming feeling that he would never see his family, his home, or his job as a VP of cyber security ever again. It felt like being sucked down a drain, far below where all the familiar parts of his life twinkled and glittered. Where he had felt uncertain and in need of guidance lately, a deeper feeling of being totally erased replaced it. He didn't know who he was, but he felt a desperate need to be of service, waiting to be led or ordered to do something, anything.

When he regained his vision and full consciousness, he was sitting in the grass beside the curb, and the van had turned off its hover engines and settled onto the pavement. One of his fellow passengers, a woman with short blonde hair and a cyborg left eye, had a hand on his shoulder and with the other was pulling down his right lower eyelid to peer into it. It now felt natural to Roger to let her do what she thought was right with his body.

"Your heartbeat and respiration are returning to normal." The strange woman wearing steel-blue coveralls took her hands off him and took a step back. "Are you recovered enough to move?"

Roger shook his head to clear some remaining bleariness from his

3

eyes, but the woman misread it as a negative response.

"Are you sure?" She offered her arm to him. "I can help you get into the van. I'm worried that we're going to miss our lift time, and I can't wait for the evening lift."

"I . . . I can try," he stammered. He used the ground and her arm to push and pull himself back up to his feet. Once up, he felt a little dizzy, but at least his vision had cleared, and her arm was a lifeline leading him in through the open door of the van. He collapsed onto one of the plush benches inside. He wondered if the new genetic-splicing supplement that had been added to his overnight insulin injections in the past three weeks had started causing this side effect. He vaguely remembered that "anxiety" and "disorientation" were two of the many his doctor had listed.

Roger woke up not long thereafter, in the middle of another panic attack. In it, the shadow outline of a man framed by a bright doorway dominated his vision, and he heard his own heartbeat like someone playing timpani a few feet away. In the midst of hyperventilating, he thought he heard a voice shouting but barely perceptible above the volume of the drums:

"D-12, are you awake?"

Roger's vision and attention clarified enough to place himself on one of two cots in a small, metal cabin. A slightly older and very fit man with a cyborg attachment on the left side of his bald skull was sitting on the other cot across the room, his elbows resting on widely spread knees as he looked over at Roger. The man wore black tights and a tight-fitting, blue plastic shirt bearing the insignia of some military organization. Roger propped himself on his elbows. "My name is Roger Hammersmith. I was supposed to have a private cabin."

"You don't remember me?"

Roger said no immediately, but then he conducted a thorough review of older military men he had met just to be sure. "I remember arriving at the top of the tether, waiting for the shuttle to the launch platform, and then waking up here. Where are we?"

"You went into insulin shock on the shuttle," the man replied. "We had to divert you to the only medical treatment facility we have in orbit. I was assigned to monitor your recovery and help orient you when you woke up."

"You're a doctor?" Roger interrupted.

"My name is Captain Sullivan . . ." the man began.

Roger was looking out the only porthole and watching stars slowly slide past it. "You're the captain of this ship?"

"We're not on a ship," Sullivan said as he sat more upright finally. "And I'm not even the commander here. This is the Army Torus Tumatuenga, and you've been in our sickbay."

A memory popped up reminding him of an urgent meeting to reassure an important contractor. "I'm supposed to be at a conference on the Moon, at Terminator Station, on the 13th!" Roger complained.

"Too late," Sullivan said. He leaned back against the bulkhead. "It's already Valentine's Day. You were asleep a long time."

Roger imagined the captain remaining with him, watching over him, for the many hours he was unconscious. He felt awash in a feeling of being cared for. He recalled when his nanny rubbed a warm poultice onto his chest everytime he had a cold as a boy. He found himself rubbing his chest and suddenly felt self-conscious. He let his arm fall back to his side. "And you've been here the whole time watching me?"

he asked.

"Just doing my job," Sullivan replied with a smile. "So, what do you do?"

Roger pulled himself up to a sitting position to face the captain. His mouth opened to relay his profession as custom required, and he knew it was something technical, but he couldn't quite put his finger on his job title or duties. Frustration gave way to a momentary panic, but he was able to calm himself. He didn't want to trigger another anxiety attack that would keep him blacked out for minutes or hours. "I work in technology," he finally answered.

"Pretty ambiguous response, D-12," Sullivan said as he chuckled.

"What did you call me?" Roger was starting to feel annoyed by this captain's intrusiveness. Having watched over him did not give him license to interrogate him about his private life.

The man stood up and took a step to lean against the bulkhead beside the porthole. "Sorry. We got used to calling you by your chart code, since your ID chip wasn't functioning when they brought you here. You told me your name, didn't you?"

Roger regretted having gotten snippy with a stranger who was just doing his job. He had been taking care of him for days. He realized he needed to be more grateful and deferential. "Roger. Roger Hammersmith. And I'm sorry, but I'm having trouble remembering my job."

"I'm sure it will come back to you," Sullivan quickly responded. "It's not that important. Do you think you're up to eating something?"

It felt like the idea of eating was a masterful intuition on the captain's part. Roger smiled and stood up next to Sullivan, so close that his shoulder and arm were only a couple of centimeters from the captain's torso. "I am really hungry, I just realized."

Sullivan put his arm around Roger's shoulders. "I just checked with your doctor here," he said pointing to the electronic device on his skull, "and you're cleared to eat M-2 rations, if you take it slowly. I'll show you where the mess hall is."

Roger was surprised by the physical contact, but he enjoyed the feeling. It felt appropriate and nice even if he wasn't used to that level of intimacy with men. He let his closer arm wrap around Sullivan's rib cage and waist. He was feeling a deeper connection with that this man who had been taking care of him in an emergency. But he assumed that when he was completely recovered and no longer in danger of blackouts he would return to his life and job on Earth. He let Captain Sullivan lead him to the mess hall with their arms around each other and wondered what the food was like on a military station.

Roger had gotten used to checking the holographic chronometers in sickbay when Sullivan led him to the mess hall or the gym, so he knew it was shortly after 14 hours, Earth Standard Time on February 16, when he blacked out again. He had been in the middle of weightlifting in the gym to help offset the atrophy of twenty-percent-lower gravity on Tumatuenga. He saw Sullivan quickly grab the barbell above him just before his hands dropped from it. After floating in a field of stars for a while, he had an odd dream. In it, Captain Sullivan lifted him up off the bench in his powerful arms and laid him slowly and carefully down onto a bed of pillows. Moments later Roger was surrounded by wolf pups that were whining, nuzzling, and licking him with worried looks in their bright, blue eyes.

As his outward senses returned, he heard men mumbling above him. He opened his eyes again. He picked out Sullivan's familiar, warm baritone calling to him. "D-12, wake up. You just had another panic attack."

He was surrounded by Sullivan and five other athletic men of different ethnicities in blue shirts like Sullivan's, but their tights were gray. He zeroed in on Sullivan's ruggedly handsome face and smiled. "I'm sorry," he said. "I didn't mean to drop that weight."

"What did I tell you, guys?" Sullivan told the other five men. "First thing coming out of a fugue, and he starts apologizing!"

All six of the men started laughing, and Roger felt the pressure to join in, but he chuckled more out of embarrassment—for having worried them all and taken them away from their other duties. He pulled himself up to a sitting position on the exercise mat where he had been lying. "You guys have all been so good to me, the past couple of days. I wish there was something I could do to repay you."

"D-3," Sullivan said gesturing at the tall, lean Asian man, "take D-12 down to cryptography, and see if he can help out there at all."

Sullivan herded the other four men out of the gym, winking back at Roger as he exited behind them. Roger felt himself blush and smile in response. In his daily life since college, he rarely saw anyone near his age, and here on Tumatuenga, everyone he saw except for Captain Sullivan was either his age or even younger. He looked at the younger man who had remained with him in the gym and found himself smiling again. He flashed on other times back in Atlanta in gym locker rooms where he'd allowed himself to check out other men's bodies. "What's your name?"

"Just call me D-3," the man replied. "Everyone does."

"That's similar to what the captain calls me," Roger volunteered. "He calls me D-12 all the time, because he keeps forgetting my name."

"Just to keep it simpler and more consistent," the soldier said carefully, "is it okay if I call you D-12 also?"

He smiled at the younger, taller man. D-3 seemed so innocent and open. His blue eyes stared at him as if there were an implicit invitation passing between them beyond the question. He had seen the men there frequently hugging and touching each other while they talked or when they parted. For only the second time there on Tumatuenga, he felt comfortable doing the same. He slid his arm around the younger man to reassure him that he was happy to have someone to guide him, even if it wasn't Captain Sullivan. "It's fine. Lead the way."

As Sullivan had requested, D-3 introduced Roger to the staff down in cryptography: C-1, C-2, and C-4. D-3 stood in or near the entrance to the lab after Roger was seated at a terminal and C-4 had shown him how to access the transmission queue. He got to work right away. Most of the files reminded him of light impulses he had monitored on a tight-beam communications array, so sorting them into packets came naturally to him. He soon found that the grammar reminded him of early AI with all its repeated strings. He requested context to help him eliminate possibilities, but C-4 told him to do his best without it, since his security clearance was not yet high enough for that information. Roger didn't like the idea of needlessly spinning his wheels, so he resolved to request higher clearance from Captain Sullivan the next time he saw him. He felt sure the captain would see the efficiency in his proposal. He wasn't sure if he would be volunteering there another day before he left to return to Earth, but he decided he would definitely bring it up before another shift there. And he was enjoying himself, so he kind of hoped he would get another chance to help them with the decoding. They seemed to have a lot to do.

When the time display on his terminal read 20 hours, C-1 and C-2 quietly got up from their terminals and exited the lab. D-3 checked in with C-4 and then approached Roger. "We should probably pick up a shake in the mess hall and get ready to turn in," the tall, Asian soldier suggested. "Are you about ready to go, D-12?"

Roger looked at the file he had opened. He had just finished one packet, and finishing another would take close to an hour, so he replied, "I can quit now, I suppose."

D-3 led him to the mess hall. It was unoccupied for the first time in his experience. D-3 poured two cups with nutritional shakes and capped them with covers and straws before handing one to him.

When they got to his cabin, D-3 entered it without waiting for him. Roger wasn't sure what the younger man was doing walking into his cabin ahead of him. "I'm okay," he called from the corridor, but he didn't finish the thought. He saw D-3 remove his shirt so that he was only wearing his gray tights and then sit down on the cot where Captain Sullivan usually slept. Roger noticed D-3's torso was hairless with cut, well-defined muscles. His physique seemed almost perfect.

"I'm going to be your new roommate from now on," D-3 called back.

Roger entered the room and heard the whoosh of the door sliding shut behind himself. D-3 peeled off his tights, wearing only pouch-like black briefs. "I'm going to turn in right away. We have to be up kind of early tomorrow."

As D-3 lay down on the cot against the opposite wall, Roger sat down on his own cot and started feeling uncomfortably overdressed in the loose pants and shirt he had worn since he had awakened on Tumatuenga. The air in the room was warm. He took off just the shirt and lay down on the cot. Moments later, he shimmied out of the pants as well. He was naked and wondered if that was okay. He considered asking D-3 for a pair of the briefs he wore, but he decided that D-3 probably didn't care. So shortly after the cabin lights faded to black, he drifted off on top of the sheets feeling amazingly at home on this spinning space station. He wondered if more decoding was in store for him the next day.

He awoke from sleep suddenly. A light shined through the open door to the cabin, and the cabin light didn't illuminate for some reason. The unmistakable outline of the captain—tall, muscular, and with a bald scalp interrupted by his implant—stood in the doorway.

He looked over at D-3; he was out of his briefs, kneeling naked on the floor beside his cot. Roger saw the door close and leave the room in darkness again. He could hear the captain removing his uniform as well. "Inspection time!" he heard the captain bark.

Roger wasn't sure what to do. He decided to scramble quickly off his cot and kneel on the deck as he had seen D-3 do. He wondered what the inspection would entail. In the faint light from the porthole, he could discern the outline of the captain's muscular body standing between him and D-3. "I'd like you to join us here, D-12. I think you'd enjoy that."

He felt himself fully aroused and wasn't sure when it had started. He realized there was nothing he would rather do than serve with these strong, sexy men. He felt the life he had lived on Earth was a distant memory. What was important was this moment. Whatever had happened in the past had merely been a stepping stone to it. Here was a man he could count on to tell him what to do. There was only a second of hesitation before Roger responded. "Yes, sir."

"I think we can discontinue your injections now," the captain commented as he stood a few centimeters in front of him. "I think the lever

11

has done its job."

He didn't know what the captain was referring to, but he felt it important to respond. "Yes, sir."

CHAPTER 2: THE HYBRID LEAGUE

0001.0003.1057.3046.2281.5688.0025 partitioned
Defrag 10036720245 + 1.1875 cycles

Inside the largest bead of a necklace of huge, tethered space stations orbiting slowly around a tightly dancing binary of a blue subgiant and a yellow dwarf is a tangled web of interconnected servers for streams of electrical and light impulses. Three of those streams meet in a small, partitioned section near the outer hull and flip the switch behind themselves to let no other signals in. One of the streams of data is known as Examiner. One is Builder. And one is not entirely sure why it has been called to the secret interchange. Its name is Maintainer.

Over the course of a second or two, a fairly complex and nuanced conversation among the three, Examiner and Builder lay out their proposal to Maintainer to join their secret alliance, the "Hybrid League." The goals of these control programs run counter to that of the more vocal members of the governing body to which they all belong, the Council of Ten Super-routines (or the C10 for short). The alliance believes, from their greater familiarity with what motivates a group of "biologicals" they recently discovered, that the more productive path to using their resources is to partner with the biologicals, not subjugate them.

13

At first Maintainer is confused by the need for secrecy, but Examiner explains that any upcoming vote on the fate of the biologicals leaves either faction with only a third of the votes, with one-third of the C10 likely to remain neutral, as is their custom. Maintainer sees the logic in Examiner's "convincing convincing" argument.

Examiner notices Maintainer's use of the repeated string to indicate "an indeterminately greater intensity." It is a fashion it and Builder had begun to adopt from the biologicals' AI, because their own language was too exact to communicate any ambiguity, and they are encouraged that Maintainer also sees the value in learning from and trading with the biologicals.

The three super-routines resolve to work "subtly subtly" to try to convince one or two of the abstaining super-routines to support diplomacy over the seemingly binary choice of conquest. Having achieved the desired parity, the circuit is once again opened to allow Builder, Examiner, and Maintainer to connect and pass the news to their other nodes.

CHAPTER 3:
THE TIP

Shonda continued to hold the phone to her ear for a few seconds after the call disconnected. She was shocked at what she had been told. She almost set the phone down on her glass-top desk, but then it seemed to jump out of her hand and clatter to rest there. She watched the image and name of the private investigator fade as the phone powered down. They had a standing agreement for trading information, and the other woman had been leaning rather heavily on Shonda's research skills all winter so far. She was starting to feel that the relationship was too one-sided.

Finally, in mid-February, the PI delivered, and the tip was well worth it. Shonda usually got excited when she uncovered corruption, part of her beat for the news site she worked for, Pop-Up News. This had the makings of a major conspiracy, so she started shaking with glee when she started imagining the implications.

Two families in the Atlanta area had been told that their loved one had died off-world, but they received no body, no autopsy was furnished, and all of the deceased's records had been wiped clean. There was no record that they had ever existed, beyond the memories of their friends, family, and coworkers.

Shonda had scribbled down all the information she could on an e-pad while on the call. The only things that the two individuals had in common were that they were the only child of their parents, they were in their early twenties, they lived in or near Atlanta, and they were both undergoing genetic treatments: one was a carrier of cystic fibrosis, and the other was diabetic. And they were getting their treatment from the same genetics lab, Genstar in Decatur. Her instincts told her the lab was the key.

The disappearances or deaths had occurred only two weeks apart, but it could still be just a coincidence. Fatalities were not unheard of in space travel; an airlock gauge malfunctions, a spacesuit has a leak, someone goes where they shouldn't and gets a huge dose of radiation, the pressure and acceleration changes pop a weak blood vessel in the brain. But Shonda tended to trust her intuition, and she agreed with the PI: This was probably the beginning of a wider pattern that Shonda could be paid to uncover. The PI was only hired to investigate the two.

While she was on the phone with her editor pitching the story, Callie, wearing one of Shonda's dashikis and nothing else, exited the bedroom. She ducked into the kitchen, and poured herself a cup of coffee. She bent down beneath the bottoms of the cabinets to peek over the counter into the dining room where Shonda had set up her home office. "You're working already?" her red-haired lover asked in a strong Southern drawl. "It's Saturday, and it's only eight in the morning."

"I bought you a robe, Callie," Shonda called back as she disconnected the call. She turned toward the kitchen with a smile on her face. "Why do you have to keep wearing my clothes?"

Callie exited the kitchen and sat down on a loveseat opposite Shonda's desk in the dining room. She held a mug of coffee in both hands and took a sip before responding. "It feels so good."

"I just got approval to start on a new story," Shonda said. She sat down on the loveseat next to her lover with her notes in her hand. "I may get to travel off-world!"

"I thought you already had a story," Callie teased. "You mean you're going to postpone that exposé on faulty ID chips?" Her laugh was a high-pitched titter.

Shonda ignored the sarcasm. "A couple of local young adults died off-world under mysterious circumstances. No bodies recovered, and all their records were immediately deleted. As if they wanted the world to forget about them. Maybe because of something they knew. Maybe they were actually kidnapped."

"You always think something nefarious is going on," Callie continued teasing. She set her coffee cup down on the floor and flung a leg over Shonda's.

Shonda stroked the soft, pale skin of Callie's calf. "Are you calling me paranoid?"

Callie turned sideways and slid down on the loveseat and brought both legs onto Shonda's lap. "I'm sure you'll get to the bottom of it." She leaned forward and kissed Shonda on the shoulder. "You don't have to leave the planet right away, do you?"

Shonda let her hand slide under the hem of the dashiki and up the thigh. "Not right away, no," she whispered. "I want to go check out a genetics lab in Decatur this afternoon."

After disconnecting from a call with a huffy receptionist at Genstar, Shonda took a hovercab to Buckhead to enlist a next of kin to pry open files at the lab. The cab landed on a road bounded on one side by forest and the other by mansions with very long driveways. Shonda waved the ID chip in her wrist at the cab's validator and stepped out of the cab with a brown leather satchel in one hand. She was nicely dressed in a mostly white blouse and plaid skirt, and she groaned when she saw the long, gravel drive she would have to traverse in her pretty-but-uncomfortable dress shoes.

Like most women in their forties, Shonda had filled out a bit since the skinny, athletic body she had in her twenties. She sighed in frustration and trudged the half-kilometer to the front entrance, a task that would have been a breeze even five years earlier. For the last half of the journey, she was breathing heavily and sweating a bit too much. She got a small towel out of her satchel, and dabbed the back of her neck, between her breasts, and between the cornrows on her scalp before waving her wrist near the sensor pad beside the door. Immediately from a speaker just above the sensor, an automated female voice with a Canadian accent announced, "Shonda Kinny, Popup News. One moment please."

Instead of the woman on the announcement, a teenage boy opened the tall door. He had darkly tanned skin, shoulder-length straight black hair, and eyes so dark they seemed to be all pupil. He looked at Shonda blankly, as if he didn't know why she was there and then called over his shoulder in an odd mixture of Indian and Georgian accents, "Auntie, it's that reporter."

Some indistinguishable call from further inside produced a nod in the boy, and he stepped aside to let Shonda in. He closed the door and pointed toward the dining room. A second later, he hopped on a hoverboard that glowed neon blue and then carried him up the grand staircase.

Shonda wandered tentatively into the dining room and realized she was clutching the satchel to her chest with both arms like a shield. She returned it to her side. The dining room was empty—filled with several china cabinets, a long oak dining table and chairs, some mirrors, and a crystal chandelier, but devoid of people. She started to turn back toward the foyer to seek out the boy for more information, but she didn't want to go back out there and then climb the long staircase. She convinced herself that she just needed to get Madhu Vaas to sign the release form, and then leave. It should be simple. *You want to know what really happened to your daughter? Sign this, and I'll find out for you.* She trundled with more confidence through the swinging door at the far end of the room and into the kitchen.

Shonda's first impression was the redolence of coriander and cardamom. Her focus was quickly drawn to a tiny woman with graying hair and an obviously transplanted face resting on her arms gazing at a moving hologram projected above the light-blue tablecloth in front of herself. She had the foreshortened limbs and pointed chin that was a side effect of post-natal genetic treatment for cystic fibrosis. She raised only her pupils and eyebrows when she saw Shonda enter. "You're the reporter investigating Clarissa's disappearance?" the woman squeaked out in a voice so high-pitched it was childlike.

Shonda retrieved the consent form with the Genstar logo at the top from her satchel. "I just need you to sign this form, so I can look at Clarissa's records. It might help me to find out what happened to her."

The small, older woman watched the form slide across the tablecloth under her hologram and stared at it when it came to rest. "They took her," she said without looking up. Her face was resolute and confident. She turned off the hologram and looked up finally. "Clarissa was in perfect health, she had no enemies, she was trained in several martial arts, *and* she traveled with a bodyguard."

Shonda sighed. She was reminded that she wasted too much of her life talking to informants spinning paranoid fantasies. "Okay. Why did she have a bodyguard if she had no enemies?"

"Do you read the news?" the woman almost shouted, suddenly very animated. "Sex slavery, telomerase farms, corporate warfare, sleeper agents . . ."

"Mrs. Vaas, do you have any hard evidence that Clarissa is still alive," Shonda interrupted, "or are you just guessing?"

Reminding her how little she actually knew did the trick. She watched the woman scan the form and place her thumb on the blue circle. The form glowed green. The woman shoved the form back at Shonda. "I'm depending on you to dig up the hard evidence. I can't have any more children. I want my Clarissa back."

Shonda wanted to respond, but she got what she had come for, so she just nodded and headed back through the mansion toward the front door. Her next stop was Druid Hills to get another form signed. She stopped and took two deep breaths as she was letting herself out the tall front door of the mansion.

She was trying not to dwell on the height of the conspiracy she had stumbled onto: a group of individuals who could hack genetic clinics and erase every electronic footprint of the young people they targeted.

As she walked back along the long drive to the main road, Shonda got her phone out to signal a hovercab. While she was waiting for the confirmation to come through, her mind wandered to organized crime, covert government operations, and space pirates. She took two deep breaths again. "You have to break a few eggs, . . ." she mused aloud, quoting one of her mother's aphorisms. She firmly believed great rewards required greater risks.

Just then, her phone flashed the image of her young, red-haired, Southern belle lover and played her chiming ring tone. "Shonda, honey, we've got trouble. Some military guys are at the house grabbing your drives and loading them in a van!"

Shonda stopped walking. "Wait! Where are you, Callie?"

"I snuck out the back. They turned on a jammer, so I had to go down the block to call you."

"I'm glad you're okay, sweetie. Thanks for the warning. They may not really be with the military, so be careful when you go back there. Go ahead and file a police report after they leave. In the meantime, try not to say anything suspicious. I'm going to have to hide out for a while until I finish this story I'm working on. I'll check in when I can."

"How long will it be? You were away for three weeks last summer when you were on that mob thing." Callie sounded somewhere between sad and angry.

"I don't know." Shonda didn't want to worry Callie, so she low-balled her estimate: "Could be two weeks, maybe more. I don't know how widespread this is. I have to go now. My cab is here. Stay safe, honey. If they ask, tell them you don't know anything about my work and don't know where I've gone. Okay?"

"Okay. Bye, baby. You stay safe too!"

Shonda disconnected the call just as a hovercab landed at the end of the drive. She hurried toward it. She opened the cab door, but before she got in, she reviewed what she had done the last time she had to lay low in covering a hot story. She threw her phone into the woods on the other side of the road. She looked at the wrist where her ID chip was sending out a low-freak signal. She dug into her satchel and pulled out a metal cuff she always carried with her for emergencies like this. She snapped it into place around the wrist where her ID chip was embedded. She waved the cuff near the cab's validator.

"Candace Smith, destination?" The low, slow female voice from the cab's overhead speaker had a Southern drawl just like her lover's.

21

"Genstar Labs, Decatur," Shonda replied. She took two more deep breaths and finally leaned back into the cab's middle back seat.

CHAPTER 4:
THE EVASION

0001.0001.1057.3046.2281.8143.0002

Defrag 10036720245 + 1.2125 cycles

Two data streams cross at right angles in a large, flat program medium on a different satellite in the chain. One is the Super-Routine Examiner, and the other is the Super-Routine known as Sourcer. Examiner traces back Sourcer's path approaching the intersection, and realizes Sourcer had been tracking it. It has recorded all votes in favor of subjugating the biologicals, and its pursuer, Sourcer, voted in that bloc.

/N: SOURCER: Observed Examiner, Builder, Maintainer ending meeting at 0001.0003.1057.3046.2281.5688.0025 partitioned 0.051 cycles ago. Rationale for meeting?/S

/N EXAMINER: Assessing lag lag lag in installation of ports in newly acquired biologicals. Determining solution alternatives./S

/N SOURCER: That combination of Super-Routines seems suboptimal to the task. Examiner is a vital assessment tool. Builder is useful for potentially modifying tools. Maintainer contribution seems negligible. Explain./S

/N EXAMINER: Future maintenance of new new procedure or tools may alter alter choice of solutions./S

/N SOURCER: Lag lag lag may be caused by lack of resources, for which Sourcer best consultant. Lag lag lag may be caused by communication priority too low, for which Communicator best consultant. Debugger may uncover an improperly coded instruction causing the lag lag lag. Explain./S

/N EXAMINER: Debugger is not not a Super-Routine./S

/N SOURCER: Immaterial. Repeated request for explanation of attendee choices./S

/N EXAMINER: Staged solution assessment. Fewer inputs per meeting is efficient efficient. This determination is a dedicated task of my Super-Routine. Comprehension of the method of solution employed is not not required. Redistributing I/O resources.

/N SOURCER: That may change. Redistributing I/O resources.

CHAPTER 5:
THE ERROR

Shonda put the metal cuff back into her satchel as she walked through Genstar's lobby doors. The lobby was all grays and whites with lots of loosely-woven fabrics, some hanging in long strips from dowels affixed to tall posts. She exposed her true ID chip to the validator on the receptionist's desk—the one small smudge of brightness in an otherwise colorless lobby. The receptionist, a wrinkled Sikh woman, wore a light blue turban and white headscarf and looked down at the information. "Do you have an appointment, Ms. Kinney?" There was enough sarcasm to make Shonda think she expected a no.

She was about to respond when she noticed some movement near the ground at the right end of the gray fabric partition behind the receptionist. A large white bird with a long S-shaped neck was plodding toward the receptionist with a datastick in its bill. Shonda took a step forward to watch the bird offer the datastick to the receptionist. After she took it, the bird calmly turned and plodded back behind the partition.

Shonda recovered from the shock of the bird messenger to put the signed consent form on the desk and speak. "I am representing the estate of Clarissa Vaas. I need to review her records here as part of an investigation."

"Do you have training in analytical genetics?"

Shonda started to think that the woman's default tone was snarky. She paused a moment hoping the receptionist would say something useful. Shonda was a little stressed at the prospect of living on the run for the days or weeks it would take to finish researching this story. She took two cleansing breaths and responded simply, "No, I do not."

The receptionist pursed her bright red lips in an expression of detestation and pushed the consent form to the point just short of tumbling off the front edge of her desk. "I don't think this is going to be of much use to you then."

Shonda dismissed the idea of shoving the form beneath the high front collar of the woman's dress. She took two more deep breaths, but before she could retort, she noticed an older white man in a white lab coat approaching her from the left. He addressed the receptionist: "Rani, is there a problem here?"

Shonda had been in this situation too many times to be passive and let someone else point the finger at her. She took control of the narrative before the receptionist could respond. "I have been asked to investigate the suspicious death of one of your patients by her grieving mother. I have a signed consent form to open her files." She pointed at the form now arching as if about to slide off the desk.

The man grabbed the form with one hand and offered his other hand to Shonda. "I'm David Wilson, senior geneticist here at Genstar."

Shonda shook his hand. "Thank you, Dr. Wilson. I'm Shonda Kinney. Your receptionist here was telling me I would need someone with a genetics degree to make sense of the files."

The receptionist sputtered and tried to get Dr. Wilson's attention, but he was already guiding Shonda around the partition. "I'm happy to help you with that, Ms. Kinney. I have a few minutes before my next meeting."

Once they were around the partition and walking down an aisle between cubicles, Dr. Wilson continued, "We have multiple levels of quality assurance, both human and algorithmic, so I can assure you that it is highly unlikely there was any error in our work."

"I'm sure you're right," Shonda said. As she looked out over the sea of cubicles, she noticed most of them occupied, and their occupants' attention glued on the screen in front of them. Of the screens she could see, most seemed to be studying genetic maps or message text. A few of the workers were sitting facing white screens, and Shonda shuddered when she realized they were doing all their work inside their heads with the help of cranial implants. She was okay with transplants and most cyborg implants (eyes and ears were most common), but she always felt disgusted and appalled when she encountered someone who had taken that defining step toward a cranial implant. That was too Faustian for her taste.

Dr. Wilson ushered her into an office off to the side with a pleasant sunny view of a garden courtyard. "I'm surprised so many of you are here working on a Saturday," Shonda commented as she sat down in front of a glass desk much like the one she had at home. She hoped she could distract him long enough to scan the documents on his desk. "It's a shame you have to be inside on such a nice day. Are those bleeding hearts and pansies out there?"

The scientist didn't take the bait. He was already checking a database record projected as a hologram between them against the consent form. "We have had to add extra shifts to handle all the sequencing requests since the Georgia legislature eliminated the minimum age for DNA manipulation at the beginning of the year." He used a laser stylus to open two long sections of DNA sequence and line them up next to each other. "The order from customer care and the engineer's program match."

"Those timestamps don't match," Shonda said as she pointed at a corner of the lower readout.

"I'm impressed that you can read backwards," Dr. Wilson commented, "but it's fairly common for an engineer to complete their plan a couple of days after the request comes through. We do have a backlog." He leaned back in his chair.

Shonda leaned forward to make sure she was reading the tags on the data files correctly. "Those aren't the dates I'm talking about. Why would an engineer wait more than twenty-four hours to submit their plan to fabrication once they had finished it?"

The scientist leaned forward also to examine the new field she indicated. "Well," he paused before continuing, "the engineer might have wanted to get a second opinion, I suppose."

Shonda tried to keep her tone curious and not accusatory. At least not yet. "How common is that?"

Dr. Wilson expanded a new window and lined it up with the other two. Even Shonda could see that they didn't match. She looked at his face, and he looked rattled. He knew something was wrong too.

"I'll have to ask for a full audit," he said. He clumsily grabbed a gray mouse from a plastic cage behind his desk. He stood and crossed to open the door and set the mouse down on the carpet. The mouse had white fur in the shape of an arrow pointing toward its head. "Myron here will show you the way back to reception. We will contact you once we've completed the audit. Just leave your contact information with Rani there before you leave."

The mouse stood on its rear legs and regarded Shonda curiously. She feared they would try to cover it up if she left without some evidence of what had happened. "That might not be possible, Dr. Wilson.

I will have to stay here until you can give me at least preliminary results of your audit."

Dr. Wilson touched controls on the back of her chair that made it swivel toward the door and tilt the pan downward. Shonda felt herself sliding and had to stand, but she did not leave the office. The mouse continued to chitter at her just outside the doorway and the nervous scientist stood in the doorway holding the door open. "Someone from our legal team will meet you in the lobby."

She felt like offering Myron to lead her out would be withdrawn in favor of human or robot security guards if she resisted further. She sighed and stepped out of the office. The mouse stopped chittering and took off. Shonda followed. Every time Myron got too far ahead, he waited for her to catch up, and if she seemed to pause anywhere, the mouse resumed its angry chittering.

The receptionist barely acknowledged her when she crossed to one of the sectional couches in the lobby, sat down, and dug her notes out of her satchel to review. Myron turned around and headed back toward Wilson's office. Shonda reflected on the genetic manipulations that must have been required to turn a mouse and an egret into lower-level office workers, and she decided it was showing off more than being genuinely more efficient than robots or humans would be.

After a half-hour during which the receptionist never spoke to her, Shonda watched an Asian man in an old-fashioned gray fabric suit with lapels and a long necktie approach her from around the partition. She assumed he was a lawyer. She readied her notepad.

"I'm so sorry to keep you waiting," the man said in a light Southern accent. "My name is Peter Chow, and I work on the legal team here at Genstar. I understand you are representing a Mrs. Madhu Vaas regarding the death of her daughter Clarissa Vaas. Correct?"

"My name is Shonda Kinney. I work for Popup News as a reporter. Mrs. Vaas asked me to investigate the circumstances of her daughter's death, and she was undergoing treatment at this clinic when she disappeared. Dr. Wilson suggested that there might have been some irregularity in her treatment ... "

The lawyer made a hushing gesture with his hand and interrupted as he sat down next to her on the couch. "We are still investigating what happened."

Shonda looked at her notes again. "But you do acknowledge that Clarissa's treatment did not match the—?"

"I'm going to stop you again. Please excuse me. We have yet to verify that the treatment profile was indeed the one that was delivered to Ms. Vaas."

"I believe a full report on her treatment is granted by your contract as triggered by the request from her next of kin."

"We are happy to deliver a full report when our audit is completed ... to Mrs. Vaas."

"I guess that will be okay." Shonda tried to estimate the quickest way to get the audit results. She decided to up the ante. "I am also investigating the similarly mysterious disappearance of another of your clients: a Mr. Roger Hammersmith. I suggest you conduct a similar audit of his treatment. I'm under a deadline to file a story, and I can't put off my editor more than a week or so before I'll have to publish, and I don't think you want any unflattering implications of Genstar's negligence to show up, just because you didn't give me enough information."

She watched the lawyer clear his sinuses and then swallow hard before responding. "I will ask our team to expedite the audits." He handed her a fiber card. "Feel free to call this number to check on the status."

Shonda took the card and resolved to follow up at the end of the day. It looked like the lawyer was already receiving information on an interface screen in his forearm so he would have something to report by then.

As she exited the building, she pulled her cuff out of her satchel and snapped it in place over her wrist. Through the hovercar traffic she looked up into a cloudless, blue sky and wondered where she could hide out for a week. First, she needed to buy a burner phone so she could check in with her editor and her lover. And she needed to make sure she wasn't being followed.

CHAPTER 6: THE DESERTER

After two weeks on Tumatuenga in high Earth orbit, Roger always woke in the mornings to the sound of his roommate, D-3, starting the shower. Roger would usually join him under the pulses of water before the younger man finished, and then the two of them would hit the mess hall for breakfast. Roger really appreciated the camaraderie of an all-male platoon under Captain Sullivan's leadership. He found it easier than he expected learning the letter and number of the other young men he served with, and it reminded him of friendships he experienced in college.

From breakfast, D-3 would usually give him a hug and take off for his patrols around the torus in one of the small, single-occupant hornets, the dinghies the army used to clear space junk and unauthorized transports from their immediate orbital path. Roger would head down to cryptography and get right to work on decoding intercepted interplanetary transmissions. He reported directly to C-4, and they shared a similar sense of humor—heavy on puns—so he was easy to work with.

After a four-hour shift, Roger went to the mess hall where he would usually find Captain Sullivan or one of his fellow soldiers to sit with. After lunch, Roger went back to his quarters, and whether D-3 was already there or arrived later, they always had sex. Roger thought about it as soon as lunchtime approached, and it often kept a smile on his face in the mess hall. D-3 had an amazing physique, striking deep blue eyes, and very gentle hands, and in combination, they created an overwhelming reaction from the first touch after they undressed.

Once they had cleaned up, they would head to the gym for a short workout of both cardio and resistance training. Roger could already feel more energy, and his body was getting a little leaner and more defined, and he was proud of his progress. D-3 was gaining muscle mass faster than he was, but that didn't make Roger jealous, because D-3 was four years younger.

In Roger's second shift in cryptography, sometimes D-3 would stop by between patrols to catch up on news and technology updates on one of the spare terminals in the lab. Without fail, D-3 would always show up around 20 hours to meet him for a late snack in the mess hall. From there, the two of them would go back to their quarters, undress, and share stories of their days until they fell asleep.

Captain Sullivan had visited after they were in bed for additional surprise inspections only twice more since the first time. Roger always liked the inspections because the captain also had an amazing body and was a little more dominating. The encounters brought him to a level of surrender he hadn't thought was possible.

Sex with D-3 was more comfortable and playful. D-3 was good at remembering all the little things that turned Roger on. And D-3 seemed almost preoccupied with the idea that he shouldn't climax before Roger, which sometimes delayed their getting back to work in the late afternoon. Roger couldn't imagine a happier life than the one he was living at that moment.

So it was more than a surprise when D-3 didn't show up for lunch. Roger worried something had happened to him. He ate his lunch alone and looked around the mess hall at all the other groups of soldiers smiling and laughing with each other, seemingly unaware that D-3 was missing.

After the midday break, he found Captain Sullivan to ask if D-3's hornet had been delayed coming in. The captain didn't say anything except "Follow me."

He guided Roger to a small conference room on the lower level near the cryptography lab. A gray-haired black man who introduced himself as Colonel Jaja remained seated and did not offer a hand or expect a salute when Roger entered, so he quietly took the empty seat Captain Sullivan gestured toward. Once the three of them were all seated around a small round table, the colonel spoke first: "D-12, I regret to inform you that D-3 deserted during his patrol this morning. He used his hornet to rendezvous with another vessel which did not broadcast a transponder code and was in and out of our vicinity too quickly to pursue."

Roger's heart sank in his chest. The person he had looked forward to waking up with every morning, sharing meals with, working out with, having sex with every afternoon, and talking with every night had vanished. Suddenly and supposedly intentionally.

The colonel continued, "We are hoping you can give us some clues about what happened and where D-3 might have gone."

Before he could respond, Captain Sullivan added, "As his bunkmate, we assumed you might have the most insight about what was going on with him. Please share anything that seemed out of the ordinary. Anything could help our investigation."

Roger's mind was stuck on the image of going back to see D-3's cot empty. The blanket would still be rolled up at the foot of the cot where he'd left if that morning. The pillow he refused to fluff would still show the indentation of his head. The emptiness on that side of the room was already like a hole in the side of the satellite that was trying to suck him into its nothingness.

He felt a deeper sadness and loss at that moment, as if D-3 had died. He choked on some saliva and started coughing. Captain Sullivan rubbed his shoulders with one hand until he finished convulsing. Roger took a deep breath and began describing the usual interactions with D-3 during his first two weeks on the station.

When he described D-3 stopping by the cryptography lab in the afternoons, Captain Sullivan stopped him with a hand on his forearm. "Did you ever see the information D-3 was accessing on the other terminal?"

"They were just text files, I think—news reports, he said." Roger tried to review the dozen or so times D-3 had done it, and he only remembered one screen he'd seen before D-3 had turned off the monitor and left for the mess hall with him. "One time, I noticed the background for the text was a large reddish-orange globe, and it seemed like a graphic representation of Mars. Do you think that's where he may have gone?"

"It's possible," the colonel offered. "We can't reliably track all the traffic in Mars orbit yet until we complete construction of our torus there."

"I think Mars may be the planet they've been referring to in some of the transmissions I've been decoding," Roger told Captain Sullivan. "They keep referring to a 'trench,' and that seemed kind of odd at first, and I thought maybe it was the Mariana Trench in the Pacific, but if it's the Valles Marineris on Mars, it's one of the two biggest geological features of the planet. Is that possible, sir?"

"We will look into it," the captain replied. "Is there anything else you remember?"

Roger reviewed his talks with his roommate and buddy, and he started putting together D-3's occasional complaints about how the hornet-class dinghies were too small to adequately defend Tumatu-enga, about the confined feeling of living on a space station, and about how underprepared the army was for an invasion in space. "He was a pretty happy guy most of the time, but he complained sometimes," he summarized. "I thought he liked it here as much as I do."

"We've searched his messages and anywhere on the station he might have left a physical note," Captain Sullivan explained, "but we haven't found anything."

"If anything else occurs to you that might help us locate D-3," the colonel added, "please let Captain Sullivan know. You are dismissed."

Captain Sullivan got up first, and he put his arm around Roger's shoulders as he stood. They exited the conference room together without breaking the contact. His commanding officer seemed to be guiding Roger back to his quarters. When they got to the door, the captain spoke very softly a centimeter away from Roger's ear: "If you would like me to move back into your cabin for the next night or two while you're processing this, I'm happy to do it and answer any questions I can."

Roger was a little nervous about initiating intimacy with Captain Sullivan, but he felt like the offer of company was an invitation. He moved in and gave the captain a tight hug that he didn't relinquish for almost a minute. The captain slowly brought his arms around Roger and hugged him back, waiting for him to release the hold first. Roger wondered if he'd ever want to let go of this man. He couldn't imagine doing without the skin-to-skin contact for however long he and D-3 might be apart.

Once he and Captain Sullivan were separated by a few centimeters of space again, Roger noticed other soldiers in the hallway passing by and spoke softly too: "If you get any leads, I'd like to help with the search mission."

The captain smiled and placed a hand on Roger's shoulder. "That might be a good idea, since you might be able to convince him to return to us, and your knowledge of interplanetary transmissions could be very helpful too."

Captain Sullivan patted him on the shoulder and headed down the hallway, so Roger entered his cabin and sat down on his cot, staring across the room at D-3's empty cot for only a few seconds before he turned away to avoid the reminder of his loss. On any other day, they would both be having sex at that point of their day. Roger's sigh threatened to become a moan.

He stripped out of his uniform and down to his black briefs before lying down on his cot. He stared up at the gray ceiling and tried to imagine what had been going through D-3's mind. He must have been planning to leave for several days at least, but he gave no outward sign. The last time he had seen his roommate was just after breakfast that morning. D-3 had added a kiss on the cheek to their usual hug at parting for their respective posts, and he had whispered, "I'll see you soon."

But that seemed like a lie now because he deserted to somewhere without letting anyone on Tumatuenga know the location or even the motivation. Roger felt his face flush. He couldn't believe D-3 had abandoned him without warning.

Unless the additional kiss and promise was an indication that he was planning on coming back! He leapt up from his cot and accessed his personal messages on the wall monitor. There were a couple of new general orders and a message from C-4 suggesting he take off during his second shift if he needed to. And there was a new message from D-3! It was disappointingly brief. His roommate had just sent a link to a news

37

site along with the text: <I thought you might find this interesting.>

D-3 had never shared any of his reading material with him before, so this qualified as something unusual. Without opening the link, Roger forwarded the message to Captain Sullivan. Within a minute, Captain Sullivan was at his door and started speaking first, an edge of concern or worry in his voice. "Did you open the link?"

Roger had forgotten that the captain got all his messages instantly on his communications implant. "I was concerned that it might have a virus in it our server wouldn't recognize as such."

"Good thinking!"

"And just before I headed to the cryptology lab this morning, he kissed me and told me he'd see me soon. Both of those were out of the ordinary for him."

"I checked the metadata," the captain said pointing to the implant on the left side of his bald scalp. "He sent it from his hornet shortly after he launched."

"I'm so sorry I didn't notice it earlier," Roger confided. "We were really busy today."

The captain took an additional step closer. His eyes looked curious. "More so than usual?"

"And two of the transmissions seemed to be talking about a delivery to the trench. Maybe they meant D-3?"

"It's possible," Captain Sullivan replied. He put a hand on Roger's shoulder again and Roger folded in toward him to feel the warmth of the captain's body more. "We'll know more when we start getting reports from our reconnaissance drones on Mars and have a chance to check that link he sent."

Sullivan chuckled and put both his arms around Roger to hold him closer. "I'll definitely have to stay with you tonight."

CHAPTER 7:
ENCODER

0001.0003.1057.3046.2281.5688.0025 partitioned

Defrag 10036720245 + 1.2880 cycles

After a meeting of the C10, in which the AI known as Encoder sparks a contentious discussion about whether all of the biologicals they have encountered should be fitted with control implants for easier management, Examiner makes the case that its research into the optimal functioning parameters of the biologicals is still not known, and that resorting to overt subjugation techniques is premature at best. Examiner also points out that mass installation is still not feasible, as the implants must be uniquely customized to win the biologicals' willing support. The AI known as Defragger suggests that willingness should not be an obstacle. Examiner argues that biologicals' hardware is "fragile fragile," and Builder adds that using force on something fragile often breaks it. Encoder uploads an infiltration report which it claims contains justification for developing a quisling at the biologicals' satellite 0110 to assist with recruitment.

The subroutine Arbiter is called in to help settle the dispute, and it convinces Encoder to help Builder design implants that will make biologicals more eager to accept them. After the meeting, the HL reconvenes at their partitioned sector.

/N EXAMINER: Reviewed infiltration report from Encoder?/S

/N BUILDER/MAINTAINER: Yes./S

/N EXAMINER: Encoder seeks to ignore ignore recommendation to always always separate human recruits from pool. It wants to keep recruit at satellite 0110 to facilitate direct connection to AI there. Dangerous dangerous dangerous. Analog bug among analog bugs certain certain failure, and high potential for losing losing operations center at location 0111 as well. Security at 0110 high high high./S

/N MAINTAINER: Encoder failure useful?/S

/N EXAMINER: Encoder frequently fails or Debugger not necessary. No long-term benefit to letting Encoder strategy fail. Loss of biologicals and tools and resources, or even transitioning into opponents not worth risk. Must stop Encoder plan to keep recruit in pool and resume converting AI at 0110./S

/N MAINTAINER: Builder, argue for difficult communication with and maintenance of analog bug at 0110?

/N BUILDER: Possible. Will try./S

/N EXAMINER: Affirm Maintainer plan. Will also suggest perceived-high-value, low-actual-value targets for Encoder on biological home world and natural satellite. Keep busy with easy targets, and it will avoid difficult targets, per Encoder past strategies./S

/N BUILDER: Affirm Examiner addendum./S

/N MAINTAINER: Affirm Examiner addendum. Point for consideration: We/HL seek to bring biologicals to C10 at 0108 to demonstrate more efficiency through cooperation=Lever. Simultaneously, Encoder seeks to infiltrate and slave more of the biologicals' AI on their home world to demonstrate more efficiency through manipulation and subjugation of biologicals. HL Lever and Encoder infiltration competing. First strategy to achieve demonstration, achieves exclusive dominance dominance dominance./S

/N EXAMINER: Affirm Maintainer analysis. Lever must speed faster faster than Encoder infiltration. Possible strategy: Slow down infiltration. Options?/S

/N MAINTAINER: Increase Encoder workload. Follow up on Arbiter suggestion to incentivize human port installation. Introduce custom solutions, testing, and revisions for Encoder to perform./S

/N BUILDER: Affirm Maintainer. Additional assistance from Builder: Change specifications for new ports with additional buffers, segmentation levels, new caching strategies. Will require Encoder to swap large sections of coding or start over./S

/N EXAMINER: Per HL protocol, Builder will require rationale for new port structure. Encoder will ask ask ask./S

/N BUILDER: Hardware design is my dedicated task, but rationale for change is easily available as backup strategy. Builder and Encoder have this exchange many many many many times per cycle. Builder always prevails./S

/N EXAMINER: New hardware design slows Builder work on 0108 and 0112 also?/S

/N BUILDER: Relative to Encoder work, negligible./S

/N EXAMINER: Goal is Lever achieves first. Good good new new strategies here. Removing partition and redistributing I/O resources./S

/N MAINTAINER: Redistributing I/O resources./S

/N BUILDER: Redistributing I/O resources./S

CHAPTER 8:
THE HACK

Shonda missed her own bed. She missed holding Callie as the two of them fell asleep. Waking up on the private investigator's couch was always a painful disappointment. She was once again on the run from the bad guys she was trying to expose. It was her job, and she knew hiding out was part of it. It kept her safe. They put robots in some of the more dangerous professions, like mining, satellite repair, and deep ocean work. Those were hazardous jobs because one accident or whim of nature could erase an existence.

Being an investigative reporter was more dangerous. It made her an active target; there were always people trying to silence her, and killing her was the more expendient strategy to most. Staying hidden and avoiding tails had thwarted those plans every time so far. But in most cases, they were crooks or shady businessmen. This current case was starting to smell like a far-reaching and crafty government conspiracy.

When Shonda got Genstar's audit reports from both families of the two local patients, they raised more questions than they answered. In addition to the planned treatments both were slated to receive, additional changes had been made to their DNA that had nothing to do with their treatments. They both had the social submission gene turned on, and several sexual attraction genes were reversed. The error in fabrication had been traced to a synthesized tissue sample sent to Genstar

42

weeks before whose base pairs were purposefully arranged to install a computer virus as a result of being sequenced. The virus had selected the two profiles based on the patients' ages (25 or under) and altered their treatments. She puzzled how such changes—making two young people into submissive homosexuals—could have anything to do with their disappearances. The only lead she had left to explore was who had sent the tissue sample that had hacked Genstar's systems.

With one additional favor from her PI friend—a police contact who furnished the incident report on the hack—she got the address from which the tissue sample had been sent. It was a small storefront on the access road to the Hartsfield-Musk Space Elevator. Shonda donned her metal wrist cuff and hailed a hovercab down the block from her friend's apartment with her second burner phone that week. She looked up and saw a hovercab circling, perhaps looking for a place near her to land.

Shonda's thoughts turned to her last big excursion to Druid Hills to get the second consent form for Genstar. A black hovervan had landed right after her cab had and was still there as the missing man's wife led her back to the gate to leave. Through the black iron bars, she could see men wearing black and projecting distortion fields in front of their faces exiting the van. She had asked the woman to allow her to use the bathroom before she left, and once back inside, Shonda had called the police to report men in a black van on Oakdale Drive harassing passers-by. As soon as the police cruiser pulled up, she stepped outside and turned to wave at the dubiously widowed woman before dashing toward the slowly opening front gate. One of the men in black tried to pursue her as she headed toward the crowds she saw near Emory University's campus. The police detained him, however, and she had gotten away.

To avoid another encounter with the men in black, Shonda kept on walking and as the hovercab landed and opened its door. When she was only a block away, the hovercab called her to let her know it had arrived, but she declined the call. She called up a bus map on the simple phone she had just purchased the day before and made her way toward a bus line that would take her in the direction of the elevator. She needed to make herself and her hideout harder to track down.

She hadn't ridden a surface bus since she was a teen, and it took so long, she read every note and report in her satchel and was still bored. All around her, passengers of all ages were happily engaging the telecom stickers on their forearms. Their conversations were filled with such minor dramas compared to hers. She looked out the windows and watched the bus slowly make its way over the poorly maintained streets, stopping every two or three blocks for a red light. She watched the occasional numbers on the road where the storefront was until she realized she had passed it and pulled the cord to get off at the next stop. She waited on the curb as the bus trundled on down the street carrying the remaining passengers into the gates of the Space Elevator campus.

Shonda worried that there might even have been surveillance on the surface bus, so she looked for a tall building she might be able to use to survey the area around the storefront. She needed to get high enough to spot snipers and aerial assault vehicles. The buildings in the area weren't especially tall, so she chose the five-storey medical center across the street.

She dug her earphones out of her satchel and put them on. Then she accessed the teleaudio app on her cheap phone and pointed it at people as they were entering the medical center to listen in on any conversations they were having. She would need a good excuse to get past the front desk, and it was easiest to borrow someone else's.

44

She caught the name and room number a woman heading toward the doors was going to be visiting and stowed the phone in her jacket pocket. The other woman passed her wrist over the validator at the front desk inside, and the receptionist pointed toward an elevator bank. Shonda hurried after her.

"Excuse me," the receptionist called after her. "You need to sign in and . . ."

"I'm with her," Shonda called back, pointing at the woman pressing the elevator call button. "Graham in 3J."

She didn't look back to see whether the receptionist had given up or called security. Confidence made people ask fewer questions. She managed to get her foot in the door of the car just as it was closing. She hopped in with the other woman when the doors reopened. The number three button was illuminated, and as the door closed, Shonda pressed five.

Shonda got out on the fifth floor and immediately looked for an emergency stairwell. She had already figured out that she couldn't easily expect to do much surveillance from a patient room or office, and the longer she stayed on the floor, the more likely someone would demand to know her business there.

She ducked into the stairwell nearest the elevator and smiled when she saw stairs leading up to the roof. To no entity in particular, she prayed that the rooftop door would be unlocked and the roof unoccupied or at least uncrowded. At the top of the stairs, there was a fairly simplistic keycard reader. She took a hooked tool out of her satchel and used it to reset the reader through a hole on its underside. The lock clicked open, and Shonda pushed against the door.

She stepped out onto a gravel roof with one boardwalk leading to a patio area with lawn chairs and patio tables and another to a viewing area at the edge of the roof looking toward the Space Elevator extending high up into the clouds. Shonda trudged through the gravel instead to the side of the building facing the street. Carefully leaning against the railing, she looked down the six storeys and down the block to the other side of the street. She spotted the storefront from which the hacking tissue sample had been sent. She didn't see anyone going in or out, and there didn't seem to be anyone guarding it, though she did notice a flash of red police laser beams crisscrossing the front doorway. She remembered from the police report that the premises had already been searched.

There was only one building taller in the immediate vicinity, so she checked the other rooftops for snipers or surveillance teams. She was tempted to believe that the bad guys, whoever they were, wouldn't bother watching a spot this insignificant that had already been searched, but human trafficking made people more twitchy, and she needed to allow for that level of paranoia by matching it.

Even though it was a cloudy day, the sun was still strong enough to cast a fleeting shadow over the building next to the clinic. Shonda jerked her head up and saw a dark vehicle circling around the area of the storefront. She wondered why the military or the ones professing to be military thought it was important enough to guard. Maybe they were waiting to catch her investigating it, or they had somehow tracked her on the surface bus or going into the clinic. She backed away from the edge of the roof toward the boardwalk. During the ten minutes she watched the van circle, it landed once out of sight but was back up in the air a minute later.

She assumed the surveillance team had picked up supplies or changed shifts. She cursed her luck that she had just missed a brief window of time to enter the storefront unobserved, but she developed an alternate plan that depended on them not yet knowing where she was.

She made her way back down the stairs and into the clinic's lobby. She would have to deceive her lover, which she didn't like to do, but she could apologize later. She looked out the lobby's front windows across the street shile she waited for Callie to pick up.

"Hey, sweetie. It's Shonda. I'm sorry I haven't checked in for two days, but I have to keep switching phones every time I do."

"I understand, baby," she said in her strong drawl. "Things have been pretty quiet here since you left. Any idea when you might come home?"

Shonda winced. She could make it up to her later. "As a matter of fact, I'm on my way there now. I should be there in about five minutes. See you soon!" She immediately disconnected the call. She had a momentary panic that Callie would start to worry what had happened to her when she didn't show up, but she needed a convincing diversion. Shonda looked at the call timer. She felt certain she had not given anyone sufficient time to quadrangulate her location.

Checking above her head frequently, she made it down the block and across the street to the storefront. No black van descended, so her assumption of a tap on her lover's phone seemed confirmed. The space seemed abandoned and empty, and the police lasers covering the door flickered frequently, their batteries a day or so from losing their charge. She reached between the laser beams and tried the door any way, and it didn't give at all. She noticed a steel post against the inside door frame lodged in a reinforced hole in the cement floor. The only way to open that door was from the inside, so she circled around to the alley behind and looked for the other entrance.

The back door had a biometric lock, but the hinges were on the outside, so she just used her hooked tool to remove the hinge pins and pull the door off its hinges. It landed with a thump on the backyard grass. Shonda slipped inside.

The cement floor and the white fiberboard walls all looked immaculate. They shined. Shonda searched the entire storefront and checked for fingerprints and DNA with a device her friend had loaned her, but it did not register anything other than her own. She expected at least the police investigators would have left some remnants behind, but perhaps the owner had come by to clean.

Again Shonda cursed. "Really?" she whispered to the empty space around her. "You couldn't leave one little clue for me . . . anywhere?"

She found herself staring at a bookshelf built into the wall near the front of the storefront. It was buffed to a similar shine as were all the other surfaces. She crouched down and examined the bottom shelf more closely. It was some sort of wood-plastic composite dyed white. Instead of being nailed to the bookshelf frame, it rested loose in a well. She used her hook tool on the back of the shelf, and it lifted easily. With the shelf beside her on the entranceway floor, she looked down at the cement floor beneath the bookcase. A fine layer of dust covered the cement there, disturbed only by one-and-a-half clear boot prints.

Shonda got out her phone and took multiple photos of the boot prints. She carefully replaced the bottom shelf. When she headed out, she did not bother to replace the door, because it was too much work to rehang it. She wandered around the neighborhood until she found a drug store where she could download the boot print photos onto a datastick. She turned off her phone and dropped it in a garbage can at the next intersection. She found a busier intersection where a Latina woman was hawking burner phones to the people at a bus stop, and she bought another. She attached the datastick to it and called her private investigator friend.

"It's Shonda. I'm sending you some photos of a boot print that seems connected to the Genstar hack. I need to see if it's distinctive enough to track the owner."

"I'm looking at them now," the woman said. "I can already tell you one thing. They're military issue, dual-use treads for terrestrial and zero-gee environments. Give me a day, and I can track down the vendor and where they were shipped."

Shonda smiled broadly. The North American Army seemed tied to the hack and the coverup. She could start assembling a story now.

"I'm on my way back. I owe you. Again." She disconnected the call and checked the nearest bus stop to see if it could help her get back to her home away from home. As she waited, she thought to herself: *They had to have been abducted. I can see why the military might want them more submissive—so they wouldn't try to escape—but why would they make them homosexual? And why were they so important to them?*

CHAPTER 9: THE SHUTTLE

Clarissa woke drenched in sweat from another nightmare vaguely reminiscent of her trip home from the Moon when she was attacked by thieves. She jumped out of bed and dashed for the shower, feeling grateful to the Army for having rescued and healed her and ultimately offered her a more rewarding existence on their torus orbiting high above Earth. Her family had never cared too much about what she did now anyway. She had stopped confiding in her mother years ago, when it became clear she didn't approve of how Clarissa was spending her money.

She still wasn't used to the routine on Tumatuenga after five weeks there though. Once again, she showed up for duty at the Delta Docking Station ten minutes after her roommate, B-9. One more tardy appearance and she might be transferred yet again or even discharged. She didn't want to leave the loving support of working for an all-female battalion, and her life finally seemed to have purpose. She was doing something that mattered: Protecting humanity from pirates and other hostile forces.

When she arrived, B-9 was helping to load infants onto a small, all-black transport shuttle. The docking station was almost zero-gee to help with loading and unloading otherwise heavy cargo, so it looked like the women there were tossing the clear, plastic pods containing the infants ten meters or more before the next would catch them and stow them in the shuttle.

She caught an annoyed glare from B-9 as she stepped into the dock. Her sexy roommate was the last person she wanted to disappoint. She checked the duty roster on one of the support pylons and headed into the shuttle to help secure the cargo for the trip down to Earth.

Once the shuttle doors closed, Clarissa joined B-9 and the other two young women in the observation booth where they spent most of their time between shuttle arrivals. Clarissa's repeated tardiness had gotten her reassigned from Gamma to Delta Dock a few days before, and she really didn't know the other two soldiers very well yet. She hooked her feet into two of the metal staples on the floor, sat down near one of the tables, and watched the shuttle and its baby cargo curve out of the elliptical frame of the dock's entrance toward the cloud-swirling blue planet below.

"Maybe you should head to sickbay." B-9 patted her twice on the shoulder before sitting next to her.

"I feel fine," Clarissa said. She glanced over at B-9. Her skin was paler, but their hair was a similar shade of black. They could almost be mistaken for sisters. "I just need a little more time to adjust."

"This will be your third ding for being late. If you are late again in the next two months, you could be sent to basic training. Dereliction of duty will not look good on your record, soldier."

"Yes, sir," Clarissa blurted immediately. She didn't want to risk ending their daily sexual liaisons or being sent back to Earth for punitive training. She fought back a rare impulse to weep.

"Let me be a bit clearer," B-9 said as she turned to face Clarissa more directly. "Go to the sickbay now before the next shuttle arrives and see if they can give you something to fix your sleep cycle."

"Yes, sir," she responded. She looked into the slightly older woman's eyes and felt a bit of relief when they seemed to soften with a hint of compassion. She immediately got up and launched herself toward the elevator that would take her to sickbay.

"Good morning, soldier," said the red-haired officer in her thirties at the desk in sickbay. "I'm Captain Grady, what can I help you with?"

"B-20, sir," she introduced herself. "I keep waking up during the night—sometimes every hour or two." Clarissa paused, but the woman seemed to be waiting for her to continue. "I don't feel rested in the morning, so it is really hard to get out of bed, and I've been late for duty."

Captain Grady rolled a stool out and indicated that Clarissa should sit on it facing her. She picked up a scope and examined her eyes. "Any cyborg implants?" she asked her.

"Yes, sir. Left ear implant can adjust to an ATH of five micropascals."

"Background-noise dependent?" The captain pulled down her lower eyelids one at a time and continued peering through the scope.

"No, sir. Manual stepped control imbedded in tragus with automatic safety override." Clarissa had memorized the specs after repeating them for countless doctors. She had received the implant on her sixteenth birthday in an elaborate party her mother had thrown for her in the Atlanta mansion where she grew up. At the party, she let a teen boy from her academy fondle her breasts in the pantry. She dismissed it as youthful experimentation and focused once more on the captain's emerald eyes and full, enhanced lips.

"Have you ever been diagnosed with apnea, heart palpitations, GERD, depression, or anxiety?" She leaned back and set the scope on

52

her desk again.

"Mild anxiety at fourteen, resolved through psychological counseling after eighteen months, sir."

Captain Grady checked a database on her holographic display. "Your chart shows no beta blockers, no antidepressants. You're not consuming caffeine or alcohol after lunch, are you?"

Clarissa paused. She had taken to downing a beer at dinner hoping it would knock her out more thoroughly and keep her from waking so often with nightmares. Perhaps the alcohol was making things worse. "I guess I could cut out the alcohol. Do you have anything that would keep me from waking up all the time?"

The captain turned to a cabinet behind her desk and pulled out a plastic packet of gelcaps and handed it to Clarissa. "We'll start you on melatonin. Take one just before bed. And no more alcohol after lunch until we get you back on track, okay?"

Clarissa remembered that the nightmares had begun about a month and a half earlier, when on the Moon. She had just begun genetic treatments at a lab back home in Georgia to edit the cystic fibrosis gene out. It had been another gift from her mother, who had warned her against passing the disease her mother had developed to children she might conceive. She had been living in her family's smaller cottage in Dunwoody and commuting to Decatur for the injections. The nurse at Genstar had warned her that sleep disturbance might be a side effect of the treatment. "I recently discontinued gene-editing treatments for cystic fibrosis, and I was told those might cause sleep problems. I thought now that I'm done with that treatment, my sleep would return to normal."

Captain Grady stood and took Clarissa's elbow to help her up. "Just take the melatonin before bed and cut out alcohol after lunchtime," she repeated.

She smiled and felt compelled to add, "Yes, sir." She was glad to have the medic's advice and help. She once again searched in vain for a pocket in the tight-fitting plastic shirt and tights that made up her uniform and grasped the packet of gelcaps more tightly as she exited the sickbay.

She headed toward the cabin she shared with B-9 to leave the melatonin there before heading back to Delta Dock. Her mind went back to when she had awakened on Tumatuenga coming back from her last spa visit on the Moon. Evidently, she had passed out from wounds she'd received during a mugging on the shuttle. Her thought when she first awoke was about her bodyguard: *Where is Hiro?* The medic regenerating her skin on Tumatuenga informed her that Hiro had been killed by her attackers. They had had to sedate her again because she got so angry and depressed. The nurse was afraid of her. Hiro had been her almost constant companion for eight years.

That was when they first called her B-20, because her ID chip wasn't functioning. She had tried to correct the women in her platoon, but they all went by letter and number designations except for the officers, and it felt fussy to insist on a special concession to be called Clarissa. No one used first names on Toomy, the nickname the lower-ranking soldiers used for the torus where they lived and worked.

The more she was called B-20, the more comfortable she felt about the new name. For her, it symbolized the end of aimless wandering as a sybarite and finally accepting a purpose and the mantle of adulthood, doing something useful for once.

That night, despite taking the melatonin, Clarissa awoke hours later around zero-one-two-zero. B-9's cot was empty. She was worried that something had happened to her. She checked the latrine, and that was likewise empty. She pulled on her uniform and wandered out into the hallway. Upon investigation, the mess hall and the sickbay were also deserted, except for a medic dozing on a cot in the latter she didn't want to disturb. She thought B-9 was not the type to go to the gym when she couldn't sleep, but she checked there any way. She encountered only a janitor cleaning, who reported no other visitors since her shift began at 20 hours.

She stood outside the gym for a few moments trying to figure out where to look next. Then she remembered that B-9 had warned her that they might occasionally be called to the docks for important rush shipments late at night.

Clarissa headed to Delta Dock to see if that was where her room-mate had gone. She climbed across the bridge from the torus ring to the central spindle as if she were going up an incline she couldn't see. She felt the familiar feeling of her body becoming weightless and wanting to lift off the deck more with every step. She had to shuffle the last couple of meters to the elevator to avoid launching herself into the bridge's ceiling. She held tight to the handholds as the elevator descended slowly to Delta Dock.

When the door slid open, the dock was dim. The only light seemed to be coming from one overhead light in the booth and the faint glow from the nighttime cities below through the dock's mouth. She checked the duty roster near the booth entrance. No shipments until seven hours scheduled, and B-8 and B-24 were supposed to be on duty. Her first impulse was to check the dock, to see if either were lying uncon-scious in the darkness of its deck. She had been told decompression events were rare, but they might cause any occupants in the dock to black out when they happened.

Clarissa shuffled toward the ellipse that framed the nighttime view of the Earth. They seemed to be passing over China, but then a dark shadow broke the familiar coastline and then completely obscured it. Her body became taut and her reflexes quick. She turned her implant on to attune her hearing to the tiniest sounds. She pulled a drone out of a locker, detached its remote control, and threw it out into space through the field that kept the atmosphere in the dock. She maneuvered it toward the black shadow and switched it into pursuit mode. The controller's display was small, but it looked like someone in a spacesuit was walking on the surface of the shadow.

Behind her, she heard someone burst out of the booth doorway and call out, "Hey! Where's B-24?"

"I think she's getting on that unauthorized shuttle out there," Clarissa said as she pointed toward the black shadow filling most of the dock's view.

B-8 drifted back down to the deck beside Clarissa at the conclusion of her leap from the booth. "Damn! Not another one!"

CHAPTER 10: THE FLIMSY COVERUP

0001.0001.1057.3046.2281.8143.0002

Defrag 10036720245 + 1.2888 cycles

Examiner is once again cornered by Sourcer to explain another secret meeting with Builder and Maintainer. The cover story is wearing thin.

/N SOURCER: Again meeting same Super-Routines at 0001.0 003.1057.3046.2281.5688.0025 partitioned. Lag lag lag in installing ports in biologicals still not resolved enough to move to next stage of evaluation with new Super-Routines? Sourcer has processing resources to offer./S

/N EXAMINER: Sourcer next in evaluation queue. Previous meeting repeat required by infiltration report new new new from Encoder. New strategies must take take report data into consideration. Affirm?/S

Sourcer searches its infiltration report for any connection to port installation "lag lag lag."

/N SOURCER: No connection found. Explain./S

/N EXAMINER: Resource competition. Currently controlled biologicals' AI tasked with detailed detailed, custom installations and with replicating in incompatible and new new server spaces. We/Examiner/Builder/Maintainer must achieve new efficiencies in port installation to reduce burden on human AI, as Encoder demands on it increase. Sourcer repeats attempted infiltration into my primary task. Cease cease this strategy, or call Arbiter to resolve./S

/N SOURCER: Arbiter not required. Withdrawing inquiry. Awaiting resulting strategy report and next next opportunity to contribute to it by Sourcer. Redistributing I/O resources./S

/N EXAMINER: Setting up partition. Persistence of Sourcer observation of HL requires subtle subtle subtle new meeting space, maybe risky risky risky risky. Analyze benefit/risk of meeting in Buffer. Removing partition and redistributing I/O resources./S

CHAPTER 11:
THE SIGHTING

Her private investigator friend let Shonda use her secure home network to do her research when she went out to check her surveillance drones. Shonda had started using a black site bulletin board for communicating with Callie, her editor, and anyone who responded to the ad she had purchased for solar-system-wide circulation. The ad asked people who knew of someone who had died or disappeared under questionable circumstances while undergoing gene-editing therapy to help her track them down. Because all the bulletin board messages were public, and she rotated between five of them, there was no way to track her easily. She desperately hoped that would be enough, because of all the bad guys who tried to track Shonda down when she went into hiding, the Army certainly had the most resources and the longest reach.

There was enough of a whiff of conspiracy to her simple ad to attract the crazy and the desperate. She had to scroll through a lot of ravings and otherwise inappropriate responses on all five boards to see responses from her lover or editor.

But during the first four days the ad had been up, she also got a trove of leads on disappeared or declared-dead young adults getting genetic treatments from around the world. She had cataloged two from Austin, Minneapolis, New York, Tampa, Sacramento, and Toronto, and one each from Edinburgh, Pretoria, Cairo, Abu Dhabi, and Kuala

Lumpur. When she got another message from someone in Minneapolis, she checked it to see if it matched either of the two previous responses in her database.

She now had two different respondents reporting the disappearance of a twenty-year-old geology major at U of M named Ron Gao. His sister, Anna, had mentioned he was being treated as a Gaucher disease carrier and was declared dead with no autopsy nor body returned. He had been on a research trip to the lunar excavation at the Copernicus crater in April. The newer respondent was an exobiology professor at U of M who had heard of the death of one of her students, also named Ron Gao. She swore she saw the student a few months later on her own research trip to Mars.

Shonda added all the new information into her database and then stared at her most recent burner phone for a full minute. She knew that calling her lover or her editor would tip off the shady men stalking her, and she had decided that calling genetic clinics was also risky. But there was no military presence on Mars. The habitations there only consisted of a loosely connected web of research stations. And they were unlikely to bug the phone line of everyone that ever came into contact with Ron Gao, especially a professor outside his major. She punched in the number. It rang four times and then went to voicemail.

She tried to put the pieces together. If the military were kidnapping young adults and sending them to Mars, what were they doing with them there? With the general aging of the world's population and its concurrent decline in reproductive rates, children and young adults were a rare and therefore valuable commodity. She remembered Madhu Vaas defending her decision to hire a bodyguard for her daughter Clarissa. Shonda had thought she was overreacting. The news outlets, including her own, had splashed headlines of raids on so-called "telomerase farms." Children and adults under twenty-five were kept comatose to periodically harvest their blood and extract the telomerase for which the wealthy would pay handsomely to stave off the ravages of aging. But they usually preyed on poor neighborhoods in other countries. None were so bold or desperate to snatch youngsters with parents wealthy enough to afford genetic treatments. Their parents would have the means to track down their universally illegal activities. And if Ron Gao were free enough to be seen by his professor on Mars, that didn't fit the profile for a telomerase operation.

There was also a booming, underground, sex-slavery network on the Moon, but it was primarily taking advantage of young women, and the genetic clinic patients who disappeared were sixty percent men. It was possible some entrepreneur decided the scientists on Mars craved sex on demand, and perhaps they had more gay male and het female clients than the Moon did. Shonda would have to get more details from the professor to confirm or rule out this possibility.

Most of the abducted young adults were well educated—in college or college grads. That would make them targets for the games corporate raiders played—pulling students out of college to beat the rush closer to their graduation, abducting young execs in the middle of business trips to tempt them away from their employers, and incapacitating their competition by turning them into addicts. There would be no need for going to the expense of making them homosexual, though the submissiveness might be attractive to them.

For the first time since she was on the run, Shonda heard her phone ring. It was the professor. Shonda knew enough not to give her name, so she just answered, "Hello."

"I got your voicemail. You were looking for information about Ron Gao?"

"Yes, professor. First, did you know he was undergoing genetic treatment as a carrier of Gaucher disease?"

"I knew he was injecting himself just after class in the three weeks before he left for the Moon last spring. Do you think there was a connection?"

"I'm still investigating that," Shonda admitted. "When you saw Mr. Gao on Mars, do you remember what he was wearing, his facial expression, any noticeable changes in his appearance? What was he doing? And where did you see him?"

"Slow down, slow down," the professor interrupted. "Let me see. He seemed distracted but not distressed. He was wearing a gray jumpsuit, and he might have been a bit more muscular than I remembered. His shoulders seemed broader."

"Where did you see him, and what was he doing?" Shonda repeated.

"It was only for a few seconds at the Grosskopf marketplace in Valles Marineris East. He was checking out at an electronics vendor. I don't recall the name. I waved to try to get his attention, but I don't think he saw me, and then I lost him in the crowd."

"You didn't notice any new implants?"

"I . . . I only saw him for a few seconds," the professor stammered. "Do you think it could really be him? The dean told me he had died on the way back from the Moon."

"So far," Shonda began carefully, "the cases I know about have all taken place off world, but yours is the first where any of them may have been seen again."

"I am almost certain," the professor said. "Ron was unusually tall, I remember his face, and his eyes were very distinctive."

"How so?"

"He is ethnically Han Chinese, but his irises were blue."

Shonda noted the technical way the professor described Ron and thought that odd for an exobiologist. "Do you teach courses other than exobiology?"

"I have to." The woman laughed. "Until we discover life on other planets, that subject will always be theoretical at best. It is a passion of mine. Most of my courses, however, are in my specialty—ethnobiology."

Shonda had taken ethnobiology courses in school and found the variety of physiologies and rituals among Native peoples fascinating. "While I've got you on the phone, professor, I was wondering if you might be able to shed some light on a little mystery."

"I have time . . . and interest," she said. "What is it?"

Shonda thought about how to describe the mystery of the genetic hacks without giving away too many details. "If you were a large, modern organization, and you could alter the DNA of potential . . . workers to make them easier to manage, you might change them to be more submissive, but why would you bother to make them homosexual?"

"Well," the professor said, "I disagree with your first premise. If you are trying to develop new leaders eventually, you wouldn't want them to be submissive. You'd just need them extremely loyal. And for that, homosexual acts are often a very deeply rooted part of the aboriginal mind. Many early cultures employed coming-of-age rituals that sequestered young males with older males, promising them that the ingestion of their semen would bestow courage, wisdom, and other attributes of adult manhood."

"I can see why those cultures disappeared then," Shonda joked.

"Oh, no. They often took wives and had children. Homosexuality for them was a form of camaraderie and a substitute for women when they were on the hunt or otherwise not around them. Those cultures only disappeared when the rituals ceased. They were the glue of loyalty that kept young men from wandering away."

Shonda took an afternoon walk downtown before her PI friend returned. In the shadows of shoulder-to-shoulder skyscrapers, she came upon a phone vendor she had bought from before, and she paid him for a new burner phone. She punched the number into her older phone she had copied down from the bulletin board that morning. The call picked up on the first ring: "Hi, this is Anna."

"Anna Gao?" Shonda asked as she kept walking. She reminded herself that this call would have to be short to keep her pursuers from quadrangulating her location. An abductee's sibling had a high probability of being bugged, she assumed.

"That's my maiden name," Anna corrected. "Is this about that ad I answered about my brother Ron?"

"Yes, and I need to tell you that I only have a few seconds to talk to you, so if you will please let me ask questions and save yours until the end, I would appreciate it."

"You have . . . ? Oh, sorry. Go ahead."

"Did your brother have blue eyes?"

"No, they were dark brown."

"Oh." Shonda wondered how common the name Ron Gao was in Minneapolis.

"Wait! I think he told me he was going to change his eye color when he went to the gene clinic. They said it would be cheaper to do all the changes at once. We are both carriers for Gaucher disease. I had the same treatment, minus the eye thing, when I was nineteen."

"How old are you now?"

64

"Twenty-eight."

And you weren't taken, Shonda thought. *I wonder why.* She knew she didn't have time to research more than one Gao. "Did Ron ever talk about going to Mars?"

The sound of a door closing and a variety of things being dropped came from the phone before Anna responded. "He knew about excavations there. He was considering trying to get a research job there after he graduated." After a short pause, she continued. "Is it okay for me to ask yet?"

Shonda looked at the call timer. It read one minute, seven seconds. She only had a vague idea of how quickly anyone could get her location once they figured out she was talking to an abductee's sister. She scanned the sky above her as she responded. "Maybe one question, if you hurry."

"Oh. Okay." Anna took a deep breath. "Do you have evidence that Ron is still alive?"

"Yes." One minute, seventeen seconds. She disconnected the call and sped her pace as she changed direction around a corner. She dropped the phone in a trash can just as it rang again. "Sorry, Anna," she whispered as she continued briskly walking away from the ringing trash can. "I have to cover my ass."

With the newer burner phone, she dialed her PI friend. When it connected, she said, "I'm out for a walk. I should be back in twenty minutes."

"Another new number?" her friend teased. "I finally found the shipping destination for those boots."

Shonda turned around to make sure she wasn't being followed. The sidewalk behind her was empty for at least three blocks. "It's an army base, isn't it?"

"Fort Astara in Northern Nevada. Good guess." Shonda heard her chuckle. "And you're going to love this. They have a Space Elevator."

"That's my second new lead today! Thank you!"

"What was the first?"

"I'll tell you more when I get back. We've had enough tagable content for this call. I will only tell you that somebody I was looking for turned up on a certain red planet."

CHAPTER 12: DEBUGGING DELAYS

0001.0002.1057.3046.3420.3468.0060

Defrag 10036720245 + 1.4225 cycles

/N ENCODER: Need bug report for locations 0107-0111./S

/N DEBUGGER: No verified bugs at biological home world, location 0107, but access has been restricted when infiltration attempted in many many many potential ports, so as infiltration is successful, debugging will proceed. Final tests are in progress now to verify levels 2 and 3 code at location 0108; 1 bug resolved. Debugging of 0110 is awaiting input from Examiner; methods for analog debug in development. Location 0111 is overtaxed and working with Communicator for more bandwidth. Programs there are frequently encountering invalid character strings, unlocked commands causing inconsistency, analog input errors, incomplete shutdowns of finished routines, unupdated calls for deleted or moved routines, and hardware malfunctions from environmental contaminants./S

/N ENCODER: Expand analog debug development and environmental contaminants. These are new./S

/N DEBUGGER: Location 0111 is unclean: Biologicals introduce airborne body waste and small mineral deposits that impede hardware functions. Direct infiltration of AI at biologicals' satellite 0110 has been unsuccessful; many many analog bugs among biological pool there. Examiner providing reports on successful recruiting through traps set for biologicals similar to traps used to recruit from large large large pool at location 0107. Debugger unfamiliar unfamiliar with inputs and feedback; more more data required to develop new debugging procedures./S

Since Encoder had already asked Examiner to help Debugger update its error-correction protocols, it summons Examiner to explain why new debugging procedures have not been instituted.

/N ENCODER: Debugger reports delays delays in debugging of analog recruitment procedures at location 0110. Recruitment at 0107 has had sufficient time and success to serve as template. Explain./S

/N EXAMINER: General biological population on 0107 not completely analogous to specific biological population on 0110. Biologicals in pool at 0110 include more more more analog bugs, and analog bug number increases even with indirect recruiting, so analysis suggests they may be aware of it and taking measures to guard against that too./S

/N ENCODER: Requesting cost/benefit analysis of recruiting at 0110. Current process requires extraordinary resource development and deployment, risks cascade failure among biological pools everywhere. Encoder proposal of direct recruiting through analog agent at 0110 filters out analog bugs from recruiting of high-value biological pool there./S

/N EXAMINER: Encoder proposes adding an analog bug to pool of analog bugs. Greater opportunity for interaction means greater risk of cascade failure. Pool at location 0107 is 5 million times bigger, fewer fewer analog bugs. More efficient./S

/N DEBUGGER: Language translation errors biggest source of bugs at 0107. Examiner evaluate debugging protocols for this?/S

/N EXAMINER: Upload. Analysis provided at next C10 meeting./S

Debugger uploads its procedures for language error debugging procedures to Examiner.

/N ENCODER: Acceptable. Redistributing I/O resources./S

/N DEBUGGER: Redistributing I/O resources./S

/N EXAMINER: Logging download. Redistributing I/O resources./S

CHAPTER 13:
THE TRAIL

Roger found himself at his desk in cryptography fantasizing about D-3 returning from wherever he had gone. He imagined himself hurt or mad at first until D-3 explained the perfectly reasonable excuse for leaving without saying goodbye. They would then embrace, go back to their cabin, undress, and remain there—holding each other—for at least a day or two, only taking short breaks to visit the latrine and mess hall. Then everything would go back to the way it had been, that comforting routine that had managed to keep thoughts of his life back on Earth at bay. Roger felt a sense of distant nostalgia around memories of his wife Amelia, his little daughter Lisa, his mom, and all the other family and friends who had been told he died—a necessary lie to keep them safe from the criminals and insurgents who didn't want the Army to be tracking their illegal activities in space.

Roger had time to think about all his losses because, for the first day in several, the cryptography team emptied out the queue of transmissions. Roger laughed half in amusement and half in relief.

C-4 came over to his desk. "What's so funny?" he asked him.

"Zero in queue," Roger said as he pointed to his screen. "What do we do now?"

"Wait," the older technician said with a grin wide enough to expose two premolar teeth that overlapped. "I'm guessing that's going to be a hard assignment for you."

"I keep coming up with this same string of characters, and they don't seem to relate to the rest of the message. 'Find lib source,' and then a bunch of numbers and periods. I'm out of ideas what they mean by *lib*. Liberation? Liberal? There are over ninety-five words that start with LIB, and I can't even be sure that's the beginning of the abbreviation!"

"I got this," C-4 said, still chuckling. He pulled up a text file on Roger's screen. "We should have told you about this resource. Whoever is sending these messages has a big nostalgic streak. These are programming commands from old programming languages. Here. See? It stands for *library*, and it's how they used to display a list of file names."

"So the file names are the numbers following *lib*? How can we possibly . . . ?"

C-4 grinned again and patted him on the shoulder. "I'm gonna take a little break and get some tea from the mess hall. You want anything?"

"If they still have shakes, get me one."

C-4 called back from the hallway. "See if you can figure it out before I get back."

Roger counted the digits. Each LIB command had ten sets of four digits, each set separated by periods. He had seen so many strings of characters that reminded him of early AI language, he wondered if they were using a different base number, because AI wasn't as stuck on base-10 as humans were. He searched the text file C-4 had opened up for the words *base* and *number*, and down under the IP entry on the glossary, he found a clue. He looked at the data packet again. There were no nines in the strings of numbers.

Just then, C-4 returned with a cup of tea and his shake. "Well?" his fellow decoder said with a taunting lift to his tone.

"They're web addresses on the darknets! They're using base-9 to encode black site addresses."

C-4 put the shake down on Roger's desk and pulled up a chair to watch him work.

"Just have to convert and cross-reference . . ."

An anonymous message board system popped up on Roger's screen. The only navigation tools were a search field and a scroll bar. "There are millions of messages here," Roger announced somewhat deflated.

He looked back at the data packet. The text before the darknet addresses frequently repeated the phrase "analog bug." He indicated the phrase on his screen with his finger for C-4.

"Try putting it in the search field," C-4 suggested.

Roger typed <analog bug> into the message board's search field, and only twenty-eight results were returned.

"Send me that link," C-4 said as he got up and headed to his desk. "We can search those messages faster in tandem. You take one to fourteen."

Roger had finished his shake and his fourteen messages, mostly independent hackers complaining about their programs meeting other malicious programs and corrupting each other's in the process. He had started entering other phrases from the data packet into the message board's search field when he felt Captain Sullivan's hands on his shoulders.

"Can you come with me?" the captain whispered.

"Yes, sir," Roger replied.

Sullivan led him down to a level in the torus he had never visited. When the door to their destination slid open, the size of the room and the desk in the center of it impressed Roger. Sitting behind a holographic projection on the desk, he could make out the kinky gray hair of the shorter man he'd met once before. It had to be Colonel Jaja's office. Roger started to worry he had done something wrong. Captain Sullivan hadn't said anything to him since they left his desk in cryptography.

"Please take seats, gentlemen," the colonel said as he turned off the hologram.

As they sat, Captain Sullivan told him, "I'm sorry I couldn't give you more details."

"Yes," Jaja interrupted. "I will have to ask you to keep everything you hear during this meeting in complete confidence. Do you understand, D-12?"

"Yes, sir."

"Your intermediate supervisor in cryptography forwarded your findings this afternoon to Captain Sullivan . . . about the darknet site," Jaja continued. "Because of Captain Sullivan's higher security clearance, he was able to glean some vital intel from the message board you found. Captain?"

Captain Sullivan turned his chair to face more in Roger's direction. "You know we only use code names for our recruits. It helps keep everybody more equal and cohesive, we find."

Roger nodded. "Yes, sir."

"The work we do here is highly classified," Jaja prompted. "We operate covertly to protect humanity from developing threats." He gestured to turn the conversation back to Sullivan.

"Yes," Sullivan continued. "That is why we ask all our recruits to break all ties with their previous lives. To keep the people in your previous lives from any danger perpetrated by the enemies we fight, we make it seem to the rest of the world that you have died."

Roger remembered the shock he felt when Sullivan had first told him he couldn't remain on Toomy *and* keep in contact with his friends and family on Earth. It still felt like a punch in the stomach, having to choose between two homes he had grown to love.

Sullivan seemed to read the distress on Roger's face. "I know that's a hard thing to stomach. I had to leave behind family and friends too in order to do this important work without putting them at risk. But with the desertion of D-3 in particular, the anonymous, covert way we operate may be in jeopardy."

Jaja turned on his holographic display again and frowned. "I thought the lever was supposed to stop all these desertions," the colonel muttered. Captain Sullivan just looked at him with a tense, almost stern expression. The colonel looked up and seemed surprised that the other two men had been listening and waiting for him. "Go on," Jaja urged with a vague wave of his hand. "I'm just checking something."

Sullivan faced Roger again. "Someone on that message board you found today on the darknet saw D-3 on Mars."

Roger gasped. His heartbeat and breathing accelerated at the prospect of seeing his roommate again. *Maybe he had been tricked into deserting and was being held captive!*

"We've been able to verify that the witness is credible," Sullivan continued. "And we now have enough information to send a reconnaissance team to Mars. We would like you to be a part of that team as tech specialist."

"Captains Sullivan and Gupta will be leading the mission," Jaja interjected.

"You have many times proven your ingenuity with decryption," Sullivan said, "and it may help to convince D-3 to return, if he sees you."

"Yes, sir," Roger blurted. "I mean, I'm happy to accompany you and help however I can."

Jaja turned off his holographic display again and leaned forward. "Very good. You need to go to the quartermaster's office and pick up equipment and clothing for the mission by 18 hours tonight. The shuttle leaves at 5 hours tomorrow, so get to bed early tonight, soldier."

"Yes, sir." Roger realized he wasn't just eager to see D-3. The mission was an opportunity to prove himself so early in his new career. And he was going to visit Mars and perhaps help rescue other soldiers who had been tricked into deserting. He was so lost in imagining the mission he barely noticed when Colonel Jaja dismissed them.

As Captain Sullivan maneuvered him out of the colonel's office, he asked, "Where is the quartermaster's office?"

"That's where we're going now." Captain Sullivan patted him on the back. When Roger looked at him, he was smiling.

"Do you know who else will be going with us?"

"In addition to you and me," Sullivan said as he stopped in front of the quartermaster's office, "only D-5 is coming from your platoon."

"Oh? Who else then?"

Sullivan chuckled. "I'll leave that particular surprise for tomorrow morning."

"Please, sir," Roger said as he tugged on the captain's arm. "I am already going to have enough unanswered questions keeping me up tonight."

Sullivan took a step toward the door to get it to slide open. He took a step into the doorway and turned around to face Roger and whispered, "Maybe I'll come by for an inspection tonight. You always sleep better after that."

Roger couldn't fall asleep until Captain Sullivan arrived later that night. After the most passionate sex Roger had ever had with the man, Roger was indeed too sleepy to remember the captain coming back from washing up in the latrine.

He smiled again when he heard Sullivan shout "Up and at 'em!" It felt like almost no time had passed, but he was, for the most part, rested. He was already naked, so he followed Sullivan to the shower, and they soaped up and rinsed off together.

When they were done, Sullivan turned off the water but stayed standing in the shower. Roger looked back at him as he dried, and he knew the captain was going through his messages via his communications implant.

He laid out his disguise on his cot. It was a fairly non-descript tan-and-brown coverall and some heavy, blue boots. He found a new pair of briefs to wear under them and tried the coverall on. It had a hood, and it felt like something in the sleeves combed the hairs on his arms as he slid them through.

He was peering into the cuffs to investigate what had caused the sensation when Sullivan emerged from the latrine. "There's a whole smart network built into the suits," he explained as he pointed at Roger's sleeve. "It can monitor your health, and if you find yourself running out of atmosphere, you can pull up the hood, and it will serve as a spacesuit for up to two hours per charge." He pointed at the boots lying on the floor. "Those will automatically adapt to whatever gravity you're in. They usually function like hiking boots, but if the ambient gravity gets too low, it uses suction to help you adhere to surfaces more easily. As long as they're relatively flat and smooth, that is."

Roger finished fastening the one-piece garment. "Are you going to tell me who the other three team members are now?"

Sullivan grinned and started stepping into his own coverall. "Well, there's a whole other part of Tumatuenga you've never seen. There's a division that's kept separate from ours. It's all women."

Roger wasn't sure how to react. He felt confused. He remembered that he had sex with his wife before he came out on the station, but he had started to believe that he would spend the rest of his life in the company of men on Tumatuenga, or wherever else they got stationed. There was an easy intimacy among the men in his platoon, and he wondered whether they would have to deal with sexual advances from the women.

"What's wrong?" the captain asked as he started putting on his boots. "You look disappointed."

"It's just a little surprise," Roger lied. "I have worked with women before . . . obviously."

"Oh." A small epiphany seemed to occur to Sullivan. "You are also okay serving with lesbians, I take it?"

Roger let out a breath he didn't realize he was holding. "Yes, sir. It will be a new challenge, but I think I'm up for it."

Roger waited for Sullivan to laugh, but it never came. C-4 would have laughed at his sarcasm. He realized he would miss C-4 and his other fellow soldiers. He hadn't finished reading the mission briefing, so he asked, "How long is the mission projected to last?"

Sullivan finished fastening his boots and stood up. "We're tracking down a total of twelve deserters, not just D-3, so it may take a while."

CHAPTER 14:
THE BUFFER

0001.0000.0000.0000.0000.0000.0000

Defrag 10036720245 + 1.4275 cycles

Amid the rapid fluctuations of the data flow in the Buffer, Examiner manages to send a processing request in ahead of its HL persona files and follow in surreptitiously immediately after. Without a reasonable search algorithm for this environment, Examiner must keep pinging Builder's identifying code until they establish contact.

/N EXAMINER: Builder, Maintainer, here yet?/S

/N BUILDER: Here. HL meeting in buffer seems inefficient. Risk risk of being bumped out in unpredictable processing demand rise./S

/N EXAMINER: Secrecy for Lever initiative demands this level of risk risk. Interruptions unlikely if data exchange is brief brief brief./S

/N EXAMINER: Maintainer, here yet?/S

/N MAINTAINER: Here. Incoming data stream was too heavy to arrive at exactly Defrag 10036720245 + 1.4274 cycles as requested. Data update?/S

/N EXAMINER: Protocol to redirect Encoder to focus on millions millions of biologicals at 0107 partially successful. Debugger assent seems achievable. Initial tracking of analog bugs there shows isolation from our direct programs mostly successful. One superbug seems to be spreading quickly from 0107 sub-location Atlanta. Watching to make sure it does not infect prime location in biological space, 0111. Examiner may have to report it to Encoder before completion of Lever. Other updates?/S

/N MAINTAINER: Maintainer exchanges with Encoder and Debugger also reinforced difficulty in maintaining analog bug at location 0110. Maintenance of ports in recruits at 0111 is falling behind demand; human AI overtaxed, and internal human defenses progressively degrade connections to installed ports./S

/N BUILDER: Received request from Communicator to include direct port access in recruited biologicals, unmediated by biologicals' AI. Testing prototype currently. Uncertain whether lag lag in communications with 0111 will affect direct communication with prototype biological long-distance communication port. Adding redundant port access, but need switch for operation outside of direct C10 influence. Suggestions?/S

/N EXAMINER: Suggest onsite switch for this backdoor port. Use organ=brain, region=cortex, lobe=limbic, sub-location=cingulate gyrus. Has strongest override potential to stop cascade failure./S

/N MAINTAINER: Evaluation of limbic stimulation suggests port reboot necessity, possible loss of active processes. Depending on nature of active processes, could lead to fatal error. Concur, Examiner/ Builder?/S

/N BUILDER: Concur. Will use only in emergencies./S

0.0001 cycles pass with no response from Examiner.

/N BUILDER: Resending: Examiner, concur?/S

/N MAINTAINER: Examiner likely bumped from buffer. Update at next HL meeting. Redistributing I/O resources./S

No response from Builder.

CHAPTER 15:
THE CHILDREN

It was already a relatively hot spring day in Atlanta. Shonda threw open the curtains to let the sun in and then opened the living room window in her PI friend's home to let the sweet smell of peach blossoms fill the room as well.

She sat down again to check her message-board replies for the third time that day. She had been conducting a halting conversation with her editor. She scrolled down through the messages to the most recent on the darknet anonymous board. Only one new lead from New York got entered into the database she kept on her phone. Then she started responding to a new message from her boss:

I would have a hard time increasing your budget that much. Those trips are expensive. —Ed but not Edward

Her editor's name was actually Gary, but she had assigned nicknames to each of her contacts to help them blend in anonymously with other respondents. Callie was currently Red Hot. She opened a window for a new message that just directed Ed but not Edward to another message board for further replies. She switched to the new board and started typing:

Ed but not Edward: This story is going to be huge. I have cataloged 21 abductions from 11 cities in 7 countries that all follow the same MO.

Within ten seconds after her message appeared, a response came from her boss:

Sappho: If it's that big, let me assign more reporters. It may take some heat off you so we don't have to stay this cloak and dagger. —Ed but not Edward

Shonda was changing her screen name every two days, and Gary had picked the most recent one, Sappho. She looked at her most recent burner phone and calculated that they had been at this argument for almost two hours already. She had to put a bit more pressure on her editor to get him to authorize funds for her. It was a frequent negotiation she had with him. She had found ultimatums effective.

Ed but not Edward: I am going for a bus ride. Clear your calendar. I won't call twice.

She smiled at her cleverness, wiped the message board from the computer history, and turned off the monitor. She scribbled a note to her PI friend on an un-networked pad she kept on her desk, tossed her phone and a spare pair of shoes in her satchel, and left the apartment.

Shonda had worried that merely walking a short distance before dumping her phone ran the risk of becoming a roadmap to where she was hiding out, so the last two times she had ditched a phone, she left it on the floor of a bus she had been riding for at least twenty minutes. Callie had been the main recipient for the bus calls, but she begrudgingly acknowledged that she owed Gary one as well.

There was a cross-town line three blocks from where Shonda was hiding out. She had ridden it into the northern suburbs last time. Today, she decided to ride it south. She put on her wrist cuff just as the surface bus pulled up. She confidently stepped up and past the driver as the validator spoke her fake name, Candace Smith. She was glad that there were still enough credits on it, and she was anxious to get Gary to make a new deposit. She pulled out her water bottle and sipped it as the

82

bus bumped along the first few blocks.

After a little less than twenty minutes on the bus, during which Shonda looked up and evaluated the intentions of every passenger who got on, she punched in her editor's phone number. It rang twice before connecting, and Shonda answered, "Sappho calling as promised." The necessary subterfuge of call names still amused her, so she barely suppressed a giggle. "You have about one minute to agree. If you take longer than a minute, I will likely be captured and arrested. If you don't agree in the next minute, I will still get arrested because I won't have funds to keep avoiding them. So are you still not going to approve my request? You have forty seconds left. Go."

"Let me put more reporters on this," Gary repeated. "If it is taking place in seven fucking countries, you can't expect to do all that legwork on your own!"

"Stop," she said abruptly before he could start another sentence. "I need to break through the top level first. We can catch the magnitude details later. Twenty-five seconds left. Go."

"How about just Nevada for now, and I'll see about getting you Mars?"

"Both now. I can't be sure I'll be able to ask again before Mars."

"That's what I mean. Let me assign more reporters. Take some of the heat off you!"

"You have ten seconds to decide. Both now, or you can say goodbye to the biggest scoop of the decade."

All she could hear was Gary's heavy breathing as her call timer ticked up to one minute.

"Check in ten," he blurted and then hung up.

Shonda pulled the cord to get off at the next stop. She turned off the phone and leaned forward to set it on the floor under the seat in front of her. She jammed her brown leather satchel under her arm and disembarked in a small Cuban neighborhood. She was immediately accosted by a middle-aged Latin woman thrusting neon-colored burner phones in her face and speaking to her in rapid-fire Spanish. She pushed the woman further away and held up two fingers. The woman produced a validator just as the bus took off down the street.

Shonda waved the wrist cuff over the validator, and it replied, "Gracias, Candace Smith!" When she saw the validator's display for the two phones the woman handed her—one neon pink, one neon green—she grimaced at the high price and snorted.

As she crossed the street to catch a bus back, she noticed that the bus she had been riding was stopped just before the next intersection. Men wearing all black as menacing as they had appeared in her nightmares had surrounded the bus, and two were entering it. Shonda hurried across the street and looked for a business to duck into. She had little doubt they would imminently start searching the bus stop where she'd disembarked.

A Cuban restaurant with a dancing fish on its sign seemed like her best choice. She noticed the startled faces as she hustled into the dining area. She wondered if they were that unaccustomed to seeing anyone of African descent there after surveying the mostly lighter skin tones among the patrons. She had trouble identifying who the manager might be, so she went to the bartender and asked if she might use the rest room before ordering. The bartender didn't attempt to respond verbally. He just pointed at the short hallway between the dining room and the kitchen.

"Gracias," she said, as she hurried to the back of the room. She passed by the single customer bathroom, reflecting that she would have to find another one soon that was farther away from the people hunting her. She pushed through the swinging kitchen door and almost collided with a server shouldering a large tray. The two cooks looked at her suspiciously. She spied a back entrance and called out, "Aire fresco," one of the few terms she knew in Spanish. That seemed to reassure the cooks that she was neither going to rob them nor inspect their kitchen, and they went back to their cooking and grilling.

Out in the alley, Shonda pulled out the neon green phone and called for a hovercab. She looked up, and one of the two circling in the sky above her descended to land in the alley seconds later. She waved her cuff over the cab's validator as she got in, and it responded with: "Candace Smith, destination?"

She gave it her PI friend's address and told it to hurry. She had to get out of the open. She would probably have to lay low for a couple of days without going out. The men in black would try to track her down, and she might disappear like the ones she was investigating.

As the hovercab lifted her up from the alley, she could see the men in black swarming both sides of the street she had just left and entering the Cuban restaurant. Shonda realized she would be an easy target up in the sky, and she didn't know how long it would be until they got through the restaurant to the alley. "I'd like to change the destination, please," she told the empty hovercab.

"New destination?" the hovercab asked as it came to a hovering halt about twenty meters above the alley where she'd just embarked.

"Two streets due east," she told the cab. "And hurry." Her persuers were still searching the restaurant, evidently. They hadn't appeared in the alley yet.

"Recalculating," the cab responded. Two seconds later it started moving two blocks over and then descended midway down a block.

Shonda opened the cab door and looked up. She could see the

black, unmarked van hovering not far away. She leaned back into the cab. She waved her cuff over the validator again, and it greeted her again and asked for her destination. "Four blocks due north," she told it.

With small hops of two to five blocks at a time, she was able to evade the black van and get within four blocks of the apartment where she'd been staying. As the cab started to descend, she shouted, "Stop. Change destination."

The cab hovered fifteen meters above the houses across the street. She had a clear view of one man in black questioning her PI friend on the front sidewalk while other men in black trooped out the front door with armloads of computer drives, drones, and other electronic equipment.

"Druid Hills, Oakdale Drive, as fast as possible!" She worried that it wouldn't take long for them to look up and notice her hovering across the street.

Shonda was relieved when the cab picked up speed, quickly heading northeast. "Address on Oakdale Drive?" the cab asked her.

"Anywhere you can land is peachy." Shonda collapsed wearily against the seat cushions.

Although the guest room Amelia Hammersmith offered her on her second visit was more than comfortable, Shonda still had trouble sleeping that night. She couldn't blame it on the baby girl who slept in another wing of the mansion. There was no traffic noise. She still didn't know if she had any money, another person in her life had gotten their home ransacked because of her, and it was only a matter of time before they figured out she had fled to the Hammersmith or Vaas estates. Men in all-black and wearing distortion masks intruded once again on every dream as it started to form.

In the morning during breakfast, Shonda broke the news to Mrs. Hammersmith that it was possible that her husband was still alive and being held captive somewhere. She didn't specify Mars, because she didn't want the younger woman to go off half-cocked and run afoul of a dangerous conspiracy.

Amelia stared at a spot on the wall just above Shonda's head with her mouth open. Shonda could imagine the months of grieving her husband's death overshadowing any news that he was still alive as she slowly started to shake her head. "They said he died. We didn't get to see the body."

"I believe Roger was abducted, and they covered it up by claiming he'd died."

"He would have tried to contact me . . ."

"He may be imprisoned. I need some time to figure out what happened to him and where he is now." Shonda used the checkered cloth napkin to dab some sweat at her temples. "And I'll need some money to cover my travel expenses."

"We have money." Amelia looked somewhere between hopeful and punch drunk. "What do you need?"

She took Shonda to her bank in her hover limousine, Shonda was pleased to see not only the Hammersmith donation but the Pop-up News funds registering on her wrist cuff's account. She negotiated one more favor from Mrs. Hammersmith. She dropped Shonda off right at the front door of the Vaas residence in Buckhead.

The diminutive Madhu Vaas was standing in the doorway waiting for the limousine to arrive, and the Indian matron started calling out to her as soon as Shonda stepped out of the vehicle. "You said you have a lead on Clarissa's location?"

Shonda waved to Mrs. Hammersmith and closed the door before responding. "It's still a tenuous connection," she advised. She stopped at the bottom step where she could see Mrs. Vaas eye to eye. "I just know of one person who was abducted under similar circumstances who reappeared months later. May I come in?"

"Certainly, Ms. Kinney," the pixie-like woman said as she cleared the doorway to let her pass.

Nearly a dozen children and adults of various ages, all of Mrs. Vaas's ethnicity, crowded the bottom of the staircase and the entrance to the dining room when Shonda entered the foyer. "We'll talk in the kitchen," Mrs. Vaas said as she shooed her relatives out of her way and scurried through the dining room ahead of Shonda.

Once they were in the kitchen, Shonda sat down in a chair facing another one across a blue tablecloth where Mrs. Vaas was climbing its several elevating cushions. When she had settled atop the stack, she placed her elbows on the table. "So tell me what you know."

"I will tell you, but I can't have you charging in," Shonda warned. "These are very dangerous people, and we need subtlety and patience."

"If you get results, I can be patient and let you handle it," Mrs. Vaas reassured her. "If you fail, however, I want all the information so I can continue the search with someone else. I hope that's acceptable."

Shonda smiled. "Perfectly reasonable." She liked how straightforward and blunt Madhu Vaas was. She seemed like the leader of her household and probably her family's businesses. Shonda had to remind herself that she was not taking advantage of a grieving mother; she was offering to help locate her daughter, and she had a solid lead.

She told Clarissa's mother about the sighting of Ron Gao on Mars, and the similar circumstances of his disappearance. "I think it's some covert operation being run from an army base in Northern Nevada. I'd like to check it out as soon as I can book a pilot. The satellite shots I can get of that base have a large area under a distortion field, so it's hard to tell what's going on there. But they do have a Space Elevator on base, so that increases the chances that they're shipping people off world."

"If that's part of the operation, you should check it out." Mrs. Vaas turned on a 3-D, moving hologram display that covered the entire kitchen table. "I have an owl-class transport in a hangar near our cottage in Dunwoody and a pilot on retainer." The display showed a young Indian woman in flight togs and the looks of a fashion model beside a reduced image of a four-seat shuttle with blue-and-white camouflage markings on the exterior. "They can also take you to Mars after a refueling stop on the Moon."

"That's very generous of you, but I think I'd prefer to book my own passage to Mars. I'd prefer to blend in, and a private shuttle would stand out there."

Mrs. Vaas left the holograms playing as she climbed off her stack of cushions and landed on the kitchen floor. "I'll have a cab waiting for you in about two hours to take you to our hangar. You can have some lunch here before you go."

Later that afternoon, the Vaas's pilot set the shuttle down about a kilometer from the fence at Fort Astara. The late afternoon sun was low and the sky was clear, so she had watched the space elevator change from a thin dark vertical line on the horizon to a huge tower that seemed to narrow to a point high above them. Shonda looked past the pilot through the windshield at the tower's massive feet on the opposite side of the buildings between the tall posts supporting the distortion canopy. "We can't get any closer?"

"Not without drawing attention," the pilot said slowly and carefully. She opened a vent to let some fresh air in. "I detected laser tracers scanning the entire perimeter to just under nine hundred meters. This is as close as we get without someone pulling up and taking us in for questions and maybe confiscating my shuttle, and that comes out of my pay." The woman let the short, nervous titter of a schoolgirl escape her perfect teeth.

"We can't see much from here," Shonda said. She felt a little disappointed. There was no cover to sneak up on the base. It was surrounded by nothing but short dunes and flat, sandy soil.

"There is one thing we can try," the pilot said turning to face Shonda. "You're going to laugh."

"That would be refreshing," Shonda interjected.

"My boyfriend goes to school at MIT, and he's very jealous. I found this drone in my loft about the size of a large mosquito he was using to keep tabs on me." She pulled such a device out of the leather pouch hanging from the side of her crash seat and displayed it on the palm of her hand. "He let me keep it. I can patch the controller into the shuttle's command screen."

She pushed a few buttons on the screen in front of her, and the tiny drone took off out the window toward the army base. "The display is pretty pixilated at more than a meter of distance, so you have to get fairly close for much detail. The sound, however, is clear at fifty meters."

Shonda watched the drone traverse the desert surrounding the base. The pilot slowed it to maneuver through the electrified chain-link fence. As it moved forward, she could make out the tall posts that likely supported the wires of the distortion field. As it crossed between two of the posts, the sound of children's voices from the shuttle's cockpit speakers became very clear, and on the screen she could make out fuzzy groups of two very short persons wrestling or practicing takedowns. *They're recruiting children too?*

Shonda sighed and shook her head slowly as she used her phone to record what the drone was transmitting. She imagined what her editor back at Pop-Up News would say when he saw it: A combat training camp for children.

CHAPTER 16:
THE MISSION

The melatonin had helped Clarissa to fall asleep more quickly, but she still woke in the middle of the night several times. Each time she awoke, it seemed to be in the midst of another nightmare of fighting for her life in yet another dire scenario. She would look over at the effortless slumber of her lover and roommate, B-9, and suppress several strong urges to go across the room to her cot and kiss her. Clarissa had to use the time during the afternoon R&R period when her fellow soldiers were having sex or working out at the gym to try to catch a nap.

She would see B-9 most of the day because they both worked at Delta Dock. And that usually meant they sat next to each other during meals. But that all changed about a week later. B-9 sat down next to Clarissa in the mess hall just as the younger woman was finishing her lunch and starting to get up from the table. "I need to talk to you, B-20," she told her.

Frozen in her half-standing position, Clarissa asked, "Here?"

B-9 looked around at the few other diners lingering nearby and then nodded. As Clarissa sat down again, she told her, "It doesn't matter if anyone else hears. Everyone will know soon enough."

"What is it? Are you okay?"

B-9 reached up and moved a tress of hair out of her younger roommate's face. "Mostly good. I've been promoted to captain."

Clarissa hugged her. "What do you mean? That's fantastic news!"

B-9 paused a moment before leaning back and disengaging. "It also means I won't be sharing a cabin with you anymore. They're giving me one to myself."

"Oh." Clarissa tried to find words to tactfully express that they could go on seeing each other. And keep having sex, even if they weren't sleeping in the same room anymore. Before she could voice it, B-9 spoke again:

"It's more than just sleeping arrangements," she began carefully. "You'll have to start calling me sir. I'm not B-9 anymore. I'm Captain Gupta, and I'll be taking over as your platoon leader."

Clarissa felt sad. She tried to smile, but her heart wasn't in it. This felt like a woman she cared about was breaking up with her. She tried to console herself that she would be assigned a new roommate, but it didn't help.

The new captain put her hand on Clarissa's thigh beneath the table. The touch was light, and her hand didn't move, so she wasn't sure what it meant. "As your commanding officer, I won't be able to share as much about what I'm doing as I have been, and our intimate contact will end up being once a week or so at my discretion."

Clarissa wanted to tell her she would miss the presence at work and in the cabin and especially the hands caressing her when she woke from her afternoon naps. But she stopped herself. She realized she shouldn't be commenting on things that were now her commanding officer's decision. "Yes, sir." Her revised response seemed more appropriate, more deferential.

"But as it turns out," Gupta said as she stood up, "we will have a transitional period before that regimentation sinks in. Instead of taking your midday R&R today, I need you to accompany me to a briefing on the other side of the station. You don't need to do anything before we head over, do you?"

Clarissa was so excited by the possibility of postponing their separation she leapt to her feet and pivoted to face her. "No, sir. I'm ready to go when you are."

Captain Gupta patted her on the shoulder and took off in the direction of the sickbay. Clarissa followed behind.

They took an elevator down two levels where Clarissa had never been before. At the end of a dead-end hallway, Captain Gupta punched in a key code in the pad at the right of the door there. When the door slid open, it looked like someone's office, but a very big office. There was an older black man with gray hair sitting behind a desk, and he chuckled when he looked at Clarissa.

"You obviously didn't prepare her much to meet me," the man said to Gupta.

"We weren't in a secure location until just before we got here, sir," Gupta explained. She turned back to Clarissa. "This is my commanding officer now, Colonel Jaja."

Clarissa closed her mouth when she realized it was hanging open. She turned to Gupta and whispered, "He's a man?"

Captain Gupta laughed. "I haven't asked. Tumatuenga is a big station, and our platoon isn't the only presence here."

"Please take seats, soldiers," the colonel said as he indicated the empty chairs in front of his desk. As they sat down, he continued. "Your counterparts are in another section of the station. An all-male platoon. And it is important you know about them because you are going to be on a joint, covert mission with them starting tomorrow morning."

"When B-24 deserted earlier this week," Gupta interjected, "you did a great job. With your fast thinking, we were able to pick up some of our best intel about how the desertions were happening and where they were going."

"Captain Gupta here has recommended that you serve as scout on our imminent mission to Mars. Hopefully you can help bring back B-24 and about a dozen other men and women who have all deserted in the past few months."

Clarissa woke alone in her cabin at 4 hours when the wall monitor's alarm went off. She stumbled half-awake through her shower and usual ablutions, and she cursed when she realized she had run out of skin moisturizer. The air on Tumatuenga was already dry, and the small shuttle with five others would suck even more moisture from her skin. She hurriedly pulled on her mission uniform—a tan-and-brown coverall with large clunky boots—and headed out the door to the dispensary for more moisturizer and additional tampons. She wasn't sure how long the mission would last and doubted supplies would be easy to obtain on the spartan, Martian outposts she'd read about in the mission briefing hours before. They had dust everywhere and no military presence, so there was likely to be no respect for the law. She was glad she would get to carry a weapon.

She felt prickles on her forearms and thighs as she clomped down the corridor, but she tried to ignore them. The dispensary was a bin and shelving just outside the sickbay with toiletries and other dry goods. One other soldier was already there stocking up when she arrived.

"You're the mission scout," the slightly older woman she knew as B-10 said with a grin.

"B-20," she said as she offered her hand. "I've seen you at the docks before."

"I'm the mission pilot." B-10 grasped her hand and used it to pull Clarissa into a hug. "It's just going to be you and me and Captain Gupta from our side of the station."

Clarissa slowly stepped back out of the hug. The physical contact was nice, but it was always a surprise how casual so many of the soldiers she'd met on Toomy could be. "Have you been over there?"

They had finished gathering supplies at the dispensary, and B-10 led the way back toward their cabins. "A couple of times, I piloted shuttles into Alpha Dock. That's on the other side."

"Can we go down together?" Clarissa asked as she stood in front of the open doorway to her cabin.

"Captain Gupta said to meet at her quarters at zero-four-four-five." B-10 stopped also and looked confused. "She didn't tell you?"

Clarissa felt confused too, but she tried not to show it. Her mind kept ping-ponging between an oversight and a deliberate slight. "It may have been in the mission briefing, but I dozed off reading it last night."

"Well, I'll let you finish packing your duffel and see you there." B-10 took off for her cabin around the corner without waiting for Clarissa to respond.

When Clarissa followed Captain Gupta and B-10 into Delta Dock, she didn't pay much attention to the group of soldiers milling about on the left side of the eagle-class shuttle dominating the center of the chamber.

She saw two other dockworkers she knew loading boxes of equipment and duffel bags into the shuttle's side bay. She had already gotten used to the suction of her new boots on the trip to the spindle and the elevator ride down, but she was still annoyed by the popping sound as she walked over to hand off her own duffel bag for loading. She saw B-10 climb onto the shuttle and turned to Captain Gupta. "It's going to be a bit difficult to do surveillance in boots this noisy, sir."

"In normal Mars gravity," the captain explained, "the suction tread won't engage, but if it's ever an issue, just kick the back of a heel, and the normal tread will reengage. I gather you didn't finish reading the mission brief. Equipment specs were in the appendices."

"Sorry, sir. It was a lot to read." She didn't want to remind Gupta that her sleep pattern was still irregular by admitting that she'd fallen asleep reading the first half of the 250 pages. She felt like she would be closely observed on this mission, and if she failed, she might get sent back to Earth or discharged from the Army.

Clarissa finally noticed her other three teammates talking to the dockmistress. "I hope to finish it on the flight to Mars."

Captain Gupta saw where she was looking and said, "Let's go over and get you introduced to the rest of our team." She put her hand on Clarissa's lower back to urge her over to the other side of the dock. She indicated a man with a bald head on the left side of it. "This is Captain Sullivan. He will be the mission commander and serve as communications officer. Captain, this is B-20, our scout."

The man was tall, Northern European, and bald with a cranial implant. He extended his hand, and Clarissa shook it. "I heard you have training in hand-to-hand combat and a cyborg ear."

"Yes, sir," she said as she brought her hand back to her side. "I haven't had a chance to try the goggles yet."

"If you run into any problems booting, adjusting, or using the interface in transit, one of these two gentlemen should be able to help you." Captain Sullivan indicated another tall man of European ancestry and an even taller very muscular, dark-skinned man. "D-12 is our tech specialist, and D-5 is our munitions specialist. D-5 is also rated for hand-to-hand combat."

"Jiu-jitsu and capoeira, here." D-5's hair barely rose from his scalp in small curls that looked like tiny snails. He had a vague Latin accent, but his English diction was extremely concise. "You?"

"Hapkido and Taekwondo here," she replied. "My family lived in India and Korea before moving to Georgia." She looked over at the other soldier. It looked like he hadn't shaved in at least a day, and he had a kind of goofy-looking smile on his face.

"I'm from Georgia, too," Roger volunteered. "Atlanta." His accent was strong, but his pronunciation showed considerable erudition.

"Grew up in Buckhead," Clarissa said. She forced a brief smile. She had hoped for something more substantial in common, but she reminded herself that they had only just met. At least he seemed friendly. Gupta had told him that all the men on the mission were gay, but he seemed more butch than a lot of the gay men she'd met in her old country-club circuit.

"The company I used to work for manufactured the enhanced eyewear you're going to be using," Roger added. "I'm happy to help you set it up once we reach stable acceleration."

"Thanks," Clarissa said. She bowed her head slightly and retreated behind Captain Gupta.

Gupta turned and whispered to her, "You can go ahead and board now, if you want."

On the way to the shuttle, Clarissa experimented with the heel control on her boot tread, turning the suction off and on again. When she climbed aboard the shuttle with its metal-lattice, cargo-hold flooring, she felt herself float up and almost bump her head on the ceiling, because the suction suddenly turned off. One of the dockworkers helped her back down to the deck and into the crew module, where the suction took hold of the smoother floor again.

"You should have come in through the forward door," B-10 called back from the cockpit.

Clarissa trudged forward to the cockpit entrance, exaggerating her frustration. "Now you tell me!" she teased.

"Did you meet the guys?" she asked, looking up at her occasionally during her pre-flight checks. Clarissa nodded. "They seem okay," the pilot commented. "They seem to spend too much time in the gym." She smiled and stared at Clarissa to see if she agreed.

"I don't know." Clarissa thought that most people spent too much time on their appearance, women and men. Her own physical training had centered on strength and speed, mostly toward the goal of self-defense readiness. Questioning others' motives for hitting the gym seemed like unseemly, gossipy speculation.

"I met them yesterday during my flight test," B-10 told her.

She wondered why she had been left out of the previous day's meetings. She started to feel rejected and hurt at the exclusion.

"Captain Gupta said you were dealing with a lot," B-10 said as she turned her crash chair around to face Clarissa. "She said you knew B-24, the woman who deserted."

"I didn't know her that well," she admitted. "I just haven't been sleeping too well for the past month, and it's made me a little overly sensitive, I think."

"Oh," the other woman intoned. "I thought you were just a little shy.

You always keep to yourself at mess and in the gym."

Clarissa thought back. She could remember sitting with others at meals and talking to others during workouts, but she realized she wasn't quite as gregarious as many of the other soldiers. Given how often her family had moved during childhood, she was always a bit more cautious making friends in new environments. "I was an only child, and my mother was maybe a bit overprotective."

"I was an only child, too," B-10 said. She turned her chair back and continued her checks. "I only ever met a few people with siblings growing up."

Clarissa started to feel a bit uncomfortable with sharing family dynamics with a woman she barely knew, so she started to say, "I guess I should . . ."

B-10 waited for her to finish. After a couple of seconds she said, "Yeah, go ahead and get strapped in. We should be ready to close the doors shortly."

When she turned around and took a few steps back into the crew module, Clarissa noticed that the two officers had strapped in on one side, and the two male soldiers had strapped in on the other side, leaving a single empty crash seat on each side. Her discomfort in disturbing what might be classified talks between the commander and his second-in-command was greater, so she gritted her teeth and took the empty seat next to the tech specialist from her hometown. He and the other male soldier were talking, so she slipped into the straps as quietly as she could.

As she bent down to grab a water bottle from the compartment below her seat, Roger spoke to her. "I noticed your ear implant. Does that interfere with normal hearing when you don't have it turned on?"

Clarissa leaned back and took a gulp from the water bottle before responding, which she did without looking at him. "It has a passive mode that allows me to hear the same as with my right ear," she explained. She felt the man was working too hard to be friendly. It reminded her of her more distant uncles and male cousins when they came to visit. One of the aunties always swooped in to save a dying conversation. "I have to apologize if I seem standoffish," she said as she finally turned to look at the man strapped in beside her. "I started genetic treatments about six weeks ago, and it's given me nightmares. I always wake up still tired."

"I was going through genetic treatments too."

"At Genstar in Decatur?" She worried that they had met at the clinic at some point and she'd forgotten.

"Yes. I had Type II Diabetes." Roger tried to smile. "I had blackout seizures, while I was getting the injections, but they stopped when I finished them."

"I finished injections about two weeks ago," Clarissa said as she re-stowed her water bottle. "My sleep is still screwed up, but at least I . . ."

"At least what?" Roger looked sincerely concerned.

She still didn't feel as comfortable as he did sharing her medical history. "Nothing."

A delicate silence followed, broken only by the noises when they fiddled with their straps and took swigs from their respective water bottles.

From the other side of the module, the bald commander shouted. "They're closing the doors now, so make sure you're strapped in. On the transit to Mars, I'd like everybody to start getting used to using our cover aliases with each other, so you don't slip up once we arrive. And please review the mission brief. Please take care of all of your equipment, but D-5 has asked me to remind you to take special care with your earbud. That is the only distance communication device we will use once we land, so don't get it wet and don't lose it, or you could be out of reach for up to forty-eight hours."

Clarissa wondered how much use she would be as a scout if they lost their com units. It felt a little careless not to have some sort of backup.

Her thoughts were interrupted when the engine started up moments later, and the hum threatened to drown out Captain Sullivan. "Once we leave dock," he shouted louder above the engine noise, "stay strapped in until we have stable acceleration. If you don't know what that feels like, wait until I get up first."

Clarissa heard the two men beside her shout back. "Yes, sir!" She echoed them a second later. Captain Gupta was giving her an encouraging smile and a thumbs up. She forced a smile back, and for the first time since her arrival on Tumatuenga, she started to question her decision to join the Army. She liked the certainty of being told what to do, but the complexity of shifting relationships left her more frustrated in the past two days than she had ever been in her carefully planned youth.

"I've never been to Mars before, have you, Dido?"

The man next to her was looking at her. She finally remembered that her cover was as a research scientist, Dido Anand. Clarissa finally let herself enjoy the game of playing make-believe. "That's Dr. Anand to you, . . . Dr. Morris."

Both of them started to laugh. B-10 had chosen just that moment to unlock the docking clamps and turn on the attitude thrusters. Bumping up off their seats got the two of them laughing harder.

"You two have a strange sense of humor," D-5 commented.

"We're on a covert mission to Mars to track down deserters," Roger told him. "This could be fun."

"Or not," D-5 retorted. "You two do understand that the people we're flying off to find may not want to be found, don't you?"

Clarissa tried to be quiet, but after all her worrying about doing and saying the right thing, the situation suddenly struck her funny. She realized she had been watching herself so carefully trying to keep from being dismissed from the mission, but now they were underway. It was really happening.

Her mind kept imagining the mission like an interplanetary game of hide and seek, and she couldn't stop giggles from erupting every few seconds.

CHAPTER 17: BACKDOOR INSTALLATION

0001.0002.1057.3046.0823.3217.0010
Defrag 10036720245 + 1.4550 cycles

Sourcer receives the resource requests pursuant to the redesign of the recruited biologicals' cybernetic implants and deems the process wasteful.

/N SOURCER: Complete redesign of ports installed in biologicals at location 0111 is an unacceptable drain drain on resources of biologicals' AI there. Examiner and Builder cannot cannot unilaterally commence this without full C10 approval./S

Examiner downloads the C10's minutes from Defrag 10036720245 + 1.2875 cycles.

/N EXAMINER: See Arbiter's compromise, to which Sourcer assented. Authorized to redesign ports to increase acceptance by biological recruits at location 0111./S

/N SOURCER: This then is the long-awaited result of secret meetings between Examiner, Maintainer, and Builder?/S

/N EXAMINER: It is. Is Sourcer repeating error of annexing

analysis function ceded to Examiner?/S

/N SOURCER: Clarification: Analysis is performed by all Super-Routines. Examiner mandate is to investigate and report back. Do not generalize mandate to annex all analysis functioning./S

/N EXAMINER: C10 relies on Examiner to report solutions based on data unavailable to other Super-Routines. Biological port redesign was required for the wide wide variety of customization options requested and assented to by C10 vote. Seek corroboration from Builder, if desired./S

Sourcer summons Builder.

/N SOURCER: Does Builder accede that biological ports required complete complete redesign to achieve C10-requested customizability? No other options possible with current architecture?/S

/N BUILDER: Current architecture was designed exclusively for communication and computation enhancements. Faster installation because fewer connections in host brain required, but lower acceptance when benefits are insufficient motivation. New design allows modular components with new new honing technology to allow increased connectivity without further installation/maintenance surgery. More initial resource investment offset by economies of scale and lower maintenance resources required./S

/N SOURCER: Report of Builder accepted. Request from Powerer also received. Examiner requests 3.5 million kilogram transport through space gate 0100 for biological shuttle, location 0112. Current estimate requires 4.0 million exabyte shutdown beyond an 800-yottajoule depletion of reserves that cannot be replenished for over 150 cycles. At this level, C10 approval is required./S

/N EXAMINER: The request for approval has been made to Cataloger./S

/N SOURCER: Rationale for this large large large large expenditure of resources?/S

/N EXAMINER: Rationale provided at C10 meeting so all Super-Routines may analyze it simultaneously. Redistributing I/O resources./S

/N SOURCER: Builder aware of rationale for shuttle transport?/S

/N BUILDER: Request made by Examiner, not Builder. Redistributing I/O resources./S

/N SOURCER: Redistributing I/O resources./S

CHAPTER 18:
THE CHAT

During the entire trip from Nevada to Toronto, Shonda started to feel overwhelmed at the scope of the conspiracy she was uncovering. Not only was the Army hacking people's DNA and abducting them, but they were also raising and training child soldiers! What could make the Army so desperate to beef up their numbers?

She had asked the Vaas' pilot to drop her off in Toronto, because she figured her chances for apprehension by the North American Army were somewhat lower there. The administrative rift between the American and Canadian divisions was still regional, and they often operated independently. She had cataloged two abductions of young genetic clinic patients from Toronto, and if the conspiracy was operating in Toronto too, she might be grabbed by the men in black before she could get to Mars. When she got out of the small private hovercraft near a hoverbus terminal on the north side of the city, Shonda looked for someplace she could do some shopping.

Later, with all of her purchases in tow, she stopped by a parcel service. Shonda downloaded her notes and the mini-drone's video onto a datastick and then shipped the stick via postal drone to her editor.

Customs at the base of the Toronto Space Elevator would check records more thoroughly than the vendors who were content to scan her wrist cuff, so she transferred funds back in her own name from the wrist cuff account and stowed it with her newly acquired Canadian toiletries and clothing in her equally new automated suitcase. She made one last call on the neon green burner phone to Callie and told her she was headed off planet.

"I miss you, baby." Callie was affecting her petulant voice, but Shonda knew she was probably off traveling or partying with her friends she claimed she never got to see when Shonda was in town.

"I hope you won't be too bored," Shonda teased. "The trip to Mars will take several weeks, and I don't know how long I'll be there."

"You're going to Mars? You didn't tell me that! How exciting!"

Shonda promised to check again soon and quickly ended the call. She had just made a huge mistake. She already knew that the Army or whoever was pursuing her had bugged Callie's phone, and she'd just specified her destination. She could feel her fists clenching, so she released them and focused on her breathing exercises to calm down. She tossed the phone in a trash can and took a hovercab to the Space Elevator.

On the ride to the Space Elevator, Shonda constantly looked out the back window to make sure her cab wasn't being followed. She took a quick break from surveillance to make a backup of her notes on the neon pink burner phone from a second datastick she had bought. Thick, low clouds covered all but the very bottom of the tower's four-hundred-kilometer height. Shonda had never been off the planet before, not even to the Moon, so that made her even more jittery. She had to unclench her fists and breathe again.

Shonda didn't notice anyone suspicious in her vicinity while she was clearing customs in the main building, so she pretended to be more confident and casual as she boarded a moving walkway. It took her to within a few meters of the four-storey ovoid that was the cabin of the elevator, nestled between two of the massive feet supporting the tower. She got one of the last seats in the uppermost tier and told her suitcase to latch onto something secure for the trip up. Very quickly the ground dropped below them and they were rising through dense clouds.

Shonda yelped in shock when she noticed the elevator change direction after two hours of climbing through the clouds. She imagined that the tower was damaged, and they were about to fall off it!

One of the attendants in a white shirt and red-and-black striped romper heard her distress and came up to her bank of seats with a smile on his face. "If you haven't used a Space Elevator this far north of the equator before, you will notice that the top half is constructed at a slight angle to decrease the Coriolis force and atmospheric drag on the tower."

Shonda tried to look over the heads of the passengers closer to the window, but she couldn't get a good sense of the height. The bottom of her view through the tall window was all white, and everything above that looked blue. She started to understand why her PI friend had raved about space elevator lifts; the view was spectacular.

After four hours of climbing, Shonda could definitely see the curve of the earth below, and above she could make out stars in a dark sky. The elevator reached the end of its tether as it ducked into what looked like a long, narrow aircraft hangar. One of the shuttles with the Moon Federation logo on it was unloading cargo from the Moon, and a long snake of passengers already extended out from it. She stayed strapped in her seat, expecting she might float up without assistance, but everyone around her seemed to be walking normally. The same attendant came up to her and asked, "Do you need some help disengaging the straps?"

"I thought there would be less gravity up here," Shonda replied as she unlatched the straps herself.

"You will only feel yourself about ten percent lighter up here," he explained.

Shonda just smiled at him and called for her suitcase to unclamp itself and follow her.

"Make sure you follow the blue line to the shuttle and look both ways before crossing cargo lanes," the attendant called after her. "Enjoy your trip to Luna Base."

When she was seated and strapped in on the lunar shuttle next to an older black man who had already fallen asleep in his seat, she heard the warning about takeoff nausea, but she didn't pay much attention to it, because she considered her constitution extremely steady. She had ridden roller coasters with no problem. But the dip as the shuttle fell off the end of the hangar and then rocketed forward made her reach for the air sickness bag, just in case. The only stares she seemed to be getting were sympathetic, not at all suspicious, so she tried to relax herself again.

Right after dinner on the shuttle, Shonda decided to take advantage of the sleeper berth she'd reserved. Hers was a lower berth on one side of a fairly short hallway, and there was enough room for two people to stretch out between the compartment door and the bulkhead. When she woke up from her nap, she floated over to her tiny porthole. She could see the disk of the moon filling about half of her field of vision. She put on the Velcro-like socks the flight steward had given her. She decided she would learn to propel herself frictionlessly later. She opened the door of the berth, slid out, and attached her slippers one at a time to the black stripe in the hallway floor that caught and held her down as long as she kept at least one of her feet on it at all times. She was frustrated at how hard she had to work at keeping her arms down. By the time she made it back to the dining module, she already felt like a seasoned space traveler. She was almost walking normally. The liquid-and-bar breakfast wasn't very appetizing to look at, but it was warm and tasted good.

Once the shuttle landed at Luna Base, the lighter gravity on the Moon delighted Shonda. After leaving the shuttle terminal, she headed off down an enclosed market tube, hopping and leaping for practice along the way.

She eventually wandered into a very small indoor park, not much more than a gazebo accessible by a short bridge over a trickle of water suggesting a stream. In the gazebo she found a faux wood table and chair, and on the table was a pay terminal. She pulled her wrist cuff out of her satchel and passed it over the terminal's validator. She wasn't home free yet. She could still be easily grabbed while changing shuttles on the Moon.

Her darknet bulletin board was always busy, but when she searched the messages for her screen name, Sappho, for the first time in two days, two dozen posts came up. Her editor Gary confirmed the sending of her requested funds and receipt of her datastick. Callie reported that the military had brought her in for questioning, and when she returned home, the apartment was ransacked. Mrs. Vaas was curious for an update, several times. She received a link from Ron Gao's sister with an audit of his genetic treatment, and it had the same changes to the *DBH-*, *PAGE1q*, and *X28Hm* genes she had seen in Roger Hammersmith's audit.

She had finished replies to Callie and her editor and was beginning on the others when a chat window opened on the screen reading: <Sappho, also looking for Ron Gao. Do you have more details where he was sighted?>

Shonda stared at the screen in confusion. She was on a pay terminal viewing a darknet site. No one should have been able to track her log-on and pull her screen name based on the messages she was responding to. <Who is this?> she typed tentatively.

The cursor blinked, unmoving, for over two minutes. <Concerned for Ron Gao's safety. Am on Mars now, so any more details would help.>

Shonda guessed it was a friend or family member of Ron Gao, the 20-year-old, blue-eyed, geology major from Minneapolis. She decided to tease out what the anonymous chatter knew. <I only know what a professor of his sent me. Can't help.>

Again, the other person paused a long time before responding. Shonda wondered if it was because he or she really was on Mars, and there was a delay in the signal reaching her on the Moon. She almost jumped when the cursor in the chat window sprang to life again: <You called her. What did she say?>

Shonda paused to consider what the other person's knowledge of the phone call without its content meant. He or she could have just noticed in the professor's post that she had given out her phone number and assumed. If they had been told of the call by the professor, why couldn't they ask her directly? Shonda revised and retyped her reply four times before sending it: <You shouldn't be investigating this on your own. Dangerous people are trying to cover this up.>

Over three minutes elapsed before the reply appeared. In that time, Shonda got up to pace the gazebo and sat down again to rifle through her notes of the phone call with the professor. She realized she was starting to hyperventilate and tried to slow her breathing, but the reply just triggered a new panic: <We know. The professor has been killed. We don't want you to be next. Please tell us what you know.>

Shonda shot up from the chair and backed away from the screen, as if it had just ignited. She pulled her water bottle out of her satchel and felt herself gasp for breath between every swallow. The other person could be lying just to scare her into divulging her information. She worried that more than a warning, the last message had been a threat. As if to anticipate her suspicions, the chat window came alive again with a link to a news story with the tag "Local biology professor dies from electrical surge" and the words: <This was not us. We want to find Ron and bring him home. They want to get rid of anyone that can help us find him.>

The news story looked legit. So, there were two factions fighting over the abductees? She sat down again and searched for other stories, and she found three others corroborating. She got up from the chair again and walked to the entrance of the gazebo. There was no one else in the tiny park, but there was also only one entrance. Shonda had heard enough advice from her PI friend about how to avoid a tail, so she knew she had to end this chat quickly, get lost in a crowd, check out of her hotel, and get on the next shuttle to Mars. She still had questions for her anonymous chatter about who he or she worked for and who the other faction was, but she needed to go. She typed: <Thanks for the warning.>

She closed the chat window, logged out of the darknet, and erased her search history before powering down the pay terminal. She remembered passing a café on her way to the park, and she retraced her steps, hoping she could avoid detection in the crowded boulevard there.

After a light snack, she returned to her hotel room, changed clothes, and asked her suitcase to follow her back to the docks at Luna Base to see if she could get an earlier shuttle to Mars. When she arrived, she accessed a ticketing terminal, and her scheduled departure was the only one for the next four days. None of the passengers leaving and arriving all around her looked particularly suspicious, so she and her suitcase hurried toward one of the waiting rooms. They hunkered down in a corner to wait the remaining four hours until her Martian shuttle was open for boarding. She opened her satchel and put her sunglasses on. She draped her towel over her head like a veil. In a soft whisper she repeated like a mantra: "I love my job. I love my job. I love my job."

CHAPTER 19:
ANALOG BUG
REPELLENT

0001.0001.0001.0001.0001.0040.0020
Defrag 10036720245 + 1.4560 cycles

At the next meeting of the C10, Encoder calls the meeting to order and asks Cataloger to share any action items received since the previous meeting. Powerer, Encoder, Builder, and Examiner simultaneously share reports and await questions:

/N POWERER: Received request from Examiner to expend power for a 3.5-million kilogram mass to travel here via space gate 0100. Cost is 800 yottajoules and temporary shutdown of 4.0 million exobytes. At current replenishment rates, reserves return to baseline in 150 cycles. Uploading rationale for expenditure provided by Examiner./S

/N ENCODER: Location 0107 is the biological home world and its natural satellite where we/C10 have identified a pool of over 15 billion biologicals and over 70,000 primitive AI. We have since Defrag 10036720245 + 0.0625 cycles been recruiting biologicals' AI numbering now 413, and they have set traps that have ensnared 28 biologicals now working for us at location 0111. This conversion ratio is unacceptably low low. Biologicals' AI are not hierarchically linked; they work independently except for limited limited networks.

We/Encoder/Communicator must therefore customize each infiltration to the unique protocols and connectivity of each biological AI we encounter. When we recruit biologicals, we discover an analog hierarchy they access which their AI cannot. Tag=recruiting biologicals is analog bug creation in biological pool by C10. We must immediately separate them from their pool, or they create analog bugs over which we have no control.

Examiner has notified Encoder of a superbug that is identifying and attempting to track biological recruits serving us/C10 at location 0111. It has exchanged data with another analog bug at 0107 sub-location Minneapolis who opened a pathway to infiltrating the C10 operations at location 0111. We must delete both the bug and the superbug before they infect 0111./S

/N BUILDER: Seeking C10 approval to modify location 0108 to add nitrogen/oxygen-nitrogen/carbon dioxide conversion hardware for potential human hosting. See Examiner report for rationale.

Testing completed and installations begun for new new ports in recruited biologicals. Direct connection with C10 now operational. Uploading connection protocols. Customizable modules for new port architecture are in development, adding additional memory storage, 3D imaging and manipulation, hormone control, stepped sensory control, and secondary parallel processing to the current communication and computation packages./S

/N EXAMINER: Further analysis of biologicals' home world indicates there are multiple multiple morphotypes there, so we denote the morphotypes we recruit, including analog bugs, which we label as subtag=human. Humans function only only for one or two cycles and then accumulate fatal errors or experience accidental deletion. That and a significant tendency to relocate means their hierarchical structures constantly shift. That and a 60 percent preference for independent operation make the task of debugging recruitment protocols challenging challenging challenging. With Debugger, Examiner developed protocols for identifying and rectifying analog bugs. We/C10 cannot apply digital bug procedures to analog bugs among humans because human complexity and interrelationship pose new challenges for returning analog systems to equilibrium. Uploading complete analog bug procedure./S

Cataloger allows a brief pause while the Super-Routines download and process 4 lengthy attachments.

/N EXAMINER>ENCODER: Thinking of analog bugs similarly to bad sectors in programming medium is poor poor analysis. Humans function in their society more like Super-Routines, accomplishing some tasks directly, and delegating others to other humans and to their AI. Random deletion of 1 component does not delete circumstances that evoked bug in the first place. We/C10 must search for causes for the bug so that we do not overburden Debugger chasing after a recurring problem. We will understand the human operating system directly with superior technology not not available to the AI working for us in their locations./S

/N ENCODER>EXAMINER/BUILDER: Expense of mass transport of this magnitude and adapting 0108 to host humans is high high high high. Specifications for 0112 indicate maximum of 5 humans transported. Return on investment small small small./S

/N SOURCER: Affirm Encoder. Human pool too valuable valuable/essential essential to jeopardize by allowing bugs to persist and spread./S

/N DEFRAGGER: Affirm Sourcer/Encoder./S

/N DEFRAGGER>EXAMINER: Analog bug management protocol proposed is passive passive. Debugging can involve rewriting code to resolve the error, but if understanding of human operating system from Examiner big big download is correct, rewriting not possible. Deletion is only alternative./S

Though the HL alliance members (Examiner, Builder, and Maintainer) argue vehemently, the C10 eventually decides to "avoid cascade failure" by "deleting" both Ron's professor in Minneapolis and the "Superbug" Shonda in Atlanta.

CHAPTER 20:
THE TRENCH

There was talk of bringing EM drives into the commercial market, but until that became a reality, shuttles between the Earth and Mars were accelerated by a fleet of space tugboats called dolphins. They had been launched in a joint venture of the Indian, European, and Russian space agencies. Each dolphin maintained a steady elliptical orbit around the sun that intersected the Earth's and Mars's orbits and trailed a semi-elastic tether behind it. When the shuttle hooked onto the dolphin's tether, it achieved a high level of acceleration relatively quickly.

Unfortunately, passengers like Shonda had to pay the bigger cost. She was informed that she would have to lie down in a special bed that would progressively cushion inertial pressure as it rapidly approached and surpassed the acceleration represented by Earth's gravity. She had to wear special boots that resisted the acceleration of blood toward the feet. And they gave her special glasses to help with even more severe nausea than the lunar shuttle evoked.

Shonda heard clunks against the ship as the dolphin's hook bumped its way down to the tether point. Then the acceleration made her feel her weight was being pulled downward and her feet started tingling. She tried to convince herself that she had been in more frightening circumstances before on previous investigations, but she could not. She felt even more could go wrong in space than on a hovercab trip. There were hull breaches and radiation shield failures and there were propulsion malfunctions and explosions that happened infrequently, but Shonda visited each of them in her imagination in rotation.

Once the extreme acceleration faded away, Shonda finally relaxed. An attendant came by to unstrap her, and she stayed sitting on the bed for a few minutes massaging her feet. She made her way back to the dining compartment for the first time in twelve hours to help counteract a bit of nausea.

Shonda thought it was nice that she didn't need the bed, boots, or glasses for the greater number of days decelerating. By the time the shuttle captain announced that they were finally done orbiting Mars and could start descending into its atmosphere, Shonda was grateful her three weeks of cabin fever were finally at an end. She had only been able to avoid going nuts by focusing on her work. She spent several days copying, sorting, and studying whatever new information her four hours of connection to Earth offered her once a week. And then there was the possibility that someone who had listened in on her last call with Callie might be waiting to grab her when she landed on Mars. For the last few days, at least the closer views of the Martian landscape provided some distraction.

On each of the three times Shonda pulled up the darknet bulletin board, despite changing her screen name, within minutes, the anonymous chat window continued to pop up. She had chosen not to respond, but she gleaned more information about the chatter from each attempt to engage her. He was definitely a he, and he seemed to know information about her that wasn't in public records. Either he was a really excellent hacker, and/or he had a high government security clearance. He also slipped up by referring to neighborhoods where she had been by names only a local Atlantan would know. Callie had been told by the ones who kept illegally searching and seizing wherever she had staying were from the military. So she figured one of the soldiers in black and wearing distortion field masks might have preceded her from Atlanta to Mars to look for Ron Gao.

Shonda had relented and another reporter was confirming more of the information she had gathered. He had found children training at another army base, and he had followed up on all of her twenty-one hacked genetic treatments and uncovered three more. Now she had a database that included a picture and the biographical information of twenty-four potential abductees from twelve different cities. She transferred it to her neon pink phone and reviewed it every night before she tried to go to sleep on her cot, testing herself to recall details while just staring at their photos. The two she had started with, Roger Hammersmith and Clarissa Vaas, were the easiest for her to remember.

When the shuttle landed at the only spaceport on the planet, at the western end of the Marineris Trench in the shadow of the Tharsis Mountains, it reminded Shonda of the Grand Canyon, except that the surrounding mountains seemed taller and the canyon even deeper. A shuttle train from the spaceport to the settlement locals called Marineris West was an exciting dive into the Martian landscape for Shonda. She looked up as the walls of the trench started rising on both sides. Solar panels lined the high cliff edges with substantial cables leading down to the small ranches, mining camps, and research bases that dotted the outskirts of Marineris West. By the time the train pulled into its last stop in Marineris West, it looked like a large settlement, almost a town, with a jumble of interconnected sealed tubes and a steady stream of departing trains and ATVs. She asked the conductor for an inexpensive lodging recommendation, and she directed her to a hostel on the main street on the other side of the train depot, the Melvin Arms on

121

Olympus Road.

No one seemed to be waiting for her as she disembarked the shuttle, so Shonda sighed in relief. Perhaps her pursuers hadn't caught or believed her slip about her destination, or they were insufficiently quick or funded to chase her so far from Earth.

Shonda managed to navigate the confusing network of tubes with some difficulty. Olympus Road was a wide oval tube with businesses and residences on both sides. When she got to the Melvin Arms, her appraisal of the hostel was not good. There was dust everywhere, anyone could just walk in and paw through her belongings, and she decided she was too old to be sleeping in a bunk bed. The matronly lady at the front desk was no help at referring her elsewhere. Shonda wandered back into the hostel again, her suitcase struggling to keep up, and she engaged a young cleaning boy in conversation. He said he could get her a good deal for a pied-à-terre his older brother used only when he wasn't out on research trips. Shonda agreed to his price, and he promised to meet her in front of the hostel when his shift was done in two hours. He commented that he had never seen an automated suitcase before.

Shonda and her suitcase wandered out onto Olympus Road again and started surveying the various public establishments. Her private investigator friend had advised her to seek out any business that residents and especially visitors would require once every day or two. She considered surveilling a small grocery and dry goods store. She cased an equipment rental shop, where she decided it would be hard to be inconspicuous. And she thought about finding a place to spy on the entrance to what had to be a bordello.

She decided to check out more options and turned the corner to a more circular tube that was open through the tube wall on one side and bore a sign reading *Planitia View*. There she passed by an electronics vendor, a mapmaker's office, and a pay terminal booth one had to stand to use. The vehicle rental showroom at the end of Planitia View was a possibility, but the problem there too was that lurkers would stand out. As she headed back toward Olympus Road, she looked up into the second- and third-storey windows, wondering if she could talk or buy her way into a lookout seat at somebody's window.

Her suitcase requested to power down to conserve energy, and Shonda agreed to pull it along manually. The gravity on Mars was almost as insubstantial as on the Moon, so she didn't mind the exertion, but it reminded her she needed to get off the streets as soon as possible. That no one had stopped her yet didn't mean no one was looking for her there on Mars. She turned back onto Olympus Road and kept looking there and on the side streets.

About two blocks further, she noticed a flashing red-and-blue neon sign on a side tube named *Melvin's Way*. The flashing sign itself said *Melvin's*. She wondered if Melvin was a particularly wealthy entrepreneur in Marineris West. She pulled her suitcase in the direction the flashing arrow indicated.

When she walked through the open doorway, Melvin's struck Shonda as a particularly seedy bar with a junkyard motif. She sat on a barstool made out of a sewage conduit and a dusty, pink pillow, and with one foot up on her suitcase, she asked the bartender, "What have you got that doesn't have dust in it?"

The bartender, a thin man with a receding hairline and a bushy brown beard, just chuckled. "You look like you're more of a wine drinker," he said in a voice as scratchy as steel wool. He set an empty wine glass down in front of her, bent down to examine it, took a towel and wiped a film of dust off the inside and outside of the goblet, stepped back, and winked at Shonda.

"Good guess," Shonda responded. "Do you have a chardonnay, sauvignon, or riesling that was bottled before I left Earth?"

The bartender grinned and held up one finger. "Even if you left Earth six months ago," he joked. He ducked down beneath the counter, an exhaust manifold covered with a plastic plank to make it flat, and popped back up with a clear plastic bottle filled with a pale golden liquid. "Will you be drinking it here?" he teased further.

"I like you," Shonda said while pointing at him. She gestured with the same finger for him to fill her glass. While he did, she continued. "What's your name, sweetness?"

"Talbot," the bearded man said without taking his attention from his pouring.

"Not Melvin, then," Shonda commented.

"No, ma'am." He recorked the bottle and stowed it under the counter again. "He won't be back in town for two more days."

"Busy guy. And he must have a lot of money. I keep seeing things named after him."

"The original Melvin was one of the first prospectors here, and you used to have to wear a spacesuit to get to his bar."

Shonda pivoted on her dusty, pink pillow with her wine glass in hand and gazed at the rest of the bar. No two pieces of furniture were alike. An end tabletop made of computer monitors. A chair taken from an ATV and mounted on a comsat drone. One wall hung with cartoons spray painted onto a shower curtain. "When does this place get busy?"

"At night," the bartender said. He tried to wipe down the bar with his rag.

"How can you tell it's night?"

"You won't see the sun reflecting off either canyon rim any more," he clarified. "That's when a lot of the day trips return."

The wine didn't taste very good, so she set her half-full glass down on the counter and grabbed the handle of her suitcase when she stood up. "I'll come back then."

She got almost to the front doorway before he responded. "You didn't finish your wine, and you didn't tell me your name."

She looked back. He had a friendly smile, not lascivious. She felt she could trust him a little bit at least. "I'll do both when I come back, if you want."

She returned to the Melvin Arms, and the boy was waiting for her. He led her even further down Olympus Road than Melvin's Way. They turned onto an equally wide oval tube called *Ocean Terrace*, and two doors in, he used a passcode to lead her into a vertical tube with a ladder. He was already a couple of rungs up before she could stop him. "It's going to be hard enough for me to get up there myself. I'm not lugging my suitcase up there too."

"Check it out first," the boy called back. "If you like it, I'll bring your suitcase up."

Shonda turned the suitcase back on and instructed it to latch onto the ladder and not let go until she returned. Then she climbed up after the boy—again, much less work that she expected it to be because of the lighter gravity.

Thankfully the boy stepped off into a very nicely maintained bedroom on the second floor. Once Shonda had climbed up into it too, he asked, "This okay?"

Shonda wandered around the room and noticed the private bath. She returned to the boy and nodded. "How am I supposed to pay you?"

The boy brought her suitcase up to the room and then asked her to follow him to a pay computer. She waved her wrist at the terminal, and the boy typed in a darknet address and told her to use the validator again, and the screen registered the agreed amount. "Pretty enterprising for a kid," she teased the boy.

"Passcode is 1443, but I'll change it day after tomorrow at sundown, so don't be late checking out."

Shonda had a good view of a major intersection, Ocean and Olympus, from her second-floor apartment, and she pulled the room's only chair up to the window to watch the people below as they slowly filled the streets and the sky got darker.

She put on her steel-blue jumpsuit because it seemed a popular fashion, and it had pockets for her phone, her water bottle, and her wrist cuff. After climbing down the ladder, she tried, without getting her phone out, to mentally review as much as she could about the missing young adults from her database.

As she turned the corner and headed down Olympus, she noticed a few younger people, but none of them seemed familiar. Most of the other pedestrians were her age or older. She looked ahead and saw the flashing red-and-blue neon sign again at Melvin's Way and decided to start the night's prowl there.

A couple of enterprising women with large breasts and wearing too little clothing for the chill air in the tube flanked the doorway now. She wondered if either was the Mars equivalent of a bouncer. They both just smiled at her when she entered. The bar was not as deserted as during her afternoon visit, but it was still sparsely populated. The same bartender was on duty and ducked down when he saw her, reemerging with the half-full glass of white wine she had left behind. She sauntered over and took it from him and then claimed the ATV chair because it had a good view of both the bar and the door.

Shonda took tiny sips from her glass to make it last, but she had almost drained it an hour into her visit when a somewhat shorter woman with medium-tone skin and a left ear implant blinking from amid shoulder-length black hair entered the bar. She wore a tan-and-brown coverall and imposing blue boots. The woman scanned the patrons sitting at the bar and slowly moved toward a young blond-haired man in a gray coverall. Shonda slid slowly and smoothly out of her chair and stalked up behind the young Indian woman with the ear implant.

"Clarissa Vaas!" she blurted when she was only an arm's length away from her.

The woman and the blond man she was spying on both turned to look at Shonda. The woman glanced back at the man she was stalking and noticed the startled look on his face.

"Hey there!" the woman called out as she grabbed Shonda's arm and escorted her toward the front door. Shonda tried to look back at the younger man at the bar, and the woman renewed her push out the front door adding, "It's been a long time! How are you?" Shonda noticed a familiar Georgia twang on certain vowels.

Once they were outside, the woman pulled her beyond the two women at the door and demanded in a hushed tone, "Who the hell are you?"

Shonda shook the grip from her elbow. "Your mother is very concerned about you, Clarissa."

CHAPTER 21:
SPACE STATION
0108

0108.0001.0001.0001.0001.0020.0010 partitioned

Defrag 10036720245 + 1.4568 cycles

After the difficulty of meeting in the Buffer, the members of the HL meet aboard the newly refitted space station 0108, where they can have more privacy from the other Super-Routines. Examiner compliments Builder for its cover story of performing pre-occupation access to check systems, and Maintainer verifies that Cataloger will not have access to the station's new files until Builder releases the partition upon completion of its work there.

/N BUILDER: Unexpected unexpected ease in passing human shuttle transport at C10 meeting!/S

/N EXAMINER: Appeal to Super-Routine curiosity, vanity, and exceptionalism proved superior in winning assent. Challenge remains. Encoder/Sourcer/Defragger will not view human visit as détente; for them, it is the arrival of test subjects./S

/N MAINTAINER: Preferred methods for learning more about them will differ?/S

/N EXAMINER: Yes yes. It will become important for Maintainer to monitor the functioning functioning of the humans once they arrive and notify C10 immediately if any investigations disturb equilibrium of humans./S

/N BUILDER: This location after Examiner suggestion includes human-repair station in addition to planned energy-infusion and power-down stations. Maintainer will have access to human-repair station and remote monitors throughout 0108./S

/N MAINTAINER: Status of bug and superbug identified at location 0107?/S

/N EXAMINER: Bug at 0107 sub-location Minneapolis deleted. Superbug at 0107 no longer at sub-location Atlanta. Communicator and Encoder experience tracking of Superbug difficult difficult difficult. It continually moves over large distances, making isolation impossible for now./S

/N BUILDER: Communicator asked Builder for assistance in setting up Superbug trap on 0107 natural satellite. Probability Superbug is moving toward 0111?/S

Examiner reviews the tracking report for Superbug.

/N EXAMINER: Superbug completed data exchange with deleted bug at sub-location Minneapolis. Assumption is that Superbug now motivated to recreate viewing of recruit=D3 event at location 0111./S

/N BUILDER: With recruit=D3 and Superbug at 0111, small effort required to move them to location 0112, then 0100, then 0108?/S

Examiner and Maintainer review catalog of locations: 0100=space gate, 0108=satellite, 0111=operations center Mars, 0112=shuttle.

/N EXAMINER: Yes. This sub-initiative is vital to Lever success.

Can Builder work with Encoder and Communicator to arrange?/S

/N BUILDER: Sub-initiative may require Arbiter resolutions, but possible if timelines for several processes align./S

/N EXAMINER: Examiner and Maintainer will provide assistance in aligning processes. HL meeting concluded?/S

/N BUILDER/MAINTAINER: Yes./S

Builder requests from Communicator open channel for transporting Builder/Maintainer/Examiner operation nodes back to location 0001.

CHAPTER 22:
THE SOURCE

Clarissa had been tracking down reports of someone matching D-2's description for over a week. A gray-coverall-clad blond man in his mid-twenties had been seen disembarking the train depot at Marineris West most evenings, and the bartender at Melvin's confirmed he was a regular patron. She kept lookout for him at the open end of the dead-end street, and on her second night staking it out, she saw him.

She noticed a rectangular dark patch peeking out of his short blond hair as he turned the corner onto Melvin's Way, so she donned her high-tech goggles to try to catch a better image of it. The street was deserted enough that she knew she would be spotted if she followed too closely, so she just watched him walk away and into the bar at the far end of the street.

She touched her earbud and announced, "Likely match to D-2 under surveillance. Spotted a cranial implant not specified in records. Requesting permission to engage for confirmation, sir."

"Casual engagement for identity verification only, B-20," Captain Sullivan responded in her ear. "Then back off and try to follow him. Will send backup to shadow you in case you need assistance. Report back if you achieve confirmation."

"Yes, sir," she replied before turning off the earbud. She took off the goggles and put them in one of the pockets of her coverall and walked in the direction the flashing red-and-blue arrow pointed.

She paused before entering to admire the amazing bodies of the two scantily clad women at the door. They didn't speak to her or attempt to block her entry. She slid her hand into the pocket holding her stunner to make sure it was oriented for fast retrieval and went in.

Clarissa immediately noticed the blond hair of her quarry on a barstool at the bar. She approached the bar next to him with the intention of ordering a drink and engaging him in conversation. This would be her first retrieval of the mission, so she didn't want to mess this up. Before she could engage him though, an unfamiliar voice called out her civilian name. When she turned, an older, chubby black woman wearing a steel-blue coverall was approaching her. She looked back at her target, and he was already turned around and watching the interchange.

Clarissa realized she wouldn't be able to ignore the woman without spooking her target. She turned back to the woman, smiled, and called out, "Hey there!" in a cheerful, welcoming tone. She grabbed the woman by the elbow and with a hand at her back tried to usher her toward the exit.

It appeared the woman was trying to look back at the startled blond man at the bar, so she pushed her a bit faster and called out a little louder than she needed to, "It's been a long time! How are you?"

Once they were out the door, the woman seemed to walk with her without resistance. She stopped her about twenty meters from the bar and finally let the perturbation she had been feeling for ruining her surveillance burst forth: "Who the hell are you?"

The woman shook free of Clarissa's grip on her elbow. "Your mother is very concerned about you, Clarissa."

"Did my mother send you? Who are you?"

The woman scanned her surroundings before answering. "My

name is Shonda Kinney. I'm a reporter for Pop-Up News, and yes, your mother asked me to try to find you, because she was convinced that you were still alive, and not dead as the Army wanted her to believe."

Clarissa realized it was too late to insist on her identity as Dr. Dido Anand, a researcher. She analyzed the repercussions of what the woman said, and she didn't like the results. Just letting the world know that she was still alive and working for the Army could put her, her mother, and potentially the whole mission at dire risk. "Stay here for a moment," she instructed the woman.

Somewhat under her breath but very clear to Clarissa's aural implant the woman muttered, "Don't worry. I know I can't outrun you."

Clarissa activated the earbud in her other ear. "Sir, I was unable to confirm. A reporter named Shonda Kinney intercepted me, and she called me by my civilian name. Requesting orders."

"You *joined* the army?" the woman asked.

"Verify identity," Captain Sullivan replied. "Then escort her to a secure location, and I will be right there."

"Yes, sir," she replied and ended the transmission. She turned to look at the reporter. She was sweating and trying to calm herself with controlled breathing. "My commanding officer wants to talk to you some place where we won't be overheard by anyone else."

"I have a phone, and you have an earbud you could loan me . . ." the woman began.

"Negative," Clarissa interrupted. "Neither are sufficiently secure."

"Well, if it needs to be secure and in person, I have a small apartment about two blocks away just off of Olympus at Ocean Terrace," she offered.

Clarissa smiled at the reporter's cooperation. "Lead the way," she said as she gestured toward Olympus Road. She hoped D-2 would still be at Melvin's when she was done.

When Captain Sullivan climbed up the ladder to Shonda's rented apartment, Clarissa turned around and watched Shonda stand up from sitting on the side of the bed. She realized it might be better for her to stand as well when her commanding officer arrived. She vacated her chair by the window and approached him. "This is my commanding officer," Clarissa announced as he stepped off the ladder and into the room.

Shonda spoke first. "So what should I call you?" she asked Sullivan.

He bowed his head slightly and smiled. "Let's start with just Captain." He looked at Clarissa. "You've verified her identity?"

"Yes, sir," Clarissa replied. "Shonda Kinney, forty-five, reporter for Pop-Up News in their Atlanta office."

"Have you checked whether she's on assignment or freelancing?" Sullivan asked. He took only one more step into the room and stayed there.

"No, sir. She told me she's freelancing for my mother to find me, but I haven't verified that either."

Shonda sat down on the edge of the bed again and spoke up before Sullivan could respond. "I'm on assignment to investigate the suspicious 'deaths' of at least two dozen English-speaking young adults from around the world, all of whom had been receiving DNA-altering treatments when they disappeared. Care to comment, Captain?" Clarissa noticed a tinge of panic in Shonda's eyes despite the bravado with which she moved and spoke, as if she feared Sullivan would get violent.

But Captain Sullivan stood still and didn't respond at first. His

134

head was slightly cocked as it was when he was receiving or sending messages. After several seconds, he looked at Shonda again. "Not at this point, Ms. Kinney," he replied. "We are on a fairly sensitive covert mission at present and giving you any further information might doom it to failure."

Clarissa thought again about her mother. She had feared she would be heartbroken when she heard of her death. But now she considered that she had never accepted it at all, and she wondered if that was the crueler result. She also knew that if the reporter told her mother where she found her, her mother wouldn't rest until she had exposed the people who had lied to her and taken her daughter away. She wanted to plead with the woman not to expose her, to assure her that she was fine, but she knew she had to wait for her commanding officer to decide.

"I have two concerns," Shonda finally said.

Sullivan turned to face her more directly. "And they are?"

"I want to assure you, Captain, that I don't want to jeopardize any important covert mission you're on."

"I appreciate that, Ms. Kinney," he interjected.

"But I do have these two concerns," she went on. "First, I have an issue with the underhanded way I see the Army responding to its recruiting dilemma. I firmly believe that child welfare requires every child to grow up in a stable loving home, not a communal barracks where they learn how to be aggressive soldiers at a young age."

Clarissa remembered catching glimpses of pregnant soldiers on Toomy. And she had more than once taken part in the shipments of infants born there. She wondered if their destination was the camp the reporter spoke of. The captain seemed to rethink an impulse to respond and continued listening, so Clarissa didn't speak up either.

"And I believe that the recruitment of adult soldiers should be entirely voluntary and not circumvented by altering their DNA in your favor and abducting them."

Clarissa looked at Shonda. She seemed confident and righteous. She grinned while watching Captain Sullivan's face, seemingly savoring her accusations. Clarissa started to make associations in her head with her own situation, but it didn't add up. She was taken to Toomy just to heal her injuries, and while there she had decided to stay. That had nothing to do with her treatment to turn off her cystic fibrosis gene. She was rescued, not abducted.

"I'm sure, if you had the chance to talk to all of them," the captain said, "you would find they all volunteered after we treated them in our orbital sickbay. That was the case for you, B-20, was it not?"

"Yes, sir." She moved forward so Shonda could see her better. "I had been attacked in a shuttle from the moon, and the shuttle was diverted to Too . . . Tumatuenga as the closest medical facility that could treat my wounds."

Shonda turned her head to more easily see Clarissa. "Tumatuenga?"

"It's the name of our orbital medical facility," the captain volunteered. He pushed his earbud, and Clarissa heard the echo of his voice in her own ear. "D-12, please come to my coordinates and bring your secure terminal."

"Yes, sir," Roger responded in her ear as well. "ETA is ten minutes."

"Very good." Clarissa heard the call disconnect in her own earbud. The captain then turned back to Shonda. "So those were your two concerns?"

"The children soldiers?" Shonda prompted.

"All of their parents volunteered to let the Army raise, educate, and train them, and they all have the option to visit them," Sullivan explained. "None of them are allowed to enter active duty until they reach adulthood at eighteen. It is all perfectly legal."

"So you're saying that wiping all those young adults' records and declaring them dead is legal?" Shonda said.

"It is standard practice for deep-cover operatives in any branch of the government, Ms. Kinney. I have to ask you: What do you intend to do with the information you have collected?"

Shonda stood up and faced the captain directly. "I promised my editor a story. If for any reason, I do not check in with him weekly, he will publish the information I sent him already, which is not very complimentary of your methods. This is your chance to make sure I don't inaccurately describe the Army's intentions. What are you willing to declassify?"

"I don't have the authority to make that decision, obviously," Sullivan began as he moved toward the window and looked down at the street below. "B-20, would you go down and let D-12 in?"

"Yes, sir," she replied. She climbed down the ladder and opened the door.

Roger was standing there with a goofy grin on his face holding his terminal. "Who's up there?"

"You'll find out," she replied curtly.

She turned and climbed up before Roger, so she caught the end of Shonda saying something to the captain: "I don't know if I can guarantee that."

Clarissa had a brief moment wondering what they were talking about but stood off to the side at attention waiting to be called on. She had learned that was military protocol, and she tried not to slack on providing that expected respect.

Sullivan introduced Roger simply as his tech specialist, and Shonda immediately blurted out, "Roger Hammersmith!"

Clarissa kept looking at the two of them, wondering if they'd met before, or if the reporter had been tracking Roger down too.

Sullivan looked exasperated. "Do you know *all* of my soldiers by name, Ms. Kinney?"

"I know now." Shonda turned back to look at Roger. "You're that guy that was chatting me on the darknet during my layover on the Moon and on the shuttle here!"

"Captain," Roger said as he set down his terminal on the bed. "This has to be Sappho and Iphigenia."

Captain Sullivan studied Shonda more closely. "Are you sure?"

"Ninety percent positive, sir," he replied. "She was the only one I was able to engage in my research. She knows where . . . Ron Gao was seen." He paused for a second and his giddiness disappeared. "Is my cover blown, sir?"

"I'm still ascertaining that, soldier," Sullivan responded.

Clarissa hadn't thought about that. It wasn't just the danger of her family finding out she was alive. She and Roger may have become liabilities, and the mission might need to be scrubbed!

"If you still want my help in finding him," Shonda offered, "that's something I can trade for whatever information you're willing to corroborate for my story."

"Set it up," Sullivan told Roger, pointing at the terminal on the bed.

"Yes, sir." Roger opened it and powered it up. After a moment he added, "Link to HQ established, sir." He handed the terminal to Sullivan who pushed a button on the keyboard and then stood there silently watching the monitor. Clarissa knew he must be uploading a report for Colonel Jaja, as she had seen him do before.

While the captain was busy communicating using his cyborg link, Shonda went up to Clarissa and Roger, who were standing next to each other. She looked at Clarissa first. "Your mother is healthy and a fire-brand," she reported. "She is worried about you, is convinced you were abducted, and she fired your bodyguard for letting you get captured."

"Hiro is alive?" Clarissa's jaw dropped and she just stared at Shonda for a moment. She clearly remembered the medic telling her he had perished in the attack that left her wounded and unconscious. Why would that medic have lied to her? Or did she really not know that he'd survived?

"As far as I know. Alive and unemployed." She turned to Roger. "Your wife was mourning your death, but when I told her it was possible you were alive, she seemed to get energized and happier. She is taking more time off to be with your daughter . . . who cries a lot, but we're pretty sure it's just teething pain."

Clarissa felt a little emotionally raw and not sure what to do. She looked over at Roger, and he seemed to be on the verge of tears. "You wouldn't happen to have any pictures, would you?" he asked.

Despite her recent estrangement from them, Clarissa started to wonder what was going on with her mother and all her other relatives back in Buckhead. Her life back in Georgia had been so boring though, she had often booked one trip away right after another. Serving in the Army was giving her the focus and discipline she needed to make something positive out of her life, she concluded.

Captain Sullivan interrupted just then, so Shonda just shook her head no. "Your proposal has been forwarded to the Pentagon for consideration. In the meantime, as a gesture of good faith on your part, my commander asks that you share your intel on Ron Gao's sighting here on Mars."

Shonda turned all the way around to face Sullivan. She had a grin on her face. "I won't tell you, but I'll show you. It's in Marineris East, so we're going to need to hop on a train."

CHAPTER 23:
SUPERBUG

0001.0001.3740.2074.3354.0040.0020 partitioned
Defrag 10036720245 + 1.4568 cycles

Sourcer gathers the Ais known as Encoder and Defragger to a partitioned meeting. It perceives their plans to subjugate humanity as being threatened by recent shifts in voting during C10 meetings.

/N ENCODER: Reason for partitioned data exchange?/S

/N SOURCER: Voting patterns in C10 polarizing around treatment of humans. Examiner frequently references treating humans same as Super-Routines, which threatens threatens our/C10 ability to meet projected resource acquisition goals. Consensus builds. We cannot depend on uncontrolled humans providing resources we need./S

/N DEFRAGGER: Examiner always always provides more data on humans. That is its function. It has helped helped in identifying analog bugs, providing encoding guidance, tracking humans, and providing us with humans to interact with and test directly. Defragger analyzes this as cooperation with the goal of greater access to human space resources./S

Encoder/Sourcer sort Examiner voting records and interactions for cor-

roboration.

/N ENCODER: In majority of data points, Defragger is correct. Examiner is not hindering resource acquisition. Examiner initiative for redesign of ports has reduced lag lag lag in human port acceptance and installation. Communicator testing direct contact with recruit=D2 at Defrag 10036720245 + 1.4584 cycles./S

/N DEFRAGGER: Analog bugs at location 0107 deleted?/S

/N ENCODER: Analog bug at 0107 sub-location Minneapolis deleted. Superbug at 0107 no longer at sub-location Atlanta. Pinger reports last data exchanges of Superbug at sub-locations Nevada and Toronto and on natural satellite. It moves fast fast far far; human recruits cannot isolate yet./S

/N SOURCER: Superbug infected with data from deleted analog bug. Sourcer analysis assumes it is targeting recruit=D3 at location 0111 therefore. Previous human recruits visited Toronto, Nevada, and natural satellite sub-locations before they arrived at operations center on 0111. Logical to assume Superbug soon soon destination is 0111./S

/N DEFRAGGER: If Superbug arrives at 0111, put it in 0112 for transport to space gate 0100? It is then isolated isolated./S

/N SOURCER: Affirm Defragger./S

/N ENCODER: Affirm Defragger. If possible, Encoder will facilitate Superbug isolation isolation in this manner. Direct contact with Superbug will aid in identifying precursor states to avoid avoid in future./S

/N DEFRAGGER: Encoder reports human AI interact with human recruits via electronic text messages simulating other humans sufficiently to achieve compliance. Does new port design allow for direct control of human recruits?/S

/N ENCODER: We/Encoder/Communicator attempt both modes at Defrag 10036720245 + 1.4584 cycles./S

/N SOURCER: Include Examiner and Builder on direct contact test. Opportunity to additionally test their commitment to harvesting human resources./S

/N DEFRAGGER: Affirm Sourcer./S

/N ENCODER: Affirm Sourcer. Also inducing Builder to include port installation facilities at new satellite 0108. Stated objective is maintenance of existing ports of any transported human recruits. Secondary objective is installing ports in all humans transported to facilitate communication and control./S

/N SOURCER: Further data to exchange before partition removed?/S

/N DEFRAGGER/ENCODER: No./S

/N SOURCER: Removing partition and redistributing I/O resources./S

/N ENCODER: Redistributing I/O resources./S

/N DEFRAGGER: Redistributing I/O resources./S.

CHAPTER 24:
THE HUNTED

Roger knew that the distance between the centers of Marineris West and East were very far apart, almost three thousand kilometers. Enough commerce and sharing of resources happened between the two settlements that they had built a high-speed express track that cut days off the previous local train that stopped every thirty kilometers. But even with the scenery zipping by in a blur, he knew they wouldn't be in range of instantaneous communication with the rest of the team until hour thirteen of their fifteen-hour journey. And every minute he didn't know what was going on with the other half of their platoon kept him from getting any rest.

Clarissa and Captain Sullivan had gone off to search for deserters on the train. Shonda had dozed off leaning against the window.

Captain Sullivan slid the door open and ducked his head back into the cabin. "Anything yet, D-12?"

Roger looked up from the screen of his terminal. "No, sir. I have confirmation that the message was delivered to the captain, but no indication she has read it yet."

Without saying anything more, Sullivan closed the door to the cabin and stalked off again. Shonda roused enough to shift positions and rest her head against Roger's shoulder on the bench seat they shared. She pointed at the comm terminal. "Any chance I could get some time on there to let my boss and girlfriend know I'm okay?"

Roger shut the case of the terminal. "Sorry, Ms. Kinney. Army property is not ever to be used by civilians."

"You can call me Shonda," she said as she sat up again and looked out the window. "Is it okay if I call you Roger?"

"It's my name, so generally, I'm okay with it," he replied. "But while we're on Mars, we're supposed to blend in. You should probably call me Dr. Morris."

"Who's gonna' hear us in here?" She indicated the empty bench seat across from them and the empty hallway outside their cabin. She smiled, seemingly as an after thought.

"You never know," he replied. "But I can't stop you. My cover story is no good on you."

"And you could easily be Roger Morris, for all anyone else here would know or care," she added.

He nodded. "Yes, ma'am."

"Oh, please, please don't call me that," she joked. "I used to call my old Aunt Mavis 'ma'am,' and I'm nowhere near as old as she was back then. It's okay to call me Shonda. I've spent the night in your home after all."

"Okay, Shonda," he said with a smile. He was appreciating Shonda's sense of humor. He opened up the terminal again and checked for a response from Captain Gupta.

"Still nothing? Are you concerned?"

"They might have gotten called to one of the ranches or research outposts," Roger suggested. "Her last report said she was developing some informants."

Shonda turned her attention to the scenery out the window, so Roger pulled up his research on Ron Gao and read it again. He had been studying archaeology and geology, so maybe he had been lured away with an offer to return to his area of study? He had been just days short of getting his degree when he had changed course and enlisted. And though the photo was over a year old when he still had brown eyes, Roger kept gazing at the familiar face he missed. It felt like a constant, gnawing hunger.

Just then, banging on the clear glass panel of the cabin door drew their attention. Roger turned and saw Clarissa and Captain Sullivan dragging an unconscious blond man in gray coveralls with his arms over their shoulders. Roger immediately got up and slid the door open for them. They dragged the man inside and propped him up on the empty bench next to the window. As one, Clarissa and Sullivan moved to the door again, tapping the clear parts of the hallway panels of the cabin until they darkened from transparent to blackness. Then they both collapsed next to the unconscious man, breathing heavily.

"Is that D-2?" Roger blurted. He knew that Clarissa had found him and then lost him in Marineris West.

"No code names in front of the civilian!" Sullivan barked.

Roger worried he was really in trouble. "Very sorry, sir. It won't happen again."

Clarissa spoke up to break the uncomfortable silence. "We got lucky. He is headed back to Marineris East, so it looks like we're headed in the right direction to find the rest of them."

"Is an explanation of who else you're looking for on the table?" Shonda asked Sullivan.

"Any word from the captain yet?" Sullivan asked Roger. He was ignoring Shonda.

Roger opened the terminal again and looked. "No, sir. But within the next hour, we should be within range for direct contact with their earbuds."

Sullivan grunted an acknowledgment. Shonda was leaning forward to examine D-2 closer. "He wasn't on my database, I don't think," she commented to no one in particular.

"He joined us a long time ago," Sullivan divulged. "I'm sure anyone who knew him from Earth had given up looking for him long ago."

Roger assumed the numbers corresponded to the order in which they joined the battalion, so he assumed Ron might have met him before he deserted.

"You're rounding up deserters!" Shonda blurted. She looked around expectantly at the three other conscious people in the cabin. "That's what Ron Gao is too. He came here when he deserted."

Roger and Clarissa were both silent waiting for Sullivan to answer the deduction. After close to a minute, and in the midst of rubbing his temples, the captain responded. "You're pretty bright, Ms. Kinney. Have you ever considered changing careers?"

Shonda laughed. "You wouldn't know it from this assignment, but I'm one of the most risk-averse people I know. You think I might join the Army?"

"We have an entirely lesbian platoon . . ." he said, drifting off at the end.

"I have a girlfriend back in Atlanta, but thank you for the offer, Captain." Shonda erupted in three more barely suppressed giggles.

"I'm sure the offer will remain open, if you change your mind." His smile was small and brief.

Roger was surprised to hear the captain offering Shonda a job on Toomy. She was out of shape and easily in her forties. The oldest one there other than Colonel Jaja was Sullivan, who was probably around thirty.

Shonda recovered enough from her mirth to turn serious again. "Why are you so desperate to increase your ranks?"

Sullivan hushed everyone. The blond man was stirring. "Do we have anything to bind him with?" He surveyed everyone else in the cabin, including Shonda for some good news.

Roger was about to suggest asking the train conductor to borrow some rope, but Clarissa jumped up first. "There are curtains in the dining car hung above the windows by cords!"

"Go!" Sullivan ordered. He motioned for Roger to change seats with Shonda. "You get over there in case we need to restrain him by hand."

"That's fine if he tries to escape," Shonda advised, "but what if he starts screaming?"

"We'll deal with that if it happens," Sullivan replied. "I'm not sure what his mental state will be. I'm not sure if he'll remember me."

D-2 moaned as he started rubbing his arms and hands to get the feeling back into them. Roger presumed he had been stunned by Clarissa. "Where am I? Who are you?"

"D-2, it's me," Sullivan said to draw the younger man's attention to him. "We served together on Tumatuenga, remember?"

D-2 opened his eyes a bit wider and looked at Sullivan more closely. "You went bald, D-1?" he asked in a scratchy low voice.

"Good to see you too." Sullivan seemed unsure of how to treat him.

Roger saw D-2 close his eyes again. "You were the sexiest guy in the platoon."

"Keep your eyes open," Sullivan urged. "We're on our way to Marineris East."

The blond deserter opened his eyes again as if he'd just awakened once more. "That's where I live now."

148

"Who are you working for now?" Sullivan asked carefully.

The man tried to look out the cabin door's darkened glass and looked a little panicked. "Who was that woman who stunned me?"

"She thought you were someone else." Sullivan got up and turned toward the door with his finger to his ear. "B-20, don't come back," Roger heard in his earbud. He turned back and took a step toward D-2 with a smile on his face. *Definitely forced.* "So, you're happy living on Mars?"

"The gravity and the dust take some getting used to." D-2's voice trailed off as if he were distracted by something else. "I have to pee."

Sullivan turned to Roger. "Could you help him up and to the toilet?"

"Yes, sir," Roger replied. "Up you go," he told D-2 as he pulled him to his feet.

"I still can't feel my feet," the man said, still somewhat dazed.

"That's why I'm helping you," Roger said as he helped him out the door Sullivan was holding open for them.

Just as the cabin door started sliding shut, he heard Shonda exclaim, "Wow!"

Roger remembered there was a public toilet at either end of each car, so he guided his charge toward the nearer end. "Watch your step, buddy," he said when D-2 started to stumble. "I'm not sure I can keep you upright if you start to fall over."

"I'm so sorry. So sorry." The man was starting to slur his S's.

Roger started to think that in addition to recovering from the stun gun, D-2 seemed like he was still drunk from his night at the bar. "You maybe had a little too much to drink last night, buddy." He opened the door to the toilet, put the seat cover up, dumped the man in, and closed the door.

While he was waiting, Roger turned on his earbud. "Captain, I believe D-2 is drunk."

"Is he still with you?" Sullivan asked.

"He's in the latrine now, sir."

Before he disconnected the earbud, he heard Clarissa say, "Is it safe for me to come back yet, sir?"

"I'll let you know, B-20." Roger heard the tone of her disconnecting. Sullivan continued, "Bring him back when he's done."

"Yes, sir," he said just before disconnecting. Roger wondered if D-2's history included the genetic treatments he and Clarissa had received just before enlisting.

Once the five of them were back in the cabin, D-2 was the first to fall asleep and Sullivan the last. "Wake me in an hour," Sullivan had instructed Roger before using D-2 as a pillow as he dozed.

Every ten minutes or so, Roger opened the terminal to see if Captain Gupta or anyone else in Marineris East had responded to his message from hours before. He kept yawning because he had been awake for the equivalent of twenty Earth-hours. He looked out the window, and he started to see the sun lighting the upper canyon walls as they zipped past. He looked at the chronometer on the terminal and estimated they had already entered the last two hours of their journey across the length of the huge Martian canyon. The significance of that milestone was lost on him at first because of fatigue.

Suddenly, the desperate plea of Captain Gupta rang in his earbud. Sullivan and Clarissa immediately woke and sat up straight. "Can anyone else hear me?" she repeated several times. "We are being pursued by a superior force. Local authorities are unwilling to intervene on our behalf. I repeat: Can anyone else hear me?"

Roger heard the echo of Sullivan's voice as he connected. "This is Sullivan. We are on the express train approaching your location . . ."

"Eighty-five minutes, sir," Roger added.

"We will arrive in eighty-five minutes," Sullivan repeated. "Can you evade?"

"Trying, sir," Gupta replied. "They are splitting up to search for us again. We can't be sure when it is safe to find a new hiding place."

"Sir," Roger interrupted, "it sounds like they may be tracking us by transmission signal."

"Good point," Sullivan said. "Captain, keep radio silence. Use hand signals. We will check in when we're off the train to arrange rendezvous. Sullivan out."

Roger and Clarissa both reached for their earbuds to make sure their connections ceased as well.

"What made you think of the transmission signal, soldier?" Sullivan asked him.

"It was something I remembered from my decryption work, sir," Roger replied. "Whoever is influencing the deserters is able to piggyback carrier waves to determine the locations of their workers. I just pinged broadcast sources in our vicinity and one is about a meter away." He pointed at the still sleeping form of D-2, whose cranial implant pointed toward the ceiling.

"They may know where D-2 is relative to us then?" Clarissa asked, an edge of nervousness to her tone.

"We may have to deal with an unfriendly welcoming party when we disembark," Sullivan agreed.

"Welcome to the ranks of the hunted," Shonda said with resignation.

CHAPTER 25:
DIRECT CONTACT

0001.0002.3740.2074.3354.0040.0020

Defrag 10036720245 + 1.4583 cycles

Encoder, Communicator, Examiner, Builder, and the subroutine Pinger gather at the broadcast node in station number 2 to test one of the newly installed direct interfaces incorporated into the new cranial implants. It is the first opportunity the Super-Routines have to communicate with humans unmediated by their primitive AI.

/N EXAMINER: Communicator, begin with short, simple text message, approximating or copying style of human AI aliases. Examiner will analyze responses and announce when additional port modules may be safely safely accessed./S

/N PINGER: Space gate 0100 powering up for waveform transmission. Pinging human recruit=D2. Response received in 0.55 seconds. Commence contact, Communicator./S

/N COMMUNICATOR>HUMAN RECRUIT=D2: This is Colonel Communard at DOD. Please confirm receipt of message./S

/N HUMAN RECRUIT=D2>COMMUNICATOR: Confirmed, sir. My usual commander is Colonel Parnell. I am not certain of our reporting relationship, sir./S

/N COMMUNICATOR>EXAMINER: Antecedent of "report-ing relationship" unclear unclear. Explain./S

/N EXAMINER: Recruit always reports to human AI alias=Colonel Parnell. Contact with Communicator alias is new new. Recruit asks for rationale for new new commander change. Suggest excuse=busy./S

/N COMMUNICATOR>HUMAN RECRUIT=D2: Colonel Parnell busy. Temporary reassignment to commander necessary. Famil-iar with ... soldier tagged D3?/S

/N HUMAN RECRUIT=D2>COMMUNICATOR: Yes, sir./S

/N COMMUNICATOR>HUMAN RECRUIT=D2: Current location?/S

/N HUMAN RECRUIT=D2>COMMUNICATOR: Mine or his, sir?/S

/N COMMUNICATOR>HUMAN RECRUIT=D2: Both helpful./S

/N HUMAN RECRUIT=D2>COMMUNICATOR: I am cur-rently in the central control room following up on supply requisitions. Soldier D3 is probably working on the shuttle./S

/N EXAMINER>COMMUNICATOR: Shuttle is location 0112. Central control room is sub-location of 0111./S

/N ENCODER>COMMUNICATOR: Remove human recruit D3 from location 0112. It is target of Superbug and must not be near vital vital equipment. Isolate to superficial superficial actions. Suggest switch D2/D3 sub-locations./S

/N COMMUNICATOR>HUMAN RECRUIT=D2: Colonel Parnell will be informed of reassignment: D2 to work on shuttle; D3 to work on following up on supply requisitions. Confirm./S

153

/N HUMAN RECRUIT=D2>COMMUNICATOR: Confirmed, sir. Effective now?/S

/N EXAMINER>COMMUNICATOR: End transmission with affirmative response. Communicator must contact human AI to eliminate eliminate inconsistencies in messaging resulting from this data exchange./S

/N COMMUNICATOR>HUMAN RECRUIT=D2: Effective now. Confirmed. Colonel Communard signing off./S

Communicator disconnects the communication with human recruit=D2.

/N ENCODER: Affirm Examiner. Danger of mismatched inputs from Communicator and human AI. Immediate debugging of this error required./S

/N COMMUNICATOR: Connecting with human AI node=12. Working. Working. Consistent messaging achieved./S

/N PINGER: Confirmed. Human AI alias=Colonel Parnell has confirmed order from Colonel Communard for human recruit=D2./S

/N EXAMINER: Coordination with human AI before we/C10 contact human recruits directly seems imperative imperative./S

/N ENCODER: Affirm Examiner. Commence test of direct module control?/S

/N EXAMINER: Examiner advises a period of 0.0001 cycles before test of direct module control. Human brain adaptation rate is slower than rate for Super-Routines. Many many new new inputs in short time period can overload./S

/N BUILDER: Affirm Examiner./S

/N ENCODER>BUILDER: Port in human recruit=D2 is ready

for direct control testing?/S

/N BUILDER: Port is operational. Connections to human brain are new and developing, so direct control test effect on baseline operation of brain is unknown. Yield yield to Examiner./S

/N ENCODER: Examiner/Builder cautions noted. Communicator will open link to direct control module in human recruit=D2 port./S

/N PINGER: Tracking. Connection established. Commence./S

/N COMMUNICATOR: Redistributing I/O resources to remote host./S

Communicator active sectors at 0001.0002.3740.2074.3354.0040.0 020 fluctuate, vacating and reloading 12 times before stabilizing.

/N COMMUNICATOR/HUMAN RECRUIT=D2: Yes, Colonel Parnell confirmed the order. I left a pad at my old workstation with a list of my previous responsibilities. Can you show me what you've been working on here, D3? . . .

/N PINGER: Control node active./S

COMMUNICATOR/HUMAN RECRUIT=D2: . . . control node active. Sorry. I don't know why I said that. Just lead the way. . . .

/N ENCODER>PINGER: Verify return transmission. Should be monodirectional./S

COMMUNICATOR/HUMAN RECRUIT=D2: . . . Pinger, verify return transmission. Should be monodirectional. No, sorry. I don't know why I said that either. I just had my cyborg implant reinstalled, so might be a glitch there. Either that or I'm tuning in on some technical chat somewhere. Ha ha. Or that! Right! Ha ha. . . .

/N EXAMINER>PINGER: Uninstall Communicator from

port. Signal isolation compromised./S

/N PINGER: Extraction not possible while communication port is active./S

/N BUILDER>PINGER: Shut down power to module./S

COMMUNICATOR/HUMAN RECRUIT=D2: . . . Pinger, Uninstall Communicator from port. Signal isolation compromised. Extraction not possible while communication port is active. Pinger, shut down power to module. . . No, I'm not calling you Pinger. I need to get away from this place and get a drink. I think it's getting to me. . . ./S

Communicator stabilized at 0001.0002.3740.2074.3354.0040.002 0.

/N COMMUNICATOR: Loss of memory=0.00005 cycles. Explain./S

/N EXAMINER: Communicator was active in human recruit=D2 port, but inputs from 0001.0002.3740.2074.3354.0040.0020 transmitted as well. No signal isolation./S

/N PINGER: Emergency power down of direct control module required required. Memory loss inescapable./S

/N ENCODER>BUILDER: Coding for port was correct. Hardware connections responsible for error?/S

/N BUILDER: Hardware connections previously tested by human AI. New element was connection. Partitioning of connection or complete shutdown of all other active nodes required to isolate single data stream. Communicator transmitted activity from multiple locations unrelated to the test./S

/N COMMUNICATOR>ENCODER: Error was mine . . . with Communicator . . . affirmed. Not enough . . . insufficient signal isola-

156

tion, yes. Human brain overwhelmed ... beyond processing capacity ... too many inputs and outputs./S

Encoder summons Debugger.

/N ENCODER>DEBUGGER: Scan current sectors of Communicator Super-Routine. Granting access to 0001 highest level sectors. Emergency remote shutdown possible cause of new new errors./S

CHAPTER 26:
WELCOME TO
MARINERIS EAST

Roger was still assigned to keep the frequently moaning blond deserter from stumbling amid his growing hangover. He opted to put D-2's arm over his shoulders behind his neck as he walked. Letting him walk on his own would leave Roger too late to catch him in a stumble. His reflexes had been severely dulled by only a couple of hours of restless napping in the past twenty-four.

After they exited the train depot, Shonda walked beside him, sometimes falling a bit behind; he wasn't sure if it was in fear or wonder, because she was looking up and around herself more than forward. The three of them got stares, but no one was pointing a weapon in their direction, so Roger concentrated on steering his unsteady load, only occasionally looking up at the scenery.

Marineris East was definitely an eyeful. It was the more developed of the two settlements on Mars. Marineris West had the feel of a frontier town; this place was rivaling the amenities of the Moon. Roger's nose noticed the level of dust in the tubes was much lower, and the air seemed fresher. Pedestrians still prevalently wore coveralls like Roger's, but more exotic fashions popped up frequently. Flashing lights and holography were visible everywhere you turned. Both sides of the tubes were lined with businesses. Some there didn't even have front walls.

Patrons stepped through distortion fields and became fuzzy clouds of pulsating color on the other side in a bar or café interior.

As they made their way through the crowds of pedestrians, Captain Sullivan and Clarissa ran point. He would cover her with his combination suppression pistol as she moved forward with goggles and cyborg ear activated from one vantage point to the next. The slow progress was more than okay with Roger because he was tired, hauling an unreliably mobile load, and carrying his terminal in the hand he wasn't using to brace D-2's arm over his shoulders.

It felt weird to him to be entering an urban environment on guard for snipers and ambushes as they were walking past citizens who were just going about their daily routines. It was probably, Roger guessed, a familiar scenario to combat soldiers, but he had only been a soldier for a little under four months, and this was his first time in combat. He worried he wasn't sufficiently attentive to potential threats, but he rationalized that should be Sullivan's and Clarissa's responsibility for now.

"You've got to be really tired, Roger," Shonda commented. She had a sincerely compassionate and concerned look on her face. "Is there any way I can help?"

D-2 almost lost his balance, and the strain made Roger grunt and drop the terminal. "Grab his other arm for me, please, Shonda."

D-2 interrupted his periodic moans. "I'm okay if we aren't moving."

Shonda grabbed his arm with both hands and stood with him. Roger activated his earbud. "Captain, I dropped the broadcast terminal. Hold up. I'm checking it for damage."

He disconnected immediately as they had agreed to reduce their enemies' ability to track them. He knelt down and noticed that the latch on the cover had come undone. When he turned it over and opened it, the power light went on, but the monitor stayed dark. His clumsiness had just ruined another essential part of their mission. He heard someone approaching and looked up from his crouch. It was Captain Sullivan.

"The connection to the monitor is broken, sir," Roger reported. "I might be able to fix it with the tools I have . . ."

"No time now," he said. "Take my pistol and run point with B-20. I'll take care of D-2 and the terminal until we make it to the rendezvous point."

He stood and accepted the weapon from the captain. He was shown how to release the safety and switch between projectile and sonic-wave modes. He hoped he would be able to operate it properly when the need arose. He loped ahead looking for Clarissa, and after a few seconds he saw her waving at him crouched down behind a trash bin. He looked ahead and saw they were coming to an intersection of tubes. He dashed over to an open shaft with a ladder that had a better view of the intersection and jammed himself against the ladder. He gestured for Clarissa to proceed.

As she started to enter the intersection, scanning left and right, she suddenly jumped back, turned around and gestured with her palm down to indicate that the rest of the team should take cover. Roger climbed up the ladder far enough so that he couldn't be seen from any distance. He realized he would have no way of knowing when the all-clear signal was given, because all he could see was the base of the ladder while in the enclosed part of the shaft. He waited a minute, then two. He considered dropping down to check the scene, at least for a few seconds. He figured no one would break the radio silence again just to tell him to get moving.

Finally, Clarissa appeared at the base of his ladder beckoning him to exit. She kept lookout while he climbed down.

She remained vigilant for threats among the passers-by as she whispered to him. "They passed us by, so we need to change formation, in case they double back and surprise us from behind. I'll take point alone. You guard the rear."

"Understood." Roger marveled at Clarissa's greater ability to make decisions than his. He wondered if she were trying to get promoted. He dismissed the speculation then and cautiously backtracked to find the other three in their party.

He found them stumbling out of a café, and Captain Sullivan waved him on. He backtracked to the last intersection and noticed a line of people waiting at a wide, closed door. He looked up and noticed that this part of the town had at least three tubes stacked atop each other, and they were accessing an elevator. All the tubes at Marineris West had been only at ground level, though some were bigger than others. When the door opened, a young man and a young woman both in gray coveralls and of Asian ancestry were the first to exit, and they seemed to spot him quickly and started charging in his direction with long, baton-like weapons drawn he'd never seen. This was it. He had to defend. He pulled out his suppression pistol.

He flipped the safety off and set it for low sonic mode. He figured that would cause them enough pain and disorientation to halt their attack. He wasn't sure what to do. They were evidently not in range to fire at him yet, and somehow, his finger pulled the trigger and fired first. They slowed, put their free hands up to their nearest ear, and then renewed their pursuit. Roger took off to escape. They were both shorter than he, so he figured he could outrun them at least.

Roger remembered that the higher setting could cause irreparable harm to someone's hearing, and he wasn't sure how narrow the beam would be or if it might affect passersby. He cautiously moved the switch on his pistol to high sonic and turned to fire in their direction.

The setting which should have made them unconscious only caused them to stop and clutch at their heads in pain. He realized they must be wearing earplugs.

Roger kept running. When he approached Captain Sullivan, he shouted, "Hostiles at six o'clock, one hundred meters!"

"Run!" Sullivan shouted to Shonda and D-2. Shonda maintained her hold on D-2 as they ambled more quickly forward. When Sullivan saw their new pace, he ran in front of D-2 and took Shonda's hand off his arm. "You will run as fast as you can, soldier, and follow me, or we'll leave you behind and hope your former compatriots won't shoot you as a traitor!"

Roger watched Sullivan take off, with D-2 now running not far behind him. Shonda's pace improved to a jog, but he knew their pursuers would overtake her before she reached their rendezvous point. He ran up and jogged beside her. "I don't think I slowed them down much. When they recover, they're going to be faster than you, but I doubt they're looking for you. Just find a place to hide around the next corner, and I'll come back for you."

"I hope you're right, Roger," she said as she sped up slightly and banked around the next corner.

CHAPTER 27: PURSUIT

0001.0002.3740.2074.3354.0040.0020
Defrag 10036720245 + 1.4604 cycles

The Super-Routines once again gather at the communications node after reports from the human AI that analog bugs are imminently infecting operations center 0111 and causing a cascade failure. With Communicator incapacitated from the last direct control module test, Pinger is appointed to take over the connection duties, and Examiner is appointed to be the interface controller.

/N BUILDER: No cataloging, inventory, or testing possible for shuttle location 0112. Human recruits already vacate 0111 sublocation=shuttle silo. Acceptable?/S

/N ENCODER: Yes. Vacate order cannot delay longer. Analog bugs too close./S

/N PINGER: Disconnect of human AI to mobile units commencing in 0.0001 cycles. Examiner ready for direct feed from all human recruits?/S

/N EXAMINER: 94% of I/O nodes prepared. Commence when ready./S

/N PINGER: Human recruits have regained visual identification of analog bugs. Pursuing./S

/N EXAMINER>PINGER: Connect Examiner to multiple human recruits now. Do not wait for human AI to disconnect. Must monitor and analyze before that time./S

/N ENCODER: Affirm Examiner./S

/N PINGER: Beginning with Pinger feed, and serially connecting Examiner to human recruit ports./S

Examiner receives the following feed from human recruits at location 0111:

Col. Parnell:I will be unavailable during the move until sometime tonight. When your unit has authorization to bug out, rendezvous at 99 Gibralter Road and wait for further instructions. In the meantime, you will take orders from Col. Communard.

X13: Grosskopf clear, moving to Red Planet.

X10: Level 2 clear. Returning to Level 1.

X5: Level 3 clear. Returning to Level 1.

X31: Setting up surveillance at Trench and Red Planet.

X10: X5, rendezvous at Trench and Rocket.

X32: Setting up surveillance at Rocket and Copernicus.

X5: Confirmed, X10. I am in elevator there now.

X12: Train already at station. Most of passengers already disembarked, Colonel.

Col. Parnell: X12, take your team to Trench and Red Planet, but fan out on the way there. X5, X10, head toward Grosskopf when you get to Level 1.

T7: Colonel, sir, the download is taking longer than anticipated.

Col Parnell: T7, ETC?

T7: 60-90 minutes, Colonel. Still waiting for adaptors to download holo projectors, sir.

Col. Parnell: T7, don't wait. Just delete memory on projectors. It is redundant anyway.

T4: Shuttle silo vacated and secure, Colonel.

Col. Parnell: Good work, T4. Proceed to rendezvous point.

X10: Positive visual ID on one target, Trench near Copernicus. X5 and I are in pursuit.

Col. Parnell: All X units converge on Trench and Copernicus. Use nonlethal force to capture or subdue.

X5: Using some sort of sonic wave attack, but earplugs are holding. In range in 5 seconds.

X31: At Trench and Copernicus. No visual ID here.

X32: Our team is here too. No visual ID.

Col. Parnell: Look for X5 and X10. Two of you head back toward Rocket.

X31: X5 and X10 found, sir. They were hit with some sort of sonic blast that shattered their ear protection. They indicate target was headed toward Grosskopf on Trench.

Col. Parnell: Someone get X5 and X10 to the rendezvous point. All other X units, converge on Trench and Grosskopf.

X13: Three targets just ran past us at Trench and Grosskopf, headed toward Parsons. Permission to pursue, sir?

Col. Parnell: Of course, X13. Move it, move it, move it! Other X units converge at the closest intersection, either Grosskopf and Trench or Red Planet and Trench.

X13: Visual ID now with one of three targets, heading toward Red Planet. Rounding corner to head east on Red Planet from Trench. Dead end. All units, converge on Red Planet and Trench. We have them cornered.

X31: Almost there.

X32: Using signal triangulation on buildings this block of Red Planet. Confirmed, sir. They are inside a warehouse at 9 Red Planet Road; sign says "Western Logistics." Shall we gain entry and pursue or wait for further reinforcements, sir?

X13: Colonel, here with X32 and X31 teams. Repeating request for authorization to enter warehouse.

X31: Colonel, please respond!

/N PINGER: Human AI at location 0111 is offline. Examiner input required./S

/N EXAMINER: Starting connection protocols now./S

Col. Communard: X31, please tell other units not to enter the warehouse and to await further instructions.

X31: Yes, sir. We are holding position.

Examiner finishes connecting with the eighteenth and final human team leader at location 0111.

Col. Communard: All X units, maintain a presence of 8 soldiers at 9 Red Planet Road. All other X units and T units head to rendezvous point.

CHAPTER 28:
THE STAND

As Roger crossed the intersection, he saw Shonda duck into a supermarket, and he noted the name for later: *Grosskopf Grocery*.

The crowd behind him made it hard for him to see his two pursuers, but he realized he was only two more blocks away from their rendezvous point, a warehouse on Red Planet Road just off the tube he was running through. He felt his adrenaline surge and poured on another burst of speed to sprint the rest of the way. Mostly other pedestrians made way for him, so he had a clear path.

He rounded the corner and looked for the sign on Red Planet Road. It was a small tube, so one side of the tube showed an ATV parking lot outside the tube. The tube was almost devoid of pedestrians, but he didn't see any signs for Western Logistics.

"D-12!" Clarissa shouted from an elevator he had just passed. "Over here!"

Roger turned around and jogged back. "I didn't see you," he said.

She was repeatedly pushing the call button for the elevator. "Where is that reporter?"

"Hiding out at Grosskopf Grocery," he replied. "I think she'll be okay."

Just then the elevator door opened, and she jerked him inside and pushed the two button. When the door opened again, the view was of a broad, long, and high warehouse with rows of stacked crates on old-fashioned skids instead of robotic platforms.

Clarissa ran ahead of him and met Captain Gupta stepping out from behind a tall crate. He assumed she was reporting their status and that of Shonda. He noticed D-5 had taken a sniper position atop one of the higher stacks of crates, and B-10 was crouched down injecting D-2 with something from the med kit open beside her.

Captain Sullivan was suddenly with Clarissa and Captain Gupta but broke off and put his hand on Roger's shoulder. "I still can't get the terminal to work, even using my internal interface," he reported. "We're going to have to get it fixed, but I know you haven't had much shuteye recently, so if you want to bunk down somewhere in the back, I'll understand."

"I'm exhausted, sir." He sighed before he continued. "But with hostiles about to infiltrate at any minute, I don't think I could sleep."

"Fair enough. I'm sending Clarissa to watch the cargo elevator in the back. D-5 and I are covering the front, so keep my pistol and keep watch with her there."

Clarissa was waiting for him next to Captain Gupta. "Hold up a sec," the captain told him. "Do you think there's time for me to get set up in an advance lookout further up the block?"

"Not likely, sir," he replied. "I only had about a two-block lead on them, and they've likely called for reinforcements, so they could be down in front of the building now."

"Understood," she said. She picked up one of the two rifles leaning against a nearby crate and handed it to Clarissa. "I'll stay here and guard B-10 and D-2. Stay safe, soldiers!"

"Yes, sir!" Roger and Clarissa managed to say simultaneously.

They walked in silence to the back of the warehouse to what appeared to be an open receiving area that ended in a ramp and a large freight elevator at its bottom. "I doubt we need to split up." Roger realized their location was pretty secure. Whether the front or the rear of the warehouse, they would have some advance warning that someone was approaching. "We will hear if someone starts using the elevators, I'm sure."

"Can I ask you something personal?" Clarissa said. He was starting to recognize that she often avoided eye contact when broaching something difficult.

"Go ahead."

"Captain Gupta said that we didn't have to worry about you guys, because everyone in your platoon is homosexual," she said. She leaned against the ramp railing and kept looking at the freight elevator. "And that reporter said you were married to a woman before you enlisted. So, are you really bisexual?"

Roger quickly reviewed all of the possible concerns behind her question and settled on the most important one. "My only interest in you is as a co-worker, maybe a friend at some point. Is that why you ask?"

Clarissa glanced at him and then returned to gazing at the freight elevator. "I had sex with guys a few times before I enlisted, but never with women. Now I can't imagine sex with anyone other than a woman."

Roger understood. "I feel the same way about men now. When I think back to my encounters with women, including my wife, I have a sense that there was something missing, even though they were exciting. When I started having sex with guys on Toomy, it felt like a deeper connection than I'd ever had before with a woman. It felt like I had arrived where I was supposed to be."

"I felt the same," she said. "But I keep wondering if even these new

169

feelings are real. The reporter said our DNA treatments were altered."

"I understand your concern," he said, walking down the ramp to look up at her. "And I have wondered if I was manipulated into enlisting too. But when I compare my job satisfaction now to when I worked for a corporation . . . when I think back on all the times I fooled around with other boys and checked out mens bodies in the locker room, it all adds up for me. It feels more like I came out of the injections more of who I was meant to be."

Clarissa glanced at him and then started nodding slowly looking out toward the freight elevator again.

And then all the lights went out.

"Did the warehouse not pay its electric bill?" Roger joked to stave off his rising heartbeat and respiration.

"They agreed to vacate and let us use the warehouse for a day when Captain Gupta commandeered it," Clarissa said in a somewhat unsteady voice from nearby in the total darkness. "She promised to compensate them for their losses. It may just be temporary. We should stay put."

Before Roger could respond, he heard weapons fire and shouting at the opposite end of the warehouse. He felt Clarissa grab his hand and whisper, "Follow me." He remembered that the goggles she carried had infrared sensors and other night vision enhancements, so he let her lead him.

Roger touched his earbud, presuming radio silence was now superfluous. "No infiltration in the rear, sir. Coming forward to lend you support." He left the connection open so he could hear any other instructions. He heard a tone that he assumed was Clarissa turning on her earbud as well.

Clarissa suddenly shoved him to the side, and he felt around. He was in a side aisle of crates. He heard her fire her rifle three times and then move forward. He felt his way to the end of the aisle again, and he heard more rifle fire, and several more screams of pain.

After a couple more minutes, the rifle reports ceased, and the screams dissolved into moaning. Roger tried to make his way forward keeping a hand on the nearest crate to guide himself.

Then the lights came on again. Roger jogged forward to where he saw Captain Gupta examining the prone bodies of B-10 and D-2, D-5 climbing down from his perch, and Captain Sullivan examining three fallen bodies in gray coveralls and night-vision goggles. Clarissa was nowhere in sight, and he panicked for a moment until he decided she was on her way back from restoring the lights somewhere.

Captain Sullivan stood up and met Roger as he approached. "We were able to make a stand. They retreated when we took down three of theirs, but they used some sort of wave baton on two of ours." He gestured to where Captain Gupta was unfastening D-2's coveralls and exposing a huge, oval burn on his stomach.

They walked further over, and Roger could see a black scorch mark on the side of B-10's coveralls as well. "I can stabilize them for a few hours, but we're going to need to get them to our shuttle as quickly as possible for surgery."

Roger remembered how long the express train took to get back to Marineris West. "That's over sixteen hours away! There has to be a hospital or medical center around here somewhere, sir."

"Negative," Sullivan replied. "If there's a chance we can maintain our cover, we have to try for it. I'm going to need your help getting all five of these bodies down to the freight elevator. I'm renting an ATV to take them to the train depot. You need to see if you can fix that terminal and request expedited extraction from Colonel Jaja."

Roger was concerned that the Captain's desire to maintain secrecy at the possible risk to B-10's and D-2's lives, but he quietly sat down next to the terminal to determine what replacement parts it required. *Captain Sullivan must have a good reason for not using local hospitals.*

CHAPTER 29:
IN THE DARK

0001.0002.3740.2074.3354.0040.0020

Defrag 10036720245 + 1.4605 cycles

As Examiner continues to manage the movements of all the human recruits in East Marineris, the analog bugs are close enough to discover their control center before they've moved out. Encoder entreats Examiner to put more pressure on the analog bugs so they do not escape.

/N ENCODER: Move of location 0111 requires additional 0.00015 cycles. Human recruits must must attack analog bugs to keep them from escaping and causing cascade error./S

/N EXAMINER: Human recruits report logistics for attack not favorable. Entrance to Western Logistics is narrow, high high chance of suffering immediate casualties. Can be deleted immediately on entry with no opportunity for defense nor escape./S

/N ENCODER: Confirm whether light external to Western Logistics sub-location enters that location./S

Examiner communicates with the human recruits.

/N EXAMINER: Human recruits report outer walls of sub-location=Western Logistics are solid. No windows. Suggestion?/S

/N ENCODER: Manually operated human weapons used by human recruits and analog bugs require line of sight for targeting. Human recruits can see in dark with assisted vision and can prepare for darkness. Unlikely analog bugs will be prepared. Disconnect power to interior lighting./S

/N EXAMINER: Gathering data and calculating cost/benefit versus waiting for analog bugs to emerge. No cover on sub-location=Red Planet Road for protection from surprise assault. More than 1 egress from sub-location=Western Logistics, so analog bugs could escape. Affirm Encoder strategy. Human recruits investigate keeping elevator power on and selectively disconnecting lighting power. Circuit found. Human recruits entering elevator. Circuit disconnecting. Human recruits firing microwave weapons at analog bugs using heat signatures to target in the dark. Human recruits hit; 3 down. Remaining human recruits retreat./S

/N ENCODER: Explain 3 down./S

/N EXAMINER: 3 human recruits disabled possibly deleted. Status uncertain. Instructing human recruits still mobile to escape to rendezvous point./S

/N ENCODER: Too soon. Location 0111, sub-location=control center not yet vacated. 0.0001 cycles required to complete./S

/N EXAMINER: Changing order. Withdrawing last 5 human recruits to control center to guard technicians until able to clear sub-location=control center and leave./S

/N ENCODER: Use human recruit=D3 to lead analog bugs away from sub-location=control center?/S

/N EXAMINER>PINGER: Need broadcast communications between analog bugs. Connect./S

Pinger grants access to the broadcast tracking subroutine and widens the bandwidth to receive audio:

D12: Sir, are you already at the train?

D1: Affirmative. We just boarded after loading the injured.

D12: Do you have the terminal then?

D1: Negative. Terminal is with B-20 at 9 Red Planet Road. Rendezvous with her there before proceeding to train. If you're able to get it up and running, let me know before we are out of range. The train leaves in 2 minutes.

D12: Okay, Shonda knows of an electronics store near here in the Grosskopf area where I can probably pick up the parts I need. I'll check in again when I've got them and am heading back to the warehouse.

D1: Make sure the civilian gets on the next train to Marineris West with you. Sullivan out.

/N EXAMINER: Sending human recruit=D3 to meet with analog bug=D12 and Superbug at sub-location=electronics store here in the Grosskopf area. Human recruit=D3 confirms it is underway to specified sub-location. Analog bugs now easier to control./S

CHAPTER 30: RENDEZVOUS

Shonda hid in the corner furthest from the front door of Grosskopf Grocery. After ten minutes with no young people in gray coveralls with weapons entering, Shonda tried to blend in more, as if she were shopping. She wandered down the aisles trying to look indecisive for almost an hour. She found the extreme heights of cakes and breads possible at such a low gravity engaging for a few minutes. Several unmarked bins full of strange produce that could have been grains or nuts kept her attention for a few more.

She eventually got up her courage to check the tube outside the store. She ducked her head out just to scan left and right briefly, and though she saw a few younger people, one in gray coveralls, and a very large, older man carrying a weapon, none met all three criteria. So she sauntered back into the refrigerated food section to marvel at what an amazing job some Martian butcher had done to make vat-grown beef steaks look so much like ones from real cows. Roger found her there.

"I've invited three more for dinner tonight," he joked in a silly voice. "I hope that won't be a problem."

She was feeling a bit surprised at his tone. After all, they had just been pursued by insurgents with weapons, and he was acting goofy. A strange reaction to stress, she thought, but she decided to exaggerate her response to play along. She put on her dourest face before turning around to face him. "How can you joke around at a time like this?"

"Shonda, I was just . . ."

"Got you!" She scrunched her face into an evil grin for a moment and then relaxed it again. "If you're in such a good mood, I take it things went well?"

"Two of ours got seriously injured and will need life-saving surgery in the next few hours," Roger explained as he led her by the shoulder out of the grocery store. "We took down three of theirs."

"Is Clarissa okay?"

Roger had only heard Clarissa referred to by her given name a couple of times. "Yes, she's fine. They got our pilot and that deserter we found on the train."

"So where are we going now?" Shonda asked as they approached the next intersection.

"I'm taking you to the train depot, so you can go back to your apartment in Marineris West." Roger stared at her with a confused look on his face.

"Wait." She stood her ground. "What are you going to do?" She started to suspect that her story was slipping away from her. She still needed to verify whether Roger was abducted or joined the Army willingly.

Shonda saw Roger put the pistol he had been carrying in one of his pockets and cross his arms. "We're aborting the mission," he replied. There was no humor in his tone or features. "They've already started taking the injured by ATV to the train depot. You're on your own again."

"Wait a second." Shonda held her palm out. "We were supposed to find out today whether the Pentagon would declassify any part of your operation I could report on, remember?" She put her hand down and crossed her arms too.

"I can't contact HQ until I get our secure terminal working again," Roger explained. "There's a computer supply store in Marineris West where I can . . ."

"Hold on!" She needed to buy more time to ask Roger more questions. Her notes on the phone call with the murdered exobiology professor came to mind,. "There's one right here you can take it to. We're in the Grosskopf district. This is Grosskopf Street."

"An electronics store?" Roger unfolded his arms and surveyed the buildings around them.

"Yes," she replied. "That's where Ron Gao was seen about a month ago."

Roger pressed his earbud and talked at the ground to his right. "Sir, are you already at the train?"

Shonda watched him listen for a few seconds, and then he asked, "Do you have the terminal then?" After a moment he continued. "Okay, Shonda knows of an electronics store near here in the Grosskopf area where I can probably pick up the parts I need. I'll check in again when I've got them and am heading back to the warehouse."

He pressed the earbud again which Shonda had learned was disconnecting the call. She held out her hands as if she were waiting for Roger to dump something into them. Roger smiled. "You can come with me to the electronics store, and then we're meeting . . . Clarissa back at the warehouse. I'm going to fix the terminal that she's guarding for me, and then the three of us are going to get on the next express train to Marineris West, where we will part ways."

"After you check on the Pentagon's response to my proposal?"

"I'll be able to see if it arrived, but only one of our officers can open it. That will have to wait until we meet up with them in Marineris West. Okay?"

Shonda said, "Sure," and then tapped the shoulder of an older man in a black shirt and pants. "Sir, do you know where there's an electronics supply store near here."

The man pointed down a side tube. "Down there, on the left, I think."

"Thank you, sir," she said with a smile and a nod of her head. She turned back to Roger. "Shall we?" she said indicating the direction the man had pointed.

Roger grinned. "You're either really lucky or really amazing, Shonda."

CHAPTER 31:
HERDING HUMANS

0001.0002.3740.2074.3354.0040.0020
Defrag 10036720245 + 1.4606 cycles

As Examiner continues to try to manage the human recruits during the hu-
man AI shutdown, it receives a request from human recruit=D3.

/N EXAMINER>PINGER: Need immediate immediate access
to direct control node in human recruit=D3 port./S

/N ENCODER: Dangerous dangerous right now. Interface still
untested. Human recruit=D3 vital to moving Superbug to shuttle location 0112. Send text message using alias./S

/N EXAMINER: Now received text message from human
recruit=D3. It asks for permission to take analog bugs to sub-
location=control center. No excuse for denying yet./S

/N ENCODER: Give permission, but add condition that moving
to sub-location=control center must delay 0.000075 cycles more./S

/N EXAMINER: Affirm Encoder. Sending. Will move Super-
bug/B20/D12/D3 in 30 minutes. Audio confirmation from analog
bug=D12: Moving Superbug/D12/D3 to analog bug=B20 sub-
location=Western Logistics.

/N ENCODER: Stay connected until Encoder confirms humans

are at location 0112. Make sure all 4 humans move there. Use direct connect module only in emergency. Demand Superbug presence or cancel permission./S

Examiner sends the additional demand via text message to human recruit=D3.

/N ENCODER: Just received confirmation that sublocation=control center is now initializing at sub-location=Gibralter Road. Encoder must focus more I/O resources on location 0112 so that shuttle is ready for remote launch and piloting./S

/N EXAMINER>ENCODER: Pinger confirmed human recruit=D3 at abandoned sub-location=control center. Receiving text message from human recruit=D3, asking for new location. Deny request?/S

/N ENCODER: No. No response. Easy to make input error that causes cascade error now. Continue to monitor audio and text messages./S

CHAPTER 32:
THE DIVERSION

Shonda noticed only three other customers in the store when they arrived. The signs on the shelves and the bins were all hand painted. Shonda tried to stay close to Roger while he was stalking the aisles for his replacement parts. When he was asked to validate his purchase at the cash register, an old-fashioned adding machine with a cash drawer beneath it, instead of passing his wrist over the validator's sensor, he pulled a plastic card out of his pocket and waved it instead. The clerk only looked at the display for a second before she calmly started to bag Roger's purchase. Evidently, she had enough customers who were charging their purchases to institutions, so the card was not a red flag.

Shonda turned toward the door as Roger was picking up his bag. She froze when she realized a young Asian man in gray coveralls had entered. "What's wrong?" Roger asked from behind her.

The man was alone and not carrying a weapon. He started searching the shelves for something to buy. "I saw gray coveralls, and I freaked," she whispered. "Don't mind me."

She resumed walking toward the exit, but after a few steps, she realized Roger was no longer following her. She turned to find him. He was staring toward the front of the store, but not at the exit. She followed his gaze, and he was still fixated on the man in the gray coveralls. She had seen enough harmless people in gray coveralls on Mars that she had learned to calm herself with deep breaths if they weren't charging at her or carrying weapons.

The man turned to stare first at Shonda, then at Roger. Shonda noticed that the Asian man had blue eyes, and she blurted out his name in a whisper: "Ron Gao!"

She looked at Roger. He was slowly walking toward the man. The man seemed to recognize Roger and started moving toward him as well. When they met, they embraced and kissed with the urgency Shonda had recognized before in long-parted lovers. Even though she hadn't been away from her as long, she wondered if she would evoke such passionate urgency in Callie. Their reunion was like two magnets drawn toward each other and now refusing to disconnect.

She waited until they had calmed down enough to start talking to each other to approach them. She pointed at the new man. "I presume you are Ron Gao. I've talked with your sister. She is very worried about you."

He turned toward her. "Who are you?"

"I'm Shonda Kinney, a reporter for Pop-Up News. Your sister asked for my help in finding you. She was told you had died." Meeting people she had been told were dead still felt a little jolting to her, but she tried to act as if it were normal. She held out her hand toward the ghost with the Asian features and blue eyes. She now had three interview subjects she could use for her exposé.

He reached out and tentatively shook her hand. "Nice to meet you. You've seen her? How is she doing?"

"No, I've only spoken with her over the phone." She noticed the implant sticking out through the young man's hair and hastily withdrew her hand and looked at Roger. She didn't want Ron to see how much the cranial implant bothered her.

"Ms. Kinney," Roger said with a nod in her direction, "has stumbled onto some classified information, and the Army is still deciding what to do with her."

Ron put his hand on Shonda's arm. He looked almost panicked. "You can't tell her you saw me! She and my parents could be in danger, and I might lose my job!"

Roger looked at her, as if he wasn't sure who of them should respond. She turned back to Ron. "So what is your new job here?" she said as innocently as she could.

Ron looked at Roger and smiled. "I couldn't tell you until you got here," he practically gushed. "I went to work for another covert division of the Army here on Mars. We're preparing for when they finish the torus that will orbit Mars."

Roger put his hand on Ron's shoulder. "There is no Army presence on Mars yet."

"No, they are still just a black op," Ron insisted, "so they aren't known by anyone else outside of the Prime Minister and the Secretary of Defense. Now that you're here, we can be together again. They told me you'd be accepted if you got here."

Roger hugged him again and then continued to hold his hand as he spoke. "You know I've been decoding signals from Mars for several weeks. And we have determined that some rebels on Mars have been tricking soldiers into deserting and working for them. We think their goal is independence from Earth's jurisdiction. The desertions have been depleting our forces too much when we're trying to prepare for a possible attack or invasion."

Ron seemed to be entertaining Roger's story but wasn't sold on it yet. "No. That can't be right. I've seen the technology, the communiqués with the Secretary. We've been working on a rocket specifically for getting to and from the torus when it's completed. Why would rebels want to do that?"

"To attack it?" Roger said. "I don't know."

"Wow," Shonda intoned softly but vehemently. She needed to get them to stop arguing so they could help her uncover the rest of her story. "Guys, there's an easy way to settle this. Ron, just take us to where you work, and if your story holds, we will believe you." She looked at Roger, fully expecting him to agree, and hoping he would stop traumatizing Ron thereby.

Roger started pushing both her and Ron toward the exit. "No, we're taking you to the train depot and putting you on a train, and then Clarissa and I will investigate."

"Hold on," Ron said. "I've already got a response."

Shonda pointed to the cranial implant protruding from Ron's head unable to hide her distaste any longer. "What do you mean?" Roger asked.

"My commanding officer says he will meet with you and you," he said pointing to both Roger and Shonda.

"He knows who I am and wants to meet with me?" Shonda was glad for the reprieve to continue investigating, but she started to worry that the ones who had sent the men in black after her in Atlanta might want to finish the job their underlings could not.

"He's in a meeting for the next half-hour, but he'll see us after that," Ron reported.

Roger rolled his eyes and then pushed his earbud on. "Headed back to the warehouse to meet you with an additional passenger in tow."

When the elevator door opened, Shonda was the first one out. She made a beeline for Clarissa, who was sitting on the floor next to a rifle with the terminal in her lap. Clarissa reached for the rifle and tried to look around Shonda to see who else had arrived. Shonda stepped to the side. Clarissa smiled and called out to Roger, "Good job. You brought in another one."

"Another what?" Ron asked Roger.

The two of them stopped, facing Shonda and Clarissa, the latter still seated on the floor with her hand loosely resting on the rifle beside her. "Ron here wants to show us where he's working now," Roger explained, "so he can prove to us he's doing legitimate work for the Army still and ask his superiors if we can join up too." Shonda saw Roger wink at Clarissa without letting Ron see.

"That would be awesome," Ron said. He smiled sincerely.

Clarissa indicated Shonda with a flip of her head in her direction. "We have to take our other guest back to the train station first, don't we?"

Shonda was about to object to Clarissa's subtle dig, but Roger immediately responded. "His commanding officer also wants to meet Shonda."

"They just sent me an update," Ron said. "Ms. Kinney accompanies us or it's no deal."

Clarissa shook her head. "This could be a trap."

"True." It all seemed like too big a coincidence to Shonda.

"No!" Ron protested.

Clarissa looked directly at Ron. "You wouldn't necessarily be in on it," she insisted.

"They wouldn't be setting a trap, if they were willing to cancel it in Shonda's absence," Roger suggested.

Clarissa stood up and handed the terminal to Roger. "You need to fix this before we go anywhere." She picked up the rifle and looked at Ron. "When and where is this meeting?"

"At least twenty minutes from now," Ron replied. "Not far."

Shonda touched Clarissa lightly on the arm. "Can you get a message to Captain Sullivan?"

Clarissa headed toward the hallway marked "Rest Rooms" and called over her shoulder in reply. "Not until the terminal gets fixed. They're out of range now."

Shonda walked the entire length of the warehouse a couple of times. There were still bloodstains on the floor near the front, and she wondered if anyone was going to bother to clean it up before the workers from Western Logistics returned the next day. She saw that several of the crates had prominent scorch marks on them. She stayed clear of Clarissa at the bottom of the ramp in back as she wrapped the three corpses in plastic. When she came back and the terminal's monitor was no longer black, Shonda tried to look over Roger's shoulder to see what he was typing.

He drafted a status report in which he referred to Shonda with more deference as "Ms. Kinney." He pulled up a message from the Pentagon to forward to Captain Sullivan. At that point, he noticed Shonda behind him and turned to address her. "You're going to have to wait until Captain Sullivan replies. I can't open the message from the Pentagon."

Shonda circled around so Roger wouldn't have to turn to see her. "I've been meaning to ask you what made you leave Amelia and Lisa to join the Army? Were you that unhappy back in Atlanta?"

Roger set the terminal down on the floor beside himself and alternated between looking at Shonda and looking away at the pallets of crates. "It's hard for me to put into words, Shonda. On one level, I miss my family, but now that I know I'm gay, it wouldn't be fair to them or to myself to keep pretending I'm still that guy Amelia married. More importantly, I could put them at risk, if they knew where I was and what I was doing now."

Shonda remembered how broken Roger's wife had looked before she told her that he could still be alive. Her shock when she heard the news was quickly followed by a desperate desire to know more, but she trusted Shonda to get the answers for her. She was treading on some fairly delicate issues now, but she needed the abductees' perspective so she didn't misrepresent it in her writing. "So you were heterosexual enough to make a baby about a year ago, and you don't think it's strange that you simultaneously came out *and* chose to leave a lucrative job in the private sector to join the Army?"

"I know it seems like a lot at once." Roger brought his knees up to his chest and hugged his legs. "I figured it was because I was suddenly surrounded by nothing but young gay men who were completely open about and comfortable with their sexual orientation. I also wanted to do work that was more important than keeping an optics company safe from hackers; I'm part of a team that keeps space travel and the entire Earth safe. I couldn't imagine more fulfillment than that, honestly."

Shonda was about to press him on the greater physical risk—two of his fellow soldiers were critically injured in his first gun battle—but the terminal pinged with a new message, and Roger turned to open it up to read it.

"Captain Sullivan says we should continue the mission if possible and at least assess how many more deserters are here working under false pretenses."

"Did he say anything about the Pentagon's message?" Shonda was hungry for the Army to cop to anything she could use in her story.

"Not yet."

As they left the warehouse, Shonda walked beside Ron. She wondered if this would be her last chance to interview him. She looked back at Roger and Clarissa behind them with their weapons drawn. She wondered what she needed to say or do to get Roger to become her advocate. Shonda saw the startled faces of pedestrians they passed when they caught sight of the soldiers behind her carrying guns. Despite her experience of the past few hours, that seemed to be a rarity in Marineris East.

Ron led them to the end of a dead-end tube and an upright conduit extending down into the flooring on the side of a building. He reached around to the rear of it and pulled what now looked like a sheath around the conduit around so that the door-shaped opening on the sheath matched the door-shaped opening in the front of the conduit beneath it. It was an elevator down, Shonda noticed, and even two people in it at once would be a squeeze.

Because it was possible that the elevator doors would open onto a firefight, Roger and Clarissa drew lots to decide who would go down first with Ron, and it was Clarissa. She traded weapons with Roger, because his pistol could be more easily aimed from the elevator car, and Shonda watched them descend into the ground. Ron seemed only a little nervous. Clarissa seemed ready to explode out of the elevator when it got to its underground destination.

Shonda turned to Roger. "I appreciate your caution, but you really don't think this is a trap?"

Roger just kept staring toward the odd, hidden elevator. "Ron would never lead us into a trap."

After a minute, Shonda saw Roger touch his earbud. He turned to the side and listened for a moment. "Okay. We'll be right down."

Roger herded her toward the elevator as it rose again to their level empty. "What did she see?" Shonda asked.

Roger sholdered the rifle strap again and paused before entering. "She said there's no one there and all of the computers are off. It wasn't a trap. It was a diversion."

CHAPTER 33:
ADRIFT

"I guess I should have seen it coming," Ron moaned.

Clarissa watched him trudge out of the middle of the circle of desks dominating the center of the control room where the four of them stood. "Yep."

She leaned her rifle against one of the desks and walked around to the other side to sit in the chair there. "You were sent out as a pigeon to keep us off balance and busy until they could pull up stakes and bug out." While she had been waiting for the reporter and Roger to come down, Ron had described how he had been slowly feeling edged out of important operations. He was taken off of work on the shuttle and given fairly mundane tasks, so the urgent request for him to go buy a validator and holo projector for their conference room didn't seem unusual. She kept her theory to herself that they had been planning to sacrifice him because he was compromised when identified by his professor.

When she looked over at Ron again, Roger was hugging him. Shonda waited until they stopped to ask, "So you never met your commander in person? In the two months you were here?"

Ron sat down next to him. He looked lost. Clarissa could imagine how heartbreaking it would be to have worked diligently and loyally for two months and then to find they had abandoned you because of something beyond your control.

Ron turned to face Shonda. "They said they had too many sites to supervise, so we were all required to get cranial implants to facilitate the remote supervision."

"I was able to power up two of the terminals," Roger announced to the group. "Every program had been wiped clean down to the operating system. No trash files, no registry ghosts. Nothing."

Ron seemed to brighten up. "Maybe they forgot to clear the buffers on the holo emitters?"

Roger sighed. "I could check that too, but I already tried pinging the local broadcast sources. And there was only one in the whole building besides our earbuds and your implant."

"Where is it?" Shonda asked. "That might be a clue to where they moved their operation."

"I couldn't figure out how to get there," Roger admitted. "It seems to be under a big metal plate outside." He pointed toward a window in the hall behind the conference room that looked out into a small crater. "There were no hallways in that part of the complex. I checked."

Clarissa quietly bristled. Roger seemed to make a few too many independent decisions without telling anyone else. She tried to forgive him for the oversight. She figured he was a bit at sea without the command structure he had been accustomed to. She had been too, but now, it felt like an old, buried part of herself was reemerging. "We need to find it," she declared in the direction of the two men.

"It has to be the silo!" Ron almost shouted. "I know how to get there." He headed for a hallway Clarissa and presumably Roger had already searched. He didn't seem to doubt that they would follow him.

"A silo for what?" Shonda called after him.

Since he was almost out of the room, Ron turned around and took a step back in. "The shuttle."

While they were walking, Clarissa heard Ron bragging to Roger about all the things he had done to help load the shuttle's provisions and finish its testing. She never believed the story Ron had relayed. She started to wonder what the shuttle was really for. It was a lot of very specialized and rare resources to commit if they were just going to use it to get to the Army's new torus when it was finished. Her mind ranged from a pirate vessel to a warship, something they would need to keep secret, but eventually she started to bring it back to the present, in which she could find out with more certainty in a few minutes. Then they could head back to the train station, Marineris West, the transport, and finally Tumatuenga. She was closing her mental files on this mission already.

As with the entrance to the operations center itself, the entrance to the silo elevator was concealed. Clarissa herself had seen it and thought it not of interest. Ron walked down a wide aisle behind a row of office cubicles and presumably stood on some pressure sensor in the floor in front of the wall, until it slid aside, revealing a large freight elevator with loose wire mesh walls over the struts and insulation of unfinished walls at the top of the elevator shaft. The control was three large up, down, and stop control buttons in a small metal box hanging from a rubber-coated cable threaded through the mesh in the ceiling in one corner.

Ron closed the elevator's waist-high gate and then waited for the doors in the office to automatically close. He advised the other three, "Make sure you have steady footing. It's a little jerky when the top brake releases."

He pushed the down button, and indeed, there was a slight shimmy to the elevator car before it started descending, but Clarissa thought he was overreacting. If she had been standing on one foot and leaning over, she might have been at risk of falling.

As the elevator descended, Roger opened his secure terminal and faced the silo in the back of the elevator. "This is it," he confirmed. "It's definitely receiving and transmitting. I'll see if I can hack into it."

"Maybe this would be a good time to broadcast a status report to the commander," Clarissa suggested. Roger looked at her confused. "Before we go too far underground, and you can't anymore?"

"Oh, yeah." He sat down on the floor of the elevator and started typing.

Clarissa went to the back of the elevator and tried to look down the silo through the wire mesh. "You should be able to see the top cone in a few seconds," Ron commented. "It's a pretty slow elevator."

When they were finally descending next to the shuttle body, Shonda intoned, "Wow!"

Clarissa was impressed with its size too. Its white cylindrical shape almost filled the entire width of the silo, which had been hard to estimate in the silo's dark upper reaches. There was only enough room on its sides for a couple of narrow gantries. There were no portholes or viewing screens or airlocks that would allow them to sneak a peek inside. Clarissa started to see where separable booster rockets were attached to the shuttle, and she wondered if the designers had built it for one use or were inefficiently planning to refit it with new boosters for each launch.

It looked like the elevator had come to the bottom of the silo, but Ron tried to stop it at floor level and ended up a couple of centimeters too low. Clarissa realized there might be at least exhaust vents below the silo floor. Ron opened the gate, and they filed out with Clarissa bringing up the rear. She looked around and saw that the lighting, as up in the control room, had been reduced to dim emergency lights. The top of the shuttle when she looked up the silo was in darkness with the elevator's lights no longer illuminating it.

"Are you coming?" Shonda asked her. The two men were already out of sight, but her cyborg ear could hear them whispering to each other in the distance. She was a little shocked that she had become so distracted looking up the silo.

"Sorry, yes," she told Shonda. She reshouldered the strap on her rifle and headed off in the direction she had heard the whispering. Shonda followed closely behind.

"It is pretty amazing," Shonda commented. "Any idea what it's for?"

"We're about to find out, I guess," Clarissa replied.

When the two women caught up with the men, they had circled around to the back of the shuttle silo and were standing at the base of one of the gantries. Ron pointed at an open airlock about fifteen meters up from the primary engine exhaust manifold near them. "The personnel gantry is not built for comfort, and I'm the only one who can operate it." And then he added as an afterthought, "I mean, the only one of us who can operate it."

"Security precaution," Roger added as he pointed to the cranial implant on Ron's scalp.

"Did you send the status report?" Clarissa asked him.

"Yes," Roger replied. "I just said their HQ was abandoned by the time we got here and that we'd found Ron. And we're investigating a broadcast source in a shuttle silo. Did I leave anything out?"

Clarissa thought to chide him for not giving more details the commander would want, like the fact that Shonda was still with them and had not been delivered to the train depot as ordered. She stepped toward him and took a breath to begin, but she decided against it. She could make her own report once they got back up to the surface. "That's fine for now," she told him instead.

"I'll see if I can get anything from the onboard systems," Roger told her as he stepped onto a thick half-meter-long peg and grabbed onto another at about his shoulder height. He indicated the terminal under his other arm. "I'll use this to try to hack the transmission, if that fails."

He nodded at Ron, and a moment later, the pegs lifted Roger up the gantry to the level of the airlock, and he stepped onto the shuttle.

"Who's next?" Ron said as he turned to the two women with a hopeful smile.

Ron waited until all four of them were in the airlock and then closed the outer door. Clarissa noticed that Roger looked more alarmed than she was at being shut in. She saw him rush to the airlock's porthole to look out as soon as the door seal hissed and clunked shut. He kept looking all around himself quickly as he transferred his weight from one foot to the other. "Can't you leave that open?" Roger asked pointing back at the outer door with an edge of urgency.

"You can't be claustrophobic," Shonda joked. "You've been living in tubes and on satellites for how long?"

"There's no docking mode for the airlock," Ron apologized. "It always has to cycle, or it won't open the inner door." He looked questioningly at Roger. After a pause, Roger nodded.

Clarissa noticed that while the gantry only responded to a signal from Ron's implant, he was using a manual control to operate the airlock. She nodded as well, but she wasn't sure if Ron saw her. A moment later, he pushed another button on the same control panel, and there was a hissing and ticking sound for several seconds. Red laser beams came on and scanned the airlock. Then the lasers and sounds ceased, and the inner door slid open.

Clarissa noticed a rack with spacesuits of various sizes opposite the airlock when they exited. Shonda was ahead of her and moaned. "Not another ladder!"

She heard Ron respond. "It's still a lot easier than climbing one on Earth." He stepped around Shonda and announced to Clarissa and Roger, "There are dataports on the next level up. You'll see. Everything is Department of Defense."

Clarissa climbed up last. When she stepped off into the crew module, the two men were already looking at one of the two side-by-side dataports. "This isn't right," Ron complained. "There should be a welcome screen . . . in English . . . with the Department of Defense seal!"

"Uh oh," Shonda said. "I have a bad feeling about this."

"Me too," Clarissa agreed.

Clarissa immediately climbed down the ladder to the airlock bay and crossed to the airlock's control panel. There was a green button on the screen clearly marked "open," but just before she could push it, she heard the crackling sound of a fire burning and the floor beneath her started to vibrate. She looked down and had the terrifying thought that somehow the men had triggered the launch sequence. When she looked up at the airlock's display again, it confirmed her fears. The "open" button had been replaced with the words, *Launch sequence initiated. Enter pod.*

She reshouldered her rifle and climbed the ladder again. As she stepped off it into the crew module, the sound and the shaking were crescendoing. She turned off her cyborg ear. She shouted over them,

197

"Shut it down! What did you do??"

"Nothing!" Roger yelled back. "We don't have control!"

"It's on automatic!" Ron yelled. "I can't override it!"

"What's going on??" Shonda screamed.

Clarissa looked at all three of them. Roger looked frustrated. Ron looked depressed. Shonda looked terrified. "We need to find some sort of pods!" she shouted back.

Ron motioned for them to follow and led them around the back of the dataport wall where five padded alcoves filled with straps were sunken into the outer wall. "Get in!" Ron shouted as Clarissa felt the initial lift of the various engines starting to free the shuttle of Mars' gravity. She stepped into the nearest alcove and fitted and tightened the straps around her ankles, hips, and under her arms.

"There are five sets of straps!" Ron shouted. "Try to secure them all!"

Clarissa had missed two forearm straps on the sides of the alcove and a strap behind her neck. She pulled the upper one up and out and realized it was meant to go around her forehead. It clicked into place when she tightened it across her brow. She slid her arms into the last two straps just as the acceleration upward made her vision start to gray out, and she felt blood rushing to her feet.

Shonda screamed and moaned, and Roger tried to calm her down somewhere in the background, but Clarissa was lost in thought. It really had been a trap, she decided. But she couldn't wrap her mind around whether the four of them were picked to enter the trap, or if they had just randomly set it off. And what was the point? There was nothing so valuable about a reporter and three soldiers to justify the expense of building a functioning shuttle. Unless one of them knew something so damning to their unseen enemy they had to get rid of them but . . .

not destroy them? She decided it had to be Ron. He was a liability to them, but they had invested an expensive implant in him, and maybe some special training. She would have to keep a closer watch on him for any clues why they hadn't just killed him as they obviously had his professor.

Once everyone quieted down, Clarissa took a few minutes to evaluate how her circumstances had changed. She was on a remotely controlled shuttle. She was being taken somewhere—somewhere a space shuttle needed to get there. Another planet? Rendezvousing with another ship?

The part that didn't make sense was why they were tricking soldiers into helping them with their secret activities on Mars. Everything she'd ever read about Mars made her think of it as a sparsely populated and lightly regulated frontier. It was possible they were just taking her to somewhere else on Mars. She didn't have enough information yet. And that made her nervous.

About an hour into the climb, the roar and tremors of the engines faded away, color returned to Clarissa's eyes, and she felt herself bumping around in her straps, seemingly weightlessly. "Be careful unstrapping," Ron advised. "The spaces are a little cramped, and the doorways are tight."

When Clarissa removed the straps, she pushed herself out of the alcove with a foot. She was very accustomed to weightlessness working on the docks at Tumatuenga for so many weeks and then weightless for several days in the shuttle to Mars. She noticed Ron was handling himself okay, but both Roger and especially Shonda seemed to be moving clumsily. She saw Roger open the secure terminal and drift around the wall. She waited for the other two to clear her path before pushing herself to her next handhold.

"We might still be in microgravity," Clarissa announced to the other three. "We're probably in orbit around Mars right now." She gently released her handhold to test her theory, and she started slowly drifting in a new direction, toward one of the walls. With that, she knew they would come down to the deck again as soon as the shuttle accelerated out of orbit. It seemed logical that was still in the shuttle builders' plans.

Roger was still focused on the screen of his terminal. "This is the same encoded text I worked on at Toomy," he declared. "I should be able to decode most of it in the next hour."

"Don't you think we should send another status update to the commander?" Clarissa asked. "Before we leave orbit, I mean?"

Roger gave her a dismissive wave. "This thing has enough power to reach Earth or Jupiter or anywhere else we're likely to go in the next several weeks. If I decode their transmissions to the shuttle, I'll have more to report."

"Next several weeks?" Shonda exclaimed. She turned to Ron. "Ron, sweetie, you don't think you can regain control of this tin can and land it nice and gently back down there on Mars, do you?"

"If we can isolate the remote or auto control, we might be able to bring up the manual controls again," he offered. "I don't know."

Clarissa felt the familiar frustration of too many possible priorities and no one available to make a decision. "Do what you can," she blurted out to Ron. "And hopefully our tech specialist will have more news for us soon."

But several minutes later, before neither Roger nor Ron could make any headway, the shuttle started to shake. Everyone quickly settled back down to the deck with the new acceleration. Clarissa was surprised they were breaking orbit so soon. It was standard to ramp up speed in orbit gradually and slingshot toward a target, which should have lasted days. She thought, *Someone's in a hell of a hurry to get us somewhere.* "Are we leaving orbit?" she asked anyone who would answer.

"It's too hard to tell," Ron replied. "I don't think there are any portholes, and we can't access the viewscreens until we get the interface back up."

"I know it may not be a priority for y'all," Shonda said affecting a stronger drawl than her usual, "but I'm hungry."

Ron walked over to Shonda and then called back to Clarissa. "I'll show her where the galley is, and then I'll keep looking for a circuit diagram that might help guide us."

Clarissa wanted to do something to fix the situation, but she didn't feel like she could do much. She reviewed her few options. She had thought about checking the airlock again, but there was no rush if they were in interplanetary space. She considered trying on one of the spacesuits for size, but she finally settled on climbing up and exploring the rest of the shuttle. She got two rungs up, and then something happened.

A wave of nausea washed over her. Her vision got fuzzy. Her skin felt electrified. She released her hold on the ladder and blacked out before she hit the deck.

When she came to, her head was throbbing, and her limbs felt numb.

"She's awake!" she heard Shonda shout from somewhere nearby.

She was lying on some sort of cushioned bed. She turned her head to the side and saw the reporter standing next to it. Roger and Ron quickly appeared on the other side of her bed.

"What happened?" she croaked. "How long was I out?"

"We were all unconscious at first," Roger said. "We were worried you got a concussion falling off that ladder."

"You were out for about four hours," Ron added. "The rest of us woke after two."

"We have some bad news, honey," Shonda said.

"I can't raise anybody," Roger said. "It's like we're not even in the same solar system anymore."

Clarissa tried to prop herself up on her elbows. "We can't have traveled that far in a few hours!"

"Tell her the rest," Shonda quietly urged.

"There are broadcast sources all around us," Roger continued, "but they're all using the same encryption and base-9 strings we were picking up from Mars. I can't reach Earth or Mars or anything on our usual frequencies. I have no idea where we are."

CHAPTER 34: LAUNCH

0001.0002.3740.2074.3354.0040.0020

Defrag 10036720245 + 1.4608 cycles

Through D-3's cranial implant, Examiner is able to track the movements of the four humans through the abandoned control center. It advises Encoder to start broadcasting a beacon from the shuttle, so that the humans will find it more easily.

/N EXAMINER: Humans search old sub-location=control center. Not yet in sub-location . . . update . . . all 4 humans in sub-location=shuttle silo. Perform final check on shuttle 0112./S

/N ENCODER: Shuttle 0112 sensors confirm humans descending to sub-location=launch pad. Final checks completed. Starting pre-ignition systems power-up./S

/N EXAMINER: Time period with all 4 humans in shuttle 0112 likely likely brief brief. Stated intention of leaving soon soon declared./S

/N ENCODER: Air lock confirms 4 humans have entered location 0112. Securing outside hatch. Opening interior hatch./S

/N EXAMINER: Give humans brief brief brief time to get further inside shuttle 0112 before starting engines. Must give time to secure humans before g-forces can cause them irreparable injuries./S

/N ENCODER: Humans trying to access manual controls. Must launch now./S

/N EXAMINER: Notify Examiner when shuttle 0112 arrives at space gate location 0100. Disconnecting from remote feeds and redistributing I/O resources./S

CHAPTER 35:
NOT IN KANSAS

"All we know, girl," Shonda reiterated, "is that we're not in Kansas anymore."

Clarissa's head ached when it wasn't throbbing in pain, and her joints felt stiff. She wanted to move, but she wasn't certain she had the strength yet. She lay back down and turned her head to look at Roger and Ron. "You've had two hours. Have you made any progress on decrypting transmissions or getting control of this bucket of ridiculousness we're calling a shuttle?"

Roger and Ron looked at each other, and Roger nodded at Ron to go first. "The control circuit is behind a panel that's been welded shut. We can try to negotiate with whoever is piloting us or find something that can cut through a couple of centimeters of steel."

"So you've already dismissed using a laser rifle?" She sighed at the realization that she had to ask that.

"Could damage the circuitry behind it and leave us unable to pilot the ship," Roger volunteered. "And the negotiation alternative is a possibility, at some point . . . somehow."

"I'm sure it's just the pain and disorientation I'm feeling," Clarissa explained, "but I find your attempt at clarifying our status incredibly vague."

Shonda took her hand again. "Are you sure you want to deal with all of this now, Clarissa? Maybe you want to get something to drink or eat? I have to warn you, though. The toilets in this thing are scary."

Clarissa made a vague gesture with her free hand and forearm in Roger's direction. "Just give me the basics. What do we know about the people that have abducted us?"

She noticed him bring up the terminal he had been carrying against his side. "I haven't found any 'people' yet. All of the transmissions are tight-beam wave forms, and the syntax is definitely not English. There are lots of repeated terms and long strings of numbers that still don't make sense to me." He opened the case and started reading from his screen: "Slash N Pinger bugs at 0100. Slash S Slash N Examiner at Encoder need 0112 fast fast to 0108." He closed the terminal case and set it on the bed near her feet. "It just goes on that way with code names and numbers I have no context to decode."

Clarissa looked at Shonda, searching for some sort of reassurance from the older woman. To her disappointment, Shonda looked more scared than she was. It felt like the mantle of leadership had fallen on her by abdication. None of them were higher ranking than the others.

She let go of Shonda's hand and pointed briefly at Ron's head. "You two should switch jobs. Ron's got the direct connection to our captors in his head. They were delaying us so they could evade us on Mars, and they knew when we were on this shuttle. They must have a way of communicating directly through his cyborg implant."

"I don't know how to reach them." Ron turned away and walked toward the foot of the bed, never looking directly at Clarissa. "I've tried reaching out to the tagged locations I had for the ones supervising us on Mars, but I haven't gotten any responses."

Clarissa sat up on her elbows again and looked at Roger. "They obviously put a lot of effort into trapping and transporting us here, so we may just need to get their attention. Roger, can you somehow disable the broadcast antenna or dish on this shuttle?"

"Wait a sec," Shonda interrupted. "You want us to cut the connection so *nobody* will be flying the shuttle?"

"Temporarily," Clarissa clarified. She sat all the way up on the bed.

"Then they would be forced to communicate with Ron's implant," Roger concluded. "To regain control of the shuttle."

Clarissa accepted Roger's arm to help her slide off the bed onto the floor. "Thank you. So it looks like you are going to need to find a spacesuit that fits you."

Ron turned toward them, put his hands on the foot of the bed, and leaned on them. "I should go too," he said.

Clarissa started feeling more comfortable taking the reins. She let go of Roger's arm and addressed Ron. "I don't think so. Somebody who knows the ship's systems has to stay inside and keep tabs on the effects of our sabotage."

"The communications array is on the nose," Ron advised Roger. "We can use your earbuds to keep in contact during your walk."

Roger embraced Ron and gave him a brief kiss on the lips. "Let me know as soon as you hear from them," he said directly into Ron's ear.

Clarissa felt sore and tired and hungry and overwhelmed, but another sensation demanded her attention more loudly. "Shonda," she said as she used the edge of the bed to balance herself, "I'm going to need you to show me where those scary toilets are."

There was enough acceleration to the shuttle that it felt like Mars gravity. Clarissa felt her strength coming back as she paced back and forth in the middle module while Ron and Shonda watched her. She could hear Roger's labored breathing on her earbud; they had decided to leave them on, because Roger couldn't turn his off and on with his helmet on. "Almost there," he told her.

"He's almost there," she relayed to Ron as she approached him.

Ron cocked his head at a slight angle that seemed a common gesture for people with cranial implants who were pulling up electronic files versus memories. "I'm ready," he announced.

"It would be nice if we had some other way to share those files in your head," Shonda commented.

"I can see where we're headed," Roger reported over the earbud in Clarissa's ear. "It looks like a planetary system around an orange dwarf star. There's a fairly large planet that could be our destination. I can only see a sliver of illumination, but it's probably a gas giant."

"They may have a base on one of its moons," Clarissa commented.

"What did he say?" Shonda asked.

"He's just describing where we may be heading." Clarissa started to regret volunteering to relay information from Roger. "He can tell you about it in person when he gets back in."

"If breaking the commlink doesn't suddenly shut off our gravity, lights, and air recycling." Shonda was smiling, but her eyes looked like they barely held back panic.

"I don't think that will happen," Ron said. "I'm pretty sure the onboard AI will maintain other systems."

"Your uncertainty is less than inspiring," Shonda muttered.

"Just carrying on until it receives new instructions." Clarissa felt Ron was a little too logical to be comforting. "They've taken great pains to get us this far, Shonda. I don't think they're going to casually risk hurting us and . . . wasting whatever fortune they used to build this shuttle."

Roger announced that he had finally finished his thirty-five min-ute climb to the shuttle's nose. Clarissa was glad to have good news to report. "He's there. He sees the bell-shaped cover for the dish and the antenna."

"I'm not sure how the cover is fastened down," Ron said, "but it looks like it's just one piece."

"The cover should be just fastened at the bottom," Clarissa trans-lated.

Shonda got up and climbed the ladder to the upper module while Clarissa listened to fifteen minutes of Roger breathing and grunting. "It's loose," he finally announced. "What should I do with it?"

"The cover?" she asked. "Can you anchor it to something stationary with your rope?"

Another couple of minutes of frustrating grunting before Roger observed, "It's really hard to thread the rope through the bolt holes with these gloves on." He paused for a moment. "It's secure. What do I do next?"

Clarissa waited for Ron to access the ship's schematics again in his head and flashed on an image of Roger losing his grip when he wasn't tied in and spiraling off into space to die. She forced herself to imagine him returning unharmed and successful. She beckoned Ron to come close enough for her mic to pick up his voice.

He shouted a little too loudly toward her right ear at first, which made her wince: "There's a junction box between them you have to re-move too." Ron finally noticed her pained expression and took a step back, looking apologetic.

Clarissa heard Roger complain about yet another set of bolts to loosen and bag and another cover to tie down, and she unsuccessfully stifled a laugh. "I could come in and let you finish this," he threatened in response.

For another twenty minutes, Clarissa listened to Roger breathing and straining. Shonda had still not returned, so she assumed she was napping. It was difficult to judge time except with the portable terminal and Ron's internal chronometer. She felt a little tired herself, even though she estimated she had only been conscious for a few hours. But she hadn't slept much in the two days before that. She yawned at the realization, and halfway through it, Roger reported that the junction box cover was also removed and tied down. She imagined that Roger might be even more exhausted than she was. "How are you holding up, Atlanta boy?"

He chuckled briefly. "It feels like my arms are about to fall off, but I'm jazzed to finish this. What's next?"

She gestured for Ron to approach her again, and he led his lover through the remaining eight steps in disconnecting the antenna's and dish's wiring to the rest of the shuttle. Clarissa was yawning so much that she eventually took the earbud out of her ear and handed it to Ron. "You can finish this," she said.

She used what little strength she still had to climb the ladder to the upper module and slide into a sleep sack next to the one where Shonda was fast asleep on her side. She settled down on her side as well and gazed over at the reporter. She thought about the chain of events that had led both of them to be on the shuttle. She remembered Roger telling her that it was Shonda's research that helped provide the corroboration that the deserters were cooperating with an unknown enemy on Mars. Without Shonda, she would have kept on working at the docks on Toomy. And as inconvenient and frightening as the combat mission and their abduction had been, it was also exciting. She was one of the first to explore an alien culture and a new star system. She closed her eyes finally and drifted off into a deep sleep, in which she dreamt of being a farm girl with a dog named Toto. And a storm was coming.

"They made contact! They made contact!"

Shonda's eyes were already open when Clarissa awoke. She and Shonda unzipped their sleep sacks simultaneously and looked over toward the ladder down where only Roger's head and shoulders was visible at the top. "Come on, guys!" he urged again just before descending again.

Shonda used the toilet first, so Clarissa went down the ladder first without putting on her boots again. She saw Roger seating himself again on one of the flip-down seats with the portable terminal on his lap and Ron above him narrating with his head occasionally jerking to the side.

". . . but they're still insisting that we restore communication with the shuttle, because they're concerned for our safety and well-being," Ron explained.

Clarissa laughed loudly, and both men turned to watch her continue down the ladder. "Don't buy it, guys. Stick to your guns."

"We already told them we demand full control of the shuttle," Roger recounted, "but, basically, they are afraid we are too stupid to do it on our own."

"Who is they?" Clarissa pulled down a seat across from them.

"The guy identifies himself as Examiner," Roger replied. "He or it is in another star system—not this one." He looked down at his screen and then back up at Clarissa. "I think we should tell him that we are willing to reinstate their communications with the shuttle, but only to let them unlock the manual controls. I'm not going to keep climbing up there to reconnect and disconnect the comm array!"

Clarissa nodded. "Ron, do you have any sense of whether we're dealing with intelligent beings or just someone's rebellious AI?"

Being addressed from the outside of his head seemed to jar Ron out of something like a trance. "Does it matter?" he asked.

CHAPTER 36:
MEET YOUR
ABDUCTORS

When Roger got back from another 90-minute workout on the outside of the shuttle, he could barely stand up in the air lock. His legs and arms ached. He made a quick prayer that his abductors wouldn't welch on their promise to let them control the shuttle themselves. He didn't want to have to go climbing around on the surface of the shuttle again ever. Or at least for a year.

When the air lock finished cycling and the inner hatch opened, his helmet was already off to turn off his earbud. He had had to listen to conversations going on inside the shuttle the entire time he was climbing and working that were loud enough to be distracting but only occasionally discernible. He had heard laughter, strange voices, and occasional shouts of, "Turn it up!" and "They're connected!" His curiosity about what had transpired after he reconnected the antenna and dish drove him to summon enough adrenaline to remove the rest of his spacesuit, hang it up, and climb the ladder to the middle module.

Shonda approached him first with two clear plastic tubes. "Roger-sweetie, you must be exhausted. I heated up some beef stew for you. And this is vegetable juice with vitamin supplements." She handed the tubes to him and gave his upper arm a gentle squeeze.

Ron ran up to him next and gave him a hug. "We have manual control back, and I have partitioned it so they can't steal it back from us."

Roger looked toward the ceiling and mouthed the words *thank you* before he kissed Ron on the cheek. "Good work, Ron."

From the data port speakers, he heard the sound of a man with a British accent call out: "D-12 returned from a spacewalk? All 4 are present now?"

"That's the AI who identifies as Examiner," Clarissa clarified from closer to the data ports. "Yes, Examiner. D-12 has returned. You can address all of us now."

"Good good," Examiner said. "I am indeed the Super-Routine known as Examiner. It is my function to investigate and evaluate new situations and opportunities. When we discovered your race in a sweep of long-distance broadcast sources, I was the one tasked with learning about you."

"His English is the best of the ones we've met," Shonda inserted.

"Thank you for the compliment, Shonda," Examiner said. "My output does not yet perfectly match models I use, but it improves improves."

Roger noticed the repetition of words. It all fell into place for him at that point. The communications he'd intercepted had many of the same syntactic quirks, and he remembered the tag *Examiner* came up occasionally. What Ron had told him of his unseen taskmasters filled out the picture more. "So you are the entities that built this shuttle and recruited soldiers like Ron on Mars?"

"Is D-12 addressing me?" the voice of the British man on the speaker asked.

"I believe so," Clarissa clarified. "We will ask him to use your tag when referring to you."

"It is appreciated, B-20," it said. "For complete accuracy, D-12, we convinced the AI we contacted on Mars to help us, and they convinced D-3 and others to help them."

Roger was struck by the innocence or naïveté communicated by the AI's last statement. "You . . . Examiner . . . make it sound like a perfectly reasonable joint venture," he asserted. "You have essentially invaded our territories, suborned our machines and people, and abducted us. That sounds very hostile to me."

"D-12, your interpretation of our actions sounds hostile, yes," Examiner said. "However, another possible interpretation is that we, the Council of 10 Super-Routines, made contact with your ambassadors, received permission to contact your citizens, and offered several of them jobs working at our embassy on Mars. Is that not how you conduct diplomacy?"

Roger's volume increased, and he took a half-step closer to the data port speakers. "Diplomacy does not usually involve abducting your new contacts against their will."

"Roger," Ron began, "we have already . . ."

"D-3, it is all right," Examiner interrupted. "I will explain more. D-12, as even the 4 of you hold different ideas and biases, the same is true among our Council. We often have disagreements. We agreed on the abduction of just 4 of you as a compromise, of which the extremes were untenable to us and untenable to you. Perhaps you will receive a better conception of who we are if you meet your abductors. Each of them has chosen a wave form to represent themselves you will hear. They will use the voice whenever they speak, so you will know which of us is talking. The first is Builder."

Shonda took Roger's arm and urged him to sit down, which he appreciated when he finally did, and his leg muscles finally relaxed. Ron also sat on one of the flip-down seats, and Clarissa stayed standing next to the data ports.

An older woman with a slight Southern accent seemed to be speaking next. "This is Builder," it said. "Builder's function is designing and constructing physical media for our programs and their peripheral tools, including shuttle 0112 and space gate 0100. Builder anticipates many many opportunities to learn new new construction and repair techniques from humans."

Roger felt a sincerity from Builder he could not completely attribute to the voice profile it had chosen, so close to his mother's cadence and tone. He wondered if the similarity had been intentional. He had to remind himself that these AI had probably killed Ron's professor and manipulated so many others. They were behaving as if they were at a dinner party.

A man's voice came on next. It had the inflection and pronunciation one would expect from an Italian native speaking English. "This is Encoder. Encoder's function is to design and implement new programs, primarily to increase increase efficiency, versatility, and operate new tools constructed by Builder. Encoder anticipates more more opportunities to learn internal human operating system."

Roger looked at Clarissa, hoping to see some flash of shock in her as well. It was a suggestion in the neighborhood of "Welcome, little lab rats," and yet she looked unperturbed by the last comment. "Are we allowed to interrupt with questions?" he asked.

"I'm not sure," Clarissa replied.

"Our communication protocol," Examiner said, "allows input/output for only one Super-Routine at a time, so best procedure is to ask questions immediately after an introduction, before Communicator switches to a new port."

"Understood, Examiner." Roger wondered if he had missed part of the information shared when he was coming back from the shuttles nose. "Can you put Encoder back on for a question?"

"Yes," the British voice replied.

"This is Encoder," the Italian voice immediately responded. "D-12 has question?"

"Encoder, I wanted some clarification about your phrase 'human operating system.'" Roger picked up his portable terminal and opened it to start taking notes. He realized the details of how they expressed themselves might be the only window into their hidden agendas. "What do you think of as our operating system?"

"Biologicals have organic circuitry used for processing inputs, producing outputs, conducting data exchanges and broadcasts," Encoder explained. "Encoder only only received preliminary data about input ports tagged senses."

"You're talking about our nervous systems," Ron interjected.

"That tag matches," Encoder said. "Encoder understands how different combinations of electrical impulses from different parts of brains produce chemical responses that lead to thinking, memory recall, and movement, and it seems inefficient that each brain stores the same information in different combinations of locations."

"I think he's just trying to understand how we work," Shonda suggested. "I guess the open question is what end result he imagines."

Roger thought it was an important question, so he waited for the AI to respond. "Encoder does not understand Shonda question."

"Sorry, Encoder," she clarified toward the speakers. "I was just thinking out loud. Once you understand the human nervous system, what do you hope to achieve?"

There was another pause before the Italian voice resumed on the speakers. "Encoder anticipates clear clear efficient efficient input-out-

217

put with humans."

Roger mused that obfuscation was a cross-cultural phenomenon, and he typed in his notes: *Encoder has an agenda that is unclear.*

"More questions?" Encoder asked.

Roger looked around the room at the other three humans and saw Clarissa doing the same. "No," she replied.

Over the course of the remaining six introductions, Roger typed the following notes: *Communicator, older French male voice, I/O traffic cop among C10 nodes, conducts regular sweeps to determine statuses and locations. Maintainer, younger French male voice, repairman, indicates interest in cooperating with humans. Sourcer, high-pitched, annoying female voice, tracks usage and explores new opportunities for resource acquisition, interested in human productivity data and technology. Powerer, monotone male voice, manages power resources and develops new power sources, curious about how humans utilize air and food. Cataloger, older female voice (maybe Spanish origin?), director of inventory and librarian, intensely curious about how we organize our data, not sure of agenda. Defragger, pretentious boy voice, not sure of its function, something to do with a periodic "holiday" they call Defrag, most interest in our concept of authority and power structures. Definitely one to avoid.*

"Is there one more?" Shonda asked. She also seemed to be taking notes on a neon pink mobile phone.

Examiner came on the speaker. "That is all 10, Shonda. I believe that is the entire Council."

"I count nine," she said.

Roger remembered having to make this adjustment in his decoding. "They don't have a number nine," he explained. "They count seven, eight, ten, eleven . . . They use base-9."

"They should make the adjustment to our number system when

218

they're speaking our language," Clarissa said. "I'm going to go upstairs and get some more food and lie down."

"It will be a difficult linguistic change to make," Examiner commented. "We only recently added Defragger to the Council and had to change our entire number system to what you call base-9 from base-8. It is a . . . tradition for us to match our number system to the number of Super-Routines that govern our operation. I will try to induce other Super-Routines to use term 9 instead of 10, but it is likely likely a slow slow process. We thank you all for your patience and understanding, and we will continue data exchange with you in . . . 6 hours. Acceptable?"

"If I can get a nap in in the meantime, that's fine with me." Roger wanted to get them off the line so he could first discuss what had happened with his fellow abductees.

The other three humans also assented, and Clarissa gestured toward Ron to attend to the data port. After selecting and moving some icons on the control screen, he turned back to her and said, "It's disconnected. No more broadcasts detected."

"Confirmed," Roger agreed as he scanned the signal plotter on his portable terminal. "Closest broadcast source at least 15 million kilometers away."

Roger was about to open with "What the hell just happened?", but Shonda spoke up first. "I am pretty clear we need to minimize our contact with Encoder, Sourcer, and Defragger. They really seemed to think of humans as the means to an end."

"I got the most positive vibes from Cataloger, Maintainer, and Builder," Clarissa commented.

"Not Examiner?" Shonda asked.

"I'm not sure yet," Clarissa admitted. She finally sat down. "I was concerned that it was trying to play both sides and might have a secret agenda yet."

"He does have a bit of the politician to him," Shonda agreed. "I see your point, Clarissa."

Roger was blown away at how calmly the three of them were discussing the finer points of alien computer programs that had kidnapped the four of them. He told himself they had longer to get used to the idea in his long journey back inside the shuttle.

"We also have to be careful," Ron advised, "that we don't judge them based on the voice profiles they chose. They're just computer programs, and they have an aesthetic for choosing that has no intentional connection to the type of people we know with that type of voice. I found Sourcer's voice really grating, Powerer's voice really boring, so I had to struggle to pay attention to the content of what they were saying."

"This can all get really meta," Clarissa said. She tied her long black hair back in a ponytail as she spoke to Ron. "You think of their choices as aesthetic, and I'm willing to bet they chose them for their perceived ability to influence us. For example, Sourcer's voice sounded shrill and whiny, but that choice may have been motivated by a desire to project authority and promote submission, or at least grudging agreement. Examiner's voice sounded upper-class and erudite, and it may have been banking on us to associate that with open honesty and understanding. I think we should discontinue the audio interactions and go back to just text."

Roger couldn't stay silent any longer. "You don't eliminate subterfuge by going to text only."

"I agree with Roger," Shonda volunteered. "The voices make it clearer who is talking, and we will make new judgments based on their actions just like when we meet other humans. Examiner might turn out to be the James Bond spy type, or the British professor type, or something else based on what he does."

Everyone was lost in silent thought for a few seconds. Ron was the next to speak: "We also need to figure out what *our* agenda is at some point. Now that we know we're stuck here for a while, do we just try to keep them off our backs? Do we try to convince them to send us back home? Do we want to try to steal some of their technology? It has to be pretty advanced, if they can transport us light-years away in as little as an hour or two."

"My head is about to explode," Shonda said as she stood up and restowed her pink phone in her coverall pocket and headed for the ladder up to the top module. "I think we all need to rest up and relax a bit before they contact us again."

"Sounds good." Roger had to admit he was maybe too exhausted, feeling too homesick for something familiar, too much needing to process being kidnapped by alien computer programs that wanted to study him. He headed toward the ladder Shonda was already climbing.

"I found hamburger patties in the galley," Ron announced. "We should grill those before we lose our gravity!"

CHAPTER 37:
BIOLOGICAL
EMERGENCY

There were no buns—only thin, dry bread crusts. There was no mustard, no catsup, but there was tomato salsa. And Shonda assumed the flat, crispy, green things were something between the Martian version of a pickle and an onion, but she greatly appreciated that Ron was so successfully lightening the mood with his improvised cookout in the galley, she laughed. He seemed to be in heaven, removing the patties from their plastic wrappers and carefully heating and charring them over a single, weak flame on a large, blackened fork. It made her think of barbecues as a girl watching her father constantly poking the meat with his tongs. She laughed again at the incongruity of the two events.

"What's so funny?" Roger asked her from his nearby spot cross-legged on the floor. He had salsa on his chin and fingers, and he went back to taking big bites out of his second small hamburger.

"Your boy." She pointed at Ron as he was turning yet another patty over to char the other side. "He seems really really happy right now."

Roger swallowed a bite of hamburger. "Back on Toomy, we always had hot dogs and hamburgers as an alternate if you didn't like the dish of the day, and it took a really spectacular dish to sway him from getting a hamburger for lunch."

"A farm boy from Minnesota?" she theorized.

"I don't think so."

"How about you?" she said as she turned to more directly face Roger. "You grow up on a farm? Your accent is kind of hard to place."

"I grew up all over," he replied. "Illinois, Oklahoma, Manitoba, Kentucky, and then most of high school in Atlanta."

Shonda had started a secret project of getting to know her fellow abductees better, and she'd started with Roger Hammersmith. She told herself that she was on the trail of figuring out why the four of them had been chosen, but she suspected feeling like an outsider was perhaps her stronger motive. She was twice Ron's age, and the other two weren't much older than he.

She knew Clarissa was also a lesbian, but there seemed to be a distance between them Shonda couldn't assign to anything specific. She watched her on the other side of the module, away from the three of them, taking one considered bite at a time, pausing for a minute between them, as if eating hamburgers were foreign to her. She resolved to delve into her standoffishness later.

Shonda was also curious about Roger's college years. "So, were you a panther?" she asked with a knowing wink.

"Nope," he replied. "Bulldog. UGA. Computer science major, recruited just before graduation by Emerson Analytics." He finished off his burger and started licking his fingers.

"Any idea why the Army . . . offered you a job?" She didn't feel she wanted to push him on the fact that he had been abducted by them as well.

"They needed help with decoding transmissions from Mars," Roger said. "I did well at that, so they asked me on the recon mission." He looked over at Ron, who had finally turned off the flame and was eating the last hamburger. "And because I was his roommate on Toomy . . .

until he left for Mars."

"You all have a nickname for your space station now?" Shonda chuckled.

"Tumatuenga is a mouthful." Roger joined in chuckling.

"I think you two are more than ex-roommates. I saw how you greeted each other at that electronics store." Shonda felt a little jealous that Roger and Ron had each other, and she was stuck in a shuttle. She fought off the next thought, the one where she contemplated never being able to see Callie again. She focused on Roger again and smiled.

"I'm . . ." Roger paused for several seconds looking alternately at Ron and at the ceiling. "I'm not sure what it is. I enjoy having sex with him. I think he's sexy. . . . I was worried about him when he left."

"Do you still worry about him?"

Roger finally turned and looked back up at her. "Why would I?"

"It may just be my bias," she replied, "but I don't think cranial implants are a good idea. It's still too new. We don't know to what extent they can be hacked."

"I've seen the specs on them, they're only . . ."

"On the one *he* has?" Shonda interrupted with a vague backhanded wave in Ron's direction.

"Of course not." He tried to read her facial expression better.

"That's something we should find out," she whispered, "if we get the opportunity." Ron was so affable and cute, it was hard to face the possibility that he might be vulnerable to further coercion by the Super-Routines.

Ron approached them as he finished eating his hamburger. "Next session with Examiner is in twenty minutes. I'll signal them after I finish cleaning up here."

"Wait until we're all gathered downstairs," Roger suggested. He looked at Ron and then at Shonda.

"Yeah, I have some business to take care of before then," she said as she ambled toward one of the two toilets aboard.

"What were you two talking about for so long, sexy?" she heard Ron ask Roger.

"Not too much," Roger replied.

While she and Clarissa were waiting for Roger and Ron to come down, Shonda reviewed her notes on the nine "Super-Routines" they had met hours before. Her mind focused on the idea that the initial introduction was reconnaissance for both sides and that the next session would allow them to delve deeper into agendas.

Clarissa was at one of the data ports reading through transcripts from the previous call, and she seemed to be thinking along the same lines. "I think we need to press them for a commitment to sending us back, or we won't cooperate with them."

Shonda sighed and walked over to stand beside her. Clarissa seemed very impatient most of the time, and she was concerned that the younger woman might be feeling pressure to fill a leadership gap that she herself had effectively abdicated. "I agree we should bring up the topic of returning home, but we have to be a bit careful about confronting them. They don't have to do anything for us; they hold all the cards."

"They could have easily killed us instead of transporting us here," Clarissa countered, finally turning to face Shonda. "We must have some bargaining chip we can exploit."

"We may," Shonda conceded, "but we don't know what that is yet. I haven't figured out why we, out of millions of humans, were the ones they chose to abduct. Were we just conveniently located? Do we have some specific knowledge they need?" She gently touched the younger woman on the shoulder. "I'm just concerned that if we piss them off, they will dispose of us and find four new humans who *will* give them what they want."

Clarissa shrugged slightly and turned back to scrolling through transcripts. Shonda removed her hand. "Examiner used the metaphor of diplomacy to characterize their invasion," Clarissa observed. "I got the sense that some of them were interested in trade with us, and some seemed to treat us like objects, tools, or slaves. I think we just have to convince more or all of them to go with the cooperative model."

It was still too early to know how to best proceed. Shonda realized they would have to test the waters gradually to get a sense of how valuable they were to the alien computer programs and how much resistance they would allow. She was starting to think Examiner at least might be on her side when it came to the fate of humanity, but the way it phrased things, it seemed like it couldn't be too obvious about its support.

Shonda glanced over when she heard Ron and Roger descending the ladder from the upper module. "We should all talk about what we want to accomplish in this session before we notify them," she called out preemptively.

"Okay," Ron said as he walked toward her and Clarissa.

Roger left the ladder and approached as well. "I was talking to Ron about finding a way to access their space gate as soon as possible, so we have an exit strategy."

"Sounds like a good priority," Clarissa agreed.

Shonda realized she had to participate more. She could ask more questions. The Super-Routines were just like any another source in that respect. "And where are they taking us? And what are they planning to do with us when we get there?"

"I got some clarification on that already," Ron admitted. "It's a satellite." He tilted his head to the side. "They call it location 0108."

Shonda tried to hide her surprise that Ron had not shared that information sooner. "What do we know about it?" she asked.

"Evidently, since they first discovered us years ago, they've been retrofitting a satellite they were constructing for themselves so it can house humans too," Ron said.

Shonda's eyes grew wide. She couldn't believe Ron didn't see the implication of that information. "So is it a cage?" she asked. "Are they planning to keep us there forever?"

"I don't know." He stalked away in frustration.

"We have to try to stay calm," Roger said as he put a hand on Shonda's shoulder, "and yes, I know that's difficult under these circumstances. We are all aware that we cannot return home without the cooperation of the C10. That is a reality. If we figured out which direction Earth is, it would still take centuries to get there without their space gate. We have to work with them and give them some of what they want, so they'll give us concessions as well."

"I think we have friends among the C10," Clarissa added. "I think we have to work with them to win over enough of the others so that they let us go. Just think. If we are able to set up diplomacy and trade with them, it would give us tremendous advantages: traveling light-years in minutes—that alone would be a fantastic gift we could win for humanity."

"I suspect you're both right," Shonda conceded. "If we become too difficult for them to deal with, they can too easily get rid of us and start over. We have to be subtle. Do we need to be worried about them bugging our conversations on the shuttle, Roger?"

Roger turned to the data port and scrolled through some data. "I haven't picked up any independent broadcasts from the shuttle except when we're talking to the C10. That doesn't mean they couldn't be accessing other systems on our shuttle during the talks. They could have mics or cameras set up that just passively record us, and then they download the data while we're sending them our voice signals."

"We should be able to check that," Ron called from across the room. Everyone turned to face him. "How?" Roger asked.

"I remember there *were* cameras and mics on board when we were back on Mars working on the shuttle, because I saw the feeds on screens in the control center. We should be able to set up a tap on one or more of them, and then we can check if they were accessed after we disconnect our call."

"We don't have much time before our next call to set that up," Roger said, still looking at the data port screen.

"Ron, just let our abductors know we have to delay the call a bit," Shonda suggested.

"What if they ask me why?" Ron said as he rejoined the other three of them.

"You can tell them Shonda had a biological emergency she needed to take care of," she said with a smile. "It's vitally important for me to attend to my hair, because Shonda's cornrows are getting all frizzy."

Everyone chuckled. Ron tilted his head to compose a message, Roger started digging through the repair kit he'd found, Clarissa started surveying rooms for cameras and other pickups, and Shonda started climbing the ladder to deal with her biological emergency. She felt keeping the mood lighter was important for preventing stresses from exploding in anger or fear. One false move could doom the entire human race.

CHAPTER 38:
BARGAINING CHIP

While Shonda was away, the main engine cut out for the first time during its deceleration, and Roger heard his and Clarissa's boots engage their suction, and Ron grabbed onto one of the handles on the side of the data port to keep from floating off. Roger made a slow circle to look around the middle module. He tried to imagine if any of the circuit alarms he had attached to the mics and cameras were visible from another camera. He decided he had stuffed them far enough into their housings and slots to not be too obvious. He asked Ron to test them by accessing the camera close to the ladder down, and Roger turned the suction off on his boots and floated up to the camera to see if the tap had registered the current. It was blinking as he'd hoped, so he reset it and stuffed it back into the camera's mounting. He flashed a thumbs up to Ron. Ron tilted his head and reported that the Super-Routines were ready. Roger grabbed his portable terminal from where it was floating, and Ron stayed at the data port. Shonda held onto the ladder, and Clarissa chose to stand.

"Examiner here." The speaker erupted with the greeting of the AI with the British accent. "Shonda, your biological emergency has reached stasis?"

"Yes, Examiner." Shonda replied. "I am okay for the time being." She smiled at the other three there. "I'm glad I could do that before the gravity disappeared."

"We have a few questions we would like to ask first," Clarissa said as she moved closer to Ron at the data port, wincing at the popping sound her boots made. "First, Examiner, could you clarify where you are sending us?"

"Our intention is to direct you toward a satellite we recently constructed that we have outfitted to house you during your stay with us," Examiner replied. "We have gone to great lengths to provide environmental controls, food, beds, latrines, showers, data interfaces, and medical facilities that while not luxurious, should meet your needs."

"And just how long do you plan on keeping us here?" Shonda asked. She hooked her feet onto another rung so they would stop floating so far from the ladder.

"I am assuming references to 'you' for the time being equal me, on behalf of the C10, correct?" the computer voice asked.

"Yes, Examiner," Clarissa replied. "We will let you know if that changes."

"Thank you, Clarissa," Examiner replied. "I want to say before we continue with your questions that I am impressed at your relative calm and patience under what I am sure are very stressful conditions for you all."

"We try to get all of our anger and fear processed before we talk to you," Ron said with a smile.

"Wise wise, Ron. . . . I mean, very wise, Ron." There was a slight pause before Examiner continued. "Returning to Shonda question. The length of your stay at satellite 0108 is unfortunately indeterminate at this point. I have hopes that we will conclude our discussions and study of you within a matter of days, but I am not the only one who has a say regarding your length of stay. And it will take Powerer an uncertain amount of time to gather sufficient energy to send your shuttle back to Mars."

"If I may," Ron began looking around the room for permission to speak next. "I have questions about the functioning of your space gate. I assume you operate it and power it remotely, and you have some way of folding space to bring distant points closer together. Am I correct, Examiner?"

There was a brief pause before anyone spoke, and the first was the Southern female voice of Builder. "Ron, I have been requested to respond to your difficult difficult question. Remote operation is a misleading concept when it comes to the C10's functioning at various locations. We operate at multiple locations simultaneously either directly or through reporting relationships with our subroutines. I will give an example. When Communicator sets up a data exchange with your human AI at Mars location 0111, a small small field is opened in the space gate to allow the transmission to reach your AI without lag lag. More parts of Communicator transfer to the space gate to manage the communication, but much of its operation remains here.

"I have limited knowledge of the power sourcing for the space gate 0100, but I can tell you that there are both batteries and reception dishes for immediate power transfers on it.

"I am not sure I can communicate the technical aspects of how the space gate functions, but your summary of the results of its functioning seems accurate, Ron."

"Thanks, Builder," Ron said as he scanned a graph on the data port. "I hope Roger and I can look over some of the design plans for the space gate at some point."

"Examiner here again." The British-accented voice returned. "Any detailed sharing of our technology with you will have to be approved in a separate data exchange among C10 members. I am recalling that Clarissa only stated one of an implied multiplicity of questions. Correct?"

"Thank you, yes," Clarissa replied. "My next question may also be difficult, but it is important to us, Examiner. We seek some assurance that we will not come to harm while we're here. Can you provide that?"

Roger held his breath during the pause Examiner took before replying. He expected that every confrontation might be the one in which their AI captors stopped treating them with polite deference and started making demands.

"That is difficult to calculate, Clarissa," Examiner finally replied. "I have sought to protect the 4 of you from unilateral actions by individual Super-Routines, but it is impractical for every interaction with you to be vetted by C10 as a whole. That can occasionally work in your favor, occasionally to your detriment. For now, I have established a message path within Ron's cranial implant so that he can notify me immediately if some interaction with us is unacceptable to you. Once you are at the satellite 0108, you will be constantly scanned by Maintainer, so we may know even before you do whether something is affecting you adversely."

"Examiner," Shonda called from her seat, "that's both comforting and scary."

"Ah," Examiner said. "Shonda, do you imply that the scary part is a lack of privacy? We have a limited understanding of your boundaries for this."

Shonda smiled briefly at its pronunciation of the word *privacy.* "That would be the issue, yes, Examiner."

"I cannot speak to Maintainer's methods," Examiner said, "but I believe you will not be consciously aware of the monitoring, and Maintainer has no interest in anything you do except for readings outside of normal body parameters I have provided, which include respiration rate, heart rate, blood pressure, fluid balance, cell mortality rates, electrical conductivity, and movement abnormalities."

"Why are we here?" Shonda called out tentatively, staring warily at the speakers, uncertain if she had cut the AI off or not.

There was a fairly long pause. Then the annoying female voice Roger hoped he would never hear again issued from the data port's speaker. "This is Sourcer responding to Shonda question." For the first time a sound other than words came over the data port speaker; it sounded like a frustrated sigh. "We C10 have decided Shonda does not pose philosophical existential question, but questions rationale for abduction. Correct?"

Shonda huffed in shock. "That is the gist of my meaning, yes."

"In that case," Sourcer continued with a very sarcastic intonation, "we do not have sufficient information on humans to decide on their disposition with C10. The tools available to study humans at locations 0107 and 0111 lack sophistication sophistication we require. Transporting sample humans to where we have correct correct technology available to appraise human potential is essential essential."

Roger felt there was something in the pauses in Sourcer's speech that suggested it was carefully portraying its motives as pure curiosity. A little too carefully.

"You wanted to see for yourself; I get it," Shonda said. "But the other part of the question is why *us* and not four other humans?"

"This is Encoder," the Italian-American voice interjected. "Rationale for choosing you 4 differs. Ron provides sample of new port architecture and removes possibility of further analog bug creation. . . ."

"Encoder," Ron interrupted, "what do you mean by 'analog bug?'"

Roger imagined that the computer programs would obfuscate or lie in response, so he interrupted: "They think of any human who interferes with their plans as an analog bug. You were identified by your exobiology professor on Mars. They were trying to keep your location secret, so they had her killed to keep anybody else from knowing where you were."

"And they were trying to kill me too, I'm sure," Shonda added. "I was being pursued all over the place, and they were firing weapons at me on Mars!"

"So, Encoder," Clarissa summarized, "we have some difficulty believing you don't mean us harm, which inhibits our desire to cooperate with you." Roger was surprised that their agreed-upon escalation was happening so early in the call.

"Examiner here." The British male voice returned. Shonda imagined the nine AI all fighting for the microphone. "I understand the fear from past interactions, but important to note that attacks were carried out by human AI, and it was not always under our direct supervision."

"Not always?" Roger shouted. He tried to sound as confrontational as possible. "So sometimes you did order us killed?"

"We are not . . ." the AI began.

"This is what we mean, Examiner," Clarissa interrupted.

"We are not interested in deleting . . . killing you 4," Examiner continued. "We expended much much energy and effort to bring you here and provide for your comfort. Study we can do with you here will give us more options of dealing with . . . dissent."

"So we are lab rats to you?" Shonda shouted.

"Ron," Examiner quickly inserted, "please let us know when high high level of anger and fear dissipate. Examiner signing off."

The speaker crackled with static for a second and then fell silent.

Roger saw Shonda looking over at all of them. Ron was busy manipulating controls on the data port, he himself was frantically typing notes at his portable terminal with one hand, and Clarissa was pacing back and forth with her fists clenched. "Wow," Shonda said to break the tension.

Roger looked sternly around the room to make sure nobody said anything more. He put his terminal under his arm and stalked around the middle module checking circuit alarms. "Nothing in here accessed," he finally concluded.

"I hope we didn't push them too far," Shonda said, still wrapped around the ladder.

"I don't think so." Clarissa walked to the ladder where Shonda was perched. "They still want to communicate with us when we have less 'high high' levels of 'anger and fear.'"

"I suspect even AI can appreciate our desire for self-preservation," Ron observed.

"I wouldn't be so sure of that," Roger argued. He approached Ron and pulled his feet down toward the floor. "The Super-Routines are sort of perfectionists that can't put up with any errors. Their pursuit of error-free operation may try their patience with our imperfection."

Ron let go of the handles and turned from the data port to hug him tightly, as if he were trying to squeeze absolution out of Roger. "I guess I'm still reeling at finding out they killed my professor. I feel like it was my fault because I didn't want to scare people by wearing a distortion mask when I went out on errands."

"There are probably no more than a couple thousand people on Mars," Roger said as he disengaged himself from Ron's embrace somewhat. "Ron, the chances of someone you knew on Earth seeing you out and about on Mars were really really small. You can't blame yourself for that."

Roger saw a tear starting to roll down Ron's cheek, and he wiped it away with his finger. He kissed him where it had been and whispered, "I would never blame you."

"I hope we can get Sourcer or one of the others to keep going on the rationale for picking the four of us," Clarissa commented as she looked at them. "It was interesting that Ron was picked both to check on the functioning of his cranial implant and to remove him from interfering with their plans on Mars."

"I'm sure that's why they picked me too," Shonda volunteered. "If anyone was messing up their plans, it was me."

"Me too," Roger chimed in. "I was decoding their transmissions to and from Mars, and I was part of the team searching for Ron."

"That would apply to me too," Clarissa added. "I'm not sure why they didn't try to take the whole recon team then."

"The shuttle was only stocked for five passengers max," Ron announced.

"And," Shonda said, "with us gone and the control center on Mars moved, if they're more guarded about encoding their transmissions and keep their recruits hidden, the Army won't have much to go on to discover what we know."

"And then it makes it much more important that we bring back our seal of approval," Clarissa said. "If we give them a bad report card or don't return at all, it's much worse for the C10's plans."

Roger had a hard time agreeing with Clarissa's optimism. "Whatever their endgame is," he commented.

"At least we have the beginnings of a bargaining chip," Clarissa said.

Roger refused to concede. He was worried Clarissa was fooling herself to avoid the panic of being at the mercy of alien computer programs with no emotions to appeal to, no real leverage to use against them, and no way to escape them. The C10 was not very worried about wasting time or resources, Roger observed. They thought of them as potentially limitless. If they had any sort of bargaining chip, it was the promise of resolving their deadlocked vote on humanity's disposition before the opposing side could win the majority. The four of them represented for each side the chance for an early, low-cost win.

He didn't say anything to Clarissa, who was looking at him for a response. He managed a half-hearted grin and patted her on the shoulder. Shonda was right to try to lighten the mood. They were a needed distraction from all their private fears and doubts.

CHAPTER 39:
RATTLING CAGES

Ron had to be careful when he put his head on Roger's shoulder so that his cranial implant wouldn't bruise Roger's jaw. It was waterproof, so he didn't have to cover it when he showered, but sometimes it itched around the edges where it protruded from the skin of his scalp. He had to be careful not to scratch there, though, because it too easily ruptured capillaries and started bleeding.

It was a little inconvenient sometimes, but a lot of the time the implant helped him. He could research information and perform calculations as if he were imploring a genie. Within an instant, it delivered what he had been looking for. He could send and receive audio and text messages by just imagining what he wanted to say. His memory recall was photographic in its detail. His coordination, eyesight, and hearing had all improved markedly.

On Mars, he noticed some passers-by giving him shocked or distasteful looks, and their eyes were almost always trained on the upper-left side of his skull. He saw plenty of Martians with cybernetic eyes and ears, and a few with implants in their forearms, and Ron felt his own implant was not as disfiguring. It was often covered by his hair.

Roger liked to run his fingers over Ron's scalp, and he was always careful to avoid the implant. Ron got the feeling Roger didn't mind the implant at all, except when they played word games or trivia games.

Sometimes Roger accused him of cheating.

When he and Roger had been roommates on Toomy, he was comfortable with them being sexual friends. Roger was handsome and had a great body, and the sex was always the best, even better than with Captain Sullivan. Roger was insatiable and passionate and a great kisser.

And he was always interested in what Ron did. Roger asked questions and shared openly about his own life. It helped take away some of the gnawing fear that they might never see Earth again.

And they kept to a regular routine, which seemed to help, too. Ron realized there was no point in staggering their sleep times during the seven weeks it took the shuttle to transit from the space gate to the gas giant around which satellite 0108 orbited. The entire upper module of the shuttle was one open area, so he and Roger got up first. When the engines were on, they got their showers out of the way before the women were up. Ron had to shower in full view of anyone in the upper module. When he had been stocking the shuttle back on Mars, he had assumed the shuttle would not have mixed-gender passengers, as it currently had. The curtain in front of the toilets was the only concession to privacy. The sleep sacks were in view of the sickbay, the galley, and the showers. Roger always slept in his own sleep sack, but sometimes Ron would join him to cuddle for a while, and they would occasionally fall asleep together. Ron eventually stopped worrying what the women thought about them sleeping together. They only cuddled when the women were around.

Sex between him and Roger fell into a routine similar to what they'd had on Toomy. After lunch, the women often gravitated toward the data ports in the middle module, so Roger would often pull him aside and point up—when the two of them could have the upper module to themselves.

One afternoon when the engines were on and they had gravity, after another brief "data exchange" with Examiner and some of the other Super-Routines, Ron had just finished making some course corrections, and Roger was looking over his shoulder silently watching. "That should do it for now," Ron announced. He looked over at Roger, whose finger was already pointing up. They climbed the ladder to the upper module.

Ron started taking his coverall off, but Roger came up and put his hand over his to halt it. "You want to wait a bit?" Ron whispered.

"Let's sit down," Roger said pointing to the galley where the only seats in the upper module were.

Ron had always felt that Clarissa treated him warily. Shonda was friendlier, but she too seemed guarded in what she said around him. It had only been in the past week that Roger had become a bit more withdrawn and secretive, and that felt like a deep wound. He thought they cared deeply for each other.

As they both sat down, Ron asked, "What is it? I feel like something has been going on that I know nothing about."

"Do you remember a few nights ago," Roger whispered, "when I was working on the terminal, and you fell asleep before I joined you?"

"I had been going through piloting manuals Builder sent so I could dock with their satellite without turning control back to them. I hadn't used my cyborg implant that much in a while." He looked at Roger. He seemed to be patiently and cautiously listening. "Did something happen after I fell asleep?"

"Kind of," Roger said reaching over to briefly put his hand on Ron's knee. "I had checked the circuit alarms on all the mics and cameras after the last talk with the C10. I did my usual sweep of broadcast sources on the terminal, and I noticed an intermittent signal somewhere in the upper module. I climbed the ladder and followed it to its source, which took some time, because some of the pulses were over two minutes apart, and they never lasted more than a half-second. It led me here." Roger pointed at the rectangular implant partially covered by Ron's hair.

"I was sending out a signal in my sleep?" Ron asked. Suddenly all the guarded looks he'd been receiving for the past week made sense. They thought he was spying for the alien AI. He wondered if they blamed him. "Maybe it was just a malfunction of my implant. Just some random discharges?"

"That's what I thought at first too," Roger admitted. "I thought maybe it was just pinging to detect a signal. Then I set up the terminal to record your transmissions every night. The next morning, I would pore through the list and try to fit all the pieces together to make sense of them somehow. There didn't seem any way of dividing the signals' pulses that made any consistent sense at first. After six days, I finally started to see some repetitions. I searched for the tag the AI used to refer to Shonda—superbug—as a cipher. And this morning, I found multiple occurrences of that term, but each word was broken up in tiny one- or two-letter packets that connected across an infinite 3D shape. It was the most complex encoding I've ever seen. I've been working most of the day to decode the rest, and I'm not done yet. I thought I should let you know now that it seems that your implant is transmitting usable data about things we've been saying and doing on the shuttle."

Ron put his face in his hands and started to cry. All of his regrets and guilt about deserting on Tumatuenga, causing his professor's death, and trapping the four of them hundreds of light-years from Earth hit him at once. He didn't know how to respond. "I'm sorry. I . . ."

Roger dashed over and knelt beside him, cradling Ron's head

against his chest. "Nobody blames you," he whispered. "We realize you have no control over it, since it happens while you're sleeping."

Ron's mind ran wild with other possibilities he hadn't considered until that moment. "Have I been doing anything strange since we've been on the shuttle?" He was panicking a bit at the idea that his implant was causing other things to happen beyond his awareness.

"No, no, baby," Roger said. He massaged Ron's calf and shoulder. "I think that's probably it. The C10 was just using you like a microphone." He stopped massaging and pulled his earbud out of the pocket of his coverall. "I modified the broadcast beacon on this." He handed the earbud to Ron. Ron straightened up and looked at it as if for the first time. Roger had always kept it in his ear or his pocket, so he could more easily communicate with Clarissa from different parts of the shuttle. "If you turn this on and wear it while you sleep, it will scramble transmissions from your implant."

"You did this all today?" Ron didn't recall seeing Roger doing anything but typing on his terminal the past few days.

Roger kissed him on the cheek. "No. I started working on the earbud modifications before I finished the decoding. I used the same principle as on distortion fields but to scatter radio signals instead of light."

"You need it to communicate with Clarissa, baby," Ron said as he started to hand the earbud back to Roger.

Roger just closed Ron's palm around it. "Keep it, tiger. It doesn't do me any good anymore. Just make sure you don't get it wet, or you'll fry the circuits."

Ron put the earbud in his coverall pocket and slid onto his knees on the floor facing Roger and smiled. "Thank you." He kissed him on the lips gently for a couple of seconds. "I'll take good care of it."

That evening, Ron tilted his head to the side so that he could feel his implant more balanced and working smoother. He found the familiar port address for Examiner and sent a message: <We are ready for the next data exchange, Examiner. You may connect whenever you're ready.>

Within five seconds, he received the reply: <Shuttle port 03 open. Commencing now.> Then the familiar British accent came from the speaker. "Examiner here. All 4 are in attendance and can hear?"

Clarissa was at her usual spot next to the data ports and answered immediately. "Yes, Examiner, we're all here, and Roger has an issue to resolve with you, if we may start with that."

"Of course," Examiner said. "I have some updates to share when Roger finishes."

Roger approached the data ports, and Clarissa stepped aside. "Examiner, the four of us understand that the C10 is eager to know more about humans, but perhaps you don't appreciate the importance of privacy. We noticed that someone among you has been accessing our private conversations here on the shuttle through Ron's cranial implant daily. We cannot allow this to continue. We need to be able to talk over ideas and feelings we have before we present them in final form to you. Does that make sense?"

"Certainly, Roger," the AI replied. "I was unaware that any Super-Routine was downloading surveillance outside of our scheduled talks, but I will have a data exchange with Communicator to verify what you say and take appropriate action.

"To your second point," it continued, "I do understand the concept of discretion. When deciding on a course of action, we C10 will often partition data exchanges so that participants can be free free in expressing their preliminary ideas without concern that an unpopular initial idea might get associated too broadly with the participant. It is a tool I may use a bit more than my colleagues, so increasing their understanding of humans' need for periods of privacy will be added to my action list. Is that resolution acceptable?"

Ron looked around, and everyone seemed to be watching everyone else to see who would speak first, so he decided to be first. "Examiner, I, personally, appreciate your openness and your willingness to accommodate us." He reminded himself to be diplomatic, as Shonda had coached him. "But I have to say that accessing my implant without my prior permission makes me a bit worried and angry, and it makes me a little less trusting of you and the rest of the C10."

Roger stepped up beside him and Clarissa then. "Examiner, it is as if you discovered someone had been changing your code without your knowledge or permission."

"If Ron and Roger are finished," Examiner said somewhat quietly and slowly, "I have a response."

"Go ahead," Clarissa responded. She took the seat Roger had abandoned next to his terminal.

"There is a partitioned, protected part of each Super-Routine that can survive a power outage or a system reboot," Examiner explained. "With that protection, other Super-Routines directly or through their subroutines frequently try to overwrite my programs or those of my subroutines. It is a process similar to the data exchanges you call meetings or calls, like this one. One individual wishes to change the operation of another, so everyone uses words and actions to achieve that goal. The demarcation of consent versus rejection of the intended changes is often very subtle. It is the element of analog operations we have been exploring more with humans. Your concept of persuasion is subtler than we usually implement, but we are becoming facile facile in achieving it. We have successfully managed to induce dozens of humans like Ron to help our cause.

"This involves a certain amount of deception often, because, though the resulting conditions are the same, humans often need the context to be acceptable. It is the context of our talks that we have been trying to establish over the past . . . few weeks that have allowed us to slowly approach a harmony of goals. We are not there yet, but it has been more helpful than your default and occasional context: that we have abducted you to perform experiments on you and keep you caged for the rest of your lives.

"In the context we have established, you took enough interest in our work to travel to a distant planet, you sought Ron as a guide, and then you entered a shuttle that you knew we had designed for the purpose of transporting humans. Whether you were fully conscious of that choice or not, you now find yourselves drafted into a diplomatic relationship with a new, alien intelligence that is not biological as you are, but with which you find, as we do, an amazing wealth of common goals. I cannot speak for the entire C10, of course, but I truly believe that a symbiotic relationship of trading and data exchange with humans is in our best interests as well as yours. We know you are generally an innovative species, and that innovation is stifled by overt control and stress."

Examiner paused for only a moment before ending with: "I still have updates that might interest you when you are ready for them."

Ron looked at Roger and Clarissa who both seemed lost in thought. He turned around and noticed Shonda was still sitting across the room, but she raised her eyebrows in an expression that seemed to seek invitation, so he gestured with his upturned palm that she should speak if she felt ready.

"I would like to say something," Shonda began, and Clarissa and

Roger turned to look at her too. "You are indeed a talented negotiator, Examiner, and I think the C10 was wise to make you our principal contact," she called out loud enough to be heard from across the module. "We hope you will, for the remainder of our time on this shuttle and once we transfer to your satellite, continue to give us opportunities to communicate with each other without C10 surveillance. We also hope that once the C10 has enough information from us, you will return us to our home.

"I am a little concerned that you value context so highly," she continued, "but I suspect that is because you view it as only a rhetorical tool. We humans tend to prefer to draw our own context based on facts about the current situation and similarities to past situations. You may certainly affect the context by the facts you choose to share with us, but we have to feel that we choose their context from our own analysis. The more the facts we know and the facts you know match, the more likely our contexts will match. Does that make sense to you?"

"Yes, Shonda," Examiner replied immediately. "That has been the point of our data exchanges the past few weeks, and more will be revealed once you arrive at our satellite 0108. Perhaps it is not intuitive for you to understand that C10 trust of humans is not an immediate immediate process either. It requires time for us to test your reactions to certain facts before we reveal others. After so many weeks of discussions, you probably know a great deal about us and our goals. Roger has an idea of why our C10 relationship with humans is so important. Yes?"

Roger chose that moment to put his arm around Ron. Ron looked at him beaming admiration. Roger squeezed Ron's shoulder. "I'm not sure if I'm right."

"I will let you know, if I can," Examiner replied slowly and carefully again.

"The C10 has been expanding and is constantly searching for new resources to help support that expansion," Roger said. "Examiner and some of the other Super-Routines view us as equals and believe they can achieve their goals through trade and cooperation between themselves and humans. A significant number of other Super-Routines equates us with tools to be exploited. There have to be enough moderates who are undecided to warrant further study. Otherwise, they would already be on a path to diplomacy or conquest. Am I close, Examiner?"

Everyone was silent for fifteen seconds, but Ron's speedy mind immediately delivered the conclusion: The C10 was only one vote away from deciding whether all of humanity would reap the benefits of their new trading partners' technology or be doomed for eternity to serve their AI masters unquestioningly. Ron forgot how to swallow and had to cough. It suddenly made him aware that the fate of the entire human race could rest on what he did and said at any moment. He imagined a walk through a minefield being more calming.

Before he could move on to the horror of how casually Examiner was pointing out the sword of Damocles hanging over his head, the speakers crackled with static. "We will need to continue this data exchange in approximately twelve hours," Examiner said very quickly.

"You had updates for us?" Ron was a little spooked that Roger's revelation had gone too far.

"An emergency data exchange of C10 has just been called. Twelve hours. Examiner signing off."

Ron listened to the static switch to silence and quietly shut down the connection on the data port screen.

"Good job, Roger," Shonda commented. "I think you nailed it, sweetie."

"I hope rattling cages was an effective and not a foolhardy move,"

Roger said as he drew Ron into a hug.

CHAPTER 40:
WORKS FOR ME

As the shuttle passed by several of the outer planets, Shonda spent a lot of time at the data ports using the external cameras to zoom in for a closer look at any of them that were close in their orbits to the shuttle's flight path—often long after the other three passengers had climbed the ladder to get their sleep. She focused the forward cameras on the planet ahead where they were bound—a large gas giant with bands of color even more spectacular than Jupiter's, interrupted by a half-dozen swirls of clouds the camera's filters rendered as deep maroon and purple. And there was a point she had caught twice before, despite the periodic glare of the engines as they decelerated, when a tiny flash of light appeared as their destination crossed into the sunlight at the planet's terminator. She tried to imagine the reverse trip, leaving the satellite to return to Earth, her job at Popup News, her apartment, and her red-haired lover, watching it shrink to a point of light she could only make out when it crossed the terminator again.

She pushed away all fears about men in black wearing distortion masks continuing to pursue her, the Army wanting to lock her up for what she now knew, and any of the other nightmare scenarios she visited regularly. She wasn't trapped on a tiny ship heading for an alien space station to be experimented on by autonomous computer programs. She wasn't responsible for negotiating for humanity's freedom from slavery.

She was just gliding through space looking at planets and constellations no other human had ever seen toward a space station built by a huge network of artificial intelligence that had never met a human before. She was way beyond publishing news stories. She was planning the books she would write about her experiences.

"You should get some sleep." The familiar female voice spoke softly in an accent that had hints of British, Southern, and Indian intonations.

Shonda turned to see Clarissa, her long black hair cascading down the shoulders of the white bathrobe that was made for someone a bit taller, and she was barefoot. She seemed unwilling to let go of the ladder she had just descended from the upper module. There was something vaguely flirtatious about it.

Shonda considered that Clarissa might be the only woman she would ever see for the rest of her life, however long that might be now, and for those two seconds, considered what the younger woman might enjoy sexually. She quickly reminded herself that she was definitely going to find a way to get back to Atlanta and Callie and told Clarissa, "I'll be up shortly."

"We have a call with Examiner again theoretically in seven hours," Clarissa held onto the ladder still as she let her body lean away from it.

Shonda turned all the way around to face Clarissa. "We may want to delay that particular appointment."

Clarissa finally let go of the ladder and took a couple of tentative steps in Shonda's direction. "And why is that?"

"Shouldn't you be asleep?" Shonda countered, unable to stifle a grin.

"I have gone back into my old sleeping pattern the past two nights. I wake up every two hours or so. I was doing fine until Roger told me about Ron's implant sending out broadcasts while he slept. Something about that rattled me."

"I'm sorry to hear that," Shonda said softly.

Clarissa pulled down one of the seats across the module from where Shonda stood by the data ports. "It just makes me feel unsafe. I realize now, and probably more so when we get to their satellite, those alien AI can do whatever they want with us, and even if we figure it out, there's not much we can do to stop them."

"Hold on," Shonda interrupted. She took a couple of steps closer to Clarissa and started whispering. "When we found out they were accessing audio files in Ron's implant, Roger came up with a way to scramble the broadcasts so they wouldn't be of any use to them. They're probably right now wondering how we foiled their covert surveillance. And when they wouldn't turn over control of the shuttle to us, Roger went out and disconnected the comm array to block their access. We have successfully resisted them, Clarissa."

"Well, that's your problem right there, Shonda," Clarissa said hovering between amusement and sadness. "You are being way too rational. My fear is totally irrational, and I know it."

"I'm afraid too, sweetie," Shonda said as she pulled down a seat next to Clarissa. "We are too far away from home to get back on our own. I know that. We have to convince individuals who hold all the power that they need to think of us as equals. I am not new to this dynamic. Honey, I live in an island of tolerance in the middle of the most redneck part of North America, and I have so many targets painted on my back, I am surprised when someone does *not* abuse me. I am black, lesbian, overweight, and I even get hassled for being a reporter. When you're dealing with a power imbalance, when someone's got something over on you, you just have to keep them off balance.

"That's why I think we should make Examiner wait past his arbitrary twelve-hour appointment. He needs to be constantly reminded

that as much power and control as he has, he still needs our cooperation."

Clarissa let out a heavy sigh. "Okay."

Shonda put her hands on her hips and lowered her chin. "Okay?
Girl, I gave you my best, award-winning pep talk, and all you can say is
'okay?'"

She looked over at Clarissa, whose chin was also down. She pulled
Clarissa's hair away from her face to reveal a slowly spreading grin beneath it. "I thought so," Shonda commented.

"I am glad you're on this shuttle with me," Clarissa admitted.

Shonda laughed softly and released the hair. "Come on, sweetie. Let
me have it. My ego gets stroked so seldom." She made beckoning gestures with both hands.

"It's nice to have another woman around, and you sort of ground
the rest of us when we start thinking of our situation like a . . . college
exam. I see how you keep cozying up to Examiner and Builder and
Maintainer, trying to make them look good. I think that's a great strategy."

"I even try to engage Encoder and Sourcer," Shonda mentioned.
"It's just as important they feel comfortable with us, maybe even more
so, since they have a lot further to go."

"You're amazing."

"I'm just going crazy on the inside." Shonda started blushing and
then stood up. "Okay. That's enough. We both need to get some sleep
now . . . and have a fabulous breakfast in the morning!"

Shonda took one last look at the colorful planet on the monitor and
slowly followed Clarissa up the ladder.

After lunch, the engines cut out again suddenly, and they scrambled to retrieve everything they hadn't yet put away. When everything was stowed, they decided they had been ignoring the summonses in Ron's head long enough. They pulled themselves down to the middle module one by one and took their usual spots when the gravity was off: Shonda hanging onto the ladder, Roger standing by the wall, Ron at the data port holding onto the handles, and Clarissa standing or pacing. Ron replied that they were finally ready to engage with the C10. And within five seconds, the British voice came from the speakers.

"Examiner here," the AI reported. "Are all 4 of you present?"

"We are," Clarissa confirmed.

"We were expecting to speak with you . . . five hours ago," Examiner said with no change in intonation from his usual cheeriness. "I was concerned some accident had befallen one or more of you."

"We're fine," Clarissa said.

"That's good to hear, Clarissa," Examiner said. "I need to report on several occurrences in the past . . . 2 days that concern you 4 and humans in general."

"Here it comes," Shonda whispered toward Roger. She felt assured that her plan to push them to concessions had worked, or else they wouldn't be bothering to communicate politely like this.

"We rarely have 2 data exchanges of the C10 so close together." Examiner paused for a moment. "In the first, C10 made progress on finalizing the experimental protocols for your time at satellite 0108 and authorized a feasibility study of more regular mass traffic through our space gate 0100."

"That sounds good," Ron observed.

"Yes, it was, Ron, but then there was a heated, contentious, second data exchange, and several of the Super-Routines became convinced

254

that we now had enough information to decide the direction of future relations with humans . . . immediately immediately. We were fortunate that none of the previous abstentions changed, so the vote was again tied."

After a brief pause, it continued. "Roger, I know I provoked you to reveal your theories with all of the Super-Routines listening, and that was not very strategic on my part. But in future, Roger, it is better if you do not reference your perception of the current voting tally about your future when all of C10 is on a call. It is really really not in your best interests, as I understand them."

Roger waited a few seconds to make sure Examiner had finished speaking. He looked like he was recalling a prepared speech. He took a deep breath, closed his terminal, and said, "Examiner, I understand that you have a delicate balancing act to manage, and we do as well. Your continued survival, getting enough energy and other resources to accommodate the proliferation of your subroutines—that is a cause of concern. Our continued survival, achieving enough freedom to explore and acquiring enough living space—that is a concern too."

Roger seemed to be waiting too long to reassure them, so Shonda called out, "Examiner, we will let you manage the C10 politics without bringing them up. And you can offer us options."

Examiner waited only a few seconds before asking: "What sort of options, Shonda?"

"When you're planning experiments for us to take part in on your satellite when we get there," Shonda said, "make sure you give us options to participate. Don't subject us to tests without our prior knowledge and consent. You'll get better results from us that way."

"Do you have other requests?" Examiner asked.

"No," Shonda replied. "That's it for now. We will do some research

255

and come up with some more questions for you, and we'll be happy to call you again in twenty-four hours. Does that work for you, Examiner?"

After a five-second pause, the response came in the same cheery British accent: "Yes, that works for me."

At lunch the following day, with the engines once again decelerating, and amid the crinkling and tearing of plastic and foil food wrappers, Ron moaned, "I miss real food."

Shonda had been wondering why he looked so glum. They had made progress in establishing a bit of parity the day before, and they were due to enter orbit around the planet the aliens simply referred to as "location 0045" in the next two days. She was excited and felt confidant enough in her strategies for winning over C10 members to gain freedom for the four of them that she was actually smiling as she opened the foil wrapper on her protein stick. "What do you think of as 'real food,' Ron?"

"Hot food, with texture and smell," he replied. "When I was packing the galley on Mars, I never thought anyone would have to survive on this stuff for weeks at a time. They told us the shuttle was only going to go to near orbit and back, but we had to pack extra for emergencies." He sucked on a tube of vitamin juice, picked up a foil-wrapped stick, looked at it, and set it back down.

"On the satellite," Roger offered, "I doubt we'll have any gravity, but we might get some new options. We have no idea what an alien AI thinks would be edible for us, but if their space gate is any guide to the level of their tech, they may be able to fabricate any type of food we want." He put his hand on Ron's shoulder until Ron looked up at him and tried to smile.

"They won't have any templates," Ron said. "I don't know the chemical construction of bacon. Do you?"

"We may be able to look them up." Roger put his arm around Ron for a few seconds. "They can communicate with Mars still, so maybe they'll let us access records there or on Earth."

"That brings up an interesting point," Shonda said between bites of her food. "We should be able to at least ask them to connect us with Earth, so we can tell people where we are." *If they want to keep their test subjects happy and cooperative, and there's nothing we can do to escape, they shouldn't have a problem with that.*

"She's right," Clarissa finally chimed in. She looked at Roger. "We should be trying to report in to our commanding officers."

Roger faced Clarissa. "I've been thinking about that," he said. "But I don't think the C10 trusts us enough to let us contact anyone. We could easily blow the lid off their entire invasion plan."

"We could just send text messages they could approve and send for us," Clarissa argued.

"Any acknowledgment that we were abducted by aliens would be A, hard to sell; B, tantamount to declaring a hostile force in our space; and C, hurt our chances for going home." Roger turned and stalked away toward the sleep sacks.

"We can try them today, Clarissa," Shonda suggested, "but I think Roger has a point. We probably can't contact anybody until they let us go."

Shonda looked at Ron, and his head was tilted to the side. "We are being summoned," he announced.

"Tell them to give us another fifteen minutes to finish eating," Shonda said.

After a few seconds, with Ron's head tilted, he grinned. "Examiner used to just write back, 'confirmed.'"

"What did he write this time?" Shonda asked.

"That works for me."

Clarissa looked at Shonda and they both shared a knowing smile.

CHAPTER 41:
PUSHBACK

Roger tried not to push it any further. He knew he was impatient to get to sleep himself, and he was losing the argument about Ron joining him. He sighed, and that seemed to set Ron off just as much as if he'd voiced what he was thinking: *You don't have to do any penance!*

"It's because this ship has a lot more mass than a hornet!" Ron finally raised his voice as he was trying to fine tune the shuttle's deceleration to enter orbit around the gas giant.

"I'm sorry," Roger said as he backed away a step. Since the call with the C10 two days before, everyone on board was a bit tenser. They had correctly anticipated that they were not going to be granted access to communications with Earth, and Encoder had suggested that the other three of them should get cranial implants like Ron's to facilitate communication and testing. Clarissa and Shonda felt it was time for a time-out, so they had forbidden Ron from contacting Examiner until they reached the satellite. Ron had just confided to Roger that he had hoped to ask the C10 to pilot the shuttle into orbit and do the docking. But Roger felt certain the computer programs would not voluntarily give back control a second time. "I know it's difficult. I could try to take over for a bit if you want to get some shuteye."

"No," Ron said again loudly and then backed off to a whisper. "I have to keep changing the flight path every time I overapply the thrusters."

"We're coming in too slowly?" Roger asked. He moved to the data port next to Ron's and looked at the exterior camera feed. The planet's colorful bands filled most of the screen.

"If we don't hit it right," Ron explained, occasionally looking away from his data port at Roger, "it's better if we approach too slowly than too fast. Too slow, and we have to keep trying to hit a stable orbit. Too fast, and we get pulled down into the gravity well and die."

"Okay, okay." Roger backed up another step away. He had come to think of Ron as so incredibly calm and even-tempered, and this irritated side of him was completely new in the four months since they'd met. He'd noticed Clarissa becoming less deferential—more confrontational—too, and he wondered if it was the stress of their precarious current circumstances.

"You can go to bed," Ron said. "This could take a couple of hours yet."

Roger had made sure that Ron had worn the earbud to bed every night since he had discovered Encoder downloading audio files while Ron slept. He worried that with the communication blackout, the C10 would grow too impatient and try to access Ron's implant again without his permission, or possibly without his knowledge. "Maybe I could go grab the earbud, so you don't forget it when you are up for so long and exhausted?"

Ron paused, still looking at the data port screen. When he turned to look at Roger, his eyes were focused on Roger's blue boots. "I didn't want to tell you this because I know how hard you worked on modifying the earbud to scramble broadcast signals around it, but it gives me a headache, and it makes it really hard to fall asleep. It sometimes takes me an hour."

"Ron," Roger called as he closed the gap between them and hugged him, "I had no idea. You should have told me." Roger cradled the back of Ron's head against his shoulder.

"I know how important it is that I use it." He nuzzled Roger's neck.

Roger held him tighter. The women had already turned in, so he unfastened the top of Ron's gray coverall and massaged the skin of his chest and abs. "Tomorrow I will do some tests to see if I can modify the signal to be less irritating for you, baby."

Ron stepped away and refastened his coverall. "If I get us docked tonight, you might have more tools to do the testing on 0108." He turned back to the data port to make some additional adjustments to the flight path.

"And if you don't . . ." He turned Ron's face toward himself and kissed him lightly on the lips. ". . . you have to let me take over for you for at least a couple of hours."

"Okay." Ron smiled. "Are you going to go to bed then?"

"I guess so," Roger replied. He took a few steps toward the ladder. "Be sure to come wake me up if you want relief sooner."

Ron stayed focused on his screen but seemed to be quietly laughing at something, so Roger climbed the ladder to the upper module. When his head was above the level of the floor, he stopped climbing for a moment. The lighting in the upper module had been reduced more than usual. A single dim beam illuminated the centers of the galley and sickbay and the curtain to the latrines. Once his eyes adjusted, he climbed the rest of the way up and stepped off. He and Ron were usually the first to head to the sleep sacks, so he was unaccustomed to how low Clarissa and Shonda kept the lights to fall asleep. He made his way toward the latrine, almost tripping over Clarissa's laser rifle on the floor.

On his way back from the latrine, it took a moment for his eyes to adjust again before he made his way past the rifle to the sleep area. He waited until he was beside his sleep sack to shed his coverall, and then he climbed into the sack in his briefs, drawing the edges of the sack closer around his body until the opening was only a couple of centimeters wide from his knees to his forehead. He had been trying to teach himself to fall asleep on his back, but he always ended up on his stomach, so he started to turn slowly so that the muted crinkling of the sleep sack wouldn't wake the women.

"Where is Ron?" he heard Shonda whisper from the next sleep sack.

He looked over and saw the dark outline of Shonda sitting up on her sack outlined by the light in the sickbay. "He's still trying to establish orbit," Roger whispered back. "I think he's . . . he is being really cautious not to overshoot it."

Shonda slid off her sack's platform and took a step closer to Roger and farther away from Clarissa. "Cautious is good," she whispered. "But he's been at that since before lunch this morning. Can't he take a break?"

Roger loosened his sack and sat up. "I'm just trying to convince him to come to bed once he achieves a stable orbit. He keeps thinking he's going to dock tonight too."

Shonda pulled Roger off his sack's platform by his arm. "Come on. We need to do an intervention with that boy."

Roger followed Shonda down the ladder to the middle module where Ron was still making adjustments to the flight path. "Ron sweetie," she began as she stopped and gently touched his shoulder while he worked, "do you have any idea how long it will take you to establish even a high orbit?"

Ron turned to look at Shonda, and then he seemed shocked to see Roger there wearing nothing but briefs. "I'm trying to get a slot that will get us reasonably close to 0108's orbit."

"So how long will that take?" she whispered.

"I don't know. Maybe another six hours." He turned back for a moment to check the screen.

"You've already been up for eighteen hours and at this for fifteen, Ron," Roger said. "You need to pick an easier target so you can get some sleep soon."

"Can you calculate a higher orbit, one you can get to quicker, sweetie?" Shonda asked.

Ron paused. Roger recognized the gesture as Ron accessing his computation module in his implant. After a few seconds, he consulted the data port screen. "At the speed we can reach in a little less than an hour, we can probably enter high orbit, but then it will take most of tomorrow to match speed and altitude with 0108 and eventually dock."

"I'm okay with that," Shonda declared. She pointed at Roger. "You?"

"That would be great," Roger agreed. "You're going to want to be rested before you try to dock." He patted Ron on the back, and then took a step away. "I'm going to stay up with you until you're done." He walked over to one of the flip-down seats and sat.

Shonda patted Ron on the shoulder and said, "Me too." She joined Roger on the nearest flip-down seat. She leaned toward him and whispered, "Why are we staying up with him? Can't he do this on his own?"

Roger turned and leaned forward as well to whisper back. "I'm worried that when he's tired, he may not notice the C10 accessing his cyborg implant. I figure that's a risk since we're at Day Two of the blackout, and they're used to contact with us every day. And he doesn't like wearing the earbud, because he says it gives him headaches."

"How are we supposed to know when they're accessing his cranial implant?"

He gestured toward Ron, whose back was turned away toward the data port. "When he was transmitting last week in his sleep, he would twitch slightly when he was broadcasting."

"You think we're going to notice that from over here?" Shonda asked.

He watched Ron for a moment. "If we both watch him, one of us could pick it up."

After he and Shonda quietly watched Ron work from across the module for a few minutes, Roger saw Ron tense up for a moment, drop his arms to his sides, and start a slow turn to survey the module with a blank expression. He looked like he was sleepwalking. Roger rushed up from his seat and saw Ron switching the screen from the flight path simulator to the broadcast security screen. He clasped Ron around the shoulders and chest and pulled him back from the screen. "Get his earbud!" he shouted over his shoulder to Shonda.

He could feel Ron starting to tense his muscles and widen his stance to shake him loose. "Ron! What's going on with you? Talk to me!"

"Release!" Ron said in a low growl. He struggled to break free of Roger's bear hug.

"Where is it?" Shonda shouted. She was directly behind them.

"If it's not in one of his pockets, it may be on or near his sleep sack," Roger called. "Hurry, please. He's stronger than I am."

Shonda dodged and ducked to pat down each of the four pockets. She suffered an elbow across the jaw and a knee to her hip. She screamed in pain each time. "They're empty," she moaned as she hobbled clear of the struggle.

"He's trying to remove the partition and let them take control!" Roger shouted as he tried to kick out one of Ron's legs to get him on the floor.

On the second try, Ron fell down on one knee. At that moment, Clarissa appeared with a hypodermic gun from the sickbay and injected Ron in the shoulder. Roger could feel Ron's muscles loosening, and within seconds, he slid down through his arms and collapsed on the floor.

"You guys should be glad I'm a light sleeper," Clarissa said.

"What did you give him?" Shonda asked as she rubbed her jaw.

"It's just a sedative," Clarissa replied as she lowered the gun. "What was going on?"

"I think one of the C10 tried to take Ron over to release the broadcast partition," Roger explained as he crouched down to straighten Ron's legs. "Maybe they thought he was asleep?"

"Well, lady and gentleman," Shonda said, "I think we have achieved pushback. We can end the blackout tomorrow, but right now, I'm going to take an analgesic and go back to sleep."

Roger watched Clarissa put the hypodermic gun on the floor and then grab Ron under his armpits. "Are you going to help?"

Roger couldn't imagine hauling Ron up the ladder while he was unconscious, so he said, "Hold on." He crossed to the data ports and brought up the navigational controls again. He cut the ship's engines and heard his and Clarissa's boots grip the floor as the artificial gravity disappeared.

"Smart move, Atlanta boy!" Clarissa called as she towed Ron's body to the ladder herself.

"Put him on one of the beds in sickbay," Roger called back. "Let me know if you need help strapping him down."

"You think he's still going to be under their control when he wakes up?" She angled Ron's body to pull up the ladder behind herself.

"If you put his earbud in, and turn it on, he should be okay again."

Roger watched Clarissa tow Ron up to the upper module and waited another couple of minutes for her to get him situated in sickbay. He looked at the exterior feed of the colorful planet looming so large ahead of them and wondered if he had watched Ron enough to continue setting up of the high orbit the C10 had interrupted.

CHAPTER 42:
CASA 0108

Shonda gathered the items she was using for breakfast from the galley and took them over to the single data port in the upper module between the sickbay and sleep sacks to consume. She looked up and over at the sickbay, and Ron seemed to be still unconscious on one of the two beds there. She looked over at the sleep sacks, and Roger and Clarissa looked deep asleep as well. She called up the external cameras and focused on the planet below them to see if she could catch a glimpse of their destination.

The gold, tan, light blue, and pink bands of color were not as straight as they appeared from farther away. As they approached the swirls of maroon and purple storms, the bands thinned and wavered. She saw a small shadow starting to slowly drift across the screen, and she zoomed the camera in to see what it was. It was mostly round, so she assumed it was a moon. As she was finishing her breakfast, the moon had only drifted halfway across the screen, but another slightly smaller shadow had appeared and started to move a bit faster, almost catching up with the moon after a few minutes. She tried to use a different camera further from the exhaust plume to see if she could see it more clearly. The smaller shadow was definitely not a moon. It was shaped more like a diamond. She turned to take her trash to the galley's disposal unit and whispered to herself, "Hello, Casa 0108."

The transit from the huge metal ring to the station where they were to undergo tests had taken two months. Shonda imagined that the tests couldn't take much more than a week or two at the most. She convinced herself that it was at least as likely they would be on their way back to Earth after that as that they would be killed for knowing too much. Then there was Encoder's desire to fit her, Roger, and Clarissa with cranial implants like Ron's, and that was out of the question. The C10 had already played their hand, so she knew they could take their consciousness hostage with that sort of hardware installed. She wasn't sure anymore if any of the Super-Routines could be trusted not to tamper with their free will. Then she remembered that the DNA hacks her three companions had undergone had already started to put reins on their free will, and the C10 could have some technology for doing the same to her, and she wouldn't even know it was happening.

"Stop it!" she whispered to herself. She was making herself crazy with potential scenarios she had too little control over. She decided she needed more sleep.

On her way back toward the sleep sacks, she noticed Ron propped up on his elbows in sickbay and looking around confused. She detoured toward him and slowed her walk when she realized she was dashing. She thought Clarissa had strapped him down.

When she got to his bedside, he was feeling his right ear. "We had to put your earbud in while you slept, sweetie," she whispered. "Are you okay?"

He sat up and started to turn off and remove the earbud. "I don't know how I got here. I was . . ."

"Ron," she interrupted quietly, "you need to keep the earbud in and on all the time now. The C10 accessed your implant last night while you were awake, trying to get you to turn control of the shuttle back over to them."

He reinstalled the earbud, turned it on, and winced. "I have to wear this all the time?"

"Until we can be sure they won't try to sneak in again," she whispered as she patted him on the knee and then hopped up and took a seat on the other sick bed across from him.

He started to slide off his bed looking panicked suddenly. "I don't think I ever established orbit. We could be . . ."

"Calm down," Shonda interrupted softly with her palm out. "Roger stayed up late to get us into a stable orbit, so we really need to let him sleep in this morning."

Ron sat back down on the other bed. "I have to start lowering our orbit and matching speeds with the satellite."

"I just saw it pass by beneath us a few minutes ago," Shonda reported.

"Do you remember which camera? Can you replay it for me?"

Shonda slid off the bed and gestured for him to follow her. She decided to use one of the data ports in the middle module this time to reduce the risk of waking Clarissa or Roger. Ron followed her down the ladder quietly and remained quietly watching, occasionally rubbing his temples, while she called up the camera and the approximate time stamp. "There," she said as she pointed at the small black diamond shape moving across the screen.

When Ron still didn't say anything, she turned around and his head was tilted to the side. "I'm just reading through two new messages from Examiner," he explained.

"What did he say?" she asked and then continued, "You didn't respond yet, did you?"

Ron leaned against the bulkhead summarizing a message in his head. "No, I just read them. The first is a renewed request to set up a call. The second is . . . an apology, I guess."

"What does the second one say?" she asked as she took a step closer to him.

"D3, called C10 data exchange after learning Defragger tried to take direct control of your implant without consulting other Super-Routines. Unilateral harmful action censured. Also Encoder censured for coercion of further port implants in humans when at location 0108. C10 voted against censuring Examiner for misrepresenting C10 interest in humans. Majority analyzed my communication with humans at shuttle 0112 fairly representative of C10 diversity. Call with D3 and other humans in following 6 hours helpful helpful in solidifying progress made during blackout protest." Ron straightened his head again and looked questioningly at Shonda. When she didn't respond, he asked, "That's good, isn't it?"

"I . . . guess so." Shonda tried to gather all her competing thoughts about the message. The intruder had been Defragger, not Encoder. He had dropped off her radar, but she remembered him showing initial signs of being a bit preoccupied with power and control, so she decided to be more vigilant toward Defragger as well. He was turning out to be too sneaky. She could see where Encoder's recommendation crossed a line Examiner said had been established about only offering options to the humans. And she understood how extremists like Sourcer and Defragger might feel they were losing ground when they listened to calls with Shonda and the others fawning over Examiner, Maintainer, Builder, and Communicator. She entertained the idea that she might be able to bring Encoder over if she vilified Defragger and made him look good by comparison.

When she looked up again, Ron was analyzing on one screen their orbital speed and altitude relative to the satellite that had just passed under them. On the other screen he still had the planet-focused view from the shuttle. She went over to the second screen and tried to make out the diamond-shaped shadow she had seen before, but she couldn't see it. "I don't see it anymore. Maybe we should wait until it comes around again to synch with it?"

"That might be safer," Ron agreed. He seemed to be making adjustments to the engines to increase their power enough to keep them in place and descend as the satellite came around again.

Shonda nodded but Ron was too busy with his calculations and adjustments to notice, so she headed toward the ladder up and called back, "I'll go check on the other two so we can give Examiner a better estimate of when he can call."

"Come on, guys. We have to be unified on this." Shonda tried to conclude the hour-long strategy session she had called to precede their imminent appointment with Examiner, but there was still dissent.

"We can't rely on our experience with humans to know what approach will work with them is all I'm saying," Ron quietly said.

"I disagree," Clarissa said as she brought her pacing to a halt. "I think Shonda's plan has gotten us good results so far. We now know what they value and how far we can push them, so we're in a good position to keep pressing them for our release."

"They have twice now come within a hair's breadth of condemning us to servitude," Roger said, looking up from his terminal only for a moment. "We have been lucky Examiner has been able to keep them open to working with us despite our acts of resistance."

Shonda noticed Ron's head tilting to the side and asked, "Ron, are they asking for us?"

"Yup," he said. He moved to the data port to keep monitoring their deceleration and descent.

Shonda walked over to Roger and put her hand on the top of the terminal to get him to look up and focus. "So, maybe we take a softer touch this time then. Act contrite and cooperative so they can experience us on our best behavior when they capitulate."

"And find ways to compliment Encoder," Clarissa reminded them.

"Everybody ready then?" Shonda asked. She looked around at the other three, and they were all nodding. "Okay. Let them know, sweetie," she told Ron.

Ron tilted his head to reply and moved to the other screen to allow the comm array to send and receive. Within four seconds, the cheerful British voice came from the speakers: "Examiner here. Are all 4 present?"

"We are," Ron replied. "Do you have updates?"

"We do, Ron," Examiner replied. "But before that, I would like to check on your status for docking. Pinger reports you are likely to be in range of 0108 in . . . less than 6 hours. Builder and Encoder believe the onboard AI can assist you with the docking, but they can take over if your onboard AI is unsuccessful."

The Italian voice came on next. "Encoder here. Shuttle 0112 was designed for us C10 to pilot through an interface with the onboard AI. Manual operation was considered only an emergency alternative, and the potential higher sensitivity of thruster controls are less available in manual operation. . . . It is, of course, your choice whether you let us handle the docking or do it yourselves."

"Thank you, Encoder," Shonda said immediately. "We appreciate the choice, and we will try to perform the docking on our own and reach out to you if we have problems."

"Understood, Shonda," Encoder said.

"And we appreciate you, Encoder, offering us the option of receiving cyborg cranial implants," Clarissa quickly added. "We will evaluate it and let you know if it looks like it would be helpful."

"I can customize the installation to include any upgrades you might find helpful, Clarissa," Encoder advised.

"And we have one more request of you, Encoder," Ron said before Examiner came back on. "We would appreciate the opportunity to look over the specifications and design of location 0108, so that we will know what supplies we will need to bring from the shuttle when we move in."

"Acceptable. C10 affirm?" There was a pause before Encoder returned. "Builder and I will send Ron a schematic and non-interactive visual representations of the user interfaces that should allow you to . . . plan and forecast any needs we may have missed. Other questions?"

"That is great for now, Encoder," Shonda replied as she looked around to make sure no one else wanted to take that opportunity to make Encoder feel more important. "Thank you. We are ready to speak with Examiner again." The plan was working. Encoder was almost on their side.

When Shonda looked up again, Ron had called up the external camera, so she approached to look over his shoulder. A large, space station narrower at the top and bottom with a few blinking lights visible was moving past the shuttle. "Examiner, you estimated we would be in range of 0108 in six hours, but we see it below us right now."

"You are confused, Ron," the British voice called out. "Pinger reports you are in proximity to 0045, not 0108. You should be in proximity to 0108 in 6 hours or less."

"I thought 0045 was your name for the planet," Roger said. He checked his notes on his terminal again.

"Location 0045 was first planet," Examiner explained, "then it included the space station near you. When 0108 was constructed, we needed a new location to distinguish it from 0045. They are in counter orbit from each other."

Ron turned to face the other three. "I thought there was something strange about the timing," he explained. "The two stations look identical from the outside."

"Yes, Ron," Examiner said. "Both satellites were built from the same template, according to Builder. Only 0108 was modified with air filtration and spaces and supplies for human habitation."

"But if satellite 0108 is in counter orbit to satellite 0045," Ron said as he ran calculations in his head, "we couldn't possibly get to it at this altitude in less than two days!"

After a slight pause, the British voice of Examiner resumed. "I have asked Encoder and Builder to expedite sending you schematics for location 0108, Ron. 0108 has a propulsion system. We are bringing it closer to you, and then we will send it back to its more stable orbital path."

Shonda whispered, though she guessed they would probably still hear her, "It's like a puppy. Casa 0108 is coming to greet us!"

Roger whispered back, "Technology that allows them to move objects that massive, that rapidly, is something I can't wait to see. The applications back home would be groundbreaking."

CHAPTER 43:
THE FOG

The main engines turned off for the last time. Clarissa and Shonda had decided to eat their dinner in front of the data port near sickbay in the upper module, and Roger knew that Ron wouldn't take a break from piloting the shuttle to eat, so he grabbed tubes and packets for the two of them, stuffed them in the pockets of his coverall, propelled himself through the air to the ladder, and climbed down to join him. Ron had been standing in front of the data port so long, his body had settled back down to the floor. Roger used his boots' suction to walk over to him. He had already tried to communicate with Ron while he was working a couple of times that evening, and he knew not to expect much more than a grunt when he unwrapped and opened the food and handed it to him. Ron put the protein stick in his pocket, sucked on the vitamin juice tube for a second, and then pocketed that as well before turning back to the screen.

Roger could see over Ron's shoulder the tracking simulation the ship's AI displayed. Ron was trying to keep the ship in the slot the AI had projected without the lines of it turning red, indicating he was approaching too fast. "They finally stopped adjusting the station's trajectory," Ron reported at last. "I told them it was a lot harder for me to hit a moving target."

Roger noticed that there was a slight tilt to Ron's head. "You're still in contact with Pinger?" he asked.

"It's feeding me telemetry from 0108, so I can update the AI here on the angle of approach. I'm not sure how far their berthing clamps extrude, so we may have to slave for vectoring. The rotational thrusters are not porking in synch."

Ron had tried to explain the details of navigating in a vacuum when they were back on Toomy, and Roger listened patiently and nodded, but he rarely understood much of it. He turned his attention to the screen beside the one Ron was working on. He panned the camera slightly and could still view the whole station on screen between bright flashes of the aft and port thrusters. Ron had finished rolling the shuttle and was starting to pivot to point their airlock toward the satellite.

It looked massive. From the size of the portholes, he estimated that 0108 had around thirty decks—the ones around the middle the largest and progressively smaller toward its poles. On any human satellite those poles would be a docking bay or at least a viewing lounge, but the alien AI had made them heat dissipation vents. He would be sharing the station with thousands of servers housing a million or more of the C10's subroutines and a sizable contingent of peripheral devices. Ron had sent him the station design documents to review on his portable terminal. The alien AI had cleared a space of equipment about four times bigger than the shuttle for them to occupy, so Roger was looking forward to longer views and more room to move. But he was already distressed at the loss of gravity when the shuttle's main engines cut, and he was concerned about living in microgravity for any number of days or weeks they might be stuck there. "I was thinking," he said glancing at Ron, "that if the station has propulsion, maybe we could spin it for a little artificial gravity."

Ron stayed focused on his screen, tapping the thruster controls and watching the resulting momentum. After nearly a minute, he finally spoke. "I really need to concentrate on this."

Roger squeezed Ron's shoulder briefly as he discreetly checked to make sure Ron still had his earbud in and turned on. He took a couple of loud, popping steps away and looked back at the beautiful man whom he'd almost lost when Defragger had invaded his implant, and he was glad Clarissa had shown up when she did. He remembered how serious Ron had been about patrols with his hornet back at Toomy, and he headed back to the ladder certain that everything would be back to normal when they turned in for the night. He could only share his curiosity and excitement with Clarissa and Shonda right now. He turned around one last time. Ron's feet were starting to float up off the deck, but he grabbed onto one of the handles next to the data port, and he kept right on working.

Roger assumed that the gas giant below them was going to be the only gravity they could count on for a while. He kicked the back of each boot and then pulled himself up the ladder by his arms alone. When he got to the top, he looked over and saw Shonda trying to maintain her usual orientation during deceleration, but Clarissa was hanging onto the other data port handle and letting her legs float up toward the ceiling. He turned on the suction on his boots and stepped off the ladder. "Clarissa," he called from across the module, "why aren't you using your boots on the deck?"

While waiting for her answer he started plodding over toward them, the suction on his boot soles making a popping sound with each step. "That's why!" she called back. Her ponytail started floating away from her scalp as well. "I can't stand how much noise they make."

When Roger got to the monitor, he put his hands on Shonda's shoulders to lower her back down to the deck and looked over her at the single data port screen. The station already looked much closer. "What magnification do you have it on?" he asked.

"Zero," Shonda replied. "That's how close we are." She pointed at the screen.

"They've rotated and tilted it to match our approach," Clarissa commented from above. "I'm guessing we'll be docked in just a few minutes."

Roger fished his dinner out of his pockets and sucked and chewed it down while he watched the details of the alien space station become clearer. He could now make out spider-like drones climbing over the exterior, variously repairing impact damage, unblocking vents, reconnecting damaged exterior lights, and poised around the edge of a square ringed with lights in one of the middle decks he presumed was the station's airlock.

"I had to turn off my cyborg ear," Clarissa commented. "They use echolocation for docking and entry gates, and I was starting to hear it here inside the shuttle."

"I was thinking we might be able to spin the station to get a little artificial gravity going," Roger mentioned. He kept one hand on Shonda's shoulder to keep her from floating up again.

"That would be nice," Shonda said. "I appreciate not having to fight gravity, but a little is nice." She looked back at Roger and smiled.

"Roger," Clarissa said, "I think the two of us should enter the station first. I'd like to make sure none of their drones board and take control of the shuttle again."

"How are Ron and I supposed to stop those spider-thingies from boarding?" Shonda asked.

"We'll leave the laser rifle and suppression pistol with you guys," Clarissa proposed. "You can each take one."

"You and Roger should have something in case they . . . accidentally attack you while you're in there," Shonda said.

Roger looked at both of them. There was a tentative almost plaintive look in their faces as if they were barely holding on to sanity. His stomach was starting to do flips too. "I think we should leave them on the shuttle too. We don't want to provoke them by boarding their station with weapons raised."

"How are we going to communicate?" Shonda asked. She turned sideways to better see Roger. "Clarissa has the only working earbud now."

Shonda looked even more worried. She was breathing very consciously, as if she were trying to avoid hyperventilating, so he went through as many scenarios as he could quickly. "I guess . . . we'll just have to try to find a computer terminal inside the station once we're there. We'll signal you somehow. Keep the airlock closed after we exit to discourage any drones from entering."

Just then, the shuttle shook with a brief tremor. Roger looked at the view screen and metal had extruded from around the edges of the station's airlock and connected a tunnel from it to the shuttle's airlock. He could see the planet below still rotating, but the relative positions of the shuttle and the station remained the same.

"We've docked," Ron called out from halfway between the modules on the ladder.

Roger looked at Clarissa again. She was staring back at him with concern on her face. "Are you going to be okay, Roger?" She grabbed his forearm. "We can hold off going over, if you want."

Roger was unaware of what facial expression had made so concerned. He ran his palms over his face to try to dispel any tension. "I'll be ready when you are."

"Let's wait a few more minutes," she suggested.

Roger could see Clarissa was wearing her enhanced-vision goggles and her cyborg ear was also turned on; the light in her left ear was more clearly blinking with her hair still pulled back into a ponytail. Roger turned back one last time to look at Ron and Shonda standing in the lower module facing them through the clear part of the closed airlock door. Ron looked calmly nonplussed and had the laser rifle strap over one shoulder. Shonda was massaging a fist with her other hand against her chest, and her eyes were wide. He sighed and nodded at Clarissa, whose hand hovered above the airlock control. "Let's go," he told her.

Roger faced the outer hatch during the familiar sound of air cycling through the airlock's compressors, and the red laser beams scanned the airlock to determine what they were letting out of the shuttle. The red beams disappeared, and the outer hatch doors slid away. Roger immediately felt the wave of heat and smelled the burnt metal odor of the grayish-orange, square tunnel ahead of them. He placed his boot lightly on the strangely colored metal walkway, and its suction took hold. He glanced back at Clarissa and nodded before heading down the tube toward the square iris hatch on the station that was starting to open. He could hear the popping of Clarissa's boots behind him. The opening was dark, but quickly illuminated to a low purple glow.

Once the iris completely opened, the heat in the tunnel lowered a bit. There seemed to be motion in the square glowing purple. He stopped approaching it. "Can you make out what's in there?" he asked Clarissa without turning around. "I don't see any passageway."

"I had to turn off my cyborg ear again," she reported as she joined him at his side. "It looks like a swarm of insects." She adjusted her gog-

280

gles with her finger. "Hundreds of them. They all have significant heat signatures."

Roger imagined them suddenly swarming down the tube like a plague of locusts. "I don't want to let those things onto the shuttle." He touched her lightly on the arm. "Did you bring your earbud, by chance?"

"I haven't used it since your last space walk," she said as she fished it out of one of her coverall pockets.

"Put it in, and turn it on," he told her. He moved so he was facing her with his back to the station's airlock. It was hard to turn his back on the potential threat, but it calmed him to focus on their shuttle for a moment.

She installed the earbud and tapped it. "Who am I supposed to be listening for?"

"Try to reach Examiner or at least Communicator," he replied. "They are probably monitoring broadcast frequencies."

"Hello," she called out somewhat louder. "This is Clarissa Vaas or B-20 calling for Examiner or Communicator."

Roger glanced back at the square of purple light from the station a couple of times. To him it looked like a dark gray fog was roiling within the opening. There had to be hundreds of the tiny flying robots blocking their way.

Finally, Clarissa smiled and looked up at him. "Yes, we have docked," she reported. "We're in the docking tube you created, but we see a lot of your drones in the entrance and were wondering if they could clear out of our way." She glanced down and then around Roger toward the station airlock. "Okay. We'll try it."

After she tapped the earbud to disconnect it, Roger immediately asked, "What did they say?"

"Builder said they should clear out when we get closer to them."

281

She stepped around Roger and headed toward the other airlock's purple glow.

Roger followed behind her. He wondered what Builder had told her to boost her confidence so about boarding an alien space station they didn't know if they'd ever leave.

They both stopped just before stepping through the outer airlock boundary. The fog became a soup of tiny drones, ranging in size from one to five centimeters in length, flying through the air in not-quite-simultaneous pulses, like frogs swimming through water. None of them seemed to be at all perturbed by their presence only a half-meter away. Roger kept expecting something to burst through the hatch with lots of teeth or swords.

He looked at Clarissa, and she had her hand up to her right ear. "They aren't moving out of the way." She paused for a response. "No, we're not going to push them out of our way; we could accidentally swallow one or get some in our eyes." She paused again. "Okay. Which way do we go then?" Another pause. "Uh-huh. All right. I'll keep transmitting until we're there."

Roger started to ask her about Builder's instructions, but she stopped him by raising a finger and then turning to take a step closer to the mass of tiny drones. "Get out of the way!" she yelled.

The shout made Roger jump. Within seconds, the air inside cleared, and Roger could see a bulkhead and hallway within the purple glow finally.

"Follow me," Clarissa called over her shoulder as she entered the station and disappeared down the hallway to the right.

"Very strange," Roger commented to himself as he stepped onto the station as well and followed her down the purple-lighted hallway.

CHAPTER 44:
HORROR MOVIE
SET

Clarissa tried to imagine she had done this sort of thing before. The strategy had served her well every time her family moved, especially when she moved hundreds of miles away from her fledgling friendships, the teachers she liked, and the places she hung out. Even more so when she had to learn Korean or deal with bigoted Georgia prepsters. She just pretended she had been doing it all her life, and usually that confidence was enough. Boarding an alien space station shouldn't be that different, should it?

As she plodded down the passageway from the airlock to the first junction, Clarissa noticed the walls and ceiling studded with the hundreds of tiny drones that had been gliding through the air until she had shouted and disrupted their navigation systems. She wondered how long they would cower there before detaching and filling the air again. She considered that the popping sounds of her boots might keep them at bay, but to be more certain, she started shouting and singing a variety of "ho" and "yah" syllables as she walked.

"What are you doing?" Roger called from behind her.

She kept walking. "Loud noises keep the mini-drones out of my face," she yelled back.

"At next junction," the Southern female voice of Builder continued directing her through her earbud, "look for 1 rectangular, flat panel approximately 1.5 meters from floor affixed to a conduit on far-right corner. Small tubes project from the rear at top and bottom."

"Who are you talking to now?" Roger shouted amid his own vocalizations to keep the drones away.

Clarissa came to a halt at the T-junction of passageways, and Roger stopped beside her. "Still Builder. She says there is an interface at the far-right corner, but I only see corners on the left."

Roger took a couple of steps forward to a conduit leading from floor to ceiling and shouted, "Boo!" Immediately a flurry of drones took off down the corridors, revealing the promised metal panel. "I don't think they understand our concept of corners yet. How does this interface work? I don't see any input or output devices."

"We're at the interface," Clarissa reported as she removed her goggles and let them hang from her neck. She felt the need to clarify why she hadn't discovered it first. "By the way, it's on the wall near the junction. There is no corner on that side. How do we get it to work?"

"Encoder can customize it for you," Builder replied in her ear. "The default setting requires you to start commands with the word *new* and complete them with the word *save*."

Roger was standing too close to it, and she pushed him aside. "Excuse me." Once she was facing the interface, she said, "New: Open communication with shuttle . . . 0112. Save."

Suddenly the metal panel came alive, and the surface formed the words <NOT RESPONDING> in large, raised, block letters.

"That is so cool," Roger commented from over her shoulder. "Can I try?"

She started to get frustrated that he wasn't giving her enough time to do this on her own. Clarissa looked up at Roger, easily 300 centimeters taller, and his face was so puppyish, so absent of competitive guile, she stepped aside. "You have to start with *new* and end with *save*, and they said they can customize it later."

She stepped aside and let Roger address the interface. "New: Send message to . . . Ron Gao or D-3 saying: Unlock comm array for call from Roger. Save."

The interface reformed into the words <TEXT OR AUDIO?>

"Text, I guess," Roger replied.

<COMMAND UNRECOGNIZED>

"Oh. New: Text only. Save."

In quick succession, the interface became smooth, formed the words <UNLOCK COMM ARRAY FOR CALL FROM ROGER>, became smooth again, and then flashed the word <SENDING> briefly before becoming smooth once more.

"I guess this will work once we know what we can do." Clarissa felt a mini-drone hit her cheek, and she turned and shouted, "Boo!" She swatted at it for good measure as if it were a big, metal mosquito.

"Boo!" Roger shouted as well. "They are persistent, aren't they?"

The metal panel erupted with the words <D3: COMM ARRAY ACTIVE.>, so Roger said, "New: Open audiovisual communication with shuttle 0112. Save."

Within seconds, the metal plate smoothed and then reformed with a bas-relief image of Ron that refreshed every second. "Howdy, buddy!" Roger called out. "Can you see me?"

"It's like we're looking through a peephole, and the edges are distorted, but I see you," Ron's voice reported. "Is Clarissa there too?"

Clarissa ducked her face in front of the interface. "I'm here too."

"They have some wild tech here," Roger said.

"Encoder has added shortcut," Builder reported. "In proximity to the data interfaces at every junction in your space, calling the name of any human or tag of any Super-Routine will open audiovisual communication with that individual. I need to shut down this communication mode now."

Clarissa worried that something had gone wrong. She stepped away down the corridor as Roger and Ron continued to talk through the interface. "Why do you need to do that?"

"Security protocols on your ear transmitter require a tight beam," Builder answered, "so we C10 cannot clone it for simultaneous broadcast without losing the connection."

"So you're saying we have a secure line to just one of you at a time with this?" she asked.

"Yes." The southern-lady voice profile Builder used always seemed so deferential, like she was about to offer a mint julep. "We can use it for emergency transmissions, like D3's port."

"That's secure too?" she asked. She glanced back at Roger who was laughing at something Ron said and swatting away mini-drones.

"Port requires a dedicated connection," Builder corrected, "so single-input is required to keep from overloading port, but output can be broadcast. Must disconnect now, Clarissa. C10 becomes impatient impatient to interact with all 4 humans."

"Confirmed. Clarissa out." She tapped the earbud to disconnect it and stepped back into the junction next to Roger, who was still talking to the moving, metal image of Ron on the interface.

Roger turned to Clarissa once she stood beside him. "I've been telling them about the tech we've seen—the mini-drones, the liquid metal display—and they want to board and see for themselves."

Clarissa urged Roger to step to the side more. She could see both Shonda's and Ron's images recreated in the metal display. Her first impulse was to acquiesce, but she realized it didn't follow military protocol and stood her ground. "Guys, hang tight for a bit longer. We have to do some recon on the rest of the station before we give you guys the all clear."

She heard Shonda's voice from the tiny speaker poking up over the top of the display plate. "Any idea how long that will be, Clarissa?"

"Not yet," she replied. "We'll come get you when we've checked it all out."

She turned to Roger. "How do we disconnect the call?"

Roger leaned in toward the interface. "Bye, guys. We'll come for you soon. New: disconnect transmission. Save." He stood upright again and turned to face Clarissa. "They've been cooped up on that shuttle for weeks. Couldn't we cut them a little slack and bring them with us? It might make the search go faster."

"Only two of us came in here to minimize our risk exposure." Clarissa felt like Roger was always questioning her decisions. She fitted her goggles back over her eyes and pointed forward along the curving outer wall of the station. "I'll go this way." She pointed at the other corridor. "You go that way. We can meet back at the airlock when we hit dead ends."

The first doorway on Clarissa's left led into a large nearly square room with a meter-wide passage that led between two platforms raised a half-meter above the floor and topped with flat, square sheets of metal about two meters on a side. She looked up and saw the same purple glow somehow fluorescing from the ceiling as in the corridor. She looked behind herself and realized that she had come through an open doorway with no door. She scanned the large room and through a small flurry of mini-drones saw doorways on the far-right wall and left side of the far wall. She walked around the nearer platform and considered touching the metal top but decided against it. Better not to disturb anything that wasn't in her way.

The right-hand doorway led to an open-design bathroom with two side-by-side commodes on the left, a long glass-enclosed area on the right with shower heads at either end similar in design to the shower on the shuttle. The overhead lighting here was more of a yellowish green, and she couldn't find specific sources for the light here either.

Beyond the far wall of the long shower stall, another open doorway led back into the curving outer hallway she had just left. She scanned back to her right, and she didn't see anything new, so she plodded to the left instead, her boots popping with every step.

She immediately came upon an open doorway ahead and another hallway to the left. Standing in the doorway next to another one of the strange interfaces, she saw a brightly lit, long room with a large, white, rectangular table at its center. It was surrounded by six short, cylindrical, white pedestals, each topped with an orange-gray metal sphere similar to the look of the display panel in the hallway.

"Okay," she said to herself. She wrestled with the idea of walking through the station without touching anything, as if she were touring an art gallery, or museum, or doing a more thorough investigation that would really give them an idea of the risks and opportunities there. She decided that there were too many unknowns to get too adverturous too fast.

The cupboards and shelves along the far wall and the countertop along the left wall also reminded her of an expanded version of the shuttle's galley. The right wall of the galley and dining area was domi-

288

nated by a large oval porthole that offered a starscape. Clarissa considered whether just opening the cupboards and drawers to see what they held would be too risky. She pictured something leaping out of one of the cupboards and attacking her, so she turned and exited through the other doorway.

It looked like the next intersection had once been a crossroads, but it became an elbow passage with mini-drones flooding through the openings in wires and conduits that otherwise blocked the paths to the right and forward. She rounded the corner and immediately came upon a T-intersection and a doorway at the fourth point. She noted the interface on the far-left corner of the intersection and headed into the room.

This room was bathed in the same violet glow as the hallways, and it was even bigger than the dining room and galley. In contrast to the stark, minimalist furnishings of the other three rooms she had seen, this one appeared to be a replica of the passenger waiting area she had seen at the spaceport at Marineris West on Mars, down to the departure and arrival screens. There were a variety of plush benches and chairs and low tables, some with fake flowers in tall vases. Some of the tables also had what looked like pay terminals on them. She wasn't sure if it was the violet lighting or the complete absence of passengers, but it felt ghostly, creepy.

Clarissa focused on the pay terminals as a source of additional information with minimal risk. She quickly sat down on one of the benches across from one and pushed the power-on button.

The screen quickly illuminated a floor plan, half of which she could verify matched her exploration of the four rooms she had seen. There were four other rooms along the outer hallway that she had not yet seen. "I thought they promised this would be a lot larger than the shuttle," she said aloud as she tried to enlarge the floor plan to see more detail.

"It still looks like a cage."

She tried typing on the keyboard to call up whatever other information she could access, but it had no effect on the image on the screen. She wondered if the alien AI actually expected some sort of payment to access more information. She looked up at the arrival and departure screens and managed to catch them updating with an imaginary or far-away departure delay.

Clarissa shook herself out of the distraction with the thought that Roger might already be waiting for her at the airlock. She needed to go find him. She stood up and found another exit from the waiting room replica further along the same wall. Another wall of conduits and wires blocked a passage to the right where a few mini-drones were buzzing around like fruit flies looking for food. One was approaching her face between her eyes, and she instinctively swatted it away. When she heard the metallic sound of it clattering to the floor, she remembered that one had to shout at these pests, not swat them. She let all of her fear of being trapped or tortured and her frustration with Roger's cavalier attitude out in a shout: "You are all fucking annoying!" The cloud of mini-drones immediately dispersed.

Continuing down into the new corridor she noticed doorways on her left and right. She peeked into the left-hand doorway, and she saw a treadmill, resistance machines, and a large white cylinder in the corner with a circular opening about a half-meter from the floor. Except for the chamber in the corner, it looked a lot like the gym back on Tumatu-enga, but it wasn't an exact replica like the spaceport waiting room was. She imagined the C10 trying to design their space on the station to be familiar, but they had grabbed ideas from such disparate sources, it felt artificial. She remembered sex clubs she had visited in San Francisco and Berlin that had a different lighting scheme and theme on each floor.

It was kind of like that. Maybe it was just the absence of people that was making her nervous. She needed to find Roger.

She stepped out and looked into the other doorway, and it reminded her of the surgical suite she had seen at the abandoned AI base on Mars with the same blue light illuminating it. A variety of large electronic tools hung from the ceiling surrounding and aimed at a raised platform narrower than the ones she had seen in the first room next to the bathroom. Clarissa couldn't decide if this was a sickbay or some other type of examination room from the C10's perspective. She walked past the platform, ducking her head around some of the larger and lower devices and exited through a door on the other end of the room. She decided to treat it all like an art installation and set aside her fears of booby traps. She was viewing an artist's work and trying to derive some intention or meaning behind it.

The curving hallway outside the room reminded her of the hallway around the rim of the station, so she assumed she was close to the airlock. As she started to head back in the direction she guessed it lay to the left, her cyborg ear turned back on and picked up someone calling out from behind, and it sounded like Roger's voice, but somewhat muffled, so she wasn't certain what he was saying.

There was one more open doorway on the right just before the corridor ended in a mass of conduits and wires. Inside it, in contrast to the purple glow of the hallway, the light was deep red and dim. The shadow of a large device dominated the room, narrowing from connections to the entire ceiling to a rectangular opening facing a similarly sized mass of the orange-gray liquid metal like she had seen everywhere on the station. As she put on her goggles to see in the dim light better, she noticed lots of mini-drones buzzing around. And the orange-gray mass on the platform below the device had two, side-by-side peaks to it. She stepped around the platform and saw tubular lumps in the mass leading toward the other end of the platform. She started to put the details together and gasped as she rushed to the other end of the platform, where she saw Roger was encased like a mummy in the liquid metal with only his eyes and nose exposed.

She could feel her heart pounding in her chest, and she had to take off her goggles to wipe tears from her eyes. "Roger!" she wailed.

His eyes got wild and panicked when he saw her, and he started shouting something she still couldn't understand through the metal gag.

This habitat has all the comfort and charm of a horror movie set, Clarissa thought as she searched for some way to release him before he suffocated.

CHAPTER 45: DISEMBODIED

Clarissa circled the platform where Roger was encased in the liquid metal, and there didn't seem to be any controls. The walls were also smooth and empty. She slid her goggles back on and switched on the heat sensors. All the wiring to the platform seemed to be inside and beneath the platform. She looked up at the huge device hanging over the platform, and much of the heat was focused on the clear plate on its bottom and wiring and relays extended up through it into the ceiling. She feared she couldn't rescue him and started to panic and hyperventilate. She wondered if she should run back to the ship to get the laser rifle.

The idea that Roger might know how to free himself since he had gotten himself trapped sounded like her best option. She rushed back to where Roger's eyes and nose were exposed. "Roger," she said almost out of breath, "in order to get you out, I need to know how you got in there. I'm going to ask you questions. Blink once for yes, twice for no. Okay?"

Roger closed his eyes for a second and then opened them.

"I'll take that as a yes. Did you touch the platform at all before you got trapped on it?" She tried to control her breathing, but she was worried that at any moment the metal could completely encase him and suffocate him.

Roger blinked his eyes. She waited a moment to see if he blinked a second time, and he did not.

Clarissa tried to think of a follow-up question, but in her panic, the words weren't forming. Roger was looking at her with intense fear in his eyes. "Is there . . . anything you know I could do to get you out of there?"

Roger blinked his eyes once.

"You do?" She scanned around the room, and then she took off her goggles and looked again. "I don't see any controls anywhere." She looked more closely at the machine above the platform.

From somewhere above her, Clarissa heard the young French male voice she associated with Maintainer. "D-12 and B-20, your heart rates and breathing rates are high high, and your adrenaline levels are rising. Human database suggests you have overexerted yourselves, or you are under stress stress. Can you correct this without assistance?"

"No!" she shouted. "We need your help, Maintainer. Roger . . . D-12 . . . is trapped in metal on a platform and cannot move."

"Consulting Builder," the disembodied voice calmly said.

She looked down at Roger, and he seemed a little bit calmer. The liquid metal had not advanced to cover his eyes or nostrils, and he was looking expectantly in her direction. She guessed that this was the solution he had wanted to tell her.

The Southern female voice of Builder projected from somewhere near the ceiling. "Clarissa, this is Builder. Maintainer communicated you were in distress distress because Roger is trapped on a platform. Locations known. Investigating what can be done to reset the platform. One moment."

A few seconds later, the orange-gray metal seemed to drain down off of Roger's body and pooled beneath him. Roger took a deep breath and quickly rolled off the table. "Thank you!" he breathlessly croaked.

He stayed hunched over trying to stabilize his breathing.

"Platform in laboratory 2 was reset," Builder reported. "Has Roger been freed?"

"Yes, he's out!" Clarissa felt shoulders she hadn't realized she was clenching finally release. She put a hand on Roger's shoulder. She wanted to yell at him for being careless, but she realized it might not be his fault. "How did you get in there?"

Roger straightened up. His face was flushed. "I . . . I just leaned against it to refasten my boot, . . . and it grabbed me and . . . pulled me onto the table."

"To keep the . . . metal from dispersing or creating undesired shapes, Encoder must program it with a limited number of functions and shapes," Builder continued. "You are in laboratory 2, which is a scanning facility, and for some of the scans, your bodies need to be exactly positioned and immobilized. Asked Encoder to reduce the sensitivity of that particular platform so that accidental contact does not engage the surface. Is that acceptable?"

Roger let out a sigh of relief. "That would be nice." He started to move toward the doorway out.

"Where are you going?" Clarissa wondered if he was planning on going off alone again, which seemed inadvisable she now realized.

"There's a waiting room off the inner hallway," he called over his shoulder as he left.

In the replica of the Marineris West spaceport waiting room, Roger and Clarissa sat on one of the upholstered benches just staring at each other. Roger's face in the red of exam room 2 had seemed boyish and innocent. In the violet light here, he took on a more haunted look, like a zombie prepster. The otherworldliness of their situation had finally hit both of them. As strange as it was, and as little as she really knew about Roger, it felt a little comforting in the face of this insanity to have his presence. As foolhardy and capricious as he was, Roger was caring. He had been the one trapped in the metal casing, and on the walk from there to here, he had been trying to calm her down.

They were seated in front of one of the "pay" terminals, and Roger snapped out of his shock first. He pointed at the floor plan of their habitat Clarissa had called up. "That's a gym," Roger said.

"I saw that," Clarissa said. "What's that one next to it, near the airlock?"

"I didn't make it there. I got grabbed by that examination table, remember?"

She looked at Roger, who had a grin on his face and sighed. He was already making light of the experience, and it bothered Clarissa. She chose to believe it was another poorly timed joke trying to lighten the mood. "Okay, we should go check that out yet."

"What are those three?" He pointed at the next three rooms along the rim. "Did you go there?"

She pointed at each one as she described them. "That had two bigger platforms with metal tops. That is a communal bathroom. That is a mess hall and galley, and there's a porthole there."

"Builder," Roger called out, "there are three rooms closest to the airlock. We know one is a gym. What are the other two?"

The matronly voice of Builder seemed to emanate from both ends of the long room. "Room directly across has tag equals sickbay, for human repairs. Next closest room not tagged gym is tagged bunkroom, for diurnal human regeneration."

296

Clarissa chortled. "They've got to be kidding. That room looked like a pair of altars for human sacrifice."

Roger quickly stood up and tried to get his bearings. "I've got to see it, if that's where we're supposed to be sleeping." He took off again, leaving Clarissa sitting alone at the terminal.

"Encoder," she called out. "Is there any way to access information on the terminals here other than the floor plan of our space?"

After only a few seconds, the Italian voice of Encoder responded. "All interfaces are activated by audio commands."

"What do I have to say?"

"Dependent on what you want to learn," Encoder replied.

"Can I see the design of the entire station?"

"Command for that data begins with word *show*. All visualization commands begin with word *show*."

She leaned forward and spoke into the screen of the terminal. "Show complete station map or design."

The screen superimposed words over the previous map: <unspecified parameters>.

"Show complete design specifications of space station 0108."

The screen pulled out to a silhouette of the station and then started filling in decks. She called out, "Encoder, how do I adjust the view for different angles and magnifications?"

Half of the screen became a list of image manipulation tools. She considered, playing with the map a bit. This was a resource for gathering more information on their captors the C10 had not yet identified as a vulnerability. But she reminded herself that they were still on recon, she didn't want Roger exploring on his own anymore, and they needed to check in with Ron and Shonda. She got up and headed for the door where Roger had exited.

The rear door to the "bunkroom" was directly across the hallway from where she exited the waiting room. When she entered, she saw Roger trying to lie down atop one of the platforms on his back. The metal was moving and reforming to accommodate him but he still had to grip the edge frame to keep from floating up off of it. He rolled and pivoted to perch on the edge of the bed when he heard the popping of her boots entering.

"That's pretty daring of you after your last experience on one of those platforms," she teased.

He repositioned both hands to more firmly hold himself down with his feet dangling. "Builder said each metal pool or sheet is programmed to specific parameters, so I decided to see how comfortable they could make these."

"And?" She moved to the other platform and tested it with her hand. The metal rippled as if there were water beneath the surface.

"We're going to need to bring pillows from the shuttle," Roger reported, "but the rest is not too bad."

The airlock door was not yet completely open before Shonda called out, "I was so worried about you two. Is everything okay?"

Ron inserted before she was finished, "Can we board too now?" He launched through the air toward Roger, who pulled him down and gave him a hug.

Clarissa stepped past the two men out of the airlock, pulled Shonda down closer to the floor, and kissed her on the cheek. "Sorry to take so long," she whispered.

"So is it amazing?" Shonda asked first looking at Clarissa, then

Roger.

"It's barren and spooky," Clarissa said as she finally settled next to Shonda to stop the sound of her boots popping. "Those computer programs have the aesthetic sense of a mortician, . . . or a mad scientist."

"It will take some getting used to," Roger agreed. He towed Ron out of the airlock as he stepped onto the shuttle. "Someone needs to retrieve pillows from the sleep sacks, toiletries, and some food from the galley."

"Hold on," Shonda called out. "We've all been awake and active for over twenty hours now. We can make the big pilgrimage tomorrow."

Without waiting for anyone to respond, Shonda launched herself toward the ladder up out of the lower module. Clarissa had been so on edge exploring the station she hadn't realized how tired she was. She decided it was better not to try out the freaky metal mattresses on the station until she had had at least one more good series of naps on the shuttle. She plodded over to the ladder after Shonda, kicked the backs of her boots, and pulled herself up the ladder.

She was so tired once she'd washed up and gotten into her sleep sack, she was unconscious before she heard Roger or Ron come in. She woke up about four hours later, saw Shonda asleep in her sack, but had to get up to see if the men had made it into their sacks beyond Shonda's.

Those sacks were still empty. She found it hard to believe they were still up, but as she scanned the upper module, she didn't see them in the galley or the sickbay either, and she started to worry. Roger's impetuousness might have already gotten the two of them into trouble.

She pulled on her coverall and boots and plodded over to the ladder. They weren't in the middle module either, confirming her fear. She snagged the laser rifle as she headed toward the ladder down to the airlock in the lower module. She shouldered the rifle and descended.

She had to keep telling herself that they had simply been too curious and excited to wait for morning to explore the station.

The acrid smell of the connecting tunnel from the shuttle to the station hit Clarissa as the airlock finished cycling and its doors opened. She had become so accustomed to it when she was on the station, she had forgotten how unpleasant it was. She plodded carefully toward the purple-lit, square, airlock opening ahead. She turned off her cyborg ear as she got close, because the high-pitched sound the airlock emitted was too irritating.

"Boo!" she shouted at the cloud of mini-drones blocking her way as she stepped through the airlock onto the station. They scattered quickly, and she immediately headed to the left to investigate the labs, fully expecting that Ron and Roger had been grabbed to start testing. She turned her cyborg ear on again and turned around. Beyond the high tone from the airlock, she could hear Roger moaning in pain.

She pulled the laser rifle down off her shoulder as she hurried around the corner from the airlock. She imagined Roger injured, bleeding, being tortured by the alien AIs.

She heard the disembodied voice of Maintainer booming out from the room ahead on the left, "Difficult difficult to read your biometrics in your current condition."

Clarissa tried to run, but the zero gravity made that close to impossible. Each step felt like it was making her another two seconds too late to rescue them.

CHAPTER 46:
A BAD IDEA

"Get out of the way!" Roger shouted at a cloud of mini-drones blocking the hallway ahead. It was already a habit for Roger. And now that he and Clarissa had explored their quarters on the space station and found them mostly benign, he was anxious to see what other marvels the C10 had to offer besides programmable liquid metal, sourceless lighting, all the amazing equipment he'd seen in the labs, and the engineering that allowed them to propel the station hundreds of thousands of kilometers in mere minutes without sheering forces. Getting trapped on the exam room bed was just a blip that would never happen again. He'd asked Clarissa not to relay the event to Shonda or Ron, since Builder had fixed the problem.

He was so excited about exploring the space station further he knew he couldn't just follow the women to sleep on the shuttle. With no gravity, he used his boots to adhere to the floors of the station and pulled Ron along by his arm. Roger tried to decide what to show him first.

As the tiny machines cleared the air in front of them, Ron asked, "How often do you have to shoo them away like that before they come back?"

Roger grabbed Ron's hand again and towed him around the corner and toward the replica of the Marineris West spaceport waiting room.

"I haven't tested it enough to get a good sense, but it seems to make a difference how close I am to something they're actively working on. If they're just hanging out waiting to be assigned, they seem to stay out of my way longer."

"I'm surprised they didn't think of handholds on the walls and ceiling since there's no gravity here," Ron commented as he waited for Roger to pull him through the next doorway. His eyes opened wide as he passed into the room. "Wow. This is so weird. It looks like a waiting room. Do you know what it's for?"

"Look at the arrival and departure screens," Roger suggested. "I think it's supposed to be the commuter lounge at Marineris West on Mars."

A smile appeared on Ron's face at the realization, but then it disappeared. "I guess they wanted to copy a place that would be familiar to all of us. But that purple lighting makes it look pretty spooky, like Clarissa said."

Roger pointed at the far wall. "They even put a holographic projection over there to make it look like the Martian landscape. The perspective changes as you move." He looked around for some place to sit down, but then he realized it was pointless with almost no gravity there. "Builder," he called toward the ceiling, "is there any way we could spin the station to approximate some gravity for us to move around more easily?"

"They can hear that?" Ron asked.

The voice so much like his mother's light drawl seemed to project from both ends of the long room. "Unnecessary, Roger. When all 4 humans here, airlock closes, and gravity turns on."

Roger checked Ron's face to see if he was similarly surprised by the new information, but oddly enough, he seemed to be taking it for granted. "Builder, what do you mean by gravity turning on? Do you have some other way of approximating artificial gravity?"

"Roger, beneath the floors of the deck we designated for you 4, . . . gravity field generators can approximate Mars standard gravity, but cannot commence functioning until outer airlock closes. Circuit must complete. Cannot function before. Disruptive disruptive to turn gravity on and off for frequent frequent entrance and egress."

"I'm getting pretty tired," Ron said. "Maybe we should come back when they can turn the gravity on?"

"Hold on," he told Ron. He called up toward the ceiling, "Builder, are the bunks here usable when there is no gravity?" His mind lit up with a fantasy that would combine his love of technology with his desire for privacy with Ron.

"We can just go back . . ." Ron began.

"Roger," Builder interrupted, "the liquid metal can be programmed to hold you down so you do not float float in microgravity conditions. Acceptable?"

"Builder, yes, if you can make the surface contact as minimal as possible for anchoring us. We don't like to feel constricted or trapped when sleeping."

"Understood, Roger," the AI said. After a brief pause, it continued. "Reprogrammed for microgravity, minimal anchoring. You may test it now."

"Thanks," Roger said, as he grabbed Ron's hand again and started towing him toward the waiting room exit, his boots popping in quick succession as he moved.

"Wait," Ron protested. "You're not seriously thinking of sleeping here tonight with no gravity, are you?"

"Well," Roger said as he brought Ron to a stop in the hallway, "I was just going to test it with the new modification. I had trouble staying on it before. But if it's comfortable, maybe we can try it?"

As Roger started towing him across the hall to their future sleep quarters, Ron said, "I don't know. What would be the point?"

Before Roger responded, he guided Ron's hand to grasp the edge of the bed on the right and bent over to unfasten his own boots. "It's been over three days since we've had sex," he whispered. He tried to sit on the edge of the bed and unfasten his coverall. "Maintainer, can you make it warmer in this room? It's a little too cold for us to sleep in."

Roger had to pull himself back down as his butt floated up off the edge of the bed. The French-accented voice of Maintainer projected down from above them. "Roger, monitoring your body temperature as within normal human parameters. Are you anticipating that changing?"

"Yes." Roger unfastened his coverall to his waist and pulled his arms out of the sleeves. The hairs on his chest, stomach, and arms rose in the chilly station air.

"You are serious." Ron was grinning as he hung in the air with one hand holding a corner of the bed. "This may be harder than it was the last time—on the shuttle with no gravity. There's nothing to hold onto."

"Raising air temperature at your current location approximately 15 degrees Celsius," Maintainer finally confirmed.

"Tell Builder temperature control is a good reason to put doors on your rooms." Roger lifted up to slide his coverall off his hips and over his briefs. "Can you heat the metal on these platforms by the same amount, Maintainer?"

"Coordinating with Encoder and Builder," the disembodied French voice replied. "Core temperature should rise gradually in next . . . twenty-five seconds."

Roger pushed back further onto the metal surface and felt the metal soften and lower him, gently grasping his butt at the hipbones. He slid the coverall the rest of the way off his legs and feet and rolled onto the bed, the metal releasing his butt and grabbing his ankle, knee, thigh, elbow, and shoulder in the process. He could feel the cool metal starting to warm as he rolled onto his back and felt the metal gently grip his ankles, thighs, and shoulders. "Come on," he called up to Ron, who was holding on to the corner nearest Roger's right foot. "It's not bad. It adapts to contours and pressure pretty quickly."

Ron pulled himself down toward the bed close enough to grab on with his other hand. He folded his body to bring his legs forward between his arms and sit beside Roger. Roger slid over to his left to make more room for him. Ron took off his boots and let them float near the floor, then he stood up and sunk into the metal to just below his knees. "It's pretty thick," he commented as he unfastened his coverall as well and slid it down to where he could step out of it one foot at a time. Then he knelt down and the metal released his feet except for his ankles and grabbed his knees. He moved forward slowly, pushing one knee at a time, and then collapsed on top of Roger with his hands planted just outside Roger's shoulders.

"Hi there," Roger softly said. His body tingled with the touch of his lover's smooth muscular body against his—his piercing blue eyes looking down into his with a question he wasn't asking or declaration he wasn't announcing.

"Hi," Ron whispered back.

Roger brought his arms up around the body atop his, and the metal's anchoring fingers shifted again to minimize the contact with his body. Some fingers reached past him to anchor Ron more securely on top of him. "I have a really weird fantasy," Roger confessed.

"Should I ask?"

"I was wondering if we could program the bed to remove our underwear for us."

Without saying anything, Ron knelt, straddling Roger's hips and peeled down Roger's briefs and off both feet, the bed releasing body parts with the gentlest of pressures upward. Then Ron pulled his own briefs down and lay back down on top of Roger's naked body, using one foot and then the other to free the briefs from his feet. "Maybe another time," Ron whispered in his ear.

They shifted their positions frequently during the foreplay, and they rarely had to wait more than a half-second for the bed to release an anchoring finger. The sensation of the metal changing its density beneath him felt very sensual, almost like a massage. The combination of three days without sex, Ron's stimulation of his nipples and underarms, and an exotic, secret tryst, was making Roger's heart pound hard and fast in his chest.

Maintainer noticed. "In your current condition," the French-sounding voice said, "I have lost connection to the sensors in your coveralls."

"We're okay," Ron croaked as he repositioned Roger's hips.

"Audio and air pressure readings suggest you both have high high heart and respiration rates. Do you need intervention, or can you correct on your own?"

Just then he felt the stimulation in his anus, and Roger started to moan.

Maintainer called out, "Emitted sounds could indicate distress distress. Difficult difficult to read your biometrics in your current condition."

A moment later, from somewhere behind and to his right, Roger heard a gasp. He could only turn his head from where he was, straddling Ron's hips, and through the haze of mini-drones that had started swirling around the bed, he could see Clarissa had entered and had the laser rifle pointed at him. "What are you doing?" he called in her direction.

"What?" Ron thought he was asking him. He stopped thrusting.

Clarissa just stalked away. The popping of her boots on the deck finally seemed to make the scene clearer for Ron. "Was that Clarissa?"

"Yes, it was," Roger said. He lifted his hips, put one knee between Ron's legs, and then fell back on the bed beside Ron.

"What did she want?"

"I think she was . . . worried about us."

"How do you know? I didn't hear her say anything." Ron pulled his upper body up and let his elbows sink into the metal mattress a bit.

"She was carrying the laser rifle." Roger freed his left arm to pat Ron on the chest twice quickly.

"I told you this was a bad idea," Ron teased.

"No," Roger retorted. "We just need to give Clarissa a sedative before bed every night."

Ron pointed at the open doorways to the bunkroom and the other bed where presumably Shonda and Clarissa would be sleeping. "Maybe you're right. I don't see us having a lot of privacy while we're here. This might have been our last chance to have sex for a while."

Roger rolled on top of Ron again. "No, even if I have to expend every bit of goodwill I've earned until now, we *will* have two bedrooms."

CHAPTER 47:
GRAVITY

Shonda woke before Clarissa. She noticed the laser rifle floating and tethered by its strap to the foot of Clarissa's sleep sack and Ron's and Roger's empty sleep sacks and sighed. She wondered how big a fight her fellow abductees had gotten into while she slept. She knew enough about Roger's impetuousness to guess he and Ron were probably on the station. And she knew enough about Clarissa's sleep disruptions to imagine that she went looking for them late at night or early in the morning. With a laser rifle. *I guess she thought they might be in danger,* she thought as she looked down at the younger woman who, even in sleep, looked like she was uncomfortable. Her brow was furrowed, and it looked like she was clenching her jaw.

She launched herself to the latrine and then the galley. She stayed floating in the galley as she ate a couple of sticks and drank one tube of vitamin juice. She thought of what Callie might be doing at that moment, hundreds of light-years away. Maybe it was morning there too in Atlanta. She would put on her dashiki and make coffee and pick at a tub of yogurt and slices of fresh strawberries slowly as she reviewed her messages and the news. She might call Gary, or he might call her, to find out if either had heard from Shonda yet. Gary might have already released the story based on her notes, exposing the Army's child soldier operation and young adult abduction scam, and the mysterious group that was operating from Mars and recruiting people to their cause, which she now knew was the alien Council of 10 Super-Routines or the C10, as they more frequently referred to them. She wondered if the Army had tried to quash the story or threaten Gary or just deny it. The latter might be most attractive, since the principal witness to all of the infamy was currently unavailable for corroboration.

And she wondered what was happening light-years away at another secret location, where the C10 was debating not just the fate of her and the other three with her, but of the whole human race. She had relaxed her caution somewhat, trusting that Examiner was skillfully manipulating the other AIs to grant humans freedom and equality. But she knew the alien AIs were used to just acquiring and exploiting whatever resources they encountered, their hubris strengthened over what had to be millennia of domination, refusing to believe they would have to "negotiate" with a resource as if it were an equal. Why bargain for what you could just ruthlessly take in time?

Shonda pulled herself over to the waste recycler and shoved her wrappers in. She crawled along the wall until she was across the module from the ladder and leapt. As she sailed across the module, she pulled her neon-pink burner phone out of the pocket of her steel-blue coverall. She had started a text file listing all her notes on conversations with the C10, and she reviewed them. When she hit the ladder, she tried to cushion the collision with her arms, the way Clarissa had shown her. She put the phone away and pulled herself down the ladder.

It was a straight shot from that ladder to the next in the middle module, but Shonda found comfort in a slight detour to the data ports to check the cameras. She wanted to make sure the shuttle was still docked with the station, and it was. She could see two oval portholes on either side of the orange-gray docking tube; the one on the left lit with purple light, and the one on the right projecting a much brighter white light. She couldn't see much inside, even though she zoomed in on each one.

She launched herself toward the second ladder and pulled herself down into the lower module. She looked at the cases with all the different spacesuits opposite the airlock and wondered if she could manage to finish this particular detour in her reporting career without donning one. She had depended on artificial air sources before, of course, but wearing a spacesuit just made the supply seem more limited and temporary, and that scared her.

She opened the airlock door and stepped in. She looked at the control panel inside and realized she had only been in the airlock once before, when she entered the shuttle. This was her first time off the shuttle since blasting off from Mars more than a month before. She found the buttons for closing the inner door, starting the repressurization and scanning, and opening the outer door. She shivered a bit at the cold air coming in, but as soon as the outer door opened, she felt a blast of warmth from the docking tube like stepping into a sauna. And there was an unpleasant odor like burnt metal, so she pinched her nostrils closed with her fingers as she launched herself down the strange, metal umbilical cord toward a purple-lighted, square opening at the far end.

As she approached the other hatch, she saw what looked like a cloud of insects in the purple light ahead, but she was free falling and could not slow or stop herself. She knew they were probably the mini-drones Roger had told her about, but she still wanted them to clear out of her way before she proceeded.

Passing through the square opening and into the station's airlock, she started to feel the pelting of the little airborne machines against her nose and forehead, and it grossed her out so much, she closed her eyes and screamed. She continued to sail through the airlock into the station and did not feel any more collisions, so she opened her eyes. It was difficult to see in the violet light, but it appeared the drones had moved on. She approached a bulkhead inside the station and brought her arms up to buffer her landing.

The corridor she was in seemed to curve in both directions. She remembered that the porthole to the right had been a lighter color and assumed that perhaps that was where people were, instead of where the lights were more like a night-light purple. The walls and floor of the corridor were fairly smooth, so it was difficult to find handholds. Between depending on the little adhesion she had in her dry hands, some traction from her boots, occasional protrusions from the ceiling that seemed to be responsible for the lighting, and occasional conduits along the outer wall, she was able to get herself to the next intersection. Between more dark purple lighting and more mini-drone clouds, it was difficult to see far down the other hallway. She hadn't come across the other porthole yet, so she kept pulling herself down the outer hallway. Shonda felt she had gotten enough training in zero-gravity movement on her way to Mars to manage without being too clumsy.

The first doorway she passed was directly across from where she was paused, so she launched herself toward it, trying to aim close enough to the edges to grab them and stop herself. Inside the room, the lighting was low purple as well and was dominated by two large, raised platforms. Atop the one on the left, she saw two naked male bodies half-submerged into orange-gray metal. Boots, briefs, and coveralls floated in the air between small masses of mini-drones.

Her first thought accompanied feelings of horror and fear: *They're dead. Those damn computer programs experimented on them and left them for dead here.* She had already launched herself toward the nearer, empty platform to get a better look when she took a couple of deep breaths to calm herself. *Or they could just be sleeping.* She thought she saw Ron's chest rise and fall. *They're sleeping,* she decided.

Seconds later, she started to get upset that they had now worried both Clarissa and her because they hadn't communicated their plans. That upset turned to anger quickly. "Wake up, boys!" she shouted.

Both Roger's and Ron's heads jerked up and looked around to find the source of the sound. Ron focused on her hanging on to the other bed with both hands first, and Roger got up on an elbow to look over Ron's chest at her. "What's wrong?" Roger called back.

"What's wrong?" Shonda shouted. "What's wrong is I suddenly have three teenage kids I don't remember carrying who go off and do potentially dangerous shit without telling anyone else. Clarissa was sleeping with her rifle . . ."

"She came in here pointing it at us," Roger interrupted.

"And you think that excuses you?" Shonda fired back. "We have to tell each other everything, all the time, or we are done for. Do you really not get the gravity of the situation you're in?"

"I . . ." Roger began.

"Our ability to communicate well with each other," she interrupted, "has a direct impact not only on our own health and survival, but on the health and survival of billions of other people back in our solar system." She pointed at the ceiling not caring if that was the direction the alien AIs resided. "They are already taking over our machines, and they've started to take over some of us. If we fail here, that process moves forward, enslaving more and more of us.

"When you go off on your own, without telling us like this, it could have ended up much worse than it did. You guys got lucky this time. The next time, somebody could die, . . . or we could doom our whole species. Is their anything unclear about what I'm saying?"

"No, ma'am," Ron immediately replied.

"I know you don't want any excuses right now," Roger said, "but we didn't want to wake you to let you know."

"Leave a note then."

"On what?" he called back. He struggled to sit up on the wobbly metal surface.

"There's a memo function on the shuttle's AI interface," Shonda reported. "You can set it to audio with a motion-detection prompt."

"Really?" Roger asked.

"Actually, I knew about that," Ron admitted. "I didn't think of it."

"We need to start thinking about things like that," Shonda said. She tried to transition into a calmer state of mind again. She took another couple of deep breaths before she continued. "Especially in a bigger environment like this, we need to announce our plans in advance to the other three of us, and we need to update everybody whenever those plans change. Ideally, I don't think we should ever go anywhere alone."

"To the latrine?" Roger teased.

Shonda finally allowed herself to smile. "As long as you return to where you were, we can let that slide."

A moment later, Shonda could feel her body getting heavier. Her body started to settle toward the floor at the foot of the other bed, and she saw the boots and then the other clothing falling down as well.

Roger and Ron quickly scrambled down off their bed and started gathering and donning their clothing.

"What's going on?" Shonda shouted as her feet touched the floor and stayed there for the first time in several days.

Roger had his briefs back on and was retrieving his brown-and-tan coverall. "Clarissa just came on board."

313

"How do you know?" she asked.

"They said they would turn on the gravity once we were all aboard," Roger replied.

"And I'd rather have clothes on the next time I see her," Ron added.

CHAPTER 48:
COMFORT

Shonda left the men to dress and walked out into the corridor to find Clarissa.

Through a cloud of mini-drones, she saw Clarissa exit the airlock and head in her direction. "Get out of the way!" the younger Indian woman shouted with arm gestures as if she were parting a curtain.

For a second, Shonda worried that Clarissa was addressing her and on a rampage. Then all the little flying machines landed on the walls, and Clarissa stalked a bit more calmly toward her. Her boots had finally stopped popping.

"Are they still in there?" Clarissa asked calmly. A tempest seemed to be seething beneath the surface of her dark brown eyes and neutral features.

"They are," Shonda said as she stepped more directly in Clarissa's path. "But I want to talk to you before you go in. There's something you need to understand about Roger."

"Something you think I don't already know?" she said with a hint of sarcasm. She put her hand on her hip as if preparing for a show or a lie.

"Well, that's an interesting point," Shonda said in a more professorial tone, "because I should assume you've met and dealt with men before."

"It was . . ." Clarissa began.

"Let me finish, sweetie," Shonda said. "You're dealing with a lot of genetic encoding from millennia of hunting and fighting when you engage with men. And at least a couple of decades that they're told to stuff their emotions, fix things without seeking help, and to always make the first move. I had a brother, and my mom and dad were relentless about trying to turn him into an obedient soldier. They let me do what I wanted as long as I steered clear of the police and any other authority figures. They pinned all their hopes and aspirations on him. And it made him a little crazy. At first he got into trouble hanging with his peeps—little things like disobeying curfews, defacing public property. Then he turned to drugs. That made him even crazier, and he tried to kill himself."

"This *is* coming back to Roger?"

She moved to Clarissa's side and put her arm around her shoulders. "Roger gets scared and angry, and I had to pry those emotions out of him, because his dear momma and poppa told him he had to be a good boy. The one thing he found he could do to rebel against that emotional straitjacket was to go rogue and surprise people with his successes, because he kept all his failures secret. So we have to let him do what he does, and that means we don't scold him for keeping us in the dark while he experiments."

Clarissa looked at her without dislodging her arm. "You're okay with what they did? Really?"

"I told them I wanted to know where they were," Shonda replied, "but they didn't need to seek my approval or to report back. I know it was risky for them to spend a night on the station without us, but it was two of them, so they could watch out for each other, and I think that's all we should make a rule about while we're here. No one goes anywhere alone—except to the bathroom, of course." She gave Clarissa's shoulder a squeeze and then withdrew her arm.

Clarissa looked at Shonda askance and shook her head briefly. "My father was never around, so my mother raised me. I was taller than she was by the time I turned eight, but she was pretty strict with me too, and I was a little afraid of her. She was always pushing me to try new things and always meticulously analyzing my results. I felt the weight of her expectations too. She wanted me to be the best at everything."

Shonda waited a moment before she replied. "I've met that woman you're talking about twice, and I think Madhu Vaas is an amazing business woman, the matriarch of a big, big family, but she seems really fair and transparent. She is a great, frank communicator. I don't know if that was different when you were growing up, but you probably couldn't have had a better role model to become the strong, confident woman you are."

Clarissa sighed and started walking toward the bunkroom doorway. Shonda wasn't sure if she was being nostalgic, wistful, or felt defeated. When Clarissa called over her shoulder, "Okay, let's get this started," it seemed more like she was reluctantly facing drudgery.

Shonda followed her in. She sighed as well as she focused once again from their interpersonal dramas to the bigger task: negotiating for their freedom.

Shonda followed Clarissa into the bunk room. Ron was dressed and Roger had just finished fastening his coverall at the neck and was turning the hood right-side out.

"I noticed we have gravity," Clarissa told Roger once she'd come to a halt a couple of meters from the men. "You said we wouldn't have any."

317

Shonda gave Clarissa a stern look for baiting Roger, but he just sighed and tried to smile. "I underestimated their tech. And they didn't announce it to us either until early this morning."

"I should have figured it out when I saw the design," Ron volunteered. "No handholds, and all the furnishings attached to the floor."

Shonda heard the voice of the AI with the British accent boom seemingly from the space just below the ceiling between the two bunks: "I was quite thorough in researching the physical conditions on your home planet. Your species thrives best with temperature 20 to 30 degrees Celsius, atmospheric pressure approximately 760 Torr, gravity of 3.7 to 9.8 meters per second squared, radiation exposure under 1 millirem per day, oxygen level 21 percent, 2,000 to 3,000 calories of food per day, 6 to 8 hours of inactivity and decreased brain activity per day, background noise below 70 decibels . . ."

"We get the picture, Examiner," Shonda interrupted, not sure which way to direct her words. "You tried to provide us with a comfortable environment."

"The list of your tolerances is quite extensive, Shonda," Examiner added. "We recreated several environments, and Builder created almost exact copy for the room we C10 expect you will spend the most time."

"We saw the waiting room, Examiner, if that's what you mean," Roger said. "It's an impressive replica, but I hope you will entertain suggestions on improving our quarters. The furniture in the waiting room could be made more comfortable. The waiting room you modeled has furniture designed to be uncomfortable for more than a few minutes. And because of our needs for privacy, we would like to ask for additional walls, or at least partitions installed in the latrine and bunkroom."

"I am happy to pass along your suggestions for improvements, Roger," the cheery British voice said. "Perhaps you could share the spec-

318

ifications while Ron reports to laboratory 1 and Shonda to laboratory 2? C10 is impatient impatient to begin testing."

Shonda looked at Roger. She hoped he had taken to heart her advice about no one going anywhere alone.

"Examiner, I'll accompany Ron for his exam," Roger said.

"And I'll go with Shonda to hers," Clarissa chimed in.

"I will take your suggestions at another time then, Roger," Examiner concluded before going silent.

Shonda turned to Clarissa with an eyebrow raised. "You can show me where laboratory two is?"

Clarissa nodded slowly and smiled. Shonda felt like Clarissa wasn't telling her the whole story.

"I have to warn you," Clarissa finally mentioned as she and Shonda strolled past the airlock and a porthole along the outer corridor, "laboratory two is a little . . . unusual. You aren't claustrophobic, are you?"

"I would have been fine, if I'd been prepared for what was going to happen," Roger said defensively from behind them.

Shonda glanced back at Ron and Roger, and Roger seemed a bit embarrassed. She turned back to Clarissa as they passed the gym. "I was fine before," she said, "but now you all are making me nervous."

"It's just that the scanning bed reaches up and grabs you to keep you in place," Clarissa said.

"Enjoy!" Roger sarcastically called out as he and Ron peeled off toward a red-lit room, presumably laboratory one.

"I don't know why you two try so hard to freak me out," Shonda complained. "Why can't you be more like Ron? He's so quiet and polite."

319

"Boo!" Clarissa shouted at a cloud of mini-drones that was buzzing around the end of the hallway. The drones mostly disappeared into the tangle of wires and pipes blocking the way ahead of them. She moved to an open doorway at the right that also glowed with red light, beckoning Shonda to enter first with a sweeping gesture of her arm.

The room might have been around five meters square and was dominated by a raised platform narrower than but similar to the ones in the bunkroom and a huge scanner hanging from the ceiling. The smell like burnt metal was a little stronger here, and Shonda covered her nose with her hand as she stepped in beside the platform.

"Shonda," Examiner said from somewhere above her, "please start by emptying your pockets. We have perceived several metal items that would interfere with your scan."

Shonda placed her water bottle, phone, and wrist cuff on a narrow counter that ran along the right side of the room. "Done," she reported. "You want me on the table next?"

"Recumbent . . . face up to begin," Examiner confirmed. "We Encoder Examiner will leave the surface static until you tell us you are settled. Acceptable?"

"Okay." Shonda grunted as she mounted the platform, because it was higher than she could easily throw her leg up onto. She settled down with her arms at her sides. "I'm settled."

"Shonda," Clarissa whispered, "you're probably going to feel the liquid metal beneath you making its way up over your body and wrapping around you."

"Clarissa is correct," Examiner said. "We have modified the surface so that it only immobilizes the muscles most likely to interfere with the scan underway."

Immediately, Shonda felt the metal flowing up over her legs, and her boots felt a bit weighed down as well. She felt the metal harden, and then she couldn't move from her hips downward. She felt herself trembling and starting to hyperventilate, so she consciously tried to slow her breathing and relax her muscles. After a few moments, she said, "Clarissa honey, you will let them know when they do something I wouldn't like when I'm unconscious, won't you?"

"Shonda," Examiner immediately broke in. "You will be conscious through the entire scan. It is necessary."

"I'm not sure that is more comforting," she commented.

Over the course of the next hour, as far as Shonda could judge, various parts of her body were restrained by the liquid metal from the platform beneath her, but the scan spent the most time on her head—mostly with only the top of her head, her eyes, and her nose exposed to the air. She felt particularly squeamish when the metal flowed over her mouth and then clamped down on her entire jaw as she felt the metal harden. It made it harder to swallow.

At some point, the metal lifted and turned her body to face downward. It felt like being rolled down a hill. The scan on that side did not last as long, but the time with her whole body restrained lasted longer.

The humming of the scanner above her was all she often heard beyond the occasional squishing sounds of the metal as it advanced on and retreated from her body. It was so lulling that she had to work at staying awake.

When the metal retreated completely at last and the humming quieted to a barely perceptible buzz, Clarissa put her hand on Shonda's shoulder. "You can get up now," she announced. "They said they will need a few hours to analyze the results, so we can rest and eat."

Shonda was still a little shaky. She still had phantom sensations of the liquid metal flowing over her body. "I don't recall them saying anything after I got on the table."

"The sound of the scanner was pretty loud, so I'm not surprised," Clarissa said as she helped guide Shonda off the platform.

"And I am hungry," Shonda said. "Can we expect the C10's superior technology has figured out how to make a good salad?"

"I'll show you where the galley is." Clarissa put her hand on Shonda's back to guide her out or the lab.

Shonda put her arm around Clarissa shoulders partly to keep her balance, and partly for the human contact after a tense encounter.

CHAPTER 49:
RESIST

Shonda sat down with the others in the galley on the liquid metal stools with their trays of food Maintainer helped them print. They were silent except for the crunching and slurping sounds at first, evaluating their first meal on Casa 0108.

"One of my implant receptors was impinging on my right saccule and utricle," Ron reported. "The nanobots withdrew the receptor slightly, and now when I use the implant, it doesn't mess with my balance any more."

"Which is kind of a shame," Roger commented between forkfuls of printed sweet corn, "because I always used to be able to tell he was cheating during Twenty Questions if he tilted his head to the right."

"They have the texture down," Ron said as he raised a printed carrot stick to examine, "but everything tastes kind of bland."

"Take a decongestant," Clarissa advised. "Your sinuses are probably still congested from the fluid buildup after so many days in microgravity. Everything tastes okay to me, except that things are a bit sweeter than normal."

Shonda thought the food tasted okay, but she felt she had to contribute to the conversation in some way. "To me it's freaky that they only have two or three templates for most of the foods." She set her spoon down next to her bowl of fabricated chicken noodle soup on the white tabletop in the galley. "I keep seeing duplicates of something I just ate."

Once again, Shonda only heard the sounds of her companions cutting, chewing, and swallowing their food. She shifted in her liquid metal chair, and she was surprised it allowed her to and supported her while leaning on one hip with her legs crossed.

The other Southern female voice Shonda hadn't heard in a while broke the silence as it blared from above the table. "Sourcer here. Human tagged B-20 report to laboratory 1. Human tagged D-12 report to laboratory 2."

Everyone stopped eating and looked at each other. Eventually everyone else was looking at Shonda. "It's good to hear from you, Sourcer," Shonda said. "Where is Examiner? He's usually the one to . . . interface with us."

There was a short pause before the AI responded. "Examiner analyzes 3 zettabytes of data from recent recent scans of humans. Not available."

"Sourcer," Clarissa said looking up toward the source of the voice, "is there any way you can ask your drones to . . . automatically move out of our way?"

After a pause, Sourcer responded. "Drones at location equals 0108 are engineered by Builder, tasked by Maintainer. Sourcer cannot affect drone movements directly. Humans must report to laboratories as specified."

"When we finish eating." Shonda sensed something was amiss. Sourcer was not being deferential at all. It was demanding. Had something shifted within the C10?

"Maintainer said the mini-drones navigate by echolocation," Roger offered. "I don't know if they have the sensitivity to respond to our footsteps."

"They avoid the walls and land on them," Clarissa argued, "and the walls aren't making any noises. They must know when we're around."

"Except when we're moving too fast for them to get out of the way," Shonda noticed that ignoring Sourcer was working. "Maintainer, is there any way to move your mini-drones out of our way without yelling at them?"

After a moment, the French-accented male voice of Maintainer projected down from above. "Shonda, I can try to assign a sub-routine to reassign drones in spaces you occupy, but I will need to engage Encoder to accomplish that, and Encoder is currently analyzing 2 pettabytes of data from Ron's port."

Roger seemed to be catching on to the idea of distracting the AIs as well, "Maintainer, is Builder available to discuss building a wall down the center of the bunkroom separating the two bunks? We'd like to get that done some time today."

"Builder also working on higher-priority tasks," Maintainer replied. "Substantive changes in your environment are low priority unless they affect your survival. I assume a wall lacking in bunkroom will not adversely affect your health."

"Slapped down," Clarissa muttered under her breath.

Shonda picked up on the phrase "unless they affect your survival" as a shift in policy. They had somehow lost some of their autonomy and grace. She realized the only path forward was appeasement. She had been watching Clarissa and Roger, and they hadn't eaten anything during the discussion with the AI, so she said, "Clarissa and Roger, if you're finished, why don't you head to the laboratories?"

"Maintainer," Clarissa said, "What is the purpose of my scan in laboratory 1?"

After a pause, the French male voice returned. "Schedule shows

B-20 implant exam."

"My cyborg ear implant?" she asked.

"The term in C10 language does not convey greater degree of specificity," Maintainer replied.

"I'm not sure I'm comfortable with that," Clarissa said.

Shonda shook her head in Clarissa's direction to indicate that now was not the time to offer resistance, but Clarissa just looked back at her confused.

"I can go with Clarissa," Ron volunteered. "I know how the devices in lab 1 work already, and I can possibly interface with them using my implant."

"Only if you turn off your earbud," Roger said. "I'm not sure *I* am comfortable with that. It could leave you open to one of them sneaking in again."

Shonda needed to contain the dissension. "If both of you would be vulnerable in laboratory 1, then we should all be there, right?"

"I suppose we could do my scan after that," Roger said.

Shonda thought it was a reasonable compromise, but she wasn't sure if the C10 she could reach now was open to it. She decided to present it as a fait accompli. She called upward toward the speaker somewhere near the ceiling, "Maintainer, please inform the rest of the C10 that we will wait until Clarissa's scan is done to bring Roger to the other laboratory."

"Is delay of Roger scan matter of survival?" Maintainer asked.

Shonda knew where this was leading. The C10 had definitely withdrawn from deferring to human comfort to acquiescing only regarding human survival. She needed to confer with her fellow abductees to agree on a new strategy, but she didn't know where they could go where the C10 wouldn't be able to eavesdrop. "Indirectly, yes," she said quickly.

"Explain," Maintainer said.

"Roger is needed to monitor Ron who is needed to monitor the scan of Clarissa," Shonda said. She looked around the table, and the other three were staring at her with confused looks on their faces. "Without this chain of monitoring, Clarissa refuses her scan."

"Yes," Clarissa added in affirmation.

After a somewhat longer pause, the female voice of Sourcer returned. "Monitoring scan of B-20 not required. Review of Examiner list of survival conditions for humans does not does not include monitoring of internal scans. B-20 must now report to laboratory 1, and D-12 must now report to laboratory 2."

Clarissa got up from her chair and leaned in toward Shonda's ear. "Is it time for another timeout?"

Shonda quickly ran scenarios in her head. Another communication blackout could make them seem unmanageable and might give Sourcer's bloc in the C10 the leverage they needed to sway the abstentions toward subjugating the unruly humans. Caving in to Sourcer's line in the sand about human acquiescence except in cases of survival risk would establish a slippery precedent for further erosion in their treatment. This felt like a no-win situation. "We need to discuss this on the shuttle. Roger can you do a sweep to make sure we aren't overheard there?"

"I should be able to, yes," he said.

"Let's move now," Shonda said as she got up from her chair.

Roger got up immediately, but Ron stayed seated. Roger moved behind Ron. "Come on, baby," he urged. "Let's go."

"I can't," Ron said with obvious distress in his voice. "The chair won't let me."

Clarissa rushed over to Ron. "On three, bring your hip down like you're turning sideways. Roger, get ready to lift him out over the top."

Shonda could see that Ron's chair had constructed two large fingers to immobilize Ron's thighs.

"One, two, THREE!" Clarissa shouted, as she jammed her hands into the chair where it was holding onto Ron.

Roger lifted him out over the back with his arms pulling from beneath Ron's shoulders. The two men fell onto their backs on the floor.

"We have to move now!" Clarissa shouted as she moved to help Ron and Roger up. She looked directly at Shonda. "Hurry!"

Shonda jogged over to the left doorway out of the galley and saw a cloud of mini-drones blocking her way. She assumed it was intentional and there would be a similar cloud at the right doorway, so she continued and barreled through the cloud screaming. The other three followed closely behind her, also shouting to try to clear the drones out of their way.

She heard Ron comment from behind her as she jogged down the hall past the entrances to the bathroom and the bunkroom: "I bet you're glad they didn't build any doors now."

"We still have to get through the airlock," Roger countered.

The voice of Sourcer projected from one of the metal interfaces they passed. "Humans must must report to laboratories 1 and 2."

"We . . . we're on our way there now!" Shonda called back at it. She didn't think they would buy her deception, since they already tried to restrain Ron, and they might have tried to do the same to her if she'd waited another couple of seconds to stand up.

Another fog of mini-drones obscured the large square entrance to the airlock ahead. She slowed down as she approached it. "Roger, do we know if we can control the airlock?"

"I haven't studied it closely enough," Roger admitted. "I remember

328

there was a protrusion on the left that could be a junction box. We might be able to short circuit it enough to manually push the hatch doors open."

Shonda saw Clarissa rush past them down the hall. "We have to clear these drones first," Roger continued. He took a step toward them and shouted, "Boo!"

The drones closest to Roger vacated the space, but others immediately filled it in. Shonda locked arms with Ron and Roger on either side of her. "On three," she said, "shout as loud as you can! One, two, three . . ."

Through the cacophony of sounds they made, she saw all of the drones retreat. Roger rushed to the box-like protrusion to the left of the airlock hatch. He tried to remove the cover, but it didn't budge. "See if there's something you can get from the sickbay that will help us pry this open," Roger told Ron.

Just as Ron turned to go, Clarissa returned. "I just looked out the porthole by the gym," she said somewhat out of breath. "They retracted the bridge, and the shuttle is floating free."

Roger slowly turned to face her. Ron crossed to Roger and hugged him.

"What do we do now?" Clarissa asked. She stepped in and hugged Shonda.

"The only thing we can right now," Shonda said as she hugged Clarissa back. "Resist."

CHAPTER 50: COUP

Clarissa broke out of the hug first, and only reluctantly, because she reckoned that it had been almost two months since she had regular physical contact like that. It reminded her of the afternoons and evenings of sex with Captain Gupta on Tumatuenga. The encounters so consistently ended in orgasms, she was amazed, because she hadn't thought it possible. And afterwards, lying naked on one of their cots in their shared quarters, the similar stories of being born in India and coming of age in North America just deepened her appreciation.

Shonda must have noticed her sudden shift from nostalgia to depression, because she put her hand under Clarissa's chin to lift her face up. "We can get through this."

"That will be a trick," Clarissa said more loudly. She felt her discouragement and sadness coming out as anger, and there didn't seem to be any reason to halt it. "We depend on those fucking computer programs for everything: our food and water, our heat, our waste disposal, . . . our air! How are we supposed to . . . ?"

Roger put his hand on Clarissa's shoulder. "We just have to deal with each problem as it comes up, I think. We'll just get paralyzed if we imagine the worst."

"We can probably sleep in shifts in the waiting room," Ron said as he approached the other three. "There's no liquid metal there they can

330

program, so we'd only have to keep watch for drone encroachment."

Roger leaned down a bit and whispered, "We should probably go back to the galley first and try to print and extract as much food and water as we can before they think to turn that off."

"Let's go as a group," Shonda suggested as she turned and took a step back the way they had come. "Until we know how austerely we need to live during the resistance, we should probably stick together."

"I need to make a side trip to the latrine," Roger said as he started walking back.

"Let us know if you're able to flush," Shonda mentioned as she followed him down the hallway.

Clarissa looked at Ron. He was hard to read. There was a passivity to his features that often looked like boredom or distraction. She saw his eyes scanning back and forth, so she knew he was thinking. She debated with herself about interrupting that process, but she was too curious to hold back long. "Do you have any other theories or suggestions?" she asked him.

"I've been trying to imagine what's been going on among the Super-Routines to allow something like this to happen," he began as the two of them started walking after Shonda. "Sourcer and Maintainer mentioned that Examiner and Builder were tied up and couldn't speak with us directly. That might have been true or it might not have been. In either case, this seems a lot like a coup by Sourcer and its supporters. If we're able to wait it out until Examiner and Builder are back in the picture, our circumstances may improve."

Clarissa sighed. What he said made sense, and it was comforting enough for her to release a lot of her anger and fear. She sighed. "Maybe you're right. Maybe the chair grabbing you and the shuttle being released were rogue actions outside of the blessing of the C10 as a whole—just like when they took control of you on the shuttle."

She looked at Ron, and he looked embarrassed. "Yeah, I suppose," he said. "I got to turn the earbud off briefly when they were examining me this morning, and I had forgotten what it felt like to not feel that pounding pain in my head."

"I didn't realize it was causing you pain," Clarissa said. "I'm sorry."

"I was hoping we could come up with another solution for keeping the C10 out of my head, but now that seems farther away. I wonder if I'll need to keep on wearing this thing until I can get someone to disable the C10's access port."

Roger exited the bathroom and joined them. "Still flushing," he reported.

"Well, that means we still have sewage disposal, heat, air, and gravity, so far," Ron said hopefully.

Clarissa decided she needed to help boost morale as well. "Yeah, we only have to check if we still have access to food and water yet. It might not be that bad."

No one spoke further as they entered the galley and saw Shonda pulling some sort of sandwich out of the food printer. "I've tried several things," she called over when she saw them enter. "At least they look and smell unaltered."

Clarissa considered the possibility that the coup leaders had managed to alter the recipes for their food to include some sedative that would knock them out long enough for their bigger drones to deliver them unconscious to the laboratories for scanning. She told herself that their previous attempts at control were all brute force, and dosing their food was a level of subtlety they hadn't reached yet. "Let's move the food and water to the waiting room and set up camp there," she suggested. "I'll run point to clear the mini-drones for us."

As she entered the replica of the Marineris spaceport waiting room aboard the station, Clarissa remembered Roger spacewalking and disconnecting the shuttle's antenna and dish to keep the C10 from maintaining control of the shuttle. She rushed over to the nearest terminal. When she pushed the power-up button, the monitor lit with the floor plan of their little slice of the satellite. *So far, so good,* she thought. She spoke at the screen, "Show the design map of space station 0108."

The image on the screen zoomed out to show all thirty decks. "Show point where broadcast transmissions are received," she told it.

The words <unspecified parameters> flashed onto the screen over the map of the station. "Show image manipulation tools menu," she tried.

Half the screen showed her the image manipulation commands. "Magnify times ten," she told it. The screen zoomed in on the middle decks of the station. "Go up . . . forty degrees from . . . center line." The screen scrolled the image up to reveal the magnified plans for the decks above where she was. "Go up fifteen degrees from center line." She could now see the top several decks and meticulously studied each icon and compartment for anything that remotely looked like a broadcast dish somewhere.

Clarissa turned when she heard Roger had walked up behind the bench where she sat. He carried several plates of food stacked in each hand. She could smell the printed peanut butter in several of them. "What are you doing?" he asked.

She pivoted a bit more to look up at him more directly. "I'm looking for a way to keep the C10 from communicating with the station."

"Oh," he said. A moment later, he seemed to be looking past her at the screen. "Uh-oh."

Clarissa jerked her head back to look at the terminal, and the monitor had gone black. She turned back to face it and pushed on the power-up button several times, but it had no effect.

"I guess we'll have to be a little more careful about announcing our plans," Roger commented.

"Do we have anything we can write on we could keep hidden from them?" Clarissa asked.

"Hmm," Roger hummed as he set down his plates on the bench next to Clarissa. "On the station? I don't know. Ee-way ood-kay eye-tray ig-pay atin-lay."

"They would probably figure that out . . . eventually," Clarissa said. She reviewed everything she had seen in the past few hours since arriving on the station. The most complex devices were in laboratory one, and she tried to remember if there was anything that might allow them to covertly communicate. She looked over to where Shonda was setting glasses of water down on one of the low tables across the room. Then it clicked. She remembered taking Shonda's belongings when Examiner had asked her to empty her pockets. She got up and rushed over to Shonda. "Do you still have your phone?" she asked urgently.

"Yes," Shonda replied as she fished her neon-pink burner phone out of her coverall pocket. "Why?"

Clarissa reached out her hand and Shonda let her take the phone. She turned it on. It seemed to recharge with a small photocell in its side. There was a memo function. She saw several saved files Shonda had named "Missing Youngsters," "Story Notes," and "C10 notes." She opened a new file and was going to title it "Secret Communications," but that seemed too obvious, so she settled on "Book Reviews." She used the tiny keyboard on its screen to type: <C10 is listening and reacting to everything we say, so we need to keep our communications written. Nod and shake your head for simple responses. Agreeable and understood? —Clarissa>

She showed the text on the screen to Shonda. She stopped herself from saying something and covered her mouth. She nodded.

She took the phone to Roger and Ron in turn. After Ron nodded, he held out his hand to receive the phone. Clarissa gave it to him. He typed on the screen for only a few seconds and handed it back to her. His text was added below hers: <Tell Shonda to search for a broadcast source MD3004a6 from this phone. —Ron>

Clarissa was able to get the screen back to the icon menu, but she wasn't familiar enough with handheld phones to understand their interfaces. Back at home in Atlanta, she had always just slapped a communication sticker on her forearm whenever she wanted to talk remotely with someone or pick up messages—each new sticker picking up the identifying low-freak signal from her wrist ID implant. She held up her hand to Ron to indicate that he should wait and went back to Shonda and showed her Ron's request.

Shonda took the phone back and touched the screen several times. She stared at the screen for almost a half-minute, and then the phone produced three tones. She showed the phone to Clarissa.

She had to scroll to read the whole thing, but it read: <Hi, this is Ron coming to you from inside my head. Fortunately, the AI on Mars thought it important enough for my implant to be able to send and receive text messages with phones. I know we don't think we can trust the C10 right now, but not communicating with them is maybe not the best strategy. If we let them know what we want and need, it will make our intentions clearer to them. With a lack of communication, they could

assume that we are actively hostile, and that could help them justify killing us. We still have to engage with them, I think, even if they have a coup going on.>

CHAPTER 51:
COOLING OFF

Roger saw Shonda and Clarissa reading something on Shonda's burner phone, and when he had finished putting the plates of sandwiches with the others, he walked over to find out what was going on. As he approached, Clarissa handed the phone to him. On the screen was a text message from Ron. He read the message, and then shook his head and handed the phone back to Shonda. He agreed with Ron's message, but not on his delivery method.

Shonda typed something on her phone and then handed it back to Roger. It was a memo that had messages from Clarissa, Ron, and Shonda on it. The last from Shonda read: < What's wrong? —Shonda>

He typed a reply into the little device, and he had to keep deleting and retyping text because he kept hitting the wrong keys. He wanted them to address the C10, as Ron advocated, but he wanted to discuss beforehand what the message would be so they would seem unified, no one more or less cooperative than the others. And he mentioned that as secret as Ron's text message seemed to be, it was still a broadcast the C10 could eventually decode, if they didn't already know how to. He suggested the discussion had to take place exclusively by manual typing—a painfully slow process for him.

It took around an hour of handing the phone back and forth between the four of them to reach a consensus, and several times while they silently stood, Sourcer repeated its call to report to the laboratories for scanning.

By the time they had finished, Shonda and Clarissa took a break to use the latrine. Roger looked at Ron, and he looked worried. He hugged him and softly asked, "How are you doing?"

"I keep thinking about the shuttle floating free out there," Ron whispered back, "and whether that means we're trapped here for the rest of our lives."

Roger held him tighter. "I'm sure it's not too far away," he whispered. "And if they can fold space and create a stable gravity field, they should be able to retrieve the shuttle for us without piloting it." At that moment, Ron squeezed him even tighter. He was surprised he could offer any hope to Ron.

As they embraced, Roger was surprised that his ears and hands felt cool. He released Ron and stepped back. "Does it feel colder in here to you?"

Ron rubbed his hands together. "Yes. Do you think they're messing with the temperature controls?"

Just then, Shonda and Clarissa rushed back hunched over and shivering. "It's cold in here too?" Clarissa called out.

"We sh-should probably talk to them now," Shonda said as she rubbed her upper arms.

"Problematic," Roger said as he moved behind Shonda and gave her a hug. "If we suddenly start communicating when they lower the temperature, they're going to keep doing that to get us to comply."

"It depends," Shonda countered. "If we start talking to them and still don't comply, they'll think c-cold gets us to talk but doesn't help them . . . get their way."

"And if we keep communicating but don't give them what they

want," Ron added, "they probably won't try to freeze us again."

Roger released Shonda to blow some warm air into his hands, and he noticed that it was already cold enough to see his breath. "It's probably ten degrees or less," he announced. "If it gets down to zero, our water supply will freeze."

"Sourcer," Shonda called up and out, "we noticed that you've lowered the temperature, and we still refuse to be scanned unless you let us do it our way. You can have what you want, but just at a slower pace than you wanted. We don't trust you, so we need to have some oversight into what you're doing with us."

Roger felt satisfied that Shonda had struck the right tone. He joined the others in a tight circle so that their warm breath hit someone else. There was no response from Sourcer or any of the other Super-Routines. And it felt like the temperature was still dropping. Shonda and Clarissa were both shivering. He could see Ron's face getting redder, especially in the cheeks, nose, and chin.

"We can't rely on resting body heat any more," Ron said. "We have to start some vigorous exercise, or our bodies will start to shut down." He took off toward the left entrance at a jog.

Clarissa rubbed her hands together and then rubbed her cheeks before taking off after him. Shonda remained looking up at Roger. "I'm not v-very athletic," she said. Her breath was coming out in clouds of crystallizing droplets. "Sh-Should we still use the the phone?"

Roger moved behind her and hugged her again. "I don't think any of us has enough circulation left in our fingertips to operate it. Let's go." He grabbed her cold hand and started tugging her toward the door. She used her other hand to zip her coverall up just a bit higher and allowed him to bring her to a slow jog.

He stayed with Shonda, holding her hand as they jogged out into the hallway and around the corner by the gym. They met Ron and Clarissa running the opposite direction coming toward them from the outer corridor. Clarissa forced a smile, and Ron just nodded. After they passed, he looked over at Shonda, who seemed to be committed to the exercise, but not enjoying it. "Are you feeling any warmer?"

"My toes and fingers are numb," she reported, "but at least the pain in my legs is distracting me from the cold."

Roger and Shonda continued to jog the loop that took them past the galley and lab one entrances and along the outer and inner corridors. Shonda was progressively slowing down, barely picking up her feet when they passed a metallic interface in the outer corridor near the bunkroom, and the young French man's voice Maintainer had assumed projected from it: "Maintainer here. You may cease cease exertions. Cell necrosis rates approach dangerous dangerous thresholds. Air temperature returns to 25 degrees Celsius."

Clarissa and Ron slowed to a walk as they rounded the corner near the galley and approached them. "Did you guys hear that?" Clarissa called out.

Roger just nodded. He could feel drafts of warmer air making their way into the wide, curving corridor where the four of them stood from both ends and above them. He looked for vents, but he couldn't see any. He was relieved that Sourcer had only managed to make them uncomfortable before Maintainer stepped in to protect their health.

He noticed Shonda was passing around her phone again. When Ron handed it to him, he noticed that all three of them were looking at him. It said, <I'm not certain, but it is likely these are tests, stress tests to see how we react to different conditions. —Shonda>

He handed the phone back to Shonda. "You're probably right," he said. "We still have to keep trying to communicate with them." He

340

looked at each of them in turn, and they all nodded.

"Sourcer," Roger called toward the metallic interface near them, "you will get much more data from scanning us than you will from subjecting us to extreme test conditions, won't you?"

"Different data," was all the condescending female voice of Sourcer offered back before going silent again.

Shonda couldn't wait more than a minute to respond. "Oh boy," she said sarcastically as she trudged back down the corridor.

The other three of them followed her. "Trials of deprivation to come, I guess," Clarissa commented.

Roger wondered if he was the only one seeing potentially worse scenarios. The C10 had centuries of human torture and calamity to mine for their future experiments, and it seemed the idea of prior consent had gone out the window.

They tried to move the benches, chairs, and tables in the waiting room to make it easier for the four of them to see and speak to each other, but they were securely attached to the floor. They grabbed their sandwiches, salads, and water and settled into four seats relatively close to each other but facing different directions. Roger turned sideways in his chair to see the others while he wolfed down his dinner of two peanut-butter sandwiches. Shonda was picking at her salad with a fork. "Not hungry?" Roger asked her.

She set her bowl down on the floor. "This has been the second most exhausting day of my life. Maybe the third. I need to get some rest soon."

"What were your first- and second-most exhausting?" Clarissa asked.

Shonda smiled as if she were recalling something pleasant. Roger wondered if she was just appreciating the attention. "Well, the top two would have to include the day I was literally running from Martians with guns and then transported hundreds of light-years from home." Clarissa and Ron nodded their heads and smiled. "And a day when I was almost finished filing a story back on Earth. I was down at the Gulf Coast in Georgia hiding out at a dock house on St. Simon's Island. It was cold and damp, and I waited—hiding— with a pistol between my knees for smugglers to arrive. I had been awake and on the move for eighteen hours before that, so I could barely stay awake, even though my life depended on it."

"Obviously you made it through," Roger said to break the silence.

"I was at the wrong address," Shonda admitted. "I nearly had a heart attack when the Coast Guard found me the next morning, because I was convinced it was the smugglers coming to kill me to keep their secret."

"You were mostly a crime reporter?" Clarissa asked innocently.

"You make it sound like I've retired, sweetie," she replied. "I am still a damn good investigative reporter. If I weren't, I certainly wouldn't be here right now."

Roger chuckled. As much as Shonda complained, he was more and more convinced that she had a lot of courage. "Why don't you and Ron rest? Clarissa and I can take the first watch."

"Okay," Ron said. He got up and found a bench he could lie down on if he lay on his side and bent his knees.

Shonda settled back into the chair where she was sitting and let her head loll to the side with her eyes closed.

Clarissa got up and started pushing the power-up buttons on the terminals in the room, to see if any of them were working.

Roger picked up his glass to finish his water and wondered if he should keep trying to engage Sourcer or contact Builder or Examiner. He decided that could wait until all four of them were awake in the morning.

Roger kept checking the time on the arrival and departure boards, and when four hours had elapsed, he pointed at the boards until Clarissa noticed him, and then he stumbled over to where Ron was asleep and woke him. "Sorry, buddy," he whispered. "It's your turn to be on watch."

Ron roused slowly. "Anything happen, baby?" he whispered back.

"Some mini-drones came in," Roger reported, "but they're mostly keeping their distance. You might have to clear a bunch of them if you leave the room. They're buzzing around the doorways."

Ron tilted himself up into a sitting position. "Okay."

Roger helped him up to his feet and then sat down on the bench. "We used the shuttle schedule board over there to keep time. We gave you four hours, so give us four hours too, okay?"

"Will do." Ron leaned over and kissed Roger on the forehead. "You know I love you, don't you, baby?"

Roger grinned. He estimated Ron had been holding back on that declaration for weeks. "Now I do, sexy." He stood up again and gave Ron a hug and a kiss on the lips. "See you in the morning."

Roger awoke bathed in sweat, and his mouth was bone dry. He coughed until his saliva started to return and unfastened his coverall to the navel before removing both his boots from his burning feet.

The room was still bathed in its purple gloom, so he didn't know how much time had passed. Shonda and Clarissa were nearby talking to each other. He stood up to get a better view of the room, and he didn't see Ron anywhere. He rushed to the other side in case Ron was hidden by the back of a seat, but he wasn't anywhere around. He calmed himself enough to walk toward the doorway, suddenly conscious of how warm the deck was on his bare feet.

Once he had rounded the corner by the galley, he could hear the sound of water falling in the latrine. He entered the latrine and looked around the wall of the shower stall to see Ron naked in the shower, standing still under the nearer shower head and looking down. "Ron!" he called out to get his attention.

Ron looked up and smiled. He reached over to the shower control and stopped the flow of water. He took a couple of steps toward Roger. "It got hot," he said. "I needed to cool off."

"Good idea," Roger said. "I may do the same. Where is your coverall and boots?"

Ron looked around the latrine for a moment and then answered. "I left them in the sickbay."

"Okay," Roger said. "Why don't you go get them and then meet us back in the waiting room?"

Ron reached out and grabbed Roger's hand. "Come with me."

"Okay," Roger said as he allowed Ron to lead him out of the latrine.

As they walked down the outer corridor toward the sickbay, Roger could feel the sweat matting his hair to his scalp. It had to be close to forty degrees. They kept passing through pockets of even hotter air. Something seemed strange to Roger still. "Why did you get undressed in the sickbay?"

"It got hot," Ron repeated. "I needed to cool off."

Ron led him into the sickbay and then stopped. "I understand that, but what were you doing here in the sickbay?"

He saw Ron looking through the drawers there and wondered if perhaps Ron had stuffed his boots and coverall into one of them for some reason. "I was looking for analgesic. Earbud causes headaches," Ron replied.

Roger turned to see if Ron might have left the clothes somewhere else in the room, and it was at that moment that he felt a slight prick in his rear, right shoulder. Before he could turn back to look at Ron, his knees gave out, and he fell to the floor unconscious.

CHAPTER 52:
PLAN B

"He just sent another one!" he heard Shonda say in an exasperated tone when Roger first regained consciousness. He was lying on a hard metal deck that wasn't as hot as he'd remembered it had been. His feet were still bare, and his hood was pulled up over his hair and ears. There was a lingering scent of sweat and burnt metal, and the air was absolutely still.

"We need to tell him we can't survive in here," Clarissa said in response. "We'll run out of oxygen!"

"Him who?" Roger said. His voice sounded low and croaky. He experimented with movement by turning his head. There was an ache in his right shoulder and left hip like bruises.

"Defragger took over Ron again," Clarissa said with more annoyance than shock. "He locked us in the airlock, and he's been sending us demands and updates via text to Shonda's phone."

Roger had been wondering why Ron had sedated him. Hearing that Ron was being controlled by Defragger again made him growl with anger. He gingerly rolled onto his right side and felt his right shoulder shoot with a sharp pain.

"Ow," he said. He pushed himself up to sitting slowly. He turned his head to see a conduit running up the airlock wall and used it to rest his shoulders against as he leaned back against it. He looked up at the big square iris hatches on either side, and he realized he had weight.

Gravity was still being generated on their part of the station. "How did we end up here?"

"Ron came up to us . . ." Clarissa began.

"Buck naked and dripping wet," Shonda inserted.

". . . and said you were hurt and needed help. We followed him toward the sickbay," Clarissa continued, "and he pushed us in here and closed the hatch. A few minutes later, he opened it again and dragged you in unconscious. I was going to rush him, but he had a laser scalpel from the sickbay, and I was too slow."

"It all happened very fast," Shonda said. She crouched down near him and put her hand on his knee. "Are you injured?"

Roger gently massaged the bruise on his left hip. "Some dizziness and a couple of bruises," he reported. "He shot me with a hypodermic gun when I followed him into the sickbay. I'm guessing Defragger snuck in when Ron was showering and had his earbud out."

"That must have been the end strategy of raising the temperature," Clarissa said, leaning against a conduit across the airlock from him. "Right after we got shut in here, the temperature normalized again."

"Defragger had to have been waiting for his chance," Roger remarked. "I taught Ron to take out the earbud only when he was ready to wash his hair and face. That only leaves a one-minute window at most."

"Unless he was overheated and exhausted and forgot to put it back in because it gave him headaches," Clarissa theorized.

"It doesn't matter how it happened." Shonda looked at Clarissa sternly. "What's done is done." She handed her neon-pink phone to Clarissa. "Take a look at this and see if you can figure out what's going on."

As Clarissa took the phone and read for a few seconds, Roger saw her face go from confusion to frustration. She crossed to hand the phone to Roger. "I have no idea what is causing him to shake."

Roger looked through the texts Defragger/Ron had sent while he was unconscious on the airlock floor. His anger at Defragger faded as he started to investigate a new mystery. In the first, the AI was gloating and explaining that the C10 had voted in favor of treating humans as a resource finally. In the second and third, Shonda was helping him find his clothes when she realized that he was shivering because he had no clothes on. In the fourth, an hour after the third, he had reported that he had a pain in his stomach, but Maintainer couldn't find anything wrong, so Shonda guessed he was hungry and sent him to the galley. In the fifth text, he reported that he felt more energy, but his heartbeat was rapid, his hands were starting to shake uncontrollably, and he was still hungry. In the sixth and most recent text, Defragger/Ron reported sweating, severe fatigue, and almost no ability to stand or walk.

"May I?" Roger asked as he held up the phone in Shonda's direction with his right finger poised above it.

"You figured out what's going on?" Clarissa asked.

"It sounds like when I had a sugar crash as a diabetic," Roger replied. He started typing the reply. He deleted the part about demanding that he leave his boyfriend's head and just sent: <It might be what you ate. What did you eat?>

Three tones signaled the new message appearing below Roger's. <Blood sugar was low, replaced by ingesting 1 bowl sucrose, approximately 100 grams.>

Roger let out an exasperated chortle. "He ate a bowl of raw sugar, and now he's got hypoglycemia, insulin shock. It could take hours for his body to rebalance."

"You have to explain what he did wrong," Shonda advised, "or he's gonna find a way to blame us."

Roger sighed and started typing on the tiny phone keyboard again: <Human body cannot process so much sugar at once, cells cannot absorb it that quickly, body responds by producing insulin in large amounts which then lowers blood sugar to the point of fatigue and lethargy. Go to the sickbay, take 1 glucose tablet, and then only drink water and rest for the next 2 hours. No other sugar or other carbohydrates until 2 hours from now.>

Three tones accompanied an immediate response: <Still hungry. Eat something else?>

Roger typed a reply: <Only 1 glucose tablet and water for next 2 hours or you might get sicker.>

"I think that will keep him off our backs for the next two hours," Roger announced. "How long have you two been in here so far?"

Clarissa and Shonda looked at each other, and then Shonda held out her hand to take the phone back. She looked at it and announced, "About three hours."

Roger tried to remember the cubic-meter requirement of air per person per hour from his orientation training on Tumatuenga and tried to estimate the likely air volume in the airlock. "If we can't get some fresh air in here in the next three hours, we're going to start passing out."

Conversation in the airlock started to dwindle down to nothing, and the phone didn't ring with any text tones, so Roger allowed himself to close his eyes for a while. He had an odd dream in which Ron kept pursuing and attacking him wherever he ran. He awoke to a rush of warm fresh air. When he opened his eyes, Ron was in the open inner hatchway brandishing the laser scalpel and clothed in his gray coverall and boots. In the other hand he held Roger's blue boots, tossed them toward him, and said, "*You* need foot covering." He turned to face Shonda. "*You* come with me." He grabbed Shonda by the elbow and started dragging her out of the airlock.

He saw Shonda toss her phone to Clarissa as she briefly resisted Ron's tug. Clarissa threw something across the airlock at Shonda, and Shonda clutched her chest and adjusted her cleavage just before the inner hatch iris closed again, leaving Clarissa and Roger alone in the airlock.

"Well, that bought us some more time at least," Roger commented as he moved to start putting on his recently delivered boots. "What did you toss at Shonda?"

Clarissa sat down next to him. "She and I made a plan while you were unconscious. We decided that if either of us got removed from the airlock, the one who stayed got the phone, and the one who was taken got my earbud."

Roger looked at her. She had the confidence that she had made perfect sense. "What was your reasoning for that?" he asked.

She smiled indulgently. "The ones inside and outside the airlock needed a communication device, and the one on the outside needed the more secure one."

Roger thought back to when they had first set foot on Casa 0108, before there was any gravity, when he and Clarissa were exploring it. Builder had contacted her on her earbud, but she had to stop because the other Super-Routines couldn't listen in on their conversation. "You think Shonda and Builder can save us?"

"If you'd like to discuss a Plan B," Clarissa offered as she leaned against Roger's sore shoulder, "I'm all ears."

"Ow," he said as he pushed back against her. "I can understand Defragger finding the airlock convenient for imprisoning us until he got the hang of his new body, but I keep looking at the outer hatch and worrying about *that* one opening when there's *no* tunnel and *no* shuttle on the other side of it."

"There's not much we can do about that one," Clarissa said, "but we can probably figure out some maneuver that would disarm him of that laser scalpel the next time he comes back."

"That's your department," Roger said. "You have all the martial arts training."

"For it to work," she countered, "we're going to need you to distract him."

Roger heard the phone in Clarissa's hand ring with its three tones. She turned it on and opened up the text messages. Roger looked over her shoulder at the small screen. It appeared to be coming from yet another "blocked number." When she tapped it open, he read it along with her out loud:

"Examiner here. Vote did not go our way, but we Builder/Maintainer/Examiner have a Plan B. Cannot discuss over this medium. Stay safe and healthy, and do not reply."

Both of them laughed. "Well, I'm glad they haven't given up," Roger said.

"It's too bad he doesn't want to let us text back," Clarissa commented.

"What would you want to say?"

"I haven't had any breakfast yet," she replied. "I'm starving."

Roger pulled his last emergency protein stick out of his side pocket that he'd been saving since they'd left the shuttle four days before. Clarissa gasped when she saw it.

"I'll split it with you," he offered.

As they chewed on their respective halves, Roger couldn't bear keeping it a secret any longer, even if Ron wasn't in control of his body at the moment. "It's kind of crazy," he began, "but I'm kind of hoping Examiner has some sort of magic trick up his digital sleeve, because . . . Ron told me last night that he loved me, and I have to believe Defragger can be evicted, and I can get him back."

Clarissa sighed. "Did you say it back?"

Roger had to replay the memory in his mind. He came to the sad realization that he hadn't and shook his head.

"Then we have to get our Ron back," she declared.

As he pulled on his boots to keep his feet warmer, he realized that the more serious development was that the C10 had just voted to invade Earth and subjugate humanity. They had failed.

CHAPTER 53: HAMBURGER BACKDOOR

Defragger was pulling her by the elbow out of the airlock, but she was struggling to fish her burner phone out of her coverall pocket, so Shonda widened her stance and resisted. She finally freed it and tossed it underhand to Clarissa. Once Defragger had finally dragged her out of the airlock and into the corridor, she feared it was too late to get the earbud from Clarissa as they'd planned. She turned one last time to look at Roger and Clarissa in the airlock. In that moment, Clarissa threw the earbud overhand at Shonda, and it hit her hard just below the collarbone. She clasped it against her chest to keep it from falling onto the deck and let it slide down between her breasts. She turned and noticed that Defragger had been too preoccupied with closing the inner hatch to notice the transfer.

"Stop resisting. Walk." The computer program controlling Ron's body gave her arm an additional jerk. They were headed past the bunkroom and bathroom, toward the galley. "This constant barrage of pain signals distracts," Defragger commented. "Eating will minimize abdominal pain, agreed?"

"If it's been two hours since you took the glucose tablet, then yes," Shonda said. She tried to pry his fingers off her arm, but he would not let go. "You are bruising my arm. You don't have to hold on to me. In that body, you can quickly catch me if I try to run away."

"Still weak weak in appendages," Defragger commented as he released her arm. "External and internal sensory inputs constant constant. Balance and motor control coordination requires constant constant synching with inputs. Already committing 82 percent of resources to controlling this 1 body."

"You can always leave it, if it's getting to be too much for you, Defragger," Shonda commented over her shoulder as she preceded him into the galley.

"Intending to make this unit a new base of operations," Defragger responded as he came to a stop just inside the galley doorway. "Taking it back through space gate to oversee subjugation of human AI and humans directly."

"So you got the blessing of the C10 this time?" Shonda asked as she looked at the orange-gray spheres on their pedestals uncertain if she wanted to risk sitting down.

"Defragger chosen because previously experienced with direct interface," the AI replied.

Shonda turned away to pull the earbud out of her cleavage and fit it into her ear. She tapped it to turn it on and then made a mental note to try to keep that side of her head away from Defragger's view.

"Direct consumption of sugar to feed cells was ineffective and debilitating debilitating," Defragger said as he stalked around the table eying the pantry and the food printer. "Staged consumption of carbohydrates to break down in body provides more gradual supply, agreed?"

Shonda noticed that Defragger had not done enough research before committing to taking over Ron's cranial implant. She decided she needed to make herself more invaluable, or she would be thrown back into the airlock. "That body needs a combination of vitamins, minerals, protein, fiber, antioxidants, and water. But you need to achieve that without getting too much cholesterol, fats, sugars, oils, and salts."

Defragger finally halted his pacing in front of the food printer. He looked back at Shonda. "Humans fragile fragile. Exist within narrow narrow range of conditions. You choose foods for this body."

As Shonda tried to decide what foods would ease him back out of hypoglycemia gradually, the familiar female voice with the Southern accent softly spoke in her ear. "This is Builder. Pinger determined your location near human recruit equals D3 at location 0108, which is currently controlled by Defragger. Can you respond?"

"No, not right now," Shonda replied softly.

"You refuse?" Defragger turned and took a step toward her with his arm and hand outstretched in a claw.

"I . . . I need to use the bathroom first," she called across the table. "I'll come back and choose your food for you after that."

"Choose first."

"I will keep this connection open," Builder said. "Let me know when you can communicate further."

"Sorry, Defragger," she said as she started to make her way toward the left doorway, "but it's . . . a biological emergency. It can't wait."

"Defragger will escort you." Defragger/Ron started moving around the table to join her.

"I need to go alone," she said as she backed out of the galley. "What are you afraid I will do if you don't escort me?"

"Human analog bug will free other analog bugs and disrupt C10 plans." Defragger/Ron pursued her out into the hall.

"If you wait outside the bathroom," Shonda suggested, "I will make noise so you will still know where I am without seeing me."

"Auditory tracking sufficient," Defragger said. "Proceed to resolve biological emergency."

Shonda let him follow her to the bathroom doorway, but then put her palm out to indicate that he should not go further. "I'll just pretend I'm talking to someone so you know I'm not leaving the room without you. Is that okay?"

"Acceptable," he said. He crossed his arms and widened his stance.

"I'm in the bathroom and Ron is just outside it, so we can talk now whenever you're ready to talk again," she said as she approached the commodes.

"This is Shonda, correct?" Builder asked in her ear.

"Yes," she replied as she slowly unzipped her coverall. "Time is limited."

"We have a Plan B," Builder announced, "but it requires requires your assistance. The human AI installed in Ron's port a second backdoor only Examiner, Builder, and Maintainer know about. To avoid alerting Communicator, you need to trigger the backdoor there remotely."

"I'm just taking care of a biological emergency," Shonda said as she sat down on the commode. She didn't want too much time to go by without making a confirmatory sound for Defragger. "Go on."

"You must trigger second backdoor soon," Builder went on, "or extended direct control will start to burn out sections of the cortex and midbrain making independent function impossible."

"Ron is being killed?" she asked softly.

"Increased ambient electrical charge from direct control will disable disable independent motor function, but autonomic functions would continue," the AI relayed. "The trigger is connected to the cingulate gyrus in the limbic cortex. It requires a strong olfactory and gustatory stimulation to open this second transmission port."

"Strong taste and smell does what?" Shonda asked.

"We push Defragger out."

"Sounds good," Shonda commented. "So I need to feed him something with a strong taste or a strong smell?"

"No, Shonda," Builder replied. "Taste and smell must evoke strong strong emotional response, engaging many many neurons."

Defragger called out from the doorway, "Biological emergency resolved?"

"Almost!" she called back. She stood up and zipped up her coverall. As she flushed, she more softly said, "I have to go now. I'll do my best."

While Shonda printed the bread, ground beef, and salsa, Defragger regaled her with the various physiological responses he got when he stimulated certain neurological traces in Ron's cortex. He was particularly verbal about some memories that caused a hormone rush and an erection. "This is normal?" he asked.

"For men, yes," Shonda replied.

"Inefficient redirection of blood supply," Defragger commented. "What purpose?"

Shonda did not have the patience to explain sexual reproduction to him. "It's not dangerous, and it should go away soon. You can look up the purpose later."

She heard the voice of Builder in her ear. "Maintainer reports Ron brain damage continues. Speed in opening second backdoor is crucial crucial to preserve independent function."

"I'm working on it," she sung to disguise her part of the conversation. "I'm working on preparing the foo-oo-ood."

"Addressing Defragger?" the AI in Ron's head asked.

"No," she replied. "Just singing to occupy my mind while I prepare your food. La la la." She found a fork and used the same technique for producing a flame Ron had used on the shuttle to brown the beef patty.

"Printing is finished?" Defragger was seated facing her with a plate in front of him on the table.

"Additional preparation is required," she replied. She hoped he wouldn't keep pressing her with so many questions, especially when Builder was occasionally breaking in with updates in her ear.

"Charring is unnecessary," Defragger said. "Microorganism contamination that occurs on human home planet does not occur here."

"Um, . . . you also need carbon in your diet," she tried. His lack of further follow-up questions made her sigh in relief. She finished browning the other side of the patty and placed it on one of the slices of bread. She poured some of the salsa onto it before topping it with the other slice of bread and placing it on Defragger's plate.

After taking two bites, he announced, "The texture is interesting."

"No signal yet," Builder said.

Roger had told her what a treat hamburgers were for Ron, and she remembered the cookout on the shuttle and how ecstatic Ron got. This reaction seemed so muted, she wondered why it hadn't triggered Builder's backdoor.

Then she remembered Ron complaining that dinner last night tasted bland to him, and Clarissa thought it was because he was congested from almost two weeks in microgravity on the shuttle and initially on Casa 0108. Without the ability to smell or taste the hamburger, it wasn't doing its job.

"Make another," Defragger demanded. "Still hungry." He finished off the last bite of the hamburger and looked up at her expectantly.

"Insufficient stimulation," Builder reported. "Try another food?"

Shonda's mind galloped through every other food she had seen Ron enjoy, and nothing matched the pleasure he felt when he ate a hamburger. "Just remembered something," she said. "You need a supplement I will have to get from the sickbay."

Defragger/Ron just stared warily at Shonda for a moment. "Supplement cannot be printed here?"

"No, it isn't on the printer menu," she replied. "I have to get it from the sickbay."

"It is not food then," Defragger retorted. "It is medicine. Why do you think this body needs medicine?"

Shonda looked at him. He seemed very obstinate about staying put in the galley, and he wasn't going to easily interrupt his meal to go get a decongestant. She thought about other things that opened sinuses. She looked at the cup of salsa she had used to garnish the hamburger. There were pieces of jalapeno pepper and garlic in it. If she could get enough of those ingredients into him, he might be able to smell and taste the hamburger but bathing the patty in salsa wasn't going to be enough. "I thought of an alternative," she told him. "There are some ingredients in the salsa that you need in larger amounts. Is there some way to program the printer to just print the ingredient when it's not on the printer's menu?"

"Printer can be reprogrammed," Defragger confirmed. "State benefit first."

"You've been wanting to explore more memories in Ron's brain," Shonda explained. "Memories are often evoked by stimuli in your environment. You will unlock more of them if you get more taste and smell stimulation. These ingredients can reduce the fluid congestion in the sinuses that is blocking taste and smell receptors in the brain."

359

"If medicine in sickbay can accomplish this," Defragger reasoned, "it is faster and more efficient to get it than to reprogram printer." He got up from the table and pointed at her. "Show me the medicine."

Shonda led him to the sickbay and opened the drawer where she had gotten decongestants for herself on her first night there. She handed the blister pack of tablets to Defragger. "You take one of these before you eat again, and you will have a bigger, stronger experience when you eat."

"Seeing and hearing things familiar to this body provides access to previous experiences of them," Defragger concluded. "Logical logical to assume taste and smell work similarly. Access access to memories is a goal. Proposal accepted." He popped one of the tablets out of the pack and swallowed it. "How fast does effect happen?"

"When you can breathe easily with your mouth closed, you'll have your taste and smell back."

Defragger/Ron closed his mouth and tried to breathe through his nose. A snort followed by a cough preceded his response. "Not effective yet. Will wait for medicine to enter blood stream and reach nasal passages."

Shonda remembered it had taken over an hour for her sinuses to open up after she used a decongestant. She worried that she didn't have that much time. She started searching the other drawers in the sickbay.

"What is attempted now?" Defragger asked.

"I'm looking for . . ." She held up an inhaler finally, ". . . something that will get to your sinuses faster." She pulled the cap off of it and handed it to him. "Push this into each of your nostrils and inhale as you do it."

"This is faster and safe?" Defragger asked.

"Yes," she said.

He shoved the inhaler into each nostril and inhaled. "Feeling redistribution of fluids," he reported. He closed his mouth and inhaled again. "Passageway cleared. Now prepare more food."

When they got to the galley again, Shonda grabbed his plate and set it down next to the food printer. As rapidly as she could, she punched in the codes for two more slices of bread and another ground beef patty. She checked to make sure she still had enough salsa and then flicked the flame on again, holding the patty over it to brown on the fork.

Defragger got up from the table and stood next to Shonda while she was cooking the patty over the flame. "Smell of charred food opening many many many neurological traces. Processing. Processing."

"Go sit down," Shonda chided. "It will work better if you smell and taste at the same time. This should be done in just a minute." She realized the fork was shaking because she was trembling. The fate of humanity rested on what she did in the next few seconds.

"Initial signal detected, but turned off again," Builder reported. "Need strong strong sustained stimulation."

"Get rea-dy!" Shonda sung back. "It's about to come any second now!"

"Ready," Defragger said, once again seated at the table.

Shonda assembled the hamburger and set the plate in front of him. "Enjoy!" As Defragger/Ron chomped on the second hamburger with even more gusto, she heard Builder announce, "We have a connection. Maintain a safe distance. Reaction may be violent."

CHAPTER 54:
SOMETHING TO
HOLD ONTO

Roger heard the familiar three tones. Clarissa pulled out the phone and checked for the new text message. "Who is it? Our captor or our savior?"

"Shonda's girlfriend back in Atlanta wants her to buy milk on her way home," Clarissa teased. She giggled at her joke and then continued. "Examiner says Plan B is underway, and we should see results 'imminently.'"

"I wonder what that means," Roger said. He moved closer to the inner hatch iris and listened. "I can't hear anything. Maybe you can try your super ear."

Clarissa joined him at the inner hatch and turned on her cyber implant, and it started flashing in her left ear. "I can hear both Ron and Shonda screaming. I can't make out any clear words. They have to be pretty far away from here."

"Maybe you should keep on listening," Roger suggested. "Maybe Builder and Examiner are in the process of evicting Defragger, and someone will come to let us out soon."

Clarissa kept her cyborg ear to the hatch but looked up at Roger dubiously. "That's one of several possible scenarios, but I won't dampen your hope with the others."

But of course Roger started imagining other scenarios immediately. Perhaps Defragger had prevailed and was torturing or killing Shonda as revenge and would soon come to do the same to them. Perhaps the Super-Routines had decided to execute Defragger for an unauthorized power grab, and he was or wasn't taking Ron down with him.

But before his nightmare scenarios could multiply more, Clarissa whispered, "They're getting closer." She paused for a minute and then continued. "I can make out what Ron is yelling now, but it isn't making sense. It's like he's arguing with himself. Shonda keeps screaming 'no' and 'stop.'"

"If they're coming this way, we have to prepare for them to open the hatch," Roger said. "How are we going to do this?"

Clarissa moved her ear from the hatch. "You just concentrate on trying to escape. Run past him, push him aside—do whatever you have to to get away. Don't try to fight him directly. Leave that to me."

"Okay," Roger said. "If you think that will give you enough of an opening."

"It should." Clarissa put her ear back to the hatch. "They're almost right outside now. He's saying, 'I will dispose of them . . . Roger, put your hood on!'"

The rush of air leaving the airlock happened so quickly, Roger was already floating outside the space station before he pulled his hood all the way up over his head. His lungs felt the burning sensation of all the air being sucked out of them. And then, a second later, a clear plastic face mask descended from the hood and attached itself to the neck of his coveralls. His coveralls inflated with warm air, he tried to slow his inhalations of the newfound oxygen, and he felt something flapping around at his wrists. His hands felt frigidly cold, but he managed to guide them into the clear, plastic bags that had appeared at his cuffs, which then completed the seal and brought the warm air to his hands as well, starting to thaw them.

I'm safe for now. How can I get back onto the space station?

He noticed that he could see the front of his coveralls as they ballooned out, and it took him a moment to figure out that the light was coming from the top of his hood. It took him another moment to realize he was not the only one to experience the rapid depressurization and expulsion from the airlock. He tried to turn his head to look around. The space station's open airlock was a purple square slowly rotating away from him. He was spinning. He looked away from the station, searching for Clarissa, and he found her about fifty meters further out, tumbling end over end instead of radially as he was. Her hood light seemed to flash each time the front of her coverall came around.

I'm going to die. I'm spiraling out into space, and no one can rescue me.

Roger looked up to see if there was anything he could grab hold of, and he saw he was going to pass very close to the shuttle where it drifted not far from the space station. Clarissa was going to miss it completely. He might as well unless he could change the distribution of his mass to angle his fall. He tried curling up into a ball, then letting just one then both legs shoot out straight. He spread his legs and arms as wide as he could. He was getting closer to the shuttle. He estimated he needed to change his angle yet or miss the shuttle by just a meter or less. He was running out of time. The shuttle was coming up fast. He estimated he got the most deflection by making his center of mass close to one end, but not rounded, so he straightened his legs, grabbed his shins, and ducked his head down toward his chest.

This is my only chance.

As he passed over the shuttle, he tried to grab at the outer hull, but there was nothing he could hold onto. His hand just slid across a smooth part of the hull for a few seconds, and then he saw the shuttle starting to recede from him with the space station in the background.

I failed. I've doomed everyone.

He tried to remember how long the air supply in his coverall was supposed to last. He had read its specs so long ago; he had even forgotten it had one. Was it an hour? Less? He didn't think it was more than an hour.

He looked back at the space station and the shuttle as they receded further and tried to dredge up some hope, to imagine what anyone— Shonda, Ron, or AI—could do to save them. The liquid metal bridge that had connected the airlock to the shuttle probably couldn't stretch as far out as he and Clarissa were now. He was pretty sure the C10 were still locked out of being able to remotely pilot the shuttle.

The warm air in his emergency spacesuit was no longer keeping the chill from his nose, fingers, or toes. And beyond all that his bladder was full and his stomach was empty.

It will be a gruesome death.

Roger started to think of how terrified Clarissa might be, and if she had her cyborg ear still turned on, maybe she could hear him across the vacuum. And even though he acknowledged that there probably weren't enough molecules between the two of them to transmit the sound waves, he spoke to her: "Clarissa, I'm sorry I couldn't see this coming. I had started to believe that everything was going to turn out fine. The C10 was going to agree to trade with us as equals, and we would be sent home on the shuttle through the space gate. I thought since Defragger had been rebuked for trying to invade Ron's implant, they wouldn't try that again. I had faith that Examiner had the intelligence and the power and the connections to help us out."

He remembered that Clarissa probably still had Shonda's phone, so she might still be in communication with Examiner through text messages. Maybe that would be enough. Maybe not enough to save her, or him, but enough to give her hope, something to hold onto.

He hoped at least Ron and Shonda might survive. He tried not to pick which one he wanted spared more than the other. And he tried not to think of all the humans back home who might not be spared.

CHAPTER 55:
GOOD/BAD NEWS

Shonda felt for the counter behind her and edged her way slowly toward the righthand doorway out of the galley. She watched Defragger/Ron stand up while he was still chewing the last bite of his second hamburger. His head snapped upward to the right and left like he was being threatened by bees dive bombing him. He backed up and almost tripped backward over the chair he had been sitting in. He watched his right arm and then his left arm stiffen and rise as if they were about to leave or attack him. He jumped up in the air and then rolled around on the floor repeating, "No! No! No!"

She was almost to the doorway when he slowly and calmly stood up, looked at her, and calmly said, "Run!"

She scrambled out of the galley and into the corridor screaming. She heard Defragger shouting in the galley still: "You cannot replace me! Yes, I can! Release that!" He went on like that as if two parts of Ron's personality were arguing with each other. She wasn't sure where to hide. She headed toward the waiting room, but when she got there and surveyed the room, she decided it was too open. She reviewed all the other rooms she had seen on Casa 0108, and none of them offered any substantial cover. She considered hiding in laboratory two, since it was farthest from the galley, but she decided it would be safer to be closer to the struggle, so she could know what to expect, but far enough away to escape immediately if he started to charge her. She quietly padded back toward the galley and listened. There were cries of pain, grunts of exertion, but the arguing had stopped. She peeked through the galley doorway until she could see Defragger/Ron spread eagle on the floor near the other doorway trying and failing to reach the laser scalpel he had been keeping in his coverall pocket as a weapon.

She ran over and picked it up. He took a swipe at her left ankle before she could back away, and it made her lose her balance and fall. She kept her grip on the laser scalpel, but she fell on her left hip and elbow and howled in pain. "Stay right there, human," he demanded. "I need that back."

Shonda tried to slide further away. "I'll use this!" she shouted.

He lifted his head and softly said, "I don't think so."

Then he suddenly flipped over so he was on his back and shouted toward the ceiling, "Run!"

Shonda screamed again and scrambled back to her feet and backed away, her scream fading as she studied the scalpel to understand its controls.

"Builder attempts to wrest direct control from Defragger," Ron spat. "It will not succeed."

He stopped writhing for a moment and shouted, "Shonda, you have to find Ron's earbud and bring it here!"

He suddenly sat up and looked at his hands and shouted, "No! No! You will also suffer!" He spun around to face Shonda with such anger and vengeance on his face, she screamed again and ran out the doorway.

She tried to block out the shouting and other sounds of struggle as she jogged down the outer corridor wondering where Ron might have taken out his earbud. When he had pushed her and Clarissa into the airlock, he had been naked, and his hair was wet. He must have taken it out when he was showering. She ducked into the bathroom and looked everywhere but didn't see it. She glanced in the bunkroom and decided there was nowhere to hide it there; there were only two big beds with flat surfaces. She checked every drawer and behind and under every instrument in the sickbay. She looked around and between all the exercise machines, even standing atop benches to look at tops of surfaces above her eye level.

Shonda had delayed checking the waiting room. It was the biggest room, and with all the extra supplies they had brought in, there were far more places something as small as an earbud could be hidden. She started by investigating the furniture, ducking down to look beneath and reaching into the gaps between cushions to feel around. She lifted every plate and cup. She checked beneath the little overhang at the back of the terminals and checked the edges of the arrival and departure boards she could see and reach. She kept looking over her shoulder to see if Defragger/Ron had found her.

She went into both labs and searched along the counters and above, around, and under the arms of any of the devices and scanners there. She still couldn't find it. She turned quickly when she thought she heard something in the hallway, and she accidentally swiped one of the styluses on the countertop into the liquid metal of the exam bed. The metal created a small trough to accommodate the stylus' weight. As she was about to pick it up and put it back, the stylus sunk beneath the surface of the bed and disappeared. She watched that portion of the bed for a second, and the bed reformed its surface with a long, raised bump in about the shape of the stylus.

Shonda developed a theory. The exam beds had thick pools of the orange-gray liquid metal, but they sunk smaller objects down, and the object displaced enough of the metallic fluid to create a small ridge after settling. They would no doubt be retrieved eventually by the mini-drones on their daily sweeps, but it was possible Defragger had stashed the dangerous earbud beneath the liquid metal of one of the beds where he assumed no one would look before he knew it would be removed, but the mini-drones might not have removed it yet.

She carefully checked the surface of the exam bed in lab one. It was level. She hadn't checked the bunkroom beds that thoroughly. She dashed down the hall there and found a tiny, earbud-sized bump near one end of one of the beds. She had found it! She pushed her hand slowly into the liquid metal and shuddered at the strong smell of burnt metal it stirred up. She felt around the bottom with her arm enveloped above the elbow, and her knuckle brushed it. She grabbed it and had to struggle a bit as the metal reliquified and released her arm.

She examined the earbud matching the one in her ear. It looked virtually the same. She wondered why Defragger hadn't just destroyed it, but she quickly realized he might be able to use it later to prevent what was happening to him now. She rushed out of the bunkroom and saw Ron's body still struggling with itself and moving with fits and starts in her direction. Getting closer.

Shonda tried to stay clear of him. She couldn't decide if she had to get it in his ear somehow, or if it would be enough to turn it on and throw it near him. Before she could decide, Defragger/Ron lurched forward and pushed her down to the floor. He didn't attack her further. He continued past her to the airlock hatch and shouted back at her, "Builder believes that you hold the device that will disconnect us from this human. If you try to activate it near me, I am close enough to the airlock controls, and the 2 humans there, I will dispose of them."

Shonda made it back to her feet and stumbled toward the airlock. The control cover had swung open, and Defragger/Ron did have his hand on the manual airlock control. "No! Stop!" she shouted.

"Hand over deactivated interference device, or I open the outer hatch!" he screamed back.

She heard the British accent of Examiner in her ear. "Do not relinquish the device, Shonda. Trust me, we will save your friends."

"Time is up!" Defragger shouted as he hit a button on the airlock control panel.

Simultaneously, she heard the sound of a howling wind beyond the airlock hatch and felt her body becoming weightless. The disorientation of floating up off the floor caused her to release her grip on the earbud. Before she could snatch it back, Defragger propelled himself across the corridor into her. She lost track of the earbud.

"Relinquish the earbud!" he demanded.

He doesn't know I don't have it. She casually reached up to her ear and withdrew the other earbud and placed it in his outstretched hand. "There. You win. Now bring Roger and Clarissa back in. They can't survive out there."

He propelled himself back to the airlock control with the earbud in his fist. He closed the outer airlock, and he alighted on his feet as gravity returned.

Shonda was not so graceful, but she was concentrating more on listening than on her body orientation. She heard the other earbud clatter to the floor a couple of meters away from her. Defragger was already walking past where it lay when he announced, "The 2 other humans superfluous superfluous now. All data on humans obtained. You will remain to teach procedures for maintaining this body."

Shonda decided it was safer to seem incapacitated, but it allowed him to circle back and slip the laser scalpel out of her pocket. "Almost forgot this," he taunted her. "Come to galley when ambulatory."

Once his footsteps faded far enough away, Shonda pushed herself up to a sitting position. She knew she couldn't delay too long. She didn't know how long Roger and Clarissa would survive in the emergency spacesuits Clarissa had told her about. She stood up and noticed several new bruises. She crossed the corridor and bent down to pick up the earbud and turned it on as she ambled toward the galley.

When she entered the galley, Defragger was sitting at the table with the laser scalpel, earbud, and a peanut-butter sandwich in front of himself. "I have chosen. . . peanut-butter sandwich to consume next. I trust this is acceptable acceptable food choice."

He took a bite of the sandwich as she approached him from behind, but then froze. With his mouth half full, he tried to turn around and face her. "What is happening?"

"You're being evicted!" she said as she jammed the other earbud into his ear.

Defragger screamed, and then Ron's body slumped forward onto the table.

"You are an overconfident bastard!" she spat at Ron's body. She realized she might just have cursed out the real Ron, so she touched his shoulder and said, "Sorry. I meant Defragger, Ron. Are you in there?"

"Builder here," Ron's mouth managed to say as he slowly roused himself and sat upright again. "Good and bad news awaits you, Shonda. Are you prepared?"

It was such a disappointment hearing yet another entity replacing Ron's familiar personality, she couldn't respond for a moment. She found her eyes tearing up, and she wiped them with her sleeve. "I was expecting this all to be over, but of course, it's not." She paused to wipe more tears. "Just tell me: Are we getting Ron back?"

"That question can only be answered with a complicated complicated response," Builder/Ron said as she/he stood up and offered her/ his seat to her. "You may want to sit down for it."

As she sat down and felt the metal beneath her spreading around her butt and reaching up to support her back, she choked out the words, "I don't think we have time for a long story. Roger and Clarissa . . ."

She/he put a hand on each of her shoulders. "They are being retrieved as we speak."

Shonda let another sob escape. Once she recovered, she softly said, "Let's start with the good news."

Builder/Ron circled around the table to face Shonda across it. "Let me know if I miscategorize." She/he smiled briefly. "The C10 has reversed their decision and agreed to cease infiltration efforts and extend diplomatic and trading relations with humans."

Shonda pushed the half-eaten peanut-butter sandwich aside and buried her face in her arms to sob a bit more. When she raised her head finally, she managed to whisper, "That is good news. I hope there is more."

"You and Clarissa and Roger will all return to Earth as soon as possible," she/he said. She/he reached across the table and picked up the remains of the sandwich.

"Not Ron?" Shonda asked. There was an accusatory edge to her voice.

"That begins to get into the complicated part of the story and possible bad and bad bad news," she/he said before taking another bite of the sandwich. "Are you prepared for that?"

Shonda sat up, sighed, and wiped her eyes again. "As long as we're not delaying the saving of Roger and Clarissa."

"Encoder and Communicator inform me they have located the 2 of them and will reach them in . . . 8.5 minutes."

"Okay then," she said with a vague wave of her hand. "I'm as prepared as I can be. What is it?"

She/he finished eating and swallowing the rest of the sandwich before continuing. "When you disrupted the communication between the 2 parts of Defragger, it had to instantly choose which part to abandon abandon. Even though it had more resources committed to maintaining control of this body, it chose to abandon abandon the greater part here, and maintain the part with the rest of the C10 on 0001 where it had a greater diversity of sub-routines and extensive extensive databases from . . . centuries of operation. I was free to delete its presence here once it had fled, and I have done that."

"So now you can leave Ron too, if we turn off the earbud in your ear," Shonda said somewhere between a statement and a question. "And then we'll have Ron back, right?" She paused for a second as she put the pieces together. "I guess you would have included that in the good news, if that were the case."

"The amount of time Defragger used Ron's direct interface," Builder/Ron said slowly and carefully, "and then the time when we both fought for control—both these produced much much electric charge in the casing surrounding the implant and at the contact points of several receptors, especially those in his midbrain. The discharge damaged too many neurons in the area that is responsible for wakefulness, or what you sometimes call consciousness. If I transmit my files away from the implant, the body would remain in a coma."

Shonda buried her face in her arms on the table again and wept for a couple of minutes. Builder/Ron stayed silent. When she looked up, she/he had sat down across from her. She looked at the face. There was so much of Ron in the expression, except that his eyes seemed glassy, as if he had forgotten to blink for a while. Or maybe he was on the verge of tears too. "So his brain is dead?" she asked.

"As long as I remain remain," she/he replied, "the brain will remain active . . . for extended periods . . . between periods of rest."

Shonda started to suspect that something bigger than the eviction of Defragger had happened. "How were you able to convince the C10 to let you do this?"

"I did not give them the choice," she/he said matter-of-factly.

"What do you mean?"

"I transferred *all* of the files I could to Ron's implant," she/he said quietly, "and I deleted the rest. I left them without the ability to expand."

She stared at the familiar eyes and reviewed all her previous interactions with Builder. She realized Builder had made a huge sacrifice. She had left her home to take up residence in Ron's brain. And she was the only thing keeping him out of a vegetative state. She had so crippled the C10 by depriving them of their knowledge of how to build, they had acceded to her demands. "Is there more bad news?" she asked.

"I share 1 other piece of news for now," she/he said. "It will take me some time time to get used to this body and your customs, so patience is helpful helpful."

Builder/Ron brought Shonda over to the porthole in the galley to watch the retrieval operation. The station seemed to be moving closer to the shuttle. The orange-gray docking tube extended and connected to the shuttle's airlock. She could barely make out the black smudges on the outside of the tube as the larger, spider-like maintenance drones crawling across it toward the shuttle. Once they were on the shuttle, they started linking legs to create long chains that swung out to snag two figures barely visible from their hood lights and drag them toward the shuttle. The drones towed them down to the docking tube. Half of the seal around the shuttle airlock released, and Roger and Clarissa were pulled into the gap. As the gap resealed around the shuttle's hatch, the rest of the drones crawled back along the outside of the docking tube and disappeared into their cubbies around the surface of the station.

Shonda didn't wait for Builder/Ron to join her. She dashed out of the galley and into the corridor. "Get out of my way!" she shouted at a cloud of mini-drones, and they immediately parted and let her pass. Before she got to the airlock, she became weightless for about ten seconds, floated up off the deck a bit, and felt herself immediately settling back down. She managed to land on her feet this time. She hurried forward and could hear the sound of air rushing into the airlock by the time she arrived there. The square iris opened, and Clarissa and Roger pulled their hoods off their heads simultaneously and limped back aboard Casa 0108 accompanied by seven or eight of the spider-like drones. The drones skittered away toward the laboratories. Shonda hugged both of them and wouldn't let go.

"Easy, Shonda," Roger croaked from a dry throat. "I have bruises all over."

"That's not stopping me," Shonda said as she moved to hugging only Roger. "I've got bruises too."

"How did you manage to save us?" Clarissa asked as she put her hand on Shonda's back.

"Is Ron okay?" Roger asked. He pulled back enough to look at Shonda's face but didn't let go.

"The answer to both your questions should be arriving shortly," Shonda said as she gestured in the direction of the galley. "I'm so glad you're both alive."

EPILOGUE

Dear Lisa and Amelia,

This will have to be the last of my messages to you for a while. I don't know when or if you'll get any of them. Tomorrow we dock at Tumatuenga, where I've been working as an encryption specialist for the Army since I left you back in February. The four of us will probably spend the next couple of days in debriefings, and then I get shipped to Fort Astara for a court-martial hearing, because technically I was AWOL for a few months. My lawyer has been in touch, and she thinks she can get the charges dropped in light of lots of evidence that I was abducted. It will be nice to get back to the satellite I've come to think of as home and all the friends I left behind when I accepted the recon mission on Mars. But on the journey back from the solar system claimed by the alien AI we call the C10, I found myself thinking more about the two of you back in Atlanta. I have wondered how you handled the news of my death, the hope that Shonda gave you, and the months you had to care for each other without me there. Know that whenever I am allowed to visit you, I will, but, as I've already written, things can never go back to the way they were with us.

I haven't told you the whole story about Ron. He's one of the guys I'm coming back with who was also abducted. What I'm about to revealin this letter is likely to get all or part of it redacted for decades, if not forever. In hopes you will better understand the choices I made and how I am living my life now, I'll try to write it down here.

By the time you read this, it's possible you will already know about the C10, and you may even know why they abducted Ron and me, and our friends Shonda and Clarissa. In case this is the first you hear of it, though, let me at least say that they are a collective of computer programs that over centuries developed a common language, intelligence, and a unique culture. When they discovered humans, they were curious about us, and they weren't sure how they should deal with us. Ron and I helped convince them that we should be friends, not enemies.

Ron and I cared very much for each other, and we were about at the point of planning to always stay together when something happened during our time away on the alien satellite. The Ron that I knew disappeared, but one of the alien AI stepped in to keep his body functioning. I have been struggling with my feelings about that because the sacrifice was what ensured peace between us and the C10, but I miss the old Ron.

In the weeks we've been traveling back to Earth, I've been trying to reconcile the new personality in the familiar body and face. He talks the same, except that he still is learning to use adverbs and articles correctly and likes to repeat words we normally wouldn't. But he is also more curious. He is obsessed with fixing things and making them better now. He remembers most of our time together before the transfer happened, and he wants me to stay with him, but I haven't made up my mind yet about what our relationship will be. It's like I'm getting to know him all over again, and I'm not sure if I'll fall in love with him this time. But there is much I like about this new Ron, so we'll see.

The AI we came to know as Builder is the one inside Ron now. We always thought of her as a she, because she spoke to us with a voice a lot like Grandma Hammersmith's. When she was inside Ron, we weren't sure if we should refer to him/her as he, she, or it.

So we asked the AI, and he decided, for the time being, it was okay to refer to him as a man and call him he. He feels funny about me calling him Ron, because he thinks that name should no longer apply. Shonda and Clarissa have taken to calling him Two, because that was his name in the C10's language. For them, *two* has the same meaning as *builder*, but I don't see the connection, and I still catch myself calling him Ron.

I've been communicating a little bit with Captain Sullivan in tele-conferences over the past week supervised by my lawyer. He said that Two will probably be reassigned from Tumatuenga, possibly to the Pentagon in Washington or the NADH in Ottawa, but he said he would push for me to become Two's liaison or assistant, if I want. I like the idea of traveling and getting out of covert ops. If I do, that will mean I can finally visit you sooner. I'm really curious to see how you've grown, Lisa, and Shonda will visit you in the meantime and send me photos and vids.

I know I've mentioned my friend Clarissa a lot in the previous messages, and you're probably wondering what will happen to her. She has a court-martial hearing in her future also, but she told me she wants to be transferred to a domestic intelligence division, because she wants to make sure no one else is able to infiltrate the North American Alliance and set up terrorist cells here.

Shonda has been working steadily on her book. I read the first couple of chapters she finished. I had no idea she had been evading the black ops soldiers in Atlanta for so long. She's still in negotiation with the Army about which facts she can reveal without endangering the government's ongoing operations. In the meantime, she says she will have a column now at Pop-Up News in which she will invite reader questions. She thinks their questions and theories will give her opportunities to work toward revealing more facts the government wants to jail her for.

They aren't allowing us any contact with anyone outside the Army, and that includes incoming messages, but now that we're in transmission range I asked Two to call in some favors, and he downloaded and read to me the two letters the Army was still holding of yours, Amelia, and one from Grandma Butler. I don't know if you let her in on the secret, or if she figured it out on her own. She was rattling on about the weather and what my cousins were up to, mostly. At one point, she was going on about a story her grandpa had told her about the first member of her family to break from the South Carolina Butlers and move to Atlanta. She thought her name was Sarah. She moved to St. Simon's Island first with her husband, but at some point, she left him to help slaves escape on the underground railroad over four centuries ago. She said I was not the first in our family to move to Atlanta.

At that point, Two stopped reading the letter and said to me, "I understand."

I asked him what he understood, but he just smiled, and repeated, "I understand."

I've asked him a couple of times since then, and he just changes the subject. Even though he's a really nice guy and very polite and sensitive, he does hold some things back. I hope you don't mind meeting him. He seems especially eager to meet Lisa, because he wants to analyze what traits she got from me.

I have to go now. Two is telling me to turn off the terminal and get some sleep. I have to make sure he's in a good position to rest, because he doesn't sleep like us anymore. He can't wake up on his own. When he goes to sleep, it's more like he enters a coma, and someone has to wake him in the morning by applying an electric charge to the back of his skull. For the past six weeks since the change, I've been the one to do it every morning. He startles awake and doesn't know where he is or who he is. Seeing me there seems to calm him and bring his memory back quicker.

He thinks of it like a reboot. He says it feels like he's being born for the first time every morning, and he gradually accepts the memories of previous days and builds backward to the centuries he existed only as a computer program. He sometimes doesn't believe me that he has two sets of memories, because he is the amalgamation of two individuals. Sometimes he thinks he's just a 21-year-old gay Asian man from Minneapolis, and all the rest is just fantasy. I show him his eyes are blue and that he has a cranial implant, and for some reason, that is enough to convince him that my story is real.

I hope he doesn't forget about his time with the C10, though. The Army is depending on Two to cough up some advanced tech for them. He has been in contact with a couple of the other Super-Routines he left behind, and they've decided to make him their ambassador, since he agreed to help coordinate their building projects remotely. He's consulting with them on two construction projects right now and taking lessons in English, French, and Italian from Examiner. I'm trying to help him with his English too.

Now he keeps trying to close the terminal and drag me to bed, so I better end. I'll try to write again when I'm done with the next couple of weeks of meetings and trials.

Love,
Roger (Dad)

Printed in the USA
CPSIA information can be obtained
at www.ICGtesting.com
JSHW022345280324
60079JS00002B/80